THE EXILED TIMES OF A TIBETAN JEW

D1471910

Jake Wallis Simons

THE EXILED TIMES
OF A TIBETAN JEW

Polygon

First published in Great Britain in 2005 by
Polygon, an imprint of Birlinn Ltd

West Newington House
10 Newington Road
Edinburgh
EH9 1QS

www.birlinn.co.uk

ISBN 1 904598 37 4 ISBN 13: 978 1904598 37 4

British Library Cataloguing-in-Publication Data
A catalogue record for this book is available on
request from the British Library

Typeset in Janson Text by Palimpsest Book Production Limited,
Polmont, Stirlingshire
Printed and bound by Creative Print and Design, Ebbw Vale, Wales

For Isobel

Life had grown hateful to me, and some insuperable force was leading me to seek deliverance from it by whatever means. I could not say that I wanted to kill myself. The force beckoning me away from life was a more powerful, complete and overall desire. It was a force similar to my striving after life, only it was going in the other direction. I fought as hard as I could against life. . . . I myself did not know what I wanted. I was afraid of life and strove against it, yet I still hoped for something from it.

Leo Tolstoy, *A Confession*

PART I

Chapter One

The first time I met my father, he was dead. After that, I got to know him. When I died, thirty years later, my father was born. I knew it would happen that way. I expected it, you could say.

When I was born, was I young or old, compared to the life I'd left? When you die, do you go back to zero or do you carry on counting?

But let's begin at the beginning. That is what is called for at moments like these, when your life flashes before you. Chronology.

Zero. One. Two. Three. As I inhaled for the fourth time in my life, my eyelids split open and my mind was invaded by a dazzling white glare. This was my moment of introduction, my personal entrance to the stage.

Five. Six. Seven. Without warning, I was struck forcefully from behind and I realised that I was being dangled upside down. Something was severed and fell, wet, to the floor. My bag of blood and sinew was shocked into a sequence of jerks, making me lose count of my breaths. Pain curled up inside my legs and I heard myself shriek as my bloody fists thrashed in the air. There was no going back now. There was no escape.

Images and sounds swirled in and out of me. The textures were all cotton and biological slime, and the colours were white, silver and scarlet. A lot of bundling took place. The air scraped my skin like sandpaper and the sounds were deafening. Measures were taken to safety-pin me into the chaos. First, I was clipped round the wrist with what I later understood to be my name: 'Tenzin Monlam, born 04:37pm, 26 March 2005, parents Tenzin Menla, Tenzin Osel.' Then I was 'bonded' with my mother – after being pushed out of her womb, I was pushed back into the smothering softness of her bosom so that the natural processes could take effect.

After a while, my mind telescoped the chaos into silence. Everything became distant until there was only myself and my mother left, a tiny island. As I lay in her arms, I tried to identify which limbs were mine and which were hers. At first I came to the conclusion that they were mostly mine; then the realisation dawned that they were mostly hers. Beneath my body, my mother's breaths were deep and hoarse; in comparison, my own were like tiny gasps. But neither were we fully separate – I could feel the pumping of my mother's blood as strongly as I could when in the womb. For a while, I enjoyed the limbo state. My identity was shifting, growing to encompass the whole world, and to the size of the tiniest atom shrinking.

Throughout my life I have thought about that moment many times, and wished that it could have been different. If my wandering mind had been blown towards a different womb, a different foetus, a different world, everything would have been avoided, all the troubles that were to come my way. But in that moment, lying there with my mother in the cool hospital air, I was blissfully happy. I had no idea where I ended and the world began, and there was nothing to fear. If I felt threatened I could simply shrink myself to the size of a speck, making myself unreachable, or expand myself to merge with the whole of existence, making myself all-powerful. I lay there for a long time, playing with the appear-ance of the world. Those first moments were the most enjoyable of my life. They didn't last long.

Slowly the peace began to fade and I felt disturbed. Like a forbidden shadow, something crept into my mind. Something sinister was glittering in my veins. I tried to expand myself outwards, and found that I could not. I tried to unite with my mother, and found once again that I could not. I yearned to relinquish my identity and ached to return to safety. But with every breath I was becoming more separate from my mother's body – and with every breath I grew more vulnerable.

Outside the window, the sun was beginning to go down. Bright golden lines appeared in the sky, slicing through the London grime. Clouds of traffic exhaust wafted in and out of view, and confusion clustered around me. Was I old? Was I young? Was I giant? Was I tiny? Who was I, and who had I been before? Who would I become? I became aware of the nurses flitting around the room, fiddling with machines and equipment. I could hear their breathing, and feel their pulses. We were all being shunted along together. Our pulses were currents in a river of blood, and our breath was the wind behind us; ahead of us lay the dark ocean, the ocean where everything ends.

Silence blotted out the noise of the nurses, and I was alone with my mother again. Her coarse fingers cupped my head, and my body rose and fell with her laboured breathing. I lay within the sounds of her body, feeling small and heavy, like a magnet.

'Mrs Tenzin, lovey? Your husband is here to see you,' came a nurse's cheerful tremolo. I felt my mother draw a sharp breath, and my body rose to a dizzying height as her lungs inflated.

'My husband . . . But that's not possible,' she said, struggling to sit up. But her voice was too feeble to be heard, and the nurse had already left the room. A lock of my mother's hair fell across my face, and she brushed it away, so gently.

After a couple of minutes, the nurse returned and put her head around the door. 'Oh, sorry, Mrs Tenzin, love. My mistake. He was looking for Mrs Saunders, next room along.'

My mother lay back once more and her heartbeat slowed. Gradually, her head lolled to one side. We stayed like that for a long time and the room darkened. I fell asleep, the noise of the hospital an uncomfortable replacement for the sounds of the womb.

Instantly I was dreaming.

I am outside, standing in long grass. The air is cold. On

5

either side of me, mountains push up to the glaring sky. Light glints off every surface. Everything is moving together in the wind; the grass, the clouds, the shadows on the mountains. I squint through the light and see a group of flat-roofed huts in the mountainside. I am relieved to be back. Two birds flutter overhead and settle in cracks in the rocks, and at the same time two children emerge from one of the huts. They are children, but they do not behave like children. They walk silently down into the valley. I approach and try to catch their attention, but they are too far away. They disappear.

I was awoken by the bang of a faraway door. I didn't know how long I had been sleeping. Every part of my body was aching. Stuffy hospital air replaced the clear mountain wind, and the sound of rustling grass fell into an uncomfortable, buzzing silence. I had never heard a silence like it; it was an agitated silence, not clean or empty. The hospital had returned, but things were not the same as before. There was a deep stagnancy in the air.

I was still lying on my mother's chest, and I could feel her hair on my face. But she did not brush it away. She did not move. There were no great breaths swooping. Her hand, clasped round my body, was not warm; her chest neither rose nor fell. She was as still as the moon. Slowly, I realised what had happened. Her mind had slipped quietly from her body as if by accident. I wobbled my head to the side and looked up into her quiet face. It was fatigued and wistful, almost translucent in the milky light. For no apparent reason, a chewed Biro rattled along the surface of the bedside cabinet and bounced onto the floor.

She looked as if she had become too absorbed in her dreams that night, and had not had enough energy to return.

Chapter Two

Chronology. That's what's needed at times like these, when your life is appearing, before it disappears for the last time. The chewed Biro came to a stop in the corner of the room. I needed to think. I needed to be free of my body. My mind spiralled up to the ceiling and looked down at the two crumpled figures in the bed. Below me, I could see my finger-arms waving. My thoughts began to race, and I was filled with a cloud of unknowing. I could hear the thud of my heart, no longer sounding tiny because my mother's great plodding pulse had ceased.

I gazed down at her quiet face. Her peace was attacking me, denying me my future. I longed to return to her life. Like vultures, other longings crept up to me and gripped me in their talons. I longed for my mother. I longed to escape the barrenness of the future. I longed to be free. Life had betrayed me before it had even begun, and I longed to escape its pulse. Life was death in disguise. I had reached a terrifying precipice, and I could neither stop nor turn round. I knew what I did not want, but I did not know what I wanted. I no longer wanted to put effort into life, but I still wanted life. I wanted not to exist, but I wanted my mother back. I wanted her past back. I wanted everything and nothing, existence and non-existence, forwards and backwards. Like a dark fire, unconsciousness closed in on me.

A powerful force beckoned me away from tomorrow, towards yesterday – a force similar to striving after life, only going in the other direction.

I opened my eyes. I was lying on my side in half-darkness, a pair of thick green curtains hanging from right to left across my field of vision. I was warm and wrapped in a coarse blanket. The curtains were pulled slightly apart. Outside, it was first light; the sun was rising over terraced roofs, coaxing light into the room. With some effort, I rolled onto my back and tried to focus my eyes. Above me was a whitewashed ceiling, in the centre of which sat a round paper lampshade. It lit up, throwing fuzzy warm light into the room. The hospital had vanished. I was in a wooden cot. Across the top of the cot stretched a string of brightly coloured plastic cubes. The lampshade vanished as a figure bent over me. My pupils contracted and the blurred face sharpened. The face was in shadow, but there was no doubt. It was my mother. I looked up at her and, despite myself, began to wail. My bare gums slid against each other with an unpleasant rubbery sensation. My mother threw her plait over her shoulder and smiled. Then she reached down and lifted me out of the cot, holding me close to her with warm, coarse hands.

Yellowish patches were on her skin, her bones were prominent and she had small lesions around her temples. I lay there for a few seconds, looking up into her face. She was ill, but alive. She carried me over to the window, and with a tired movement dragged the heavy green curtains apart. Dawn was breaking, warming the frost. As we left the room we passed a full-length mirror, and I caught a brief glimpse of her. She had the square frame common to those from eastern Tibet, a long, winding plait and a round, nomadic face that would have been full and rosy had she not looked so sickly. I saw myself in her arms, bundled up in a brown yak-hair blanket, my arms moving automatically, feeble and helpless. She carried me downstairs.

On the wall by the stairs there hung a picture of a diminutive, neurotic-looking man. A white Tibetan scarf, a *khatag*, hung across the top of the frame, and a butter-lamp had been lit below as an offering to the dead. In his eyes I saw the slightly surprised look of the newly deceased. Below the picture was a handwritten tribute, 'Tenzin Menla Tulku, reincarnation of Holy Abraham, 1975–2005 – shall be dearly missed.' My mother hurried past it and into the sitting room.

8

As we entered, I was surprised to see a man dressed in white and green robes sitting on the sofa, sipping tea and thumbing his beard. The whole room was infused with the salty-sweet smell of butter tea. My mother sat down opposite him in a red velour armchair.

'Good morning, Rabbi Chod,' she greeted him, bowing slightly, instinctively, in the Tibetan way. He nodded solemnly to her, then leant over and placed his finger in my palm by way of acknowledgement. My fingers gripped it of their own accord. Then he sat back and sipped his tea.

'Ah, *po cha*,' he said, heartily. 'Tibetan tea. Perfect thing. You made this yourself?'

'Yes, Rabbi, of course,' replied my mother.

'You managed to find the genuine, traditional ingredients? And all kosher?'

'Well, you know, I cut a few corners here and there. Lapsang Souchong, salt, Tesco dairy products . . .'

'Wonderful, wonderful. Top banana! Now today, at least, I shall not get back-ache.'

Rabbi Chod sipped his tea, clearly impressed by the flavour. In the corner of the room was a small shrine, in the centre of which was a framed picture of a person who looked uncannily like him. My mother sat in her armchair, cradling me in her arms and matching him sip for sip from a crystal glass. Was I dreaming? I closed my eyes tightly and opened them again. Nothing had changed. There was nothing to indicate it was a dream. Everything was solid and concrete; the blank plaster walls, the red velour armchair, the lumpy sofa, the glass coffee table, the bay windows, the view out onto cramped terraced houses, the sun climbing upwards between the chimneys. My mother removed some dribble from my chin. I closed my eyes once more, and opened them again. Still nothing had changed.

Rabbi Chod was wearing gaudy robes, and wearing them proudly. The central image emblazoned across his chest was a stylised close-up of a snarling face with bared fangs. Beneath this had been embroidered 'Wrathful Yahweh, God of Moses,

Leader of the Israelites' in faltering Tibetan script. The whole thing looked slightly homemade.

'Well, my dear Osel,' he said, clearly bolstered by the tea, 'I trust you are feeling well this morning, and not too discouraged. Might I suggest that before breakfast we briefly discuss the fate of the corpse of that fine man, that is, my second cousin, your hubby, the late Venerable Menla, who died so tragically last week.' He gestured with his teacup towards my father's picture. 'Menla was unique among those of us who are proud to be known collectively as the human race, and will be sorely missed. Out of respect, we must not relax until he is laid to rest in accordance with his last request.' Rabbi Chod took another gulp of tea and sighed. 'It is indeed most admirable that our most dear, and now deceased, Menla's commitment to our tradition is so strong that it extends even beyond the boundaries of his lifetime. His desire to be laid to rest in the distinguished manner of the Tibetan sky-burial is most noble, and we must continue to do our very best to fulfil his last request – whatever the obstacles. We shall overcome, Osel. We must do everything we can.' My mother began to say something but Rabbi Chod didn't hear her. 'Of course,' he continued, 'I personally shall remain by your side throughout this ordeal. I am happy to carry on staying with you in your home, as your guest, to give you help and support. I, personally, shall pick you up when you're feeling down. I shall be with you every step of the way. I shall hold your hand and, in the words of Joss Stone, I'll be there. Personally.' He emptied the contents of his teacup down his throat, gazing at my mother intently from under his tangled black eyebrows. He was unusually hairy, for a Tibetan. 'Is there any more tea, lotus petal?' My mother obligingly refilled his cup with thick grey liquid. As he blew away the steam, she found an opportunity to make a grateful reply, her fingers straying towards her plait.

'You're so sweet, Rabbi, thank you ever so much. You are a pillar of strength to me – and of course to baby Mo.' I pretended to be asleep, and tried a small snore. 'Please feel welcome in my house. You are welcome to stay here as long as you see fit.' She coughed, unhealthily. This disturbed me and I began to cry. She stroked my head and rocked me gently in her arms. I was feeling overwhelmed. What had happened? Was my mother alive or dead? When was I? Rabbi Chod lowered his teacup and leant forwards with a cut-to-the-chase air.

'Now, Osel, lotus petal, to business, without further ado. Let us recap our position.' He cleared his throat. 'As you know, Tibetan tradition calls for the deceased to be, shall we say, separated out – that is, dismembered – by those accomplished in this holy art, in this case being my good self, and left for the vultures. This highlights, in no uncertain terms, the impermanence of life, and encourages us to focus our minds on spiritual matters, for the purposes of self-furtherment. For, as you know, once the soul has departed from the body, travelling to its next incarnation, the body is no longer any use to anyone. Indeed! How true that is. Thereupon the corpse is exposed for forty-nine days to the vultures. Forty-nine days, my dear Osel, is indeed the amount of time that Venerable Moses, Leader of the Israelites, spent in lofty meditation and communion with God on Mount Sinai. Indeed! I remember it as if it were yesterday, all those lives ago. What a time I had, what a time! Thunder, lightning, the voice of God Himself . . . and the tablets of stone . . . what a sight. To mention nothing of the golden calf, of course. But! To business. After this period of exposure to the elements, the bones, stripped of all fleshly lumps by lowly birds of prey, are collected and buried in the ground, as outlined in the Jewish law.'

He slowly sat back and steepled his fingers. My mother remained silent, sipping her water. 'I have encountered two obstacles to the full implementation of the rite in this particular case,' continued Chod. 'The first is the following: finding a suitable site for sky-burial in London. In Tibet, of course, our motherland, it would be carried out on some remote lofty peak. Over the past week I, however, have been focusing my minds and heart on the local venue – that is, the site – commonly known as Hampstead Heath. This prominent location will make a bold statement that Tibetan Jews are truly part of the fabric of British life. Like the Zoroastrian Towers of Silence in the heart of Bombay. This morning, I have managed to arrange an interview with the City Corporation at Guildhall to arrange it. No, no, don't mention it. The interview is scheduled for half past ten. You shall, of course, accompany me to this appointment. The second obstacle is as follows: the most definite and unfortunate lack of vultures, or other birds of prey, in our area – that is, London, north-west section.' My mother began to cry softly to herself, and it upset me. She clutched me tightly and rocked me to and fro.

Rabbi Chod noticed our distress and leant forward in sympathy, producing a large handkerchief from his robes and offering it to my mother. 'Dear Osel, do not cry, do not despair. Do not lose hope. Rabbi Chod will ensure that Menla's last request will be fulfilled. There may not be vultures in our corner of the world, but there are indeed most certainly crows, and pigeons, and many other species of fowl, all of which I am sure have healthy appetites. It is indeed tragic that my second cousin should pass away, especially so young – indeed, at least twenty years younger than my good self! Tragic. But at least we can lay him to rest as he would have wanted. Let me get you a cup of *châng*, Osel. Strong, healthy Tibetan *châng*. To steady your nerve endings.' My mother shook her head and rubbed her eyes. He crossed the room and gazed pensively out of the window.

Eventually, my mother's sobs faded and her tears dried. She chewed her fingers anxiously, and sipped more water. After a minute or so, she blew her nose and murmured, 'May I offer you some *tsampa*, Rabbi? Or some *kyo-ma*?'

'Thank you, Osel, that's very kind but no, thank you indeed, very much. Are you all right? No more sniffing?'

'Thanks, I'm OK now, I'm OK. These last few weeks have been like a nightmare, Rabbi. And I just don't know what's to come, or what the future holds. It's . . . And the thought of Menla being buried like that . . . I mean, we had our differences, and he had his faults, but . . . what an awful way to end a life.' She coughed violently into her sleeve, and I began to whine again.

'Indeed,' replied Chod. 'Most certainly. It can be done, Osel, you must think in the positive at all times, that's my motto. We will make that sky-burial happen. Lotus petal, never give in. We shall fight them on the beach, and all that. Indeed. Menla's dying wish will certainly be fulfilled, mark my promise. What dignity. What courage. My second cousin. What a man!' He looked at his watch. 'Now you must prepare yourself to go out. The meeting at the Guildhall is in forty-five minutes. Be heartened. Be strong. Rabbi Chod is here. Now go and get ready.'

'Yes, Rabbi, of course,' my mother sniffed, still sobbing. She placed me gently on the sofa, asked the Rabbi to watch me, and padded demurely out. I wailed even louder. My mind was in turmoil. What was going on? When was I? Chod lumbered over and sat down heavily next to me, causing my small body to bounce up and down. Then he reached into a voluminous pocket and withdrew a copy of the *Daily Mail*. The newspaper rustled and a large sheet of print filled my field of vision. I stopped crying. Rabbi Chod opened it up and the front page appeared: '25 March 2005'. I looked over at my wrist, which was still flapping uncontrollably. The tag I had been given, with my name and date of birth on it, was not there.

Chapter Three

When I was a baby, I dreamt frequently about another place. Just after I was born, the dreams were extraordinarily vivid – more vivid than real life. They crept up on me at the slightest opportunity, transporting me without warning to another world. I would fall asleep several times an hour, which was immensely inconvenient. Just as I was beginning to work things out, I would spiral into oblivion. But, however hard I tried to stay awake, I couldn't manage it for more than an hour, at best. Whether I was in my little wooden cot in my parents' room, or lying on a piece of muslin on the carpet in the sitting room, or being carried helter-skelter across London, strapped to my mother's back with a large swathe of striped blanket, my head bobbing violently in all directions, I invariably fell asleep. As a result I found it very difficult to piece the world together, since my knowledge was filled with gaps and blank areas, where I had fallen asleep in the middle of an interesting event.

When my mother, Rabbi Chod and I went to the Guildhall for the meeting, we initially decided to catch a bus; Rabbi Chod's car had broken down, apparently, and had been scrapped. It was about nine o'clock in the morning, the sky was overcast and a fine drizzle was spraying from above. My mind was still in confusion. I had been wrapped in layer after layer of rough Tibetan blankets, and was wearing a tiny yak-hair hat that felt like sandpaper against my forehead. Although my mother was very weak, she insisted on carrying me. But she allowed Rabbi Chod to shoulder the bag of nappies and babywipes. We stepped out into the sharp grey air, down the steps at the front of the house, and turned left down the street, the garden gate clunking behind us. Rabbi

Chod walked slightly behind us, holding a small red umbrella and gently shepherding my mother along. We went towards the main road, along a narrow roadworks walkway, past a group of school children having crafty cigarettes, past a frail woman wheeling a shopping basket behind her, past a couple of dishevelled city workers holding newspapers above their heads. Cars swept past with a *hrim, hrim* sound, headlights flashing. Still we had not reached the bus stop. As the rain thickened and my mother slowed down, Rabbi Chod abandoned the idea of the bus and hailed a taxi instead. He stepped out into the road, and was jubilant when a black cab immediately drew up in front of him. He hunched his shoulders against the rain, tossed the nappy bag into the cab, and helped us into the back seat. As we got in, the driver made odd noises at me.

It was the first time I had been in a car. I was apprehensive. Doors slammed. I cried, and my mother comforted me. The driver got into the front seat, there was a rumbling like a second womb, and everything began to vibrate. Just as I was trying to work out where we were, and who the driver was, and how long we were going to be there, and what that stuffy smell was, and why my mother was gripping the small grey handle on the ceiling so tightly, and why the driver was sitting with his back to us, and why he was glancing over his shoulder out the window with a strange expression of bored urgency, just as I was in the midst of all this intrigue, without warning I passed out.

Immediately, I am dreaming. The parallel world springs into view, fully and all at once, as if it has been waiting in the wings. The taxi vanishes and in its place there appears cold air, and vast space. Silence falls around me. At first, I am dazzled. Then, slowly, things begin to come into view. Under my feet appear knobbles of rock, tufts of grass and occasional blue flowers. This rock expands from side to side, stretching up and down in writhing peaks and falls, dipping into the distance. A small stream is ahead of me. Next to it is a pile of white stones inscribed with black paint. Knife-edged

15

mountains come into view in the distance, so vivid they almost glow.

Again I feel as if I have returned, but I do not know where from. The square huts and the children are nowhere to be seen. The air is sharp and thin and I begin to walk. My mind feels strangely clear. I pass over a ridge of rock and begin to descend into a valley. The grass and flowers become denser. A fat, hairy animal lumbers into view, eyes me insouciantly and continues on its way, liquid dripping from its nose. Now a fine mist hangs in the air. I have no idea who I am or where I am going. But it doesn't matter. I stop and sit down on a patch of grass, looking up at the sky and the mountains.

The scene was cut rudely short by a jolting, and a stuffiness, and a rumbling and blaring of horns, and the stench of exhaust, and rain-sleeked buildings and neon signs, and my waking world rushed violently back. I remembered where I was and felt relieved, despite the noise and the grime. My life was completely uncertain. I had no idea what would appear next – the waking world, the dreaming world, or something other. It didn't matter, so long as the hospital didn't appear again. So long as my mother was still alive.

Eventually we arrived at the elaborate stone façade of the Guildhall. We paid and left the taxi. Rabbi Chod tried to disguise how intimidated he felt by the imposing architecture by swaggering confidently in. My mother tied me to her back with a blanket and followed. We passed through a metal detector. The ceiling was high and domed, and the floor was marble. Everything echoed; even the echoes echoed. We were directed through a network of echoes to Room 3151B: a surprisingly simple room with a desk, and behind that a man, smelling weakly of egg sandwiches and beer. The door closed. The echoes stopped. The man blinked and peered at us as if through a fog. We sat down. Rabbi Chod introduced himself and opened the proceedings.

The Man Behind the Desk widened his eyes in disbelief when he heard what a sky-burial involved; at the words 'Hampstead Heath', he pushed his chair away from his desk and scratched his belly in bemusement. Here was a direct conflict between the official policies of religious toleration and public health – heads could roll. The meeting was interrupted by a Nokia ring tone, blaring from Rabbi Chod's midriff. With effort he produced his phone and began a loud conversation in Tibetan, twisting round on his chair and pressing a stubby forefinger into his free ear. The only English phrases that he dropped from time to time were 'albino hamsters', 'very cheap', and 'top banana'.

'You see, sir, it was my husband's dying wish to be buried this way,' pleaded my mother, taking over.

'Sorry, his what?'

'Albino hamsters! Albino! Idiot!'

'His dying wish, his dying wish, you know?'

'What price? The hamsters? Five cases?'

'His last request. Sir, this is a very difficult time for me . . . My husband died about a week ago now, and apparently Jewish law says that the dead should be buried as soon as . . .'

'OK, OK. Top banana. Three cases. Don't say I didn't warn you. Idiot.' Chod hung up.

'Of course,' my mother continued, 'I understand that this isn't the kind of thing you're used to . . . but in the spirit of . . . multicultural . . . er . . . ism, maybe you could consider granting us permission?' She tailed off, sounding rather flat, and gnawed her fingers, nervously. I had been tied to her back very tightly, and was beginning to get uncomfortable. The Man rose from his chair and walked over to the window. Then he returned to his seat, cleared his throat unhealthily and began to speak in a diplomatic voice.

'Mr Chod – Mrs Tenzin. May I ask, why Hampstead Heath? Why don't you apply for permission to transport the body out into the countryside, and carry out the burial there, maybe on some private land? Somewhere in the Highlands of Scotland, maybe? Or Wales?'

Chod snorted. 'We are a proud people, sir. We are Tibetan Jews. We have never hidden away before, and we shall not hide away now. Indeed, for we have nothing to hide. We

17

need to make a stand for religious freedom and, as such, we demand the right to carry out our traditional burial rites in a prominent London site. Look at the mosque in Regent's Park, the Hindu temple in Neasden, the London Eye. The Towers of Silence in Bombay. Surely it is perfectly legitimate to bury our dead on the Heath? Or it should be, in Blair's multicultural Britain.'

The Man sighed. 'Well, I appreciate your views, and it is by no means my intention to undermine your religious beliefs. We are a multicultural society and an open-minded organisation, and we try to uphold, um, religious toleration wherever possible. But this proposal, unfortunately, directly contravenes certain major health and safety regulations, and as such is entirely impossible. I do apologise. Thank you for coming here today.'

Rabbi Chod spluttered with emotion. 'I understand, my friend, that you have certain rules and regulations, or shall we say, legislation, that you are required to adhere to at all times,' he replied. 'But this, my dear sir, is an important issue. It is vital. This is a man's last request we are dealing with. A Tibetan man. An ethnic minor. Indeed, my dear sir, let me tell you something.' He leant forward and lowered his voice. 'The deceased, my good friend and second cousin Menla, was none other than the reincarnation of – Abraham! Our Holy Forefather! You have no idea who you are dealing with, dear sir, no idea. This, to my right, is my late second cousin's wife, Osel, reincarnation of the famous biblical heroine Sarah, wife of Abraham.' My mother straightened in her chair. 'And I, my good self, am, I shall have you know, my dear sir, none other than, wait for it, for here it comes, none other than Moses, Leader of the Israelites, himself. I split the sea. I brought the plagues on the Egyptians, through my wrath. I remember it all as clearly as I am seeing your good self this morning. Therefore, I say, reconsider your verdict. Please. I beg you, reconsider.'

The Man Behind the Desk looked bemused, stuck his hand under his armpit and wiped his brow. 'Look, Mr Chod, I'm awfully sorry, but there is simply no possibility of feeding a human corpse to the birds on Hampstead Heath. Think of the health hazard . . .'

'I assure you, my dear sir, the crows are ravenous this time of year. He'd be polished off in no time.'

'Mr Chod, I'm sorry but my decision is final. Disregarding the appetite of the wildlife, I am giving you until the end of the week to dispose of your corpse through the acceptable channels. Then I will arrange a local Council cremation myself. I will obtain a court order, if need be. A court order.'

Rabbi Chod flushed and sprang to his feet, knocking over his chair, his Tibetan accent becoming more pronounced as he responded. My mother got up and slipped out of the office, unnoticed. Once outside she leant against the wall and began to cry, rocking to and fro. My head waved from side to side and the fluorescent lights on the ceiling seesawed. Her moans and sobs resonated through my whole body. Raised voices came from the office. Finally the door opened and Chod appeared. He looked dejected, and gave a small shrug. Then he trudged off along the corridor, beckoning for my mother to follow him. She dried her eyes and tried to catch up. The matter was settled. There had never been a Tibetan sky-burial on Hampstead Heath, and there never would be. My father was destined for the furnace, like everyone else.

Chapter Four

The following morning, I was awoken by the sound of somebody opening the curtains. I looked over, and was relieved. It was my mother. Maybe this was becoming my life, I thought. Maybe my mother was back. Maybe the hospital would never appear again. But when was I?

She was coughing hard. Her lungs sounded as if they were full of thick liquid. She picked me up and took me downstairs to the kitchen, still wrapped in my blanket. All around the house, wet clothes were hanging. The air was moist and smelt of laundry. Five or six sets of Rabbi Chod's robes hung flag-like from the banisters, dripping onto the carpet. Large, wet underpants were draped on the back of all the chairs, and several pairs of trousers were drying over the doors. All the radiators were obscured by shirts, and he had even hung his vests on the lampshades. When we entered the kitchen Rabbi Chod was already sitting at the table, fiddling with a small novelty radio in the shape of an elephant.

'Ah, good morning, Osel, Monlam, good morning. Today: laundry day. Cleansing the vestments cleanses the soul, that's my motto. I have been scrubbing and scrubbing, all morning, just like that character, what's her name . . . Lady . . . Lady MacDeath? From Shakespeare, you know it? You've seen the film? A Tibetan Lady MacBuff. That's me, Rabbi Chod.'

My mother sat down at the table. The radio crackled and a voice appeared. 'Good morning, London, on this *Gloomy* grey day, ha ha, well this is London *Isn't* it Trev, capital of the world and we can't *Even* control the weather, you're listening to London Radio, we *Welcome* you today, the 24th of March 2005, we hope you have a super day, ha ha, especially if you're commuting in the *Rush* hour, ha, *We've* got something to liven *Up* your day, something for everyone, even commuters, ha ha, you miserable bunch, *What* a programme we've got for you lucky folks today, ha ha, first *Up*—' The radio went dead. Rabbi Chod snorted and tossed it into the sink. 'Bloody machine, it's kaput-ted,' he said. 'Now, how about breakfast? A nice kosher breakfast? Something English for a change? Eggs? I'll fry the eggs if you do the toast. And tea – but Tibetan tea. I shall never get used to the English variety. Indeed. Unhealthy.' He and my mother set to work preparing the breakfast while I lay on a piece of muslin on the table. The kitchen filled with smells, noise and steam. 'Today, Osel,' said Rabbi Chod, raising his voice above the splutter of the eggs, 'I will telephone the Guildhall and arrange a meeting with an official, to discuss the possibility of holding a noble sky-burial for your dear late hubby, and my dear late second cousin, the Venerable Menla, in accordance with the dignity of his last request. On Hampstead Heath, no less. Do you have any plans for tomorrow? Morning?' My mother shook her head. 'OK, top banana, I will, then, arrange the meeting for tomorrow morning, say ten o'clock, or half past. We will overcome, Osel, mark my trousers. Your hubby's sky-burial will happen. Think in the positive – like Andy Warhol.'

'Where is the Guildhall?' asked my mother.

'Not too far away, my dear lotus petal, don't worry about a thing. We can take the bus.'

'It's quite a long walk to the bus stop . . .'

'Or failing that, of course, if you are too frail, that is, too exhausted to walk, if you don't feel up to it, we can take a taxi. I, Rabbi Chod, shall pay for a taxi, should the need arise. I will care for the sick. The underprivileged. Indeed! What an offer. What a man.' He flipped the eggs with gusto. As they cooked, I began to feel overjoyed; I had left the hospital, and my mother's death, behind for ever.

My mother, being too sick to breastfeed me, filled a bottle with special, warm milk and fed me between occasional mouthfuls of egg and toast. Surrounded as we were by Rabbi

21

Chod's sopping clothes, the act of eating felt uncannily like being part of his digestive system. After breakfast, Rabbi Chod rose from the table and swept upstairs to 'prepare a surprise', instructing my mother to wait in the kitchen.

She gathered the soiled plates and mugs around her as if for sympathy. Then she began to rock me gently in her lap, her long plait brushing my face, and I noticed how fatigued and thin she looked. She fumbled two white tubs from a fold of her dress and shook a capsule from each onto the table. I craned my head to bring the printed labels into view: 'Retrovir, AZT nucleoside' and 'Epivir, 3TC nucleoside'. From another fold, she produced a third tub, grey this time, together with a small brown bottle. These were labelled 'Indinavir, protease inhibitor' and 'Procrit, Epotin alpha'. Two more brightly coloured capsules bounced onto the table, increasing the collection to four. She poured another large glass of water and forced the pills down one by one, wincing with each swallow. Then she concealed the tubs in her dress again, clutched me to her cheek and sat motionless for a long time. The crown of my head became damp.

Presently, Rabbi Chod stepped into the kitchen with a canvas bag under his arm and, with an impish smile on his face, asked my mother to join him in the sitting room for the surprise. She gathered me up in the blanket and followed obediently. For some reason I began to feel nervous.

We padded into the sitting room, our eyes adjusting to the morning light flowing in through the smeared bay windows. There were two Rabbi Chods in there; one in a frame on the shrine, and the other bent busily over the coffee table. He had spread a piece of Tibetan brocade across it like a tablecloth, and on this he was arranging the contents of his canvas bag, humming happily to himself. Rolled-up bandages appeared, followed by pads of cotton wool, bottles of antiseptic and other bottled medicines. Beside these he placed an array of scalpels, gleaming like fish-fins. My mother hung back near the door, clutching her stomach and pursing her lips suspiciously.

He turned his phone off, and gave it to my mother to hold. Then he took my tiny bulk from her and laid me on the sofa.

'Surprise, dear Osel, surprise! This is a day of joy and thanksgiving. I had a dream last night: the Lord God revealed to me that today is the day of dear Monlam's circumcision. What a day! A cause for celebration, and no mistake.' He turned to his collection of scalpels. 'These blades,' he went on, 'are plated in the finest Tibetan gold, and have circumcised scores of men who have become to be noble and upstanding members of the Tibetan Jewish community – that is, true luminaries of our time, my dear Osel.' He undid my nappy in a matter-of-fact way while continuing his speech over his shoulder, raising his voice over my wailing. 'Indeed, I myself, personally, circumcised your dear hubby Menla with this very blade, and likewise his father, Grandpa Pagpa, when I recognised him as the reincarnation of Isaac. Or was it the larger blade? In any event, one of these.' He squeezed my cheek affectionately. 'The circumcision is a most rich and beautiful aspect of our Tibetan Jewish tradition. I have read all about it in various Hebrew texts, and have educated myself in the art of how to carry out the act, from beginning to end, from inception to fruition. Indeed! And I have had a lot of practice, on all the male members of my flock, in fact. Not a single failure yet. Well, maybe one . . . Poor Jogpo, he's never fully recovered. But. That was the only failure, Osel, that was the only one.'

'Rabbi, do you think . . . ?'

'Yes, exactly! I knew you'd be overjoyed. I am so glad. Not at all, not at all. I am just performing my duty. Have nothing to fear, Osel, regarding baby Mo, your dear son. Just rejoice, be happy, come on, let's celebrate! He is too young to feel anything, even without an anaesthetic, and he will never remember this when he's older, anyway. His private parts – that is to say, his genitals – are in my capable hands. Indeed, my father was, I believe, a professional doctor. Now, without further ado. First: the anaesthetic.'

23

He selected a bottle from the range on the coffee table, tipped some liquid onto a cotton-wool pad and held it to my nose, between finger and thumb. I began to feel woozy. My gums went numb, but the rest of my body remained sensitive. Then he raised a leather-bound prayer book to his nose and began a gruff chant, eyeing his target and dangling his blade between his fingers.

Minutes later – after the pain – as darkness closed in on me and I was panicking, hoping that the anaesthetic would start to kick in, the last thing I heard was Rabbi Chod's voice saying: 'Do you want me to do his tonsils as well?'

Chapter Five

The pain throbbed for at least a month. Even now I can almost feel it when I think about it. After the circumcision, a bluish haze engulfed me and lingered for several days. A single drop of blood had fallen on the sitting-room carpet, and the pain seemed to intensify when I caught sight of it. The following day, it was gone.

Several days passed, and I got used to the rhythm of reversal. At first, I did not think about what it meant; it was enough to be leaving my mother's death behind.

At midday on 15 March we sat down together for a lunch of sausages and steamed bread. I lay quietly in my mother's lap, feeling the warm squirt of bottled milk against my tongue. The adults ate without speaking, my mother not allowing me out of her lap, Rabbi Chod intent on his food. He ate incredibly slowly, putting his cutlery down on his plate between mouthfuls and chewing like a camel.

Eventually, my mother spoke. Her voice sounded weary. 'Rabbi, could I please ask you a favour, please? I've got an appointment at the hospital this afternoon, and, well, the queues are going to be really long. It's nothing major, just a blood test, a routine thing. But the bus will take for ever. I don't think I can manage it with baby Mo. Do you think you might be able to watch him, just for a few hours, please? I can't face dragging him across London.'

'When?'

'Well, right now, really. I'll be back later on this afternoon.'

'My dear lotus petal. How could I refuse? Of course, it will be my pleasure, nay, an honour. I have a few things to do at the shop, but I can always take little Mo along with me, don't you agree?'

25

'Well, he . . .'

'Exactly. No problem at all. Off you trot. Rest assured, he is in my competent hands. I personally will take every pleasure in caring for dear baby Mo. Mark my words. Don't worry, be happy.'

I noticed that during his speech a shard of sausage skin had begun to go hard on the side of his knife. He sat back with a broad grin, shrugging off my mother's thanks with a small pout of the lips. My mother cleared the plates away, gathered up her Medical Lab Chart and Chem-24 Report, kissed me goodbye, left some brief instructions for Rabbi Chod and headed out to her appointment. The door clunked behind her and Rabbi Chod recommenced his breakfast while I tried unsuccessfully to control the saliva that ran down my chin. The hardened globule of sausage remained stubbornly on his knife, regardless of the friction of sawing through piece after piece of steamed bread. Once the last morsel of food had been consumed he set to the washing up, sending soap suds in all directions and singing snatches of *The Mikado* happily to the ceiling. He washed and dried each plate three times, with great vigour, before he was satisfied. Then he swung me under his arm and strode into the living room, where he deposited me on the sofa. Sinking into my mother's red velour armchair by the window, he licked his lips thoughtfully and picked up a copy of the *Daily Mail*.

I found the equanimity of the sunlight almost impossible to comprehend, as it gave Rabbi Chod the same glow, the same halo, as it gave my mother when she sat there. The haloed figure in the armchair sighed, raised its left buttock with its hand and farted like a klaxon. Then it began to scrape its robes, where a rogue drop of curd had landed earlier.

After several minutes he put the paper down, looked at his watch, rose and began to wander leisurely about the room. At intervals he would pick up an ornament and blow the dust off it, or pluck a book off the shelf and read a couple of para- graphs, or rub a smudge off the glass surface of the coffee table. When he came across a black-and-white photo of my father on the sideboard, he gingerly picked it up and cradled it in his hands. 'Where did you come from? Where are you going to?' he muttered forlornly. Finally, he put it back on the sideboard and contemplated it again. Then he blew his nose, shook his head sadly and resumed his circuit of the room. He glanced at me and I blew a bubble.

Arriving at my mother's writing desk, he sat on the worn, leather-topped stool and leant heavily on his elbows. A disorganised pile of papers and photos caught his eye and he craned his neck to have a look. He picked up a few photos, glanced at them casually and tossed them back one by one onto the desk. Then he turned his attention to a bundle of hand-written poems, grunting or chuckling from time to time. After a short while he replaced them as he had found them, raised his thigh and klaxoned again, in a higher pitch this time. He turned to me and smiled, then blew a raspberry. I tried to smile, obligingly, but burped.

'Dear, dear, baby Mo, peeka-boo! The plan for this morning is thus: first, we must visit my shop. I have some appointments there, and I cannot trust Jogpo to run it alone, the thieving monkey. He really has never been the same since his circumcision all those years ago. Peeka-boo!' For some reason, I found the way he hid his face and revealed it hilarious. But although I laughed on the inside, my face didn't correspond to my feelings. 'Peeka-boo!' he said. 'Peeka-boo! Hee heee heee. But. To business. Then, after my appointments, back here again. At your service.' He broke off and wrinkled his nose. 'Is that you or me?'

It was me. He approached bent almost double, sniffing towards my bulging nappy. Cursing loudly in Tibetan, he disappeared upstairs and returned with a fistful of incense sticks. These he lit and set out in a semi-circle around the sofa. Immediately, the thick smoke aggravated my lungs and I began to wheeze. He disappeared upstairs again.

I drifted off to sleep, and a dream starts to emerge. First the sky, then the mountains—Suddenly I found myself fully awake again, being pressed into Rabbi Chod's armpit as he strode out into the street, holding aloft a fistful of incense sticks like a Roman standard-bearer. He swung open the door of a battered yellow Fiesta and secured my small, wheezing body in the back seat by winding the centre seatbelt three times round my body, like a miniature Egyptian mummy. He wedged the bundle of incense in the dashboard to ward off noxious odours, slammed the door twice, gave the key a sharp twist and bounced his foot on the accelerator. 'This car has kaput-ted three times this month so far!' he cried. 'If it kaputs again I will have to send it to the scrapyard, do not pass go, do not collect two hundred pounds! Fini-to!' An immense cloud of grey exhaust floated into the air. Curtains all along the street twitched at the uproarious revving, and a few bothered heads appeared in windows as the Fiesta rolled slowly away.

Rabbi Chod was a bad driver. He rarely used third gear and abused the first two by pushing them to ridiculous speeds, the engine squealing like a lawnmower. He controlled the car with his left hand, for his jaunty right elbow never left the window. This meant that he had to let go of the steering wheel each time he changed gears, causing the car to veer precariously from its course until restored by an alarming yank of the wheel. When he turned corners it was by rotating the wheel with the heel of his hand. The vehicle seemed to come with a fat bluebottle as standard; it fizzed around the front seats and batted against the windscreen. Chod waved his hand when it came close, releasing and catching the steering wheel dangerously each time. To make matters worse, he stopped every minute or so to allow a car to pull out in front of him, smiling kindly, oblivious of the honks from behind. In short, his driving filled me with distress.

After what seemed like an age, we drew up outside a bustling parade of shops on Golders Green Road. Ignoring the icy stares from other motorists, Rabbi Chod parked on the pavement, unravelled me from the seatbelt and carried me out onto the street. For a minute we became part of a crowd of mid-morning shoppers and it made me feel comforted to be part of a great body of life, all overhung by a throbbing grey sky.

My right cheek was pressed against the shoulder of Rabbi Chod's silken robes; slippery, luxurious, odious. The odd smell of sweat, incense and straw, mingled with a pungent stench of animal, slid straight into my lungs, making me gag. We thrust through the crowds and into an alleyway behind the shops. Piles of rubbish lay in corners; red-brick buildings towered above; the street was cobbled and was covered in a kind of greyish slime. Shadows fell across and around us. The smell of straw and animal intensified as we neared a dingy storefront, above which were painted the words 'Chod's Animals – fine and exotic pets' in English and Tibetan; and then, with a sharp tinkle of chimes, we were inside the shop itself.

We were greeted by a flurry of noise. The main sound was a great cacophonous chirping, coming from the hundreds of assorted birds that populated the ceiling in cages, on perches, with feathers of every conceivable colour. They chirped, croaked, screeched, cawed, cooed; and one fat blue parrot, sitting sullenly on its imitation plastic branch, which had been stuck to the wall with huge quantities of brown packing tape, made a sound like a low, greasy fart. For a moment, Rabbi Chod became a latter-day Francis of Assisi as he greeted his livestock, going from bird to bird, petting, smoothing, purring, caressing. A carnival atmosphere filled the air as they jubilantly welcomed him home. Punctuating this wash of birdsong came barks and miaows from dogs and cats crouching in their cages and baskets around the edges of the shop, excited to see him; and over the top of the medley came the piping hoot of a conch shell, being blown with great gusto by a human behind the till.

'Rabbi! Welcome!' exclaimed the man, removing the conch from his mouth and wiping his lips on his sleeve. He was a squat, stringy-haired, leathery-skinned, scruffy Tibetan of uncertain age, whose body looked as if it was the wrong way round, and who suffered from a severe squint. He wore a tatty set of oversized robes identical to Rabbi Chod's, and was covered from head to toe in flecks of straw.

'Jogpo, I've told you once, I've told you a thousand times,' barked Rabbi Chod, his beard bristling, 'the conch shell is only to be blown for sacramental purposes – on the Sabbath, at festivals, and so on and so forth. Not for fun.'

'Sorry, Rabbi, I just wanted to welcome you in style . . . I got a bit carried away, a bit, a bit, a bit, overexcited. Welcome, anyway, Rabbi, welcome. And also, welcome, little Mo.' He directed a stretched grin in my direction – his squint got worse under the pressure of the smile. I tried to smile back but I had not yet learnt how to control my face. He stuck out his finger and, involuntarily, I gripped it. Chod clapped him heartily on the back, sending a cloud of straw into my face.

'So, Jogpo, my gabbeh, my deputy, my old disciple, my second-in-command; how has business been this morning? It seems pretty quiet.' Indeed it was quiet – at least so far as humans were concerned. Not a single customer could be seen.

Jogpo replied distractedly. He seemed to have a particular fascination with my fingers. 'Well, Rabbi, business has been good, good. I have only made one sale – but it was a large one. I have just managed to sell Aeesha, to a very good home, a very respectable family, I think.'

'Aeesha?' asked Rabbi Chod, affectionately picking at the feathers of the blue parrot on the plastic branch, which responded with the low farting sound.

'Yes, Aeesha. You know Aeesha . . . the jaguar cub?'

'Of course, I remember Aeesha! Why didn't you tell me you were selling her? Now I'll never see her again. And I didn't get the chance to say goodbye. Dear Aeesha. How I'll miss you.'

'Sorry, Rabbi, but the customer was in a hurry. And they paid cash.'

Rabbi Chod held out his hand expectantly. Jogpo dug a bundle of notes out of the register and handed it over with a soft rustle.

'Come, Jogpo. Where's the rest?'

Jogpo grimaced, shook his lank locks and produced another small bundle of notes which he gave Rabbi Chod.

'Jogpo, I know you better than you know yourself,' said Chod loudly, setting off a great jabbering among the birds. 'When will you learn, honesty is the best modesty? And now, if you please, the last bundle.' Jogpo groaned, flushed, and handed over the final stash of money from his trouser pocket. 'Well done, Jogpo, well done. Now, follow me, walk and talk, talk and work, time management is the secret of my success, I must teach you to do the same.' Chod spun on his heel, and we continued to the back of the shop, past a row of tropical aquariums and a pile of hamster cages, past a baby monkey tethered to a post by the wrist, towards a glass door with 'His Holiness Rabbi Chod Tulku' inscribed in an arc across it. A *khatag* hung across the lintel. Jogpo scuttled in after us; the blue parrot squawked; we all entered, and Chod rattled the door closed behind us.

The office was in disarray. Wherever I looked was the kind of detritus that could only have accumulated over many years. Everywhere were piles of paper, unopened letters, old bowls of rice, dog leads, sacks of rabbit feed and articles of clothing, none of which appeared to have been moved in a long, long time. I even spotted a couple of Bibles and rosaries in the chaos. There was no window; the room was lit by three rows of flickering butter-lamps on the small altar in the corner. I had a chance to study the altar briefly, before Chod whisked me by: on the left, a picture of the Dalai Lama as a young man, smiling from behind his sunglasses; on the right, a small Torah scroll covered in green velvet; and in the centre, in a large, ornate frame, a photo of Rabbi Chod in ceremonial dress. In front of these relics were a bowl of dusty incense and the butter-lamps, their flames dancing and fluttering in the air. On the walls there were dog-eared posters of scenes from Tibet, alongside images of Jerusalem. A string of plastic Israeli flags hung limply from the ceiling to the floor in the corner; once, many years ago, they probably would

31

have hung across the room. And all round the room, where the walls met the ceiling, hung a silken Tibetan canopy, striped in yellow, green and red ruff, stained here and there with dark blotches, covered with strands of straw, and layered in a thick mat of dust. The entire room had an uncanny, discordant atmosphere. Everywhere I looked, Jewish symbols had been self-consciously positioned within an otherwise Tibetan environment, with a hint of Englishness of course; and by the looks of things, very little had changed in many years.

Rabbi Chod lifted me away from his shoulder, dangled me in the air and laid me down in a gerbil cage on a small side table behind the desk. He closed the door and locked it. Almost immediately I let out an almighty sneeze, which went unnoticed by all but the small gerbil by my ear, which woke up with a start, shot to the corner of the cage and hid in the straw, trembling with fright.

'So, Jogpo, what appointments are in store for my good self this bright day?' asked Rabbi Chod, flexing his body in his leather armchair and stretching his feet onto the desk.

'Well, Rabbi,' said Jogpo, consulting the diary, 'I was just going to remind you. Just about to. First there is a lady, Machig, coming with her son, Mukpo. She thinks her son – and herself – may be reincarnations of famous Jewish figures. She wants you to accept them as your followers.'

'Damnation and hellfire, Jogpo, I hate doing these blasted things. So tedious, there's no mistake. We do not need any more followers. I remember when I started this movement, back in the late seventies . . . do you remember, Jogpo? You were there, by my side, from the beginning, my trusty left-hand man. You always believed in me. Through thin and through thick. I greatly enjoyed recognising *tulku*s back then, accepting money, expanding my following. But now . . .' He sighed, dramatically. 'This community does not value its Leader's time, that's the problem. This is not the kind of thing a fifty-year-old Spiritual Leader should be doing. What else?'

Jogpo pulled a pocketbook from his robes and consulted his notes. 'Well, Rabbi, the only thing left this afternoon, the only thing on your schedule, is your interview with the *Jewish Chronicle*, the interview, which—'

'Oho!' Rabbi Chod scratched his beard with glee. 'That is, indeed, more like it. This I much prefer. Publicity. Exposure. Well, well. There's no such thing as publicity, Jogpo, that's my grotto. And—Oh damnation! Look, she's arrived, that woman, what's her name. Ro-ma?'

'Machig. And her son, Mukpo. Right. I see.' Jogpo waved through the glass door, and the woman waved nervously back. 'Shall I show her in?'

'Yes, yes, show her in. Let's get this over with, without further ado,' replied Chod, thumping his feet down from the desk. Jogpo left the office and went to greet Machig.

She was an incredibly thin woman, with coiled plaits pinned up on either side of her head. She was standing at the till wearing traditional Tibetan dress, her head to one side and a watery smile on her face. As she came into closer view, I saw that she was being led by the hand by a small boy, not more than five or six, marching determinedly towards the office – with his lowered brow and powerful jaws, he bore a startling resemblance to a piranha.

Jogpo swung the door open and the visitors entered the room, smiling broadly. Machig was respectfully stooping almost double to ensure that her head did not rise above the level of Rabbi Chod's. She drew a *khatag* from her pocket and presented it to Rabbi Chod, who received it graciously and draped it round her neck, in the traditional way.

'Take a seat, my dear lotus petals, take a seat,' grunted Chod phlegmatically, waving his hand towards the two green plastic chairs in front of him and leaning back into his battered leather armchair. Jogpo closed the door and scampered off, mumbling something about making tea. 'Now,' said Chod, 'I am very pleased to make your acquaintance, dear Machig and, of course, little Mukpo. I am Rabbi Chod, who you must already know by reputation. Top banana.'

'I'm a Muslim,' replied the piranha boy, unexpectedly.

'Oh, Mukpo, you silly little darling!' cooed his mother, picking him up and sitting him gently on the chair. 'I do apologise, Venerable Rabbi. My son has such a childish sense of humour.'

Rabbi Chod looked confused. 'Did he just say . . . ?'

'I do apologise on his account, Venerable Rabbi. But boys will be boys.'

'Yes, of course . . . So, er . . . tell me about yourself, and why you are considering the very wise and noble decision of requesting me to accept you and your son as my disciples.' He peered warily at the boy across the desk.

Machig reached into her bag and pulled out a large pink lollipop, which she unwrapped and slid between the jaws of the piranha boy. Mukpo looked delighted and began to suck animatedly, the stick revolving in his lips. The gerbil scampered across the cage and moved some straw aside, giving me a better view.

'Well, Rabbi, you are very kind. Where to start? Let's see. I moved to England six years ago. My parents live in Dharamsala, and are originally from Kham in eastern Tibet, as you can maybe tell from my son's build?' Rabbi Chod grunted, and Mukpo remained inscrutable. I sneezed again. Machig started and squinted in my direction. 'Wait – is that a baby in that cage?' she exclaimed.

'Yes, indeed it is, my dear lotus petal. Indeed. Best place for them, I find.'

She looked concerned. Mukpo slid off his chair and toddled over. For a moment my vision was obscured by his leering face pressed up against the cage, the lollipop stick jutting through the bars and poking me violently in the stomach. I tried my best to wriggle out of range.

Machig collected her thoughts and continued. 'I grew up in Dharamsala, in the Tibetan community in exile. I was an only child, and my parents worked very hard and saved all their money to send me to England. All that my father could think about was the Chinese, and how they pillaged our land

34

like wild animals. He was haunted by what he had seen. How they smashed the monasteries, tortured the monks, and used the ancient statues of Buddha as target practice for their tanks. His brother – my uncle – was killed in the fighting along the Huang river, and my father lost two of his fingers in the battles around Kumbum monastery. He was imprisoned, like many of us, and tortured for eight years. Eventually he was released, miraculously found my mother, and escaped to India.

'In India, things were very hard. We had no money, and no freedom. The climate was very bad for my father's lungs, and he became very sick. All the time, he dreamt of being able to send me to study in England. He thought that England must be like a paradise. I studied very hard at school, and somehow my parents managed to scrape together the money to send me here, together with grants and scholarships. At first, it seemed to be true – England was luxurious beyond my wildest dreams. These days, though, I often wish I could go back to Dharamsala.

'I came here to study medicine at the University of London. Just before I left India, I became pregnant. It was an accident. I didn't find out until a few weeks later, in England. I didn't say anything to my parents; it would have been too shameful. That was six years ago – and my parents still don't know about little Mukpo.'

Mukpo, lollipop still between his lips, turned round at the mention of his name, and his mother smiled at him. Then he turned back and continued trying to fit his fingers through the bars of the cage. The gerbil and I were both terrified, and huddled together in the straw.

'Did you continue your studies after Mukpo was born?' asked Rabbi Chod.

'Yes – I am now in my clinical year and I will be completing my course next summer. I have been looking after Mukpo all the time, all through university, for six years. It has been very hard, very difficult, but I cope. I work nights in a petrol station. But I have managed, so far. Not much sleep!' She laughed, wryly.

'And your parents still don't know about him?'

'No.'

Rabbi Chod paused and leant back in his chair, scratching his beard and stifling a yawn. 'Well, well, well, my dearest Machig, you have my sympathy. Indeed, I am very moved.' He smiled and rubbed his eyes. Mukpo had found a ruler on the floor and was prodding the gerbil, which was skittering around the cage in panic. I was helpless and began to feel sick with nerves. 'So tell me, Machig, if you would be so kind,' Rabbi Chod went on, 'your precise reasons for coming for an audience with Rabbi Chod this morning.'

'Well, Rabbi, over the last couple of years I have become very interested in Judaism. The Jews have been persecuted in the Diaspora for hundreds and hundreds of years, yet they have managed to retain their identity despite it all. They are a noble people, Venerable Rabbi. The chosen people. You believe in one God, and one God alone – there is so much strength in that belief.

'I feel a great desire for that strength. I need it. The Jewish nation is a strong nation, a mighty people. For thousands of years they have been persecuted, displaced, dispersed, systematically killed, but despite all that they now have a land of their own, a strong land, and one of the best armies in the world. We Tibetans have a lot to learn from the Jews, I think, Rabbi. We need the same strength in our Diaspora identity. We need to get our land back, and we need a strong army to defend it. We need so much courage. And the Jews . . . Rabbi, I dearly want to be one of you. I want to be part of the Jewish faith, and I want to bring that strength to the Tibetan people. I want to be your disciple.' Rabbi Chod nodded slowly and steepled his fingers. Machig leant forward and continued, her voice wavering with fervour.

'Although I am sure you haven't noticed me, I have been attending your Sabbath services here at the pet shop for over two months,' she said. 'I spoke to Venerable Jogpo about wanting to convert, and he said I had to make an appointment to see you, so that you could establish whether or not

I was Jewish in my previous lives. He said I couldn't convert – either I was already a Jew from previous incarnations, or I wasn't.'

'Indeed, this is the case,' replied Chod. 'Unlike mainstream Jewish traditions, in which the gentile can convert to the Jew, my philosophy does not allow for such transgressions. Rabbi Chod and his followers hold as Jewish only those who were Jewish in previous lives; reincarnated Jews, if you will. These reincarnations are the real Lost Tribe of Israel. There are no other Jews.'

'Yes, I am a reincarnated Jew, Rabbi, I can feel it in my blood. I have never been more convinced about anything in my life. I am a Jew, a reincarnated Jew. I know it. I'm sure of it.'

'We'll see, my dear lotus petal, we'll see. Don't dump the gun, indeed, hold your forces. First things worst. Let's get this show on the street. For a small fee – which will go towards the synagogue funds, of course – I will be able to carry out the appropriate divination.'

'Of course, of course – I have been saving up.' She brought out a small brown envelope and slid it across the desk to him. He opened it a fraction and glanced inside. Then he consulted some books and astrological charts that were scattered on the floor around his feet, knitted his brows and went into deep meditation.

He opened his eyes and asked, 'What is your date of birth?'

'Fifteenth day of the fifth month of the Iron-Bird year,' she replied.

'Was it raining when you were born?'

'No, snowing.'

Rabbi Chod returned to his meditation, sitting motionless for many minutes. Finally he opened his eyes and leant across the desk. 'Congratulations, dear Machig, lotus petal,' he said. 'The Almighty has communicated with me this day. In his kindness, he has informed me that in one of your previous lives you were none other than a courtesan in the court of holy King David. This means – you are Jewish.

Tibetan and Jewish. Join the party! Congratulations again, or, as we Jews say, *Mazal tov*. Welcome to the community. I shall expect you at the service this Sabbath.' Machig looked overjoyed, and began to thank him. He interrupted, modestly waving all appreciation aside. 'Now, how about your little son . . . Mukpo? Hey, Mukpo, come over here.'

This came in the nick of time for the gerbil, which was cornered at one end of the cage. I had managed to get Mukpo to drop the ruler through the bars, and he was trying to get it out in an increasingly violent manner. But when he heard his name he ran over to his mother, crunching the remains of the lollipop in his powerful jaws.

'Yes indeed, Rabbi, my Mukpo is a very special child, everyone says so. Our little precious Rinpoche! I have always known he was special, ever since he was small. He is a prodigy, no less. I feel quite convinced he is the reincarnation of a famous Jewish saint.'

Mukpo finished the last of his lolly. 'I'm a Muslim,' he said, spitting the stick out onto the floor.

'Mukpo! Please stop for Ah-ma, yes? You promised, remember? Ah-ma will give you a humbug, OK?' She handed him a fat, striped sweet, which he unwrapped noisily and pushed into his mouth. 'He doesn't mean anything by it, Rabbi, he's just got an incorrigible sense of humour. He doesn't really understand what he's saying. You know what they say about us Khampas – the best fighters, the best saints?'

'I see,' mumbled Rabbi Chod. Evidently flustered, he got up and walked briskly round the periphery of the room. Then he sat down again, rummaged around on the floor by his feet, and retrieved a pad of paper and a stubby pencil. 'While dear little Mukpo enjoys his confectionery, Machig, I wonder if you would answer a few questions. First, has your child ever revealed the identity that he used to have in his previous life?'

'No – not directly, no,' replied Machig, glancing warily at her son.

'Has he ever spontaneously spoken another language? Sanskrit, say, or Aramaic?'

'No, I don't think so, not really. Although when he was a baby he did make noises that sounded as if they might have come from another age.'

Rabbi Chod raised an eyebrow and wrote something down. 'Does he frequently mention another country or historical period? Does he have an unusually developed skill of some kind? Does he have recurring dreams? Can he remember who his parents were in the past? Does he . . . feel an affinity with any particular religion?'

Machig was beginning to look uncomfortable. 'No, Rabbi, nothing like that.'

'None of these things?'

'Well . . . no.'

'So, Machig, if you don't mind my asking, why, in fact, and, indeed, wherefore, did you begin to suppose that your dear son here, Mukpo, is a reincarnation, a *tulku* – or in Hebrew a *gilgul* – of a famous Jewish saint? For whatever reason? Just because you yourself are Jewish doesn't mean he is, you know.'

'Well, the night before I gave birth, I had a dream—'

'I want to be an Imam,' said Mukpo, having finished his sweet.

'Mukpo!' tutted Machig, pushing another sweet into his mouth. As if by magic he fell silent once more, grinning a piranha's grin and sucking noisily. There was a long pause.

Rabbi Chod sat back, slowly, in his seat. 'So . . . so when was Mukpo born?'

'The twenty-fifth day of the third month of the Earth Rabbit year,' replied Machig, affectionately stroking her son's hair.

'Right,' said Chod, suddenly pulling himself together and snapping his book closed. 'I have done my calculations, I have worked it out. I have meditated and received a divine message. It was quick but things like this are often quick with an expert like my good self, so quick, blink and you miss them, do not pass go, poof! Like that. Your son, my dear Machig, was nothing other than . . . a Kashmiri Muslim butcher.'

'*What?* A . . . Mukpo was never a butcher! He must have been a scholar, or a saint, or a great leader. Not a Kashmiri Muslim butcher.'

I glanced at Mukpo, who was looking rather pleased.

'Yes, I am afraid so, Machig,' Rabbi Chod replied sympathetically. 'From now on, little Mukpo will be known as "Kashmiri Muslim Butcher Tulku", or "Kashmiri Muslim Butcher Gilgul". I will inform the community this Sabbath, before prayers, that another *tulku* has been recognised. He will be instated as such. Now please leave. I have work to do.' Machig's distress overwhelmed her. She clasped her hands to her head and her lower lip wobbled violently. One of her plaits came unclipped and uncoiled itself down her shoulder. She was just about to reply when she was interrupted by Mukpo.

'I'm a—'

'Mukpo!' squealed Machig, unwrapping another sweet, 'Please!' She pressed the sweet into his mouth.

Rabbi Chod got up and pointed towards the door. 'My dear Machig, please take dear little Kashmiri Muslim Butcher Tulku and leave. I am an exceedingly busy man.'

'But Rabbi, Rabbi, please!'

Chod closed his eyes and gestured aggressively for them to leave. I could see Jogpo peering in through the window, holding a giant steaming teapot, wondering what was going on and not daring to enter. 'Venerable Chod, have mercy! This will be the end of us, Rabbi. Our good reputation will be ruined for generations. We will be a laughing stock. Have pity. Have pity.' Rabbi Chod pursed his lips imperiously and shook his head. All of a sudden, as a last resort, Machig reached deep into her handbag, sending lipsticks and crumpled tissues in all directions. She pulled out a fistful of twenty-pound notes and scattered them on the desk. Through the window, I saw Jogpo's eyes widen. 'Rabbi, please.'

40

Chod opened his eyes a fraction. There was a deathly silence, punctuated only by the sound of Mukpo crunching the remains of his humbug. Machig reached into the bag of sweets, to no avail. It was empty. There wasn't much time.

'Rabbi?'

'Very well,' announced Rabbi Chod, gathering up the money and slipping it into the top drawer of his desk. 'I see now that I have made a mistake in my calculations. This little boy, Mukpo, is not actually a Muslim butcher *tulku*. I declare him Isaiah Tulku, Isaiah Gilgul. We haven't got one of them yet. Happy? Now get lost.'

'Isaiah! I knew it! I was reading about him only yesterday. Oh, thank you so much, Holy Venerable One, thank you! God bless you, God bless you! Your powers of clairvoyance are unparalleled—'

Chod smiled, with difficulty. Machig shot him a grateful look and bustled Mukpo – or Isaiah Gilgul – out of the door. Jogpo gestured with the teapot in confusion as they passed him. They were about to leave the shop when Mukpo turned, his piranha jaw set, his brows knitted, bits of sweet still in his mouth. He waved a podgy hand and smiled.

'Peace be upon you,' he said.

Chapter Six

Rabbi Chod sat for a few minutes in silence after Machig and Mukpo had left. I comforted myself with the thought that when I went to sleep and woke up the following morning, Mukpo would be erased for ever from my future. He would, of course, remain in Rabbi Chod's future, but I didn't particularly mind that.

Jogpo was about to come in and ask what all the fuss was about. But as he began to open the door, a Tibetan man with leathery skin, a gleaming pate and a pecking manner entered the shop, leaning heavily on a walking stick, and started to ping the service bell on the counter, squinting to see if there was anyone in the back office. Jogpo froze for a moment, unsure what to do; then Rabbi Chod jerked his head for Jogpo to go and welcome him. He put the teapot down on the desk and hurried back into the shop, shooting worried glances at Rabbi Chod over his shoulder. Steam wafted from the spout and gave Rabbi Chod a misty halo. He dug around in the detritus on the floor, and managed to unearth an old teacup with a broken handle. Then he poured himself a cup of thick butter tea and sat back in subdued silence.

For a while, I was so relieved to be free from the predatory Mukpo that I felt almost relaxed in the gerbil cage. The gerbil and I had been united by our struggle against a common enemy; it crawled onto my chest and lay there, exhausted. I could feel its tiny heart racing, ten beats to every one of mine. Slowly I felt my head become heavy and the sounds around me became harsh and crisp. Then they faded away. Snatches of speech shot across my consciousness. Then blackness descended, turning in on itself and folded outwards, becoming a huge vista; this slowly separated out and dissolved away, leaving a vast empty space behind.

A new scene begins to emerge, first the most prominent details and then the colours, textures and noises. I am in a very, very cold place, surrounded by thick snow. Rocks and slabs of ice push out of the snow around me, and a few metres ahead a precipice drops vertically into an unseen valley. I turn once in a full circle, and see towering mountain peaks stretching into the high air above. It is bitterly cold, yet incredibly clear; I can see for many miles around. I feel as slow as a cloud.

Suddenly I hear a sound like a small, sharp pop rising on the breeze towards me, followed by a succession of high-pitched clicks. I make my way forwards, stumbling a little in the snow, then fall into the coldness and peer over the edge of the precipice. Sharp air pierces my body. Far below are great edifices of rock and snow, many miles across, all twisted together, churning in a great valley, rolling down towards a broad river which flows from left to right across my field of vision. Two or three small stone reliquaries (*stupas* in Tibetan) dot the occasional peak, their strings of brightly coloured prayer flags stuttering in the wind. There are more clicks, a couple of loud pops, and a bang. A cloud passes away from the face of the sun. As the valley brightens, the river becomes more vivid and I can make out movement on the water. As my eyes focus, a beetle-like boat appears in the centre of the river. It is spinning slowly on its axis, and seems to be out of control. There is movement on the boat; I can just make out several figures darting to and fro, their heads flashing as their steel helmets reflect the sunlight.

In the tiny trees along the riverbank, shadows flit in and out of view, aiming guns at the boat and ducking into cover. The pops and clicks and bangs become more frequent. One man crumples and becomes stationary. Another runs over and drags him into the trees. Two figures fall from the boat and disappear in the water. There is an explosion in the very centre of the boat, throwing debris into the air. I feel sick.

The boat begins to break up, its shell cracking and dislocating. One by one, its occupants flail overboard and splash around. Then they jolt and become still, some sinking, some floating. Their steel helmets are buffeted around in the waves. The water seems to change colour, to become darker. The men on the riverbank are gaining confidence, coming out of the thicket and raking the river with bullets. Strings of white appear on the surface of the water, piercing the waves. Nothing that these shadowy men are wearing glints in the sun; they have no helmets, no uniforms. Then a cloud passes in front of the sun again, and the scene becomes a dusky blur.

All at once there was a tremendous rasping sound, and I was dragged roughly back into consciousness. The imposing figure of Rabbi Chod was pulling open the cage door. He lifted me out and spun round, making my legs scythe through the air. Then he clutched me to his chest and there was a blinding flash.

'Great, that was a lovely shot. One more?'

Flash. Turn. Flash-flash.

'Lovely, Rabbi, lovely. And again to the other side? Rest your hand on the desk? Hold the baby up? Lovely.'

Flash-flash. Flash. Flash. Spin. Flash-flash.

'One more? One for the road?'

Flash. Flash-flash-flash.

'And again? To the left? Move the baby's arm? Lovely.'

Turn. Tilt. Flash flash flash flash flash. Nausea.

'Okey-dokey, great, that's a wrap. That'll do us, I think. All done. Thanks. Those'll come out lovely, I reckon. Lovely light. Lovely. Great with the baby. As for me – love you and leave you. You be all right now, Phil?'

'Yeah, sure, mate. Don't bother sticking around. I'll see you back at the office.'

'OK, then, we'll stay in touch. Good to meet you, Rabbi.'

'On the contrary, my dear sir, the pleasure was all my own, that is, it is indeed an honour for you to meet me, but the pleasure was, I assure you, all mine . . .'

44

'Great. See you.'

'Yeah, later, Andrew.'

'Farewell, my dear sir, so long.'

As the room stopped turning and my eyes recovered from the dazzling flashes, I found myself being cradled in the lap of Rabbi Chod in his leather armchair once more. He must have got used to the smell from my nappy, as it didn't seem to bother him. The wavering light from the butter-lamps mingled with the mid-morning sunshine filtering weakly in through the glass door. The desk shone bronze and scarlet, like a sacrificial altar. Opposite us, perched in the green plastic chair that Machig had recently vacated, was a gangly, intelligent-looking English man with flushed cheeks, horn-rimmed spectacles and hair that was somewhere between incredibly messy and incredibly fashionable. He wore a tight-fitting T-shirt which said 'Born astride a grave' in pink lettering, and a bracelet made of beads that clattered against the desk as he fiddled with a Dictaphone. I burped and, to my surprise, a little bit of puke spilt out of my mouth and down my chin. The dizzying photo shoot had taken its toll. Rabbi Chod wiped my face with a splutter of disgust and, as a curative measure, began to jog me up and down with great swooping movements.

'Well, Rabbi,' said the bespectacled man, getting the Dictaphone working and sitting back in his seat, notebook in hand, 'that's the photos over and done with, thank you. I think Andrew got some great shots there.'

'Yes indeed, my dear Mr Phil, yes indeed. My profile, I think you'll find, is especially striking on celluloid. I have every trust in Mr Andrew and his professionalism. Now, to work: interview me, without further ado.'

'Oh yes, of course, erm, let's get started. First of all, thank you, Rabbi, for agreeing to do this article for the *Jewish Chronicle*. I'm sure it will be a big hit with our readers. Oh, for the record,' he said, bending towards the Dictaphone and checking his Russian Army watch, 'the time is now 15:30 hours on Tuesday, the 15th of March 2005.' He paused, as if expecting a reply from the machine; then sat back and consulted his notes. His voice assumed a journalist's tone, and he punctuated his sentences with little stabs of his pencil. 'First off, Rabbi, would you mind telling me a bit about your childhood, your early years, where you grew up, early influences, that kind of thing?'

Rabbi Chod grunted, pushed his chair back from the table (I could feel the grate of the legs against the floor all the way up my spine) and pulled his beard contemplatively. 'You know, young Mr Phil, my very earliest memories are of my motherland, the Land of the Snows. I treasure these memories. Even after thirty-five years in exile in the corrupt West – that is, the UK – I still feel that Tibet is my home. Tibet is . . . a very special, unique place, very spiritual; one which you Westerners can only dream about. The roof of the world. Indeed, the point may be best illustrated by a traditional folk song my old mother, Uma, used to sing me when I was but a tiny nipper snapper. May I?'

'Oh, go for it, please do,' Phil replied, re-crossing his thin legs and ruffling his hair.

Rabbi Chod took the Dictaphone and held it to his mouth, Tom Jones-style.

'On the lofty mountain pool,' he warbled in heavy Tibetan,
'There are thousands and thousands of swans.
When the sun, the swan of the sky, rises gently into the blue,
The mountains are drenched – the mountains are drenched – the mountains are drenched with gold.'

He cracked his neck and replaced the Dictaphone on the desk with an air of great solemnity.

'Would you mind translating that for me, please?' asked Phil.

'Mr Phil! It is untranslatable. The beauty – that is, the artistry – lies in the Tibetan. The Tibetan. It is unimaginable to translate something as wondrous as that. It would amount to sacrilege. Ha! Sadly, for you it must remain a mystery. Unless, that is, you learn Tibetan.'

'Yes, yes, of course. Apologies. Do go on.'

'Hey, Mr Phil. Would you mind holding baby Mo? I've had enough.'

The reporter's mouth gaped like a guppy's; I was hoisted into the air and pressed into his uncertain arms, dirty nappy and all. 'But my notes—'

'Nonsense to your notes, Mr Phil. Use your radio recording instrument, Mr Phil. In Tibet people would give their left arm for such a contraption. Now, where was I?'

I began to feel sick again, but tried to hold it down. The reporter's fingers were nervous, puce and tight, and they were digging into my ribs.

'Yes, of course, my childhood, indeed. That folksong casts my mind back to the lofty clouds and majestic mountains of Tibet even now. I shall take that song with me in my heart to my dying day, and I shall be buried to the sound of its golden tones.' Phil scribbled the phrase, 'golden tones' awkwardly in his notebook, clutching me tight with one hand. 'I have always had a particular talent and ability in the field of musical arts,' Chod went on. 'Even now, at the distinguished age of fifty years young, I have a strong and avid interest in popular music. I am a long-standing member of the respectable amateur singing group, the Gilbert and Sullivan Society, or GASS, and I religiously follow the top ten in the popular charts. I could have become a famous musician, if I didn't find my calling in leading my people, in the religious sense, if you will. Do you have an affection, a passion, for the musical arts, Mr Phil? You strike me as a musical man.'

'Yes indeed I have, Rabbi,' replied Phil, flattered. 'As a matter of fact, I used to be in a band with Andrew – you know, the photographer? – in my student days. I play the electric bass,' he said, jogging me on his knee. 'Andrew's dad used to be in a rock band, you know. Queen, was it? Or The Doors?'

Rabbi Chod slapped his thigh and replied with enthusiasm. 'What a coincidence! I my good self, in fact, my dear Mr Phil, auditioned for the Queen in the early days,' he said. 'Ha! I see your surprise. I was almost picked, as well. Indeed. It was between me and Teddy Mercury. But I think that in the end Brian May was a bit intimidated by my talent. Second fiddle and all that, eh? And' – he leant closer – 'I wasn't a gay. At least . . . not really.'

Phil looked taken aback, adjusted his spectacles and jogged me faster on his bony knee. 'OK, thanks Rabbi, I'll take your word for it. This is not what I . . . Now, let's move on.'

'The other boy was a lot older than me. He was maybe a gay . . . but I was just experimenting.'

'OK, Rabbi, that's enough. Now we'll move on, if you don't mind,' snapped Phil.

Rabbi Chod snorted and took a sip of tea. 'Don't put that in your article, in the paper, OK? I warn you, Mr Phil, I can be terrible when aroused.'

'Yes, Rabbi. Of course. Now let's not mention the gay community any more. We . . . Anyway. You were talking about your childhood?'

'Butter tea? Or, as we say in Tibetan, *po cha*?'

'No, thank you.'

'Suit your good self, Mr Phil. Mr Sensitive.' Rabbi Chod pouted moodily. '*Po cha* is one of our most famous and well-loved beverages. Indeed, I myself get terrible back-ache if I drink any less than five cups a day. Terrible. Just here, along the spine, the ache occurs. But, to a foreigner . . .' he shrugged. 'Now, where was I?'

'OK, Rabbi, I'll ask you another question, how about that?' said Phil, his voice rising slightly. 'How do you respond to the accusations made against you by influential members of the Jewish, and indeed Tibetan, community, such as, and I quote from the Chief Rabbi's recent article, "Chod is an abhorrent con-man, a charlatan, an impostor; the foremost heretic of our times, a modern-day Shabbetai Tsevi, whose tiny following does not reduce the seriousness of his crimes?"

Similarly, the Office of the Tibetan Government in Exile has denounced you as, I quote again, "a barefaced cheat, whose absurd religious principles are as unsubstantiated as they are self-serving". What, Rabbi, if I may, is your response to these attacks?' He poked the air with his pencil, sending shockwaves through my small body. I felt a dribble of puke slipping unnoticed down my chin.

'Ha, Mr Phil! Good question. Let me tell you. My flock, the Tibetan Jewish community,' declaimed Rabbi Chod, the blood rushing to his face, 'are the modern-day scapegoats, the oppressed, the downtrodden, the lowly worms of the twenty-first century. Indeed. My disciples and my good self have, as you kindly pointed out, been subject to a heinous quantity of abuse, slander, racism and religious persecution ever since our formation almost thirty years ago. Heinous! We are dogs, Mr Phil, dogs!' He was warming to his theme, and despite myself I filled my nappy again. 'In theological terms our religion is perfect, flawless, tight as water in a boat, from every conceivable angle. Let me explain, Mr Phil. Let me explain.' He got to his feet and gestured in the air.

'The doctrine of reincarnation is key to my philosophy, dear sir, and once you accept reincarnation as truth, you will see I am proved right in every way. Fact number one, Mr Phil: reincarnation is fundamental to Judaism. Not just to us Tibetans. Fact number two: in Hebrew, the reincarnate is called a *gilgul*. The truth is – there is no doubt about it – we have many lives. So, therefore, with regard to my followers, we are Tibetans, we are Jews, we are Asian, we are Semitic. We are Tibetan Jews. That Torah scroll you see on the shrine behind you – no, no, the other side – to your right – yes, there, you see? It is written not in Hebrew but in Tibetan, Mr Phil. Tibetan! It is the first of its kind, the first ever Tibetan Torah, translated by none other than my good self, with some adaptations and embellishments, of course.

'We Tibetan Jews are, each of us, as you know – for you have done research, have you not? – reincarnations of

Jewish figures throughout history. This, sir, is proven. That boy you are holding in your arms, for example, is the son of the reincarnation of Holy Abraham himself. And his grandfather is the reincarnation of Holy Isaac. And Jogpo, who I believe you met, is the reincarnation of Holy Jacob. That is, Mr Phil, our spiritual inheritance is stainlessly, spotlessly pure. We are, no less, the true Lost Tribe of Israel, which has been scattered throughout the world for hundreds of years, hundreds of generations, reincarnated in hundreds of different lives. The Lost Tribe wasn't lost through geographical misplacement, Mr Phil. It was lost through death, and anonymous, unrecognised reincarnation. Now, this period of history is the long-awaited Quickening. At long last, in the twentieth and twenty-first centuries, the Lost Tribe of Israel has begun to come together. After all these long years, we are found! And I myself, their leader, am, as I am sure you are aware, none other than the reincarnation of Moses himself – what an honour! Indeed, I can remember splitting the Red Sea as if it were yesterday, as clear as so many whistles. *Whoosh!* it went, just like that. Just like that! Dry land from here to the other side, my shepherd's staff in my hand, raised aloft like this – *whoosh!* Like that. *Whoosh!* Oh, how the Israelites cheered.

'Verily and indeed, Mr Phil, these scandalous, evil accusations reveal the religious intolerance – nay, downright bigotry – that corrupts most religious institutions today, in modern times. I myself am a true prophet, a visionary, a messenger from On High, a Saviour, a redeemer, a liberator. Indeed, Jesus had it bad, did he not? He was persecuted? You've seen the film? The Mel Gibson? Likewise: my good self.' Rabbi Chod ended his speech with a flourish, retched in the Tibetan style and hacked a gob of phlegm into the wastepaper bin.

I could tell that Phil was beginning to notice the fresh smell coming from my nappy, because he held me nearer and nearer to the floor. My unsupported head began to dangle awkwardly. 'Thank you, Rabbi, most informative,' said Phil. 'Moooving on, then. Why do you think the Lost Tribe of Israel would take rebirth in Tibet, of all places?' He untwined his legs and recrossed them, intellectually.

'Aha!' exclaimed Chod. 'That, Mr Phil, is an interesting point. A point that I am thinking of illuminating in a work of non-fiction. I haven't written it yet but am planning to shortly.'

'Oh, really? I've written a work of non-fiction too, Rabbi. It's called *The Horn-rimmed Spectacle*. I'm trying to get it published.'

'Yes, exactly. Yes! Anyway . . . Indeed. As you are aware, Mr Phil, the Jewish race is often known as the Chosen People. What this actually means and signifies, on a day-to-day level, is a matter of some theological debate. Nevertheless and moreover, the Tibetans, likewise, have become a kind of Chosen People over the last thirty years, in the eyes of the increasingly morally degenerate and materialistic Western world, which, as I am sure you will agree my dear friend, is a sorry state of affairs. A sorry state. The corrupt West has, in recent decades, elevated Tibet and her people as a saint-nation, a last vestige of purity in a defiled world, a Utopia, a Pegasus, a unicorn, a pinnacle of humanity and purity, a pineapple. In this sense, the Tibetan race is also a Chosen People.

'Allow me to elaborate, Mr Phil. Sit back, relax, and take notes. Let me illustrate with an example. The recent persecution of the Tibetan people by the bastard Chinese army was taking place just before reincarnated Jews were first recognised, by none other than my very good self, among the Tibetan community. This is, let me tell you, no coincidence. None at all. The Jews have been the scapegoats throughout history. As soon as they take rebirth in Tibet, then poof! Do not pass go! Persecution follows directly, not even collecting two hundred pounds. Wham! Whang! Whoof! My disciples, the Lost Tribe of Tibetan Israelites, the Chosen of the Chosen People, are instantly oppressed. Persecuted by not only the bastard Chinese but also the

Tibetans, the Jews, everyone. Everyone. Everyone hates us. The bastard Chinese, the Tibetans, the Jews – all anti-Semites. Every last jack-man. Anti-Semites! Ptchah!' With this last burst of emotion, Rabbi Chod collapsed into his chair and ran his hands passionately through his beard.

'You're suggesting that mainstream Jews are anti-Semites?'

'Precisely.'

'Very . . . interesting. So, Rabbi, why are the Jews always oppressed, even in Tibet? What is the reason for the persecution of the Jews? Throughout the ages? Constantly? According to your philosophy?'

'How should I know?' replied Chod moodily. 'You tell me, Mr Phil. Anti-Semites.'

There was a pause. Phil glanced at his notes, letting me slide dangerously through his hands in the process. Chod sipped his tea, which by now must have gone cold.

When Phil spoke again, his voice was more balanced. 'One final comment, Rabbi, if you would be so kind. To finish off: a brief word on the current Middle East situation?'

'Well, my dear Mr Phil, it is very simple. I am a pet-shop owner, that is what I do – among other things, granted, but that is, shall we say, my day job. If there are two dogs fighting, what do I do? I separate them.'

'Er, OK,' said Phil, knitting his brows.

'Yes. Yes indeed. I separate them. That, Mr Phil, is wisdom enough for anybody, don't you agree? Two dogs; fight; separate them. Fine. Finito.'

Phil's mouth opened and closed a few times. He wrinkled his nose and coughed weakly, then lifted me up and laid me gently on the desk.

'Rabbi, I really think this baby might need changing,' he said in a conspiratorial tone.

'Oh, indeed, Mr Phil?' Chod looked genuinely surprised. 'Well, then, why don't you—'

'Rabbi, sorry, but I'm going to have to dash,' said Phil quickly, glancing uncomfortably at my nappy and his watch.

'But Mr Phil, infants come first—'

'Thank you so much for giving me the opportunity to interview you—'

'Women and children first, Mr—'

'This has been a most interesting interview, Rabbi, and I'll send you a copy of the article when it comes out. But now, I must be off.'

Rabbi Chod snorted and shook his head disapprovingly. Then he reached over, plucked me from the desk and slotted me back in the gerbil cage. Phil got to his feet, stowed his Dictaphone away and shook Rabbi Chod briskly by the hand.

'Also, Mr Phil, one more thing before you go. Do you think you would be so kind as to request Mr Andrew to send me copies of the original photographs of my good self, when they are developed? I may be able to use them for religious and publicity purposes. And when you leave, please consider purchasing a goldfish, or even a stick insect or a baby koala – discount at ten per cent for you, just speak to Jogpo.'

Phil made a hurried exit. The gerbil scuttled over my legs and nuzzled against me, trembling. My mind was bursting with the sheer volume of new information. My nappy was becoming almost painful, and the smell of puke was getting stronger. I tried to block out the raised voices, and felt glad to be in the relative safety of the cage. For a moment I envied the small brown gerbil. I had no idea what my life would force upon me in the years to come; but judging by the way it had started, I found it difficult to be optimistic.

Chapter Seven

When we arrived home that afternoon, Rabbi Chod laid me on the sofa and surrounded me again with incense. My body felt as if it was being filled with smoke and my lungs felt stuffed with sand. Chod walked over to the mirror and began to pluck his eyebrows. After that, he leant on the mantelpiece and buried his face in his hands. He remained motionless for a long time. For once, he seemed very small and fragile. I closed my eyes and tried to forget everything. He left the room and ascended the stairs. I heard a door open and close, and heavy footsteps cross the ceiling. Bedsprings growled and then all became still. Rabbi Chod had taken refuge in sleep.

Before I realised that I too had dozed off, I was awoken by the sound of keys in the front door. There was a soft thud as my mother dropped her bag under the hat-stand; then she padded into the smoke-filled room and gave a little squawk of surprise. Immediately, she took all the smoking incense through to the kitchen and there was a loud hiss as she extinguished it in the sink. She came back into the sitting room and gathered me into her arms. In her frail grasp, I felt comforted. Before long I was relieved of my overloaded nappy and felt immensely liberated. She carried me through to the kitchen, where she put me on a blanket and gulped down a glass of water. The table was dirty – Chod had forgotten to wipe it after lunch. My mother cleaned it with a rag, but the food stains still remained in the wood. For my mother, they were indelible; but for me they would disappear the following day. On the counter beside the toaster was an old typewriter. I had no idea why she kept a typewriter in the kitchen, but it looked as if it belonged there. She fisted her smeared eyes with her knuckles.

Thankfully, there was no sound from upstairs. Rabbi Chod was in the habit of going to bed and getting up very early, and I was glad about that – there was a good chance he would remain asleep for the rest of the evening. My mother sat with me in her lap. A deep quiet settled in the kitchen, made all the more noticeable by the hum of the fridge and the occasional clunk of the pipes. The sun was beginning to go down and the kitchen became intimate, darkness wrapping round us like a blanket. My mother began to hum an old Tibetan song to me, her voice low and cracking but beautiful. For a moment I could almost smell the crisp snow. She ended, holding the final note until it merged with the darkness. Then she began to speak.

'My baby, my baby, all my love, my child. What will happen to us, Monlam? What will become of me? Ah-ma loves you, always know that, won't you? For ever. Whatever happens.' She coughed painfully. 'Shall I tell you a story, Mo? Would you like that? Let me think . . . OK, how about this? It is a story my mother told me about her father – my grandfather, your Great-Grandpa Dorje. He was a great warrior, you know, in his time, a brave, strong Chamdo fighter. My mother used to remember him leaving the house late at night to fight the Chinese, making offerings to the wrathful gods, his rifle hanging on his back like a snake. He used to carry a knife twelve inches long! He was special, your great-grandfather. All his comrades wore fur-lined *chuba*s, shawls and camouflaged clothes for fighting. But Great-Grandpa Dorje was a traditional man – when he went to battle, he always wore huge Chamdo tassels of red silk. It made him easily visible, but he said it gave him courage. Maybe that's what killed him.

'I remember this particular story; my mother used to say it was her favourite one. He always told it to her before she went to bed, by the dung fire while sipping a bedtime cup of *châng*, striped by the shadows from the lengths of raw pork-fat hanging from the ceiling. She told me this story many times. She said that the shadows from the flames made his eyebrows swoop up in great triangular peaks, and his face looked bright red in the firelight. He looked like a protector deity himself – a great, wrathful Mahakala. My mother and grandmother sat close to the fire, wrapped in thick blankets, and he told them this story. And even though they'd heard it a hundred times before, it always sounded different.

'One day, Grandpa Dorje was with four of his comrades, travelling secretly by foot along the Tongtian river towards Kermo, where they thought the Chinese were camping. They wanted to ambush the enemy under cover of darkness. Dorje and his gang always used to attack at night, appearing out of the darkness like evil spirits and melting away again. Or so my mother said. They were walking along the ridge that overlooks the river, and they saw a boat carrying thirty Chinese soldiers across the water.

'Of course, they were outnumbered six to one. But they had not been spotted, so they had surprise on their side. They hid in the trees and had an urgent meeting, their breath forming bitter clouds in the air. Dorje and his old friend Gönche wanted to slip down to the riverbank and mount a surprise attack on the boat, while it was still in the water. The other three were Amdo men, less experienced and more cautious. They didn't want to take the risk. They wanted to continue on their way, according to the original plan. In the end, Dorje and Gönche persuaded the younger fighters to help them attack the boat. They all crept down the slope under cover of the trees and when they got within range they opened fire.

'The Chinese didn't stand a chance. They lost control of the boat and it began to spin in the water. One of the Amdo men was wounded. But Gönche was incredibly old and strong. With an almighty effort, he threw a grenade all the way from the riverbank into the boat, and it exploded. The boat broke up and sank, and all thirty Chinese soldiers died. What a hero he was! Everyone told the story – it spread from village to village all over the whole of Kham and Amdo, and even as far as U-Tsang. Mothers would tell their children that if they didn't go to bed, the fearsome Gönche would eat them. Although he was reviled by some religious people for his violent ways, he soon became a national hero.'

She paused and took a long drink of water. By now it was almost dark, and through the window a few resilient stars had pierced the London clouds. My mother's low, soothing tones made me happy; it didn't matter what she was saying, the sound of her voice was enough.

'Later on, Gönche felt he had become too old to fight. He gave up his role in the resistance, left his home in Chatring and fled to India. Great-Grandpa Dorje never heard from him again. He thought he was dead. But then, several years later, he met a monk who was passing through Chamdo on pilgrimage to Mount Kailash. Of course, the pilgrimage was a cover story. In reality the monk was on a secret mission, plotting the escape of an important Tibetan, the Karmapa, I think. Anyway, Dorje offered him a bed for the night. Knowing he was a member of the resistance, the monk accepted. Although food was very scarce and many people were starving, Grandma managed to prepare a special meal of *thukpa*, *mo-mo* and sweet barley, which must have been delicious: she was such a good cook. Late that evening, Great-Grandpa Dorje sat up late with the monk, sharing a bottle of *châng* – what a naughty monk, Monlam, what a naughty monk! Drinking! I think Great-Grandpa Dorje must have talked him into it. They were both under a lot of pressure, as well.

'They talked and drank for hours, discussing the struggle against the Chinese. It grew very cold and dark, and still they talked. The fire burnt down until just the embers remained, and still they talked – like secret yogis. I could just imagine them in the shadows, hunched over their *châng*, their eyes glowing like berries. At that time, around the New Year of 1959, the tension in Tibet was very high and all over the country people talked of nothing but the

57

Khampas and the Chinese, the Chinese and the Khampas. The monk said that the High Lamas had made many divinations and had consulted many oracles, and they all predicted the same thing: that Tibet would be lost, and many dreadful things would happen. As they were talking, Dorje happened to mention his old friend Gönche, wondering what became of him.

'The monk's eyes widened as if he couldn't believe his ears. "Gönche Rinpoche?" he exclaimed. "*The* Gönche Rinpoche? He was your friend?" He pressed his hands together in awe. "I myself had the honour of meeting Venerable Gönche once, a few years ago in Dharamsala."

'Dorje was confused. He didn't know what the monk was talking about. So far as he knew Gönche was a terrible ruffian, always getting into fights, very quick with his dagger. But it turned out that Gönche had become quite a celebrity in Dharamsala – a saint, even! Gradually, the story emerged.

'After leaving Chatring, Gönche had made his way to Lhasa on horseback, just before the uprising of 1959. The city was full of refugees from Amdo and Kham. Being a seasoned fighter he smelt trouble in the air, left before the uprising began and continued his journey, slipping across the border and eventually arriving in northern India. Like many Tibetans at that time, he found work building the remote high-altitude roads. A few years later, after the Dalai Lama's escape, he settled down in Dharamsala and got a job as a lowly shoe-mender, working with leather, and lived there for several years. However, after some time he became seriously ill. He reflected on the course of his life, and began to feel intensely guilty about killing so many people. Having nowhere to turn, he decided to attend a teaching given by the famous Buddhist master Kyabje Trijang Rinpoche, tutor to the Dalai Lama, on the subject of Universal Compassion. This teaching affected Gönche deeply, and made him profoundly regret his life of violence. Although by this time he was quite sick, he packed a small bag, moved to Nepal and went into a long retreat in a hut in the distant hills, far away from everything. He remained in retreat for several years, practising Tantra.

'While still in retreat, he died. On the day of his death, the air was particularly clear; and all the local people, monks as well as ordinary folk, saw bright, beautiful rainbows fanning out from the roof of the hut – for several hours. Three days later he was cremated, and this time an ocean of rainbows appeared above the funeral pyre. The High Lamas did a divination and declared that the rainbows were signs that Gönche had atoned for all his past sins and become a very pure, holy person. He had become a saint.

' "Gönche?" spluttered Dorje. "I don't believe it! That old rogue? A saint? If you weren't a monk, I'd kill you!" He laughed so loudly that the walls of the house shook and he spilt his *châng* on the ground.

Immediately, he opened another bottle of *châng* and flicked a drop into the air as an offering to the spirits, and towards the earth as an offering to the gods. Then he and the monk drank the whole bottle together, in memory of the rogue-saint, his old friend Venerable Gönche. They got very drunk that night, and fell asleep in their chairs.' My mother faltered and began to cry. 'You see, baby Mo, even the most evil people can become holy – when they die.' She rocked me gently to and fro, wiping her eyes on her sleeve from time to time. By now it was completely dark, and a thin line of moonlight creased the ceiling. After a while my eyes became heavy and I fell into a profound, dreamless sleep.

I awoke at dawn, to the hydraulic groan and wheeze of a dustbin lorry. I was lying in my mother's lap, and the air was thick with slumber. The kitchen was nowhere to be seen; we were in the sitting room, crumpled together in the armchair. My mother was still asleep. The first butter-coloured light of the West Hampstead dawn was spreading across her furrowed brow, and I could see a small lesion on the underside of her chin. How had we got into the sitting room? Then, as my mind cleared, I remembered. It was a new day, the day before. That night, under cover of disabling darkness, another

59

uncanny reversal had occurred. Again, I had awoken in my mother's yesterday. Again, nothing that I had experienced had occurred. I could hear a faint snore coming from upstairs. I closed my eyes and waited as my backwards life resumed.

Chapter Eight

One morning, Rabbi Chod moved in; the morning after, he had not yet done so. When he moved in, grunting under the weight of his bags, complaining that the place needed a good clean, vowing to support a widow in her hour of need, promising that he would organise a sky-burial for my father, it was 13 March; and, according to my estimation, it was 12 March when he had not yet done this. When he moved in, on 13 March, I was thirteen days old, constantly frustrated by my uncontrolled limbs and puking several times an hour; when he had not yet done so, on 12 March, I was fourteen days old, trying to gain authority over my facial muscles and shitting myself more frequently than I care to mention.

My mother had spent the whole of 12 March sitting in her red velour armchair, sobbing, with me in her lap, while Rabbi Chod offered her a continuous stream of cups of tea and glasses of water. As evening drew grimly in, Chod said he would move in the very next day, indeed, it was the least he could do, given the circumstances. My mother thanked him tearfully, and he smiled.

On the morning of 11 March, when I had been on the earth for exactly two weeks and a day, and Rabbi Chod was nowhere to be seen, my mother burst into my room, snatched me from the cot, tied me to her back and dashed down the stairs, wiping her face on her *pangden*. Although I was still drowsy, and dizzy (my head bounced violently with every step), as we descended the stairs I noticed that the shrine to my father's picture had vanished from the wall. Instantly, I knew what the panic was about. My mother hurried through the streets towards the hospital. Her hair was unplaited and unkempt, and restricted my view considerably. That was the

61

only time I ever saw her without her hair in a plait. She hailed a taxi. It was the only time I ever saw her do that, too. I was already showing signs of developing pollution-induced asthma, and by the time we arrived at the hospital I was finding it extremely difficult to breathe. My mother didn't notice my wheezes – I was tied to her back out of sight, and she was in great distress. She bolted awkwardly up the concrete steps, past a group of smock-clad patients smoking cigarettes, past a frail woman wheeling a stand with a drip-bag attached to her arm, past a couple of dishevelled doctors, and into the disinfected air of the hospital. She hastened over to the information desk and tried to catch the attention of the inscrutable nurse behind it.

'Is he here? My husband, I mean? Hello? Where is he? In the ward still? Excuse me?' she blurted.

'Mr Parker in ward five, bed three, and . . . Sorry, love, talking to *moi*? What did you say?'

'My husband. Tenzin Menla. Is he still in the ward? The Tibetan. I got a call an hour ago.'

'And you are . . . ?'

'Tenzin Osel. His wife.'

'And which ward—'

'He was put in the Baskerville ward. Yesterday evening.'

The nurse began to hum, consulted her computer, stopped humming, winced and exhaled through her teeth. 'I'm terribly sorry, Mrs Tenzin. He passed away just half an hour ago.'

'There's no mistake, then? Perhaps you . . . Can I see him?'

'Mrs Tenzin . . .'

'I should have known he'd never make it through the night. Why did I leave him there alone? I knew he was . . . Maybe I could have . . . Shit.'

'Mrs—'

'Is Pagpa there? His father?'

'No one there at the moment, Mrs Tenzin.'

'So my husband's still in the ward? Not been moved?'

'No, he's not been moved yet. They're waiting for you to arrive before they take him to . . . well, to . . . you know, the morgue. Mrs Tenzin? If you'd like to follow the nurse?' My mother's hair streamed into my face as she scuttled up the sterile stairs, a nurse two paces behind.

When the hair parted, I looked around curiously. This was the first time I had returned to the hospital since I was born, and it seemed a different place. Then, everything had seemed bright and shining; now, a few days on, it was smooth, smudged and dull. It must have been my mind that changed, since the place was now several days newer. We hurried past a long row of beds in which frail pensioners tried to outlive the operation waiting list, past a broom-cupboard in which a drunk had collapsed, past a group of someone's anxious relatives, fidgeting and muttering to each other. The nurse pulled aside a flap of grey material and we entered my father's little curtain-room. Fabric flapped heavily around us like the whale closing its jaws on Jonah, and the world outside was reduced to a silent collection of ankles.

The bedsheet went back; for the first time, I came face to face with my father. The image of his corpse filled my mind to the edges. He lay there as if he had exhausted his allowance of words, or used up his quota of breaths. There was nothing like his face, dead – his eyes glued shut with a resigned finality, his skin sagging from the bone. His head was an object, a roughly sculpted slab of pork. It sat motionless atop his freshly vacated body. His hands rested quietly on the NHS blanket as if about to scratch an itch, and his knees were slightly bent and turned to the side, looking poised to swing out of bed. But all his actions had ended; my brooding, introverted father was quieter than he had ever been. The flat electronic drone of the heart monitor, lamenting mortality in one continuous note, swarmed around us like a dark cloud of flies.

I tried to sleep through the rest of the day, not wanting to see my mother in the throes of grief. It was not a problem to sleep; my difficulty had always been staying awake. All I wanted to do was get through that day as painlessly as possible, because I knew that when dawn broke on 10 March it would all be over; my father would be alive again, my mother's symptoms would be improving daily, and I would be getting older and stronger. In my naïvety, I felt fairly optimistic. Things were looking up; my backwards life was working to my advantage, at least for the moment. I slept on and off all day, while my mother was dashing about, distressed. When darkness fell, I was put in my cot for the night. As I welcomed the first wave of sleep, I tried to intensify my longing to wake up on the day before. I had to make sure that my backwards journey didn't stop here, that I continued to head towards better times. As longing overwhelmed me and mingled with the shadows of slumber, I felt a deep satisfaction. I was taking advantage of the system. I was about to make my nightly about-turn and allow my pulse, my breath, and the river of blood to carry me in a better direction than everybody else. Within minutes, I was sound asleep.

Chapter Nine

Morning broke. 10 March. My father bent over the cot and picked me up. I recognised him instantly from the pictures, and from the corpse. He looked exhausted; his eyes were ringed with red and black smudges and lesions stippled his skin. As if in a dream he carried me downstairs. There was an absence of the shrine-picture of him on the wall. His hands were delicate and he carried me very high up on his chest while I marvelled at the sight of his bare feet in animation. He took me through to the kitchen, put me gently on the table and commenced what seemed to be a pill-taking ritual. My skin prickled as I gazed at his living face. He had the precision of a creature of habit, and the way he pecked his head and moved his limbs was vaguely familiar, like an echo from my future.

His small plastic case contained seven compartments, each filled with an identical combination of pills. He removed Friday's consignment and laid them out in front of him, his fingers trembling. A short while later my mother padded into the room, throwing her plait nervously from one shoulder to the other, and sat down opposite. A sour noise-lessness passed between them as she produced her own tubs of pills. The minutes passed and the atmosphere became heavier, the tension curling in the corners of the room. My mother's movements were staccato and aggressive; my father's were feeble, yet haughty. He plucked up his capsules, placed each one on his gungy tongue and swallowed with independent gulps. Then he hunched over the table and gazed distractedly into my face. His eyes were hollow, and shone like beads. I looked over at my mother swallowing the last of her pills and coughing.

I thought they were about to engage in conversation, but instead a third adult entered the room. For a moment I expected Rabbi Chod, and was surprised to see a diminutive man with leathery skin and a gleaming pate shuffle in with the aid of a walking stick to sit quietly beside my father. Far from defusing the atmosphere, however, his presence seemed to make it even tenser. His fingers were forever micro-fidgeting in front of him on the tablecloth, and he looked around the room as if he was inspecting the wallpaper. My father finished taking his pills and glanced about. Although his face was markedly softer than that of the man next to him, the way they moved their heads was almost identical.

My mother broke the silence. 'Grandpa Pagpa, it's so nice to have you here for the day. Would you like some break-fast? What do you usually have at home nowadays? Would you like me to make the same?'

Grandpa Pagpa got up, went to the typewriter on the counter and typed a couple of sentences. Then he unwound the paper and passed it to my mother. She read it, and dropped it on the table. I could just about see it from where I lay. It said, 'i hav come to see my ill sun not yoo leeve us alone yoo. maik me no food I mite catch something dirty of yoo dirty just like my son dyd.'

'Look, Grandpa Pagpa, we've been through all this before. Let's give it a rest, just for today, shall we?' My mother's eyes became angrier as she said this.

Grandpa Pagpa moved the typewriter to the table and sat down with a flourish. He evidently was preparing for battle. The keys popped and banged and another inflammatory piece of paper was dropped on the table. 'just go awai osel we dont wont yoo here. Yoo infektid my sun and you inficted yorself so just leav us alon ok.'

My mother covered her face and turned away; then she plucked up her courage and answered back, her face flushed. 'Come on, Pagpa, it's not my fault we're ill. I don't know how we caught it . . . from needles or . . . I don't know, you're the Oracle, you tell me.'

This induced more aggressive typing. My father looked from one to the other, giving nothing away, too weak to respond.

'd●nt give me that ●sel this kind ●f disis is ●nly c●rt by gays and h●res and pi●ple having affeirs lyke y●● pr●bly.'

'What? What?' Tears were spilling out of her eyes and she was on her feet. 'I've done nothing wrong. I've done nothing – *nothing* – apart from marry him and get related to you. If anyone's to blame, it's your son. That's what the rumour is. It's the talk of the fucking community.' Grandpa Pagpa turned away and made a show of ignoring her. She picked up a spoon and sent it flying violently across the room. It struck the base of a frying pan hanging on the wall, making it ring like a gong. Despite myself, I began to cry. Grandpa Pagpa jumped to his feet, jerked his head viciously at my mother and began to type, a vindictive look in his eyes.

'Oh, give the typewriter a rest, you mean . . . Can't you just swallow your pride . . . speak like everybody else?' She was sobbing fully now. 'I've done nothing, I'm innocent. Just treat me like a . . . Just treat me . . .' She seemed caught between rage and despair. I heard my howls loud in my ears. She kicked her chair backwards and it bounced loudly between the lino and the cupboards before toppling over. Grandpa Pagpa ripped his page out of the machine and slapped it down on the table in front of her. She picked it up and tore it violently in half. 'Menla! Menla! What's happening to us? We're married, Menla. Why can't we be on the same side for once? We're both heading for the same place. Are you to blame for all this, Menla? Menla?' My father was slumped over the table with his head in his hands. He didn't move. 'Menla?'

Grandpa Pagpa leant over and put his hands on my father's shoulders. His head lolled to the side. Strings of puke covered his chin.

'Oh, oh, oh, oh, Menla, my . . .' cried my mother, going towards him as Grandpa Pagpa recoiled. 'Don't just stand still, Pagpa – ring someone – an ambulance!' she implored.

Grandpa Pagpa stumbled into the hall, his face aghast, and I heard him dial 999. My mother pressed her head close to my father's and began to wipe his face, whispering inaudibly in his ear.

A tinny voice rose softly into the air. 'Police, fire, ambulance, which service do you require?' There was a pause. 'Police, fire, ambulance, which service do you require? Hello? Hello? Police, fire . . .'

My mother hurried into the hall and snatched the receiver. 'Now is not the time, Pagpa, for your fucking silence! Hello? Yes, ambulance please. It's my husband, he's not well . . . He's passed out, he's been sick . . .'

The period of waiting for the ambulance was long. My mother sat hunched over the motionless figure of my father, wiping the puke from his mouth and mopping his shimmering brow. Try as I might I couldn't stop wailing, but nobody took any notice. Grandpa Pagpa hovered uncertainly in and out of the kitchen, leaning heavily on his stick, obviously distressed. Eventually, there was a ring at the doorbell. Two green-clad people came in and stretchered my father out. There was some discussion as to who would accompany him in the ambulance, as my mother and Grandpa Pagpa refused to go together. The paramedics were impatient to get my father to hospital. My mother said she didn't want to go, anyway, and she would leave the son in the care of his bastard father. Grandpa Pagpa went back into the kitchen and picked up the typewriter to take along. The door slammed behind him and the siren faded into the distance as the ambulance ground away. My mother sat at the table and took me in her trembling arms. I had never heard her swear with so much venom as she did that day, and I have never heard her swear with so much venom since. I felt that the worst had passed, and was looking forward to my future.

Chapter Ten

A few months passed, and I learnt to sit up and to crawl. It was a huge relief to have some mobility, and to be able to investigate things in more depth. I looked forward to deciphering the mystery of walking. Admittedly, it seemed a scientific impossibility, the way you had to balance on one foot, then on the other, and kind of jig along. But I became expert at crawling, and could reach quite high speeds when I put my mind to it. My parents took to dressing me in a turquoise Baby-Gro, which perpetually had greyish-brown patches on the knees, and flappy toes that hung from my feet like a Dr Seuss character's.

I was sitting in my bouncy seat, suspended in the doorway of the sitting room. I had ambiguous feelings towards that seat. On one hand, it was downright undignified to sit in a harness that allowed your legs to poke through, attached by lengths of elastic to a doorframe. On the other, I had to admit it was great fun. I loved pounding the floor with my feet and bouncing up a foot or two into the air, watching the shrine in the corner of the room bob violently up and down. The only time I was reluctant to do this was when we had company.

It was, if I remember correctly, a Sunday afternoon and my mother had gone to do the shopping – and visit her old friend Dazel. She had been reluctant to tell my father she was going to see Dazel, but he had guessed and she had admitted it. Now my father was sitting in the red armchair, opposite Grandpa Pagpa, who was sitting on the sofa with his back to me. I was bouncing gently, the elastic creaking. The large bay windows allowed a great deal of light to pale the room. Between them was the glass-topped coffee table, with a typewriter on it facing Grandpa Pagpa, a virginal sheet of paper curving from it. My father was taking pills. As they were both quiet men, the time they spent together was largely spent in silence, just sitting with one another, each absorbed in his own thoughts, sharing their isolated worlds for an hour or two. Grandpa Pagpa still communicated only through type. My father did speak on occasion, but he was careful with his words; he was an anxious, systematic person, and there is no system more rebellious than language. When he spoke, it was in a strong Tibetan accent; he often mistakenly replaced the sound 'f' with 'p'. And, when his sentence ran away from him and he didn't know how to finish it, or was afraid of finishing it wrongly, he would fill the ensuing silence with 'la-la-la'.

My father concluded his pill-taking ritual, replaced the lid on his pill-box and slid it circumspectly into his pocket. I couldn't see Grandpa Pagpa's face; the only way I could ascertain his emotional state was through interpreting the colour of his bald head from behind. As my father took his pills, the head flushed, and Grandpa Pagpa's shoulders hunched with each swallow, empathetically. Then they engaged in the following stuttering conversation, Grandpa Pagpa communicating slowly, tapping the words out and handing the paper over, and my father speaking self-consciously, squirming slightly in his armchair. I could just see the words from where I was suspended.

Pop pop pop pop. 'H●w l●ng hav wee g●t until ●sel returnz?'

'She is being out with her priend, Dazel. Probably she will be being some time, la.' There was a pause.

Pop pop pop. 'H●w is she handlyng the dign●wsis?'

'I am not knowing, Dad, la. Honestly.'

Pop pop pop pop pop. 'Y●● d●nt kn●w?'

'No.'

Another pause. Then again pop pop pop. 'And h●w are y●● handling it?'

'The doctor is saying we should be having some years

70

before the end, la. He is saying Rabbi Chod's herb is helping. We have been taking it por years, la. It is preventing disease prom developing quickly. So it could be worse, la-la.'

Pop pop pop pop pop. 'W●rse? Dyd the d●ct●r sai h●w y●● c●ntraktid the disiase?'

'He saying there is being no way of telling.'

Pop pop pop pop *pop*! Pop pop pop *pop pop pop* pop pop *Pop*! 'W●t d●● y●● meen n● way ●f tellyng? It is a sex dysease, like gay and h●res get!'

'There is also other ways of getting, la . . .'

Pop!Pop!Pop!Pop!Pop!Pop!Pop! 'N●, it is a sex diseyse! Sex disyiase! H●w did my s●n get a sex dysease?'

'Well, it is not always being, what you call, sexy transmitting, la-la-la . . .'

Pop pop *Pop*! Pop pop pop *Pop*! 'What d●● y●● meaen, sexuly transmiting? Sexulally transmiting wh● bai? Menla, my sun, wh●?'

There was another pause and both men pecked their heads around, obviously uncomfortable. Finally my father said, 'Osel is seeing Dazel again. She very prendly with him, la.'

Pop pop pop pop. 'Dazel? S● w●t?'

'You know, the smoker? The one who is cleaning Monlam's nappy, la?'

Pop pop pop pop pop' 'Of k●rse I kn●w. But s● wh●t?'

'She is really very prendly with him, la.'

The bald head began to flush again. Pop pop pop *pop*! 'What d●● y●● meaen?'

'Well, it not impossible.'

Bright red. Purple veins, pulsing. *Pop Pop Pop POP POP! Pop! Pop! Pop! POP!* 'S● Osel is t● blaim, the dirty h●re! It is her sex disyse givin t●● my sun!'

'I'm not saying that, la. I'm just saying . . . it's not me. It's not my fault. Osel and Dazel . . . it's not impossible, Dad, la. That's all. I'm not accusing . . . I'm not wanting . . . la-la-la . . .'

71

Deep puce. Shiny. *POP! POP!POP!POP!OPO!P!O!P!O!P!*
'The   DDDERJI   dirty   HOREW   the   di●rtyi
wh●hi●ewr●j!!!!!!!' Grandpa Pagpa pushed the typewriter away in fury, setting the bell dinging, and sat back on
the sofa. Both heads jerked, and all became still. They sat in
silence.

Chapter Eleven

I grew. The toes of my Baby-Gro no longer hung loose; it was as if I had a second, turquoise, towelling skin. And through a frustrating process of trial and error, I finally managed to take my first steps. But I was rather wobbly on my feet, and it still seemed an unnatural thing to be doing. Walking was better than crawling because I knew that once I got the hang of it I would be able to run about; but at the beginning I could crawl faster than I could walk. Nevertheless, I persevered. Whenever I lost my balance, I tried to land nappy first. That helped.

I was in the sitting room again, in the afternoon, but this time with my mother. She was looking healthier by the day. Although she was still noticeably unwell, the lesions on her face were beginning to close and her rosy cheeks were returning. I was a quiet child, and spent many happy hours sitting in her lap by the writing desk, the soft material of her *chuba* against my face, watching lazily as she wrote extensive entries in her diary with an old, chewed Biro. From time to time, she would put her pen down and play a little game with me. I greatly enjoyed those games. For reasons I found impossible to analyse, when my mother hid behind the curtain and suddenly jumped out, I was struck by great hilarity. Especially when she said 'Boo!' at the same time. It was as if she had disappeared from the world, only to re-appear; the whole thing was so ridiculous that I couldn't stop laughing. When she did it under the table, it was even funnier. Sometimes she hid behind the sofa and popped out, and when she did that I laughed so much my sides ached. Often, I filled my nappy with delight.

I was gaining control over my face. I had managed to get

my mouth to pronounce a few words; the usual things. My best English word was 'again', which came in useful on a variety of occasions, such as when playing with my mother, wanting more food, even demanding to have my nappy changed. Frustratingly, I found it impossible to finish a word with a consonant, so 'again', when I pronounced it, generally sounded like 'agé'. I had to tell myself not to be such a perfectionist – people knew what I meant, and that was the main thing. My favourite Tibetan word was '*shepa*', which meant 'laughing', and I came out with it whenever I found anything amusing. It always seemed to make the adults chuckle. Although I never got the joke, I used it to my advantage.

This afternoon, however, my mother seemed tenser than usual, more distracted and anxious. She had prepared my lunch absentmindedly, dropping at least five things on the floor. Now she sat at her writing desk, scribbling feverishly as if she didn't have much time, and chewing her fingers. Occasionally she arched her back, stretched, and cracked her knuckles. She had a habit of pulling each finger, making it pop in its socket, when she was trying to think. Intrigued, I crept over to see what she was writing.

'Tuesday, 27 January 2004

'I have started combination-therapy. That's what Dr Thromby calls it. Twice a day for the rest of my life I have to eat cap-sules. They look so modern. Dr Thromby said they have been made expertly. When I roll them in my hand I can believe that they are going to make me better. But in my heart I know that they are not going to make me better. Dr Thromby's experts are very clever but cannot change fate. The cap-sules can only make me more comfortable, and give me more time in which to live, Dr Thromby said.

'I am sad I didn't trust Rabbi Chod enough, and traditional-Tibetan-medicine. But I was so tired and always had a headache. I couldn't bear the suffering any more. So I went to see Dr Thromby. Menla came too. I think he was a bit scared. Everything was very clean and official. A nurse stuck needles into our arms, drawing thick-red-threads into

74

syringes. Then, last week, in the afternoon, we went to receive the results. We went in together. When we sat opposite Dr Thromby and watched him open-the-files, I felt-afraid. The doctor had to give the diagnosis five times before we understood. Dr Thromby was very kind and sympathetic in a professional sort of way. He smiled a doctor-smile and started to give us advice. But Menla lost his temper, it was ugly. He grabbed the doctor by the neck and pinned him against the wall. He wanted to force him to reveal why things went wrong. This isn't meant to happen, he told him. Things aren't meant to go wrong. We're living in modern times, this isn't Asia, this isn't Tibet, you should be able to cope with things like this, la. Later, he calmed down. He apologised. He knew it wasn't Dr Thromby's fault.

'I realised that we have fallen into a blind-spot the doctors couldn't see. They couldn't cure us. All they could offer were doctor-smiles, serious-eyebrows and bits of fake-sounding doctor-sympathy. And lots of options.

'The main-decision was about our "therapy-strategy". This is what Dr Thromby asked us: Do you want to go for the traditional-option of starting with softer-drugs and saving the powerful-combinations for later? Or do you want to begin with the hard-stuff straight-away? That's what Dr Thromby asked us. Then he said: Either way, alternating the drug-combos is really the-thing-to-do. The virus is adaptable and will build up a resistance, so the larger the combo, the slower the resistance. On the other hand, if you use all the drugs at once, you will have less up-your-sleeves for later. And then there are the side-effects; would you prefer to have lots of minor-ailments, or one major-one? Do you want diarrhoea, anaemia or fatigue? That is what Dr Thromby said. I felt as if I was lying naked in the snow, rolling over and over, trying to freeze slower.

'We are not going to turn-up for our counselling-appointments. But of-course we will eat the cap-sules. I have gone for the traditional-option and started-soft. Menla is taking the other-approach, and starting-hard. But I'm drawing-the-line at going for counselling. We both are. We told Dr Thromby, he didn't like it very-much. He couldn't change our minds. He took me away from Menla for a minute, and asked me why I refused to attend my counselling sessions. I didn't want to tell him. But he kept asking, so I told him. I said: the counsellors aren't sick, so how could they know what it is like? Counsellors are like doctors, pretending that they are in control of things, like one drowning-person trying to save another. They are just as vulnerable to disease as me, only they haven't caught one yet. That is what I said. He said: I take your point, but having said that I think it is still a good idea to give it a go. I told him I'd think about it, and thanked him for his concern.

'Before we left, I asked Dr Thromby how we had caught the disease. He said he didn't know, and although it was usually sexually-transmitted there have been cases of transmission taking place through needles-and-the-like. This made me very confused. So I asked him again: where did this illness come from? How did we contract it? Who gave it to us? And he didn't reply. So I said: I thought it was something that only happens in Africa, or to gay-people, or sexy-people. Not to me and Menla, husband-and-wife, Tibetan-people. Jewish-people, too, believers in God, members-of-the-Lost-Tribe. How can this be? Dr Thromby didn't answer. Menla said: Rabbi Chod thinks it is to do with Spirits. He is probably right. Maybe a powerful-Spirit infected us somehow. That is what he said. After that, we left.'

She carried on writing, hunched over, whispering to herself. A couple of times she dropped her pen, blew her nose and wiped her eyes. She didn't play any games with me that day. My mind began to drift and I fell asleep, rocked by the rhythm of her writing hand.

Immediately a dream arose, but not the usual dream about mountains and space. This time I am sitting in the corner of a hospital room. It is very bright and lucid. My parents are sitting on one side of the desk, looking shocked and pale.

A doctor is sitting opposite them, and talking. As he speaks, a motley collection of beings topple out of his mouth and mooch about on the desk. The first is a warty virus, toad-like with veined eyes and a flapping mouth. Its bloody stomach is split and gapes open, emitting a fetid reek. It keeps shoving its claws into its flesh and yanking out its inner organs with a slimy, ripping sound. When it has extracted enough flesh, it sets about building new versions of itself by kneading, moulding and shaping. Bizarre, wicked-looking tools are scattered around its feet and from time to time it picks up a saw, or a sickle, or a mallet, and violently uses it on the gory mass to sculpt a swelling army of clones. On the other side of the desk hides another band of cartoons; a troop of effete, chivalrous knights. Their armour tinkles as they gear themselves up for battle, trepidation on their civilised faces. They keep patting their comrades gently on the back and encouraging them to keep stiff upper lips. When the doctor introduces them, they pause in their preparations and enact absurd little bows in the direction of my parents. On their shields are inscribed their crests and family names; Videx, Hivid, Norvir, Viramune. From time to time they muster their forces and mount gallant attacks on the army of toads, trumpets squeaking. The toads fight back viciously, and blood and limbs spray across the desk, staining the doctor's prescription pad and clogging his computer keyboard. I am surprised to see that he doesn't seem to mind. After each skirmish the knights regroup and the process starts all over again.

Chapter Twelve

One morning I woke up appallingly early in my little bed. Again, it was yesterday. Dawn was breaking, and the darkened room was perfect for rhinos. Sinister black and yellow rhinos would slink out from their hiding places in my room when it was gloomy, and lumber up to my bed when I wasn't watching. I had to keep turning on my bedside light to send the creatures scurrying back to their crannies, but they inevitably returned when darkness fell again. I stumbled out of bed, untwisting my Spiderman pyjamas. I still wore nappies at night, and they were fairly uncomfortable by morning. I needed to be changed. I passed the rhinos' lowered horns and crept into my parents' room. My mother was a diminutive lump in the side of the bed, huddled as far as possible away from my father, who was on the side near the door. He lay so still that for a moment the image of his future corpse swam before my eyes. I toddled round the bed and noticed a pile of my parents' clothes hanging over a chair. I decided to try my father's clothes on. His shoes were easy enough to wear, although my feet skidded about in them. I struggled with his trousers for about five minutes, but eventually I managed to pull them on. They were huge and heavy, and I got tangled up in the braces. I thrust my hands into the pockets to keep them up.

Deep in the left pocket, something rustled against my fingers. I pulled out a bundle of paper, crumpled but neatly folded together. There was something compelling about it; it looked secret. Slowly I unfolded it. It was a badly photocopied booklet, with grey smudges along the top. On the cover was a picture of a thin lady in her mid-forties, with peroxided hair and heavy make-up. Beneath the photo were the words 'In memory of Madeline McBretney (1959–2002). RIP.' I opened the booklet. It was full of hymns.

My father stirred in bed and began to smack his lips sleepily. Quickly, I replaced the booklet in his trouser pocket, unwound myself from the braces, removed the trousers and shoes, ran over to him and patted his face. The slight breeze of his breath fluttered his moustache and his eyes cracked open.

'What is that, la? Where is Mr Midget being? And Mr Silk, with his umbrellas? And Mr Swahili, with his swimming trunks? In the garden maze, la? Why are the North Olive Onion Police at war with the South, la? Am I a sunflower seed, la?' he asked. Blearily, he looked at his watch, dragged his body upright and hauled himself out of bed, scratching hard. His crisp light-blue pyjamas had several sharp creases cut into them, as did the side of his face. Without waking my mother, he took me through to the bathroom and removed my nappy. Immediately I did a little celebratory, bare-bottomed run around the bathroom. It was an incredible relief; I felt sleeker, faster, more mobile. Day-time nappies had been left behind, and I wouldn't have to wear another one until bed-time. I was proud. I went to the toilet, more as an expression of freedom than out of necessity. I had a plastic step which enabled me to reach the correct elevation. Also, my mother had floated an orange ping-pong ball in the toilet water, to help me aim. I hit it without a problem.

My father washed and dressed while I worked on my Lego project in the corner of the room. My mother was in a deep sleep, and didn't stir. I was trying to construct a house for my favourite Lego man, Plastic Bag. I called him Plastic Bag because I had found him in one. My mother had tried to encourage me to change his name to Phuntsog, but my father said that Plastic Bag looked like a Plastic Bag, and didn't look like a Phuntsog. I think that, in reality, any toy with a proper name would have made my father jealous. Plastic Bag had a blue body and a standard-issue yellow Lego head, but was set aside from the other Lego men by a deep scratch along the left side of his face. It was for this reason that he was my favourite. I was building him a house to protect him from suffering. Needless to say, it would never work, but it made me feel oddly at peace to keep going with the construction all the same.

My mother remained motionless, her feet just visible in the corner of the wrinkled bed. I considered the logistics of building her a house, too. Presently my father came out of the shower, getting dressed. As was his habit, he yanked his trousers up so high that the fabric tightened to an unsightly degree. His buttocks became extremely pronounced, and an unfashionable quantity of goose-skin ankle was revealed. He stretched the braces over his shoulders and snapped them against his belly. Then he put his shoes on and took Plastic Bag and myself downstairs.

'It is now breakpast time, Mo, my son,' he mumbled as he carried me into the kitchen. These words were incredibly valuable coming from a moustache which so seldom spoke. They had a ring of satisfaction about them, as if he was pleased to have made such a coherent sentence, uncorrupted by the slippages of language. It was always a victory for him if he managed to articulate a sentence in its entirety, without having to resort to la-la-las. When he was nervous, his speech became almost incomprehensible. He sat me gently on the table and set about preparing our breakfast in a methodical fashion.

For me at that time, breakfast meant yoghurt, with either *tsampa* or Frosties. For my father, breakfast was synonymous with coffee, the first of the day, meticulously sweetened by both a single brown sugar cube of medium size and a saccharin tablet, and delicately clouded by three small dribbles of milk which he measured out with a teaspoon. Method characterised both his internal and his external worlds. Every area of his mind was ordered and systematised save the dark jungle beneath, of which he was unconscious. His routines kept him alive. He was a slave to them, and this protected him: since he had already enslaved himself, he could never be enslaved by somebody else. This reliance on self-enslavement stemmed from his deep vulnerability. The vulnerability came from a profound mistrust of everyone else. And this natural mistrust had something to do with his unwholesome relationship with his father, Grandpa Pagpa. That in turn was caused by the fact that Grandpa Pagpa's wife had died while giving birth to my father. All these stems on a big rotting plant – I was backing into a hollow family tree, with roots beginningless.

My father poured me a bowl of cereal with yoghurt and I began to eat, still sitting on the table. He took an experimental sip of coffee, smacked his lips and paused; then he nodded to himself and took his seat. He tightened his braces and contemplated the steaming mug in front of him. He always used the same one, a chipped yellow mini-bucket with indissoluble circular stains on the inside. He gazed at his pocket-watch intently until exactly two minutes had elapsed. After that, the coffee being sufficiently cooled, he commenced the laborious process of drinking, whereby each individual sip was swilled around the mouth in the manner of the wine taster, swallowed, then contemplated in a kind of internalised post mortem, for there is death in each moment.

Meanwhile my mother had drifted into the kitchen, her eyes heavy with sleep. She stifled a yawn, touched her lips to the crown of my head and glanced at my father.

'Morning, Menla,' she sniped. He nodded curtly, without looking up. Her exaggerated pronunciation put me on my guard. Occasionally, at more amiable moments, he called her 'Bunch', a derivative of 'honey bunch', and she called him 'Mo-mo', after the dumplings – the result of a humorous confusion between the English words 'darling' and 'dumpling'. When they used these nicknames, I knew I was safe. But they rarely did. I guessed that in better times the nicknames had been common currency. But those times had long since faded – or, from my point of view, were yet to come.

My mother set about preparing a brew of herbal medicine. These days, both my parents felt sick and dizzy, and were constantly gripped by cruel migraines. She boiled a pan of water and tipped a packet of dried flowers and herbs into it, producing a sweet, metallic aroma. When this had simmered for a few minutes, she poured it into two mugs, placed one ungraciously in front of my father and began unloading the washing machine.

'How was your sleeping being, la?' asked my father.

'Awful. You took all the blanket again. I felt horrible, really sick. I got no sleep,' she replied over her shoulder.

'You were asleep this morning,' I put in. Despite herself, my mother shot me a withering smile.

'I too was having a horrible head, my head was, what you call, spitting, la. Spitting head. Not punny. But I am peeling better this morning,' said my father.

'Nice for you,' she replied. There was a pause. 'Menla,' said my mother, not taking her eyes off the washing machine, 'I think . . . maybe . . . I think we should make an appointment with a doctor. A real one – a Western one.'

'What? Why?'

'Well, our health is so awful, and neither of us is getting any better.'

'Is Tibetan medicine not being good enup por you, la?'

'Well, yes, but . . .'

'Well, then, la.'

There was a long silence. My mother finished unloading the washing machine and began to comb her hair.

My father spoke again. 'Rabbi Chod is diagnosing us, telling us what is wrong, la. We are having a *Lung* disorder, a disease of the aura, a disease of the psychic wind, la. The *Lung*. What Western doctor can be curing that, I am asking you, la? I am spending a lot of money on Rabbi Chod's medicine, and consultation. He is saying that with Tibetan medicine things are often getting worse before they are getting better, la.'

'But, Menla, we've been taking this stuff for years. And it's been getting worse for years. When will it start getting better, for heaven's sake?'

'The medicine is gathering the disease up, then it is destroying it, la. The symptoms are getting worse, then later they are disappearing, la. It costing a lot of money, Osel, You know that.'

'Yes, but it's not working. The illness has been gathering and gathering and gathering . . . When will the bloody destroying bit happen?'

My father snorted, shrugged and returned to his coffee. My mother rolled her eyes, banged the table and carried on pulling tangles out of her hair.

For several uncomfortable minutes they remained opposite one another while I sat cross-legged between them, like a tiny Buddha, in Spiderman pyjamas. I had learnt that it was dangerous to interrupt a silence between my parents. As the noiselessness gathered around me, I felt like a Gurkha in a jungle clearing, surrounded by a web of trip-wires. I held my breath for as long as I could. Whenever either of them caught my eye, they showed me an identically tense smile. I loved them for trying to conjure up an illusion of security for my sake; but it was clear that they were incapable of alleviating their own suffering, let alone mine.

I became acutely aware of the sounds in the room. The scratching of my mother's comb and my father's gulping seemed to constitute a conversation of their own. Eventually, my father had finished. He retrieved Grandpa Pagpa's typewriter, loaded it with a sheet of A4 and began to type, each stroke of the keys resounding like a thunderclap. He tore the paper out of the typewriter and slid it across the table to my mother. She ignored it. He glanced at his watch, pulled his trousers up, tucked his shirt in and swept me up from the table. Then we left the house, giving my mother a wide berth.

Although my father was a small man, he always liked to carry me when we went out. Some of the time I preferred to walk, but mostly I didn't mind being carried. He held me so high up on his chest that I all but obscured his vision as he ambled down the street, ignoring the postman's greeting as usual. He always carried me either too high or too low, so I felt either that my heels might get caught beneath his feet, or that I might topple over his shoulder at any moment. It was the kind of February morning that felt like May, apart from the few leaves that creaked underfoot from time to time.

I am always surprised by how long it takes for an unconscious experience to make its way to the conscious mind. For example, my father always smelt of coffee, as long as I'd known him, yet I never really noticed it. Wherever my father was, the smell of coffee was inevitably present. It was so obvious that it was almost undetectable. There was rarely any aftershave, or sweat, or any bodily odour. Just coffee. Coffee is severe, it is harsh. It takes no prisoners, and once it has been absorbed, there is no escape from the inevitability of the caffeine rush. This made it an ideal way for my father to assert control over the world; he relied on it to prove to himself that once a system has been set in motion, there is no stopping it. Coffee made him feel safe for, unlike language, it represented a reliable chain of cause and effect that he could control, and hold in his hands, and spark off at will, knowing that it would not pause until its routine had been completed. He was in love with coffee; an occupational hazard of the coffee-shop proprietor, I suppose. First he created his environment, but then his environment rose up and created him – a coffee-man. Now I think of it, he had been a coffee-man from the start. He thought that he was choosing his profession, but in reality his profession chose him. His only option ever was coffee; the comforting ritual was always already internal to him.

When the coffee-man and I turned on to West End Lane, a large white van was parked on the corner. The words 'Dazel's Dirty Diapers' were emblazoned in bold pink type on the side, set in a semi-circle above a crude cartoon of a baby. Below this was inscribed 'Pure Cotton Nappy Laundry Service', in smaller, more angular letters. Someone had fingered a message in the grime on the bonnet of the van, just legible in the dappled coins of sun tumbling from the overhanging oak. It was underlined three times, and read, 'Ageing is like an immovable mountain.' Makes a change, I thought.

Dazel was the launderer of my nappies, but he was far more than that; he was my mother's best friend. My father always tried as far as possible to stay out of the nappy launderer's way. A thread of smoke was spiralling lethargically from the front window of the van, which was slightly open. As we passed I caught the eye of Dazel, the bearer of the cigarette; a blue-faced, mole-like man whose discoloured spectacles had been smoked like a pair of haddocks. Behind them his eyes were round and light – his mother was Tibetan and his father English. He inclined his head politely to us as we passed, and I waved Plastic Bag at him. My father ignored the salute. Within a surprisingly short time, we had meandered to our destination.

My father's café was his main object of love. As he fumbled for the keys I observed its façade, illuminated by the chilly glow. The name was etched on a plain white background: 'The Hush Hush Café, West Hampstead branch'. The hand-painted lettering was so meticulous that it could easily have been mistaken for type. Contrary to the boast, this was the one and only branch. The sign was a relic from many years ago when Grandpa Pagpa, who founded the business, had been ambitious to expand. The front of the shop, sandwiched between an ice-cream parlour and a greengrocer's, was made of sheet glass, and there was nowhere present a single smudge or smear, or a poster of any description. All that was displayed in the window was a square white label which read in the same precise script, 'Rules. Silence must be maintained at all times. All forms of antisocial behaviour prohibited. All forms of sociable behaviour prohibited. The management will eject anyone not compliant.' This was my father's mantra. He sprang the catch and entered with a careful tiptoe, closing the door quietly.

The blotting-paper blinds were drawn, coating the room

in a soapy light. Clouds of dust particles were suspended in the air like plankton. With a sharp tug, dry sunlight invaded the café, sending scared shadows darting. The place was white, and intensely so. The walls were white; the ceiling was white; the coffee-stained, muffling deep-pile carpet was white; the tables were white.

Towards the other end of the shop was a broad platform, accessed by three shallow steps and surrounded by a white banister. In its centre stood a decrepit pool table, covered in such an incredibly thick layer of dust that it, too, was practically white, with balls like grimy marshmallows. My father flicked a silent switch and the café was illuminated further by the kind of hidden lighting that is used in art galleries, chosen because of its especially low level of noise output. This gave the place the vivid, rarefied feel of a museum. My father sat me on the immaculate white counter, slipped round it and disappeared behind a curtain. I sat Plastic Bag beside me in his house and began to take the few extra cubes of Lego I had brought with me out of my pockets. I heard a double-glazed door slide open and shut, producing and cutting short a brief hum of traffic noise. My father had gone into the kitchen.

A few minutes elapsed. Plastic Bag looked comfortable in his house, the scratch on his face gleaming like a laser beam in the morning light. I perused the counter. There was not much to peruse. The addition of me, Plastic Bag and his house brought the number of items on its surface to five. On my left stood a replica of the list of prohibitions in the window. On my right was the Hush Hush menu, which consisted of a single item: a fading photograph of a cup of foul-looking black coffee, £3.00.

Presently, the white curtain ballooned and my father emerged from its folds, approaching the counter more noiselessly than he had left it. I noticed that he had changed into his work shoes, a pair of discreet-looking stocking-slippers. He was carrying a small can of WD40 and he gave a quick squirt into the runners of the cash drawer to ward off the slight possibility of squeaks, as he did every morning. Needless to say, simple drawers would always be preferable to noisy tills in such a decorous establishment. Then he gathered me onto his upper chest, I gathered up Plastic Bag, and my father carried us both through the curtain.

The kitchen that lay behind the sliding door could not have been more dissimilar to the rest of the café. It was cleaned only when Health and Safety inspectors were due to visit. It was one of those rooms where all the pipes and plumbing fixtures of the building converge in a tangle of arteries and organs. The air was damp and the wallpaper was peeling in brown dragon's tongues. A smudged smell of milk, coffee and carpets clung to everything, and a fridge buzzed like a hornet. Admin was scattered about. In the centre of the thinning lino was a chipped, lipstick-red wooden table, littered with polystyrene. An ancient coffee machine hulked in the corner, supported by a stack of packaged coffee beans that partially obscured the light from the fingerprinted window. White coffee cups and saucers, in various stages of cleanliness or decay, spilt over the large sink to lurk all around the room like little predators. The base of each cup and the centre of each saucer had been covered with a layer of sound-deadening felt.

My father sat me on the table and was beginning to collect the coffee cups into the sink area when a tremendous thumping jerked in from the main room. He put the crockery down slowly, then hurried into the front of the shop. Presently he returned, followed by someone I instantly recognised: a large Tibetan man with a short but unusually thick charcoal beard, resplendent in flowing robes of emerald and white.

'Rabbi Chod, I am thanking you so much for dropping, la. It is always being such a . . . what you call . . . a pleasure, a genuine pleasure, to be seeing you, especially being so early in the day, and . . . la-la-la,' my father said, losing control of his sentence. He hated Rabbi Chod's visits to the shop just as much as Rabbi Chod did. They made him nervous.

87

The policy of silence did not agree with the holy man's nature, and he usually hustled my father into the kitchen for a 'quick word'. This irritated my father more than anything else, as he liked to maintain the rule of silence everywhere in the café, including the kitchen; but he was too intimidated by the Rabbi's authority to let it show.

'Not at all, my dear second cousin Menla, reincarnation of Abraham, Abraham Tulku, my friend, indeed, not at all,' said Rabbi Chod, ruffling my hair absentmindedly. 'Your politeness is indeed extremely foolish. I am an early worm. I always arise as soon as the cock grows – at the crack of a growing cock. Indeed! Cock grows: Chod arises. Great men always delight in rising early, in order to steal the day. Churchill, Gandhi, Thatcher: likewise my good self.' My father began to offer him a coffee but Chod declined.

'To business, to business,' he said, 'I am in a hurry. Two things. First: I have brought you some more medicine. Jogpo will send you the bill.' He dropped a small brown package on the table, among the cups. 'To be taken three times a day, and chewed well. Otherwise, the pills will straight through your body, whoosh! Like that. Like this: whoosh! Also, if you don't chew, you will not be able to taste it. The taste is vital – vital. It makes the mouth and digestive tract secrete. No taste, no benefit! As the Chinese say, bad taste shows good medicine. You must chew, or it won't work. And if your strong Tibetan teeth have weakened due to illness, you can wrap the pills in a handkerchief, and smash them with a hammer. Top banana.'

My father took the package of pills and squeezed it, contemplatively.

'But. Enough medical talk. This is neither there nor here, nor roundabouts. Don't distract me. I am in a hurry. Without further ado – second point.' My father perched uncomfortably on the corner of the scarlet table while his visitor gestured grandly. 'As you, my dear second cousin Menla, know very well, this week we Tibetans will celebrate the Tibetan New Year, or Losar. It is February 2002 – the year of the Water-Horse is coming, Menla, it is coming. Auspicious. So. As today is Friday, tonight we Tibetan Jews will celebrate Sabbath-Losar. Together. According to God's will! Indeed. Therefore, I popped in to suggest to you this morning that we engage in the festive meal together, tonight. That is, would you like to come over to mine tonight? For Sabbath-Losar? Just do it?' He slitted his eyes, anticipating a reply.

'This is being very kind of you, Rabbi Chod, la. But the thing is my wipe, Osel, already is intending to be visiting her prend Dazel tonight, to be writing poetry . . . Dazel is not being a Jew, so . . . and . . . la-la-la.' My father was jittery and his words ran off again.

'That, my dear second cousin Menla, is of no concern. Of course, the Venerable Dazel can come as well, the more the merrier. But Osel must come. We need her to cook. Sadly, I cannot cook, my good self. I live on ready-meals, mainly. And these, I regret to say, are not fit for Sabbath, or indeed Losar, as I'm sure you agree.' My father murmured that he did. 'Thusly, my dear Menla, I shall request your dear wife to journey to my home this afternoon and carry out her Sabbath cooking there. Have you given her some money already, with which to purchase provisions?' My father murmured that he had. 'Very good. She may need some more, as there is the addition of my good self to cook for, as well as this Dazel. If you pay out, Menla, I shall reimburse you at a later date. Excellent. Most undeniably excellent. I shall contact Osel by way of my telephone, and I shall expect your humble family no later than seven o'clock tonight. If you wish to bring a gift for the host, a nice bottle of Chardonnay would be gratefully accepted, or else any CD from the current top ten – particularly Ricky Martin. Samba, ha ha! Without further ado.' He spun on his heel and strode out through the curtain. The front door thundered behind him.

My father heaved a profound sigh, hoisted his trousers up restlessly and lowered himself onto one of the three-legged

89

stools at the table, gazing into the middle distance. He picked up Plastic Bag between his toe-like thumb and forefinger and pretended to eat him. I snatched Plastic Bag to safety and crawled to the other side of the table. It was things like those that made me distrust my father. After a few minutes, his eyes gradually became fixed on one coffee cup in particular. It was half full of some unidentified solid substance, smothered in many layers of lava-like dust. Slowly, a kind of absent presence came over him, as if a spurt of troublesome thoughts had burst into his mind. He covered his coin of baldness with his hands, completely still, and became unaware of his surroundings. All his senses began to constrict, to focus, to zoom in, until they were capable of experiencing no object apart from that odd, unhygienic cup. His eyes were static, not blinking, not moving, not crying.

Motionless he sat, as the clock on the wall crept through its cycles. I was disturbed by this display, all the more dramatic through its lack of drama, especially when compared to the boisterousness of Rabbi Chod's visit. I clutched Plastic Bag anxiously to my chest. Minute after minute after minute. Somewhere, something distant banged in a pipe. The bare light-bulb shone quietly to itself and the sunlight, seeping through the dirt on the windows, created lies of light in the room. The minutes passed and still my father sat. I crawled over and patted his forearm in an attempt to break him out of it – to no avail. His shoulders hunched. His head in his hands. His elbows on the scarlet table. Internalised, unaware, motionless, minute after minute after minute. In the dingy corners of the room, the traffic noise swelled and swarmed like a cloud of flies. Eventually, he said a single word: 'Bye'.

After a while he sighed and lifted the strange cup in his stumpy fingers, taking great care not to spill even the tiniest amount of dust. Then he opened the pedal-bin and lowered the whole thing sadly to the bottom. Finally, he left the room, his head low. For a while, I was left alone. Then he remembered me, came back, and took me through to the café.

It was not long before the first real customer of the day

came in. There was an absence of chimes above the door as it swung open and closed, and a coiffed girl in unusually pointed shoes sauntered in, glancing curiously around her. I was sitting on the floor beside the counter with Plastic Bag in my hands, and she shot me a dazzling smile as she meandered round the tables. I felt my father bristle; he disliked newcomers at the best of times, especially the young and frivolous. This was a place of silence, of contemplation; a place to sit and mull over the weightiness of life, not to recline and drift and daydream. Certainly not a place for dazzling smiles. She leant on the counter, sporting an expression my father clearly found disagreeable.

His scrawny neck tensed with annoyance as she pointed at the picture on the menu, unnecessarily mouthed 'Coffee', and shot him a quick thumbs-up. Nevertheless, he steeled his jaw, produced his notepad from his trousers and scratched down her order, as he always did; he would condescend to go and brew her a coffee. She began making faces at me. I tried to oblige her by putting my fingers in my nose and spluttering my tongue but my father shot me a glare. Then he swept through the white curtain to prepare the order. The girl glanced around and pulled her hair. At length, she slid into a seat by the window and dumped her voluminous bag on the table. She sat at an angle, one leg propped on the other, a pointed shoe dangling casually from her toes. After a great deal of noisy rummaging, interpolated with face-yanks for the benefit of myself, she drew a *Telegraph* out of her bag and spread it out in front of her. There was a pause. She turned a page, and her shoe dropped from her toes with a soft clump. Casually, she poked it under the table, smoothed her fringed skirt and continued to read, chewing her lip.

The perfect simultaneity of what happened next was dream-like. Just as the curtain billowed, heralding the arrival of my father with her cup of foul coffee, a phone went off. The ring tone stung through the air like a serpent, accompanied by the sound of the handset vibrating. The *Telegraph* flopped to the floor as the girl hunted through her bag, twisting to one side and burying her arm up to the elbow while directing an anguished expression towards my father. He was placing her coffee on the counter next to me, his moustache bristling. The ringing suddenly trebled in volume as she snatched her phone into the open air. It was pink and had butterfly stickers all over the back. She fumbled at the buttons and the ringing was abruptly replaced by a metallic voice. I stifled a giggle, pressing my hands over my mouth. Agitated, she reached for her fallen newspaper, not noticing my father rushing silently over to her table, weaving in and out of chairs like a slalom skier and almost falling over in his haste. As she looked up, her apologetic features were illuminated by the glare of his Polaroid flash. A black square slid out of the camera into his hand, and he brandished it triumphantly aloft. She made pleading gapes at him with her mouth but he shut his eyes dismissively and continued to waggle the Polaroid. In the end she swung her hair round her face in a mixture of chastisement and resentment, stuffed the *Telegraph* back into her bag with a terrifically loud crumpling sound and left the café, a voice still coming from her phone. Out of the window I saw her cross the street and head primly for Regent's Park Café, our closest competitor. The door gulped back its silence.

For many minutes, my father stood at the table as if he had witnessed a rape. Gradually, decorum returned. When all was calm again he glided behind the counter and pinned the overexposed Polaroid picture on a huge cork noticeboard, alongside scores of other photos of people with expressions of bewilderment and panic. He stood back, scanning the Gallery of the Banned with an air of disapproval.

From afar, I began to examine the noticeboards. Although the subjects were of all ages and sexes and from all walks of life, the uniformity of the glared faces and startled expressions created an element of continuity on the vast cork noticeboards. One thing could be said of my father: he was certainly fair in implementing the rules of his café. I later discovered that he was as willing to ban a customer who had been offering patronage for many years as one on their first visit. He understood from the moment he met someone that parting was inevitable, and could be startlingly unsentimental when he felt that the time of separation had presented itself. A black rectangular box appeared from his jacket pocket and he turned it on. It had a display panel on the front and a bank of five switches. He readjusted the settings and slipped it back into his pocket. I had seen it before but had never known what it was; I was overcome with curiosity. I toddled over and tried to take it from his pocket. He shooed me silently away.

The door opened again, indicating the start of the breakfast rush. Seven or eight customers entered in succession. Those new to the café began queuing at the counter to order their coffee, while the regulars simply took their seats. A couple of them had evidently been frequenting the café for many years, for they entered like ghosts, barely detectable, and blended into the surroundings, without the slightest acknowledgement. I carried on playing with my Lego. I wished I had brought more pieces with me, because I soon ran out of ideas; but I had been trained to sit patiently for long periods.

My father began serving. The ritual of scratching down the orders in his little notebook was strange, considering that his menu consisted of only a single item; but it was an essential part of the system. Every ritual, as it develops, necessarily spawns other rituals around it, to enhance it and keep it safe. Sub-rituals sprout automatically, like fungus on a tree, and eventually the tree rots away and nothing but a maze of hollow ritual remains.

He was about to disappear into the curtain to prepare the coffee when he paused abruptly, his mouth slightly open. I wondered if he was about to keel over, then understood that he had been hit by a realisation. He made an about-turn and prowled over towards one of the tables at the back of the café, where a rhinoceros man in leathers was sitting. My father peered at him intrusively. He was fearsome to behold, his face covered in leech-like tattoos. My father scrutinised him for a long time and he glared sullenly back. Suddenly my father, unthreatened by his intimidating appearance, beckoned authoritatively to be followed back to the counter. Rhinoceros Man, clearly taken aback at the confidence with which my father expected him to obey his commands, instantly complied, dwarfing him as they walked. My father motioned for him to stop behind the counter and began scanning the photos on the Gallery of the Banned. Rhinoceros Man became increasingly flustered, and his scowl began to collapse into the panicky squint of a guilty schoolboy. My father, with a little jump of recognition, reached on his tiptoes for a photo at the very top of one of the noticeboards. Plucking it off, he spun round and held it up. In the photo, clearly visible but with fewer tattoos, was the face of Rhinoceros Man. My father's head pecked left and right. But in place of Rhinoceros Man was now only empty space. He had slipped out of the café and was hurrying off down the street. My father was pleased. He glowered triumphantly around his domain, his moustache bristling. The newer customers bowed their heads in embarrassment while the older customers nodded in deep approval of the display of alertness and vigilance by the fierce protector of their silence. The real veterans made no reaction at all. I had to admit it – I was impressed.

The sensation of victory pleased my father in a way that words never could. But at the same time he began to doubt himself and became agitated. He examined the people dotted around the room, peering into their faces and comparing them one by one to Polaroids on the Gallery of the Banned. Eventually he had satisfied himself that all the customers were kosher, and he disappeared behind the curtain to prepare their coffee. Before doing so, however, he brought out the little black box again, along with a dog-eared instruction leaflet. I was in a better position to see it this time. It was called the Lax™ Stress Controller and, the leaflet claimed, emitted a range of electromagnetic fields that influenced the brainwaves in a prescribed fashion, paving the way to 'an easier state of mind and the science of a better way of life'. There were five settings, with corresponding switches: Sleep, Communication, Memory, Stress Release and Optimism. My father adjusted the setting to Stress Release and put it back in his pocket. The curtain flapped, and I was left alone with the customers.

I tried hard to remain polite, but could not bring myself to respond to the grimaces that several of them directed at me once my father had left the room. I was astounded at how invasive adults can be when trying to win the favour of a child. What were they trying to achieve? They were all fascinated by me in one way or another, even the most seasoned and solipsistic of them. The distracted eyes of the pale faces rushing by me were gazing at me in curiosity and incomprehension as I sped the other way. The powerful aroma of coffee was beginning to make my head spin, and having all those eyes on me made me feel nervous. I held on to Plastic Bag for comfort, and mentally prepared myself for the day ahead.

Chapter Thirteen

When my mother came to pick me up at lunchtime, the silence that passed between her and my father was thicker, heavier, more pregnant with meaning, than any of the surrounding silences in the café. It was not a mere absence of communication, far from it; its nature was communication, and it communicated on the deepest level. The superficial layer of conversation had been stripped away, laying bare the struggles beneath. The friction in my parents' relationship made me feel stabilised – in the few short years I had been alive, I had already learnt that the worst relationships often offer the profoundest sense of security. At least you know where you are with them, and you haven't got so much to lose when they break down. Not that security is ever anything other than an illusion, and not that any relationship is anything other than defunct. But if you're fortunate enough to be given the illusion of security, what's wrong with maintaining it for as long as possible?

My mother left the café and tottered down the street, holding me in her arms. It felt very different from being carried by my father. Whereas I was constantly afraid of toppling over my father's shoulders or being trampled beneath his feet, in my mother's arms I couldn't shake off the feeling that I was in danger of being dissolved back into her body, like a sugar cube into coffee. Her body was excruciatingly frail, a set of coat hangers with a layer of cellophane stretched over it. It was craving extra bulk, and seemed in danger of sucking me in. I was never afraid that my mother would let go of me; but at times I was afraid of suffocation.

When we came to the corner of West End Lane again, Dazel had disappeared from his van. He must have vanished fairly recently, because a thin cloud of yellowish smoke still hung around the steering wheel; this meant he had been sitting there all morning. My mother peered through the windows as we passed, but he was nowhere to be seen. The caption etched in the grime on the bonnet of the van had been slightly altered; it now read, 'Decay is like an immovable mountain.' The message gave me an odd jolting feeling, and I was glad when we finally reached the safety of our house.

My early life had fallen into a strict routine: my father took me to work for the first half of the day and my mother looked after me in the second. This meant that every day Plastic Bag and I were the sole spectators of both my father's pre-work rituals and my mother's secret writing. These days, her green-topped writing desk was usually littered with scraps of typed notes passed to her by Grandpa Pagpa and my father, saying things like 'need m•r bred' or 'gas_bill_paid,_£350'. Some were more cryptic, such as 'well_y•u are_kn•wing_ why', or 'he_is_smelling,_it_is_unacceptable,_I d•n't_trusting_that particular_man.'

We arrived home and had lunch. As usual she made me a plate of boiled beans and meat, arranged in the shape of a smiley face, adding to the collection of empty smiles my parents tried to comfort me with. She herself picked at a small clump of *tsampa* and a bowl of *thukpa* and *tingmo*, little steamed dough buns. Then we shared a plate of apricots. After lunch I helped her vacuum the house. I was in charge of carrying the wire behind her. Then I amused myself in my den behind the sofa while she wrote her private words, her head appearing anxiously over the top of the cushions from time to time as if I was in danger of evaporating. She sat down at her desk and painstakingly scratched out a short poem entitled 'Noise'. I crept across and read it over her shoulder.

'Noise that annoys,
Between girls and boys,

97

Is what I need,
To help me to breathe.
To release my fears,
To cry lavender tears,
To break the illusion,
To shatter the confusion.'

This small piece took her a great deal of time to compose because of her laborious process of writing, each word being invariably followed by an endless period of Biro-chewing. Moreover, she never continued to write on a page where she had made a mistake; this meant that a vast amount of paper was wasted before she completed a poem – if that moment ever arrived at all. Often she abandoned her efforts in frustration, but today she met with success. She read through her poem several times, her lips fluttering; then she folded it and added it to the rubber-banded bundle. Slowly she raised her spindly frame from the seat. She was not worried that my father would find her poems; his interest in the written word was limited to his typing.

As my mother stood up, the sound of her creaking joints was augmented by the ring of the telephone. I had spent the afternoon constructing a thick wall round Plastic Bag's house, using the extra Lego that I had been keeping under my bed. I had made it without a door so that no ageing or decay would ever be able to get through. Plastic Bag looked safe enough in his new, improved sanctuary, so I left him there and followed my mother into the hall. As she answered the phone in a soft murmur, I twisted myself in her long skirt. Rabbi Chod's voice pulsed fuzzily from the receiver for several minutes while my mother listened in silence. I couldn't catch what he said. After a time there was a crunch and his voice was replaced by the dialling tone. She stood listlessly in the hall for a while, listening to the buzz of the handset. Eventually, with great effort, she galvanised herself into action and asked me if I needed the toilet. I didn't. She made me go anyway. Then she heaved several bulging plastic bags from the kitchen table, told me to hold on to her skirt and led me out of the house, staggering under the weight of the groceries.

The wait for the number 328 was lengthy, and I was glad I had brought Plastic Bag and his house, though I had to leave the protective wall behind. The wait was more difficult for my mother, as she refused to put the bags down on the ground. Her fingers bulged under the pressure of the handles, and began to turn maroon and yellow. By the time the bus came into view, she seemed in serious danger of toppling unconscious into the grumbling traffic. But she didn't, and the severely overcrowded bus pulled up with a scrape of brakes and a hot cloud of exhaust. People crammed them-selves in as if it was bound for Shangri-la, and we battled on alongside them. My mother kept asking me to put my Lego man in her bag, but I wouldn't; this caused a certain amount of friction between us, and the other passengers gave sighs of disapproval at our bickering. The odours of exhaust, perfume and sweat became overpowering.

We were standing near a man in African dress, sitting serenely upright and smelling strongly of blackberries. My mother still wouldn't let go of the bags, so whenever the bus went round a corner she would flail ignominiously into his lap. This occurred with such frequency that he stood up and, with a stiff bow, offered her his seat. She refused; he insisted. After a while she gave in and collapsed into the vacant seat, her bags clustering round her feet like ghosts and her head lolling against the steamy window. I squeezed in next to her, careful to protect Plastic Bag from harm, and was squashed against the coarse orange upholstery. The bus jerked and jolted along for another couple of miles and then, merci-fully, we arrived. The shit-strewn pavement and murky air of Finchley Road were blissful compared to the stuffiness of the bus, and I began to think that it had been bound for paradise after all.

The effect didn't linger. We arrived at Sneath Avenue and,

as a special treat, my mother let me ring Rabbi Chod's door-bell. I appreciated the reconciliatory gesture. However, before I pressed the button, Chod swung the door open and hurried past us to his car, muttering that he was late for a meeting. We entered and the door closed behind us, of its own accord. Chod's bluebottle appeared, fizzing round our ears. My mother heaved the shopping bags along the hall and into the kitchen. The first thing I noticed was that Chod evidently had the habit of urinating before and after leaving the house, as he had installed a most fascinating and prac-tical architectural feature just beside the front door: a yellowing urinal, complete with a blue block of freshener. I gave a wide berth to the several small, discoloured puddles on the floor by its base, and followed my mother down the hall. The house was somewhere between Tibetan chic and suburban dilapidated, and had a functional messiness and eccentricity that indicated a non-sexually-active bachelor. Bags of rabbit food squatted in corners, and the carpet was flecked with bits of straw. I went into the kitchen.

Everything was conspicuously clean, and smelt strongly of Mr Muscle. The freezer was padlocked. On the window-ledge above the worktop I noticed a black-and-white picture of a formidable-looking woman with glowering amber eyes and a jutting chin. A *khatag* was draped over the picture, and offerings of yoghurt and tea were below it, indicating that she was dead. The first thing my mother did was slosh down two glasses of water. Then she began to unpack the groceries onto the worktops, rubbing her sore arms.

She laboured all afternoon at preparing the Sabbath-Losar meal, fuelling herself with glasses of water, pausing only to take me to the toilet. She had brought a ping-pong ball with her to help me aim, and even though I felt slightly humili-ated, I was glad of the extra help. I played with Plastic Bag for a while under the table, then left him in his house and sat quietly in the corner, watching my mother work. The after-noon wore on and her efforts showed no sign of flagging. I couldn't comprehend how someone so low on energy could toil so assiduously for so long. Her red cheeks became redder with effort. She seemed afraid that if she gave herself a break she would never be able to get up again. The process of preparing the Sabbath meal had become more like a grim battle for survival than anything else. By the time Rabbi Chod came home, thick savoury smells had fattened the air and she was wiping the worktops. He must have been at the pet shop – his robes were speckled with straw. They billowed behind him as he made his entrance.

'Very good, lotus petal, very good. Most top of all bananas. Indeed, you remind me of my own dear mother, Uma, blessed is the True Judge and blessed is her soul.' He opened the oven in a cloud of steam, and inspected the cooking food. 'Excellent, excellent. The most wonderful selection of traditional dishes. Wonderful. Indeed. I bet they taste even better than they smell, eh, Osel? Now, please ready your young child for the evening prayers. We must be sure he does not soil himself at synagogue, indeed. For that would be most embarrassing for all concerned, especially me.' I started to protest at this insult but my mother gestured for me to be quiet. I stamped my foot, unnoticed. 'Now I am off upstairs to prepare myself for the Sabbath. Carry on, Osel, carry on.' He vanished.

I had never liked the formality of synagogue or festive meals, and I cringed at the thought of what lay ahead. My mother stood looking vacantly at the doorway for several minutes. Then she sighed, tilted the remains of her glass of water down her throat and resumed wiping the worktop with a *shmateh* rag. Presently, a noise like Pavarotti at a football match came from upstairs; Rabbi Chod was giving a rendition of '*O sole mio*' to his shaving mirror, which almost drowned the subsequent knock at the door.

My mother put down the *shmateh*, and went to answer it, followed by Plastic Bag and myself. She had to tug the door many times before it opened, revealing a hazy figure standing on the top step. The smoke cleared slightly to expose the blue-faced, mole-like Dazel. He looked uncomfortable in a stiff grey suit and had large quantities of Brylcreem in his hair, which he had scraped formally across the high dome of his head. Yellowish cobwebs of smoke curled round his brown glasses from a smouldering cigarette which stuck out from beneath his heel. The exertion of climbing the five shallow stairs to the door had evidently taken its toll; he was supporting himself on the doorframe, wheezing like Darth Vader. The inverted V of his legs framed a patch of street, in which I could see his nappy van slotted in behind Rabbi Chod's Fiesta. The message in the grime on the bonnet had changed yet again, and was written in letters so big that I could read it from the house; this time it said, 'Sickness is like an immovable mountain.'

'Dazel, hello. Come in. *Tashi delek*, happy New Year. Welcome to Rabbi Chod's place. Sorry to have changed venues on such short notice. Do you want a drink?' asked my mother quietly, wiping her hands on her skirt. Dazel, who was severely out of breath, proffered a bunch of grey-tinted chrysanthemums by way of reply. 'Oh, thank you very much, Dazel. But Rabbi Chod is the host now, so you'd better give those to him.'

A wounded look crumpled Dazel's face inwards and he was gripped by a violent coughing fit. He stumbled past her and collapsed on the sofa, moaning and wheezing into the flowers and clutching his heaving ribcage. A trail of yellow smoke followed him, clinging unpleasantly to the upholstery. I inhaled some of Dazel's smoky aura and immediately felt my chest tighten. My mother hurried to the kitchen and returned with a glass of water, while Dazel's coughing vied with Rabbi Chod's operatics for sonic dominance. I hung back, trying to keep my distance from the smoke while remaining close enough to observe the proceedings. Furtively, I slid Plastic Bag into my pocket to keep him safe; I had enough to worry about already. Meanwhile the bluebottle hummed in, harmon-ising with the snatches of '*O sole mio*' that continued to reverb-erate around the house. It was instantly attracted to Dazel.

My mother knelt by the sofa, holding the glass of water and waiting for his coughing fit to abate.

Dazel, however, felt compelled to speak at any cost. 'Osel,' he panted, his words forming small beige clouds in the air, 'I need to . . . to speak to you.'

'Dazel, don't talk until you've stopped coughing. There's nothing to say, anyway. Nothing to talk about. Nothing at all.'

The bluebottle buzzed from one to the other, following the conversation closely.

'But, Osel, there is. I mean there . . . look . . . arararahem! . . . Read the card in the . . . in the flowers. I wrote you a . . . po . . . em.'

My mother parted the discoloured chrysanthemums and found a greetings card with a Monet print on the front. She scanned the contents and looked up, frustration and sadness on her face. 'Dazel, you're very sweet but—' She broke off and turned to me. I swiftly pulled Plastic Bag from my pocket and pretended to be playing. 'Mo, into the kitchen, please. You've got ears like an elephant, big, flappy ears. Ah-ma wants to have a private chat.'

Reluctantly I obeyed. I sat on the rubbery kitchen lino as close as possible to the doorway, straining to catch snippets of their conversation.

'Dazel, we've talked about this so many times, it's making me ill. You know I'm not very well at the moment, I can't handle it! You're my best friend but . . . if my husband were to read this card, I . . . he would not be very pleased.'

'But I've seen him at it.' replied Dazel, breathlessly. 'Everybody in the community knows. The whole of Tibet knows. The whole of North West London knows. How can you stand it? Ahahahem! I beg you, listen . . . hack, hack, huum!'

'Look,' said my mother, her voice rising, 'unlike you, Dazel, I do not believe in rumours. There is absolutely no proof that my husband has . . . has . . . done you-know-what behind my back, with anyone. I have accused him so many times and he's always, always denied it. There is no evidence, only rumours, only gossip, you know. I can tell when he's lying – we've been married long enough – and this time he's not. He's telling the truth, Dazel, I know it. It's slanderous, that's what it is, slanderous. People in the community are just bloody jealous that Rabbi Chod recognised Pagpa as Isaac, and Menla as Abraham. They say it's because we're Chod's family, malicious bastards! My husband can be a bad-tempered old git, I know, I know, I know, even if he is the reincarnation of Abraham, but that doesn't mean he's done anything wrong. I—'

'But he doesn't, hahaharrumph! Hack, hack, hack, he doesn't make you happy any more.'

'Dazel . . . I . . . You're right. I know. I know. But that doesn't mean . . .'

The talking was cut short and a fumbling silence ensued. I got up and toddled through to the sitting room in time to see my mother standing up from the sofa, her face flushed, smoothing her skirt. 'Dazel, stop it! I'm sorry. This isn't right. I'm a married woman and I've got a child, for God's sake, whatever my husband has or hasn't done.'

As long as I knew Dazel, he was smoky. His clothes were smoky, his hair was smoky, his lungs were smoky, his breath was smoky. Even his smoke smoked with a smoky smoke. Smoke pervaded his insides and hung all around him – at least, as far as I could tell, because the border was hazy. He was the kind of smoker who sets his alarm clock every couple of hours during the night to allow him to have a cigarette in bed. He dreamt about smoking. Smoking had begun as an act of rebellion and had then overgrown him, strangling him like a weed, usurping his personality like a cancer; though, as ever, smoking was always already internal to him. Now he was smoke and smoke was him; everything in his life was about addiction, and taking in, and decaying, and giving out. Even his friendship with my mother was based on addiction, on their secret habit of inhaling and exhaling bad poetry, to the severe detriment of their health. He lived in a flat in Hendon which he shared with his eighty-two-year-old father (whom no one had ever seen) and a mechanical parrot. This he had bought to replace a real one, which had died of asphyxiation a week after he purchased it. That parrot replaced a cat which had crossed the Styx due to asthma; the cat had itself replaced a pair of budgerigars, and so on. All these various animals were replacements for human interaction, of which he had very little. The mechanical parrot had survived for a good three years, although its bright-red paint had become mottled with grey and brown, and the bottom of its cage was filled with cigarette stumps. Like Dazel, it enjoyed little human contact because it was difficult to locate; everything in Dazel's flat was hidden in a thick cloud of smoke which hung almost to the ground, and the only way to identify things was by feeling around for them. So nobody ever saw the parrot, or realised that it was discoloured; and no one would have been any the wiser if one day the smoke got too much for it and it perished.

Dazel lay on the sofa, looking up at my mother, breathing hard. Each laboured inhalation and exhalation took at least four times as long as that of the average person; his throat sounded as if was stuffed with gungy cotton wool. My mother stood looking down at him, turning the card over and over in her fingers, the Monet print flitting in and out of view. She folded it and put it in the top pocket of her blouse. The bluebottle perched on the lampshade.

'You lie here for a while, Dazel, and I'll go and tell Rabbi Chod that you've arrived. Mo, look after Dazel for me, there's a good boy.'

We both nodded resignedly. She left the room and began to climb the stairs, her plait swinging heavily. There was another knock at the door and she stiffened. The knock was repeated. She made an about-turn and headed back down; something in her gait suggested she recognised the knock. She unlocked the door and, catching a glimpse of the person outside, hurried away up the stairs.

My father, realising that the door wouldn't be opened for him, pushed it open himself. Then he entered the room and sat down in an armchair, sniffing the smoky air, his eyes flicking around the room to avoid making eye contact with the prostrate figure on the sofa. I ran over and grabbed his legs by way of greeting. He hoisted me up and cradled me affectionately in his lap. Somehow, I felt sorry for him. Then he plucked Plastic Bag out of my hands and pretended to eat him – and my feelings of sympathy vanished. I managed to regain possession of Plastic Bag and put him in my pocket. Nevertheless, I didn't leave my father's lap; I sat on his crisp navy Sabbath suit, looking up at his recently trimmed moustache and pulling his tie. He took his Lax™ Stress Controller out of his pocket, checked that the setting was on Optimism, and put it away again. The familiar smell of coffee, mingled with the metallic odours of Right Guard and Brut, competed with the pungent aroma of smoke billowing from the sofa.

A few minutes elapsed. I began to feel light-headed from the overpowering combination of smells. Dazel became increasingly uncomfortable about the silence in the room; still clutching the grey flowers to his chest, he tried to engage my father in small talk.

'Good afternoon, Menla. *Tash . . . tashi delek*! Ahem! How's life treating you and yours?' He began. My father inclined his head slightly but said nothing. Dazel panted on. 'How's the . . . the café getting on?'

'As usual, it is being, what you call, ticking along, la-la-la.' I was surprised that he responded. It must have been the Sabbath-Losar spirit.

'Oh, good, good, great. Glad to hear that. Are things busy this time of year?'

My father gave no reply this time. The Sabbath-Losar spirit went only so far. There was a pause.

'Nice wea . . . weather we've been having. Ho . . . how's your father? Pagpa?' Silence. Not even any eye-contact.

Presently, Rabbi Chod came down the stairs with my mother in his wake. The two men in the sitting room stumbled clumsily to their feet. I scuttled to the corner of the room to keep as far away from the Rabbi as possible, clutching Plastic Bag in my pocket.

106

'Ah, my guests. Objects of my generosity.' he enthused, shaking them each violently by the hand. 'Welcome, Venerable Menla, welcome Venerable Dazel. Welcome, welcome, and once again, welcome. I trust you got here safely and are feeling fine. I shall now recount to you the schedule of this evening's proceedings for the benefit of the gentiles among us, that is, specifically you, my dear Dazel, for I take it you are not a Tibetan Jew? That is, you are Tibetan, or at least half Tibetan, but not a Jew? I have never recognised you as a Jewish reincarnation?' Dazel shook his head, causing a large smoke ring to rise from his hair. 'Right. Ahem. Well. Anyway. We are planning to partake of a ceremonial Sabbath meal, as our Lord commanded us on Mount Sinai all those years ago, in conjunction with traditional Losar celebrations. Prior to that – that is to say, as a prequel to the feast – we men are obliged to offer our prayers and thanksgivings to the Lord, blessed be His holy name. This we shall do in an establishment known as the Pet Shop Synagogue, of which I am the spiritual leader. It is so called because during the week it is, in fact, a pet shop – Chod's Animals, to be precise. You may have heard of it? Indeed, for it is owned by none other than my good self. The service begins in twenty minutes; therefore I am indeed grateful that you have both arrived promptly. Would either of you acquiesce to a swift pre-service beverage, perhaps? A tipple?' His flustered guests both nodded with a combination of relief and apprehension. I nodded, too, and they all laughed.

Rabbi Chod saw the limp bunch of chrysanthemums in Dazel's hands and, assuming that they were for him, grabbed them and began waving them about with theatrical magnanimity. 'Flowers. Excellent. Flower power. Ha, ha, ha. Now, without further ado: tipples are good for the souls, as I always will say. Osel, bring the vodka and three glasses.' My father, anxious not to be outdone by Dazel, hunted earnestly in the pockets of his suit. Eventually he produced a gift wrapped in a ball of newspaper and handed it to Rabbi Chod, who ripped his way through the layers of 'Lonely Hearts' and instantly broke into a broad grin.

'Ah, Ricky Martin! What a surprise! Very, very much my favourite.' He shook the CD with glee. 'Thank you indeed, my dear second cousin Menla, come here till I embrace you.' My father hated being embraced, but he accepted the bear hug with sufferance.

My mother arrived with the glasses of vodka and Rabbi Chod passed them round. '*L'Chaim*. Down the hatch. That is to say, down it in one go.' They downed their vodkas, and Dazel was immediately thrown into such a violent coughing fit that he collapsed onto the sofa again. The bluebottle, obviously concerned, sprang from the lampshade and hovered around his head, while Chod clapped my father heartily on the back. My mother bent over the prostrate figure on the sofa and proffered a glass of water, but he waved her away, trying to stifle his coughs. Declaring that it was time to go, Rabbi Chod helped him to his feet, gripped my father by the elbow and seized me by the wrist. Then he led us out of the house, thrusting the flowers and CD into my mother's hands as he did so. She closed the door behind us, waving to me. I was surprised to see that the message on the bonnet of Dazel's van was different again. This time it said, 'Death is like an immovable mountain.' We set off down the road, forming a motley procession; Rabbi Chod strode on ahead, with Dazel and myself lagging behind. Bringing up the rear was my father, yanking up his trousers with one hand and scurrying awkwardly along.

Chapter Fourteen

Before long we arrived at Chod's Animals, which had been transformed for the occasion. The usual stench of straw and shit had been masked by the smell of incense, and an atmosphere of festivity was in the air. There was not an animal in sight apart from the baby monkey, which looked well groomed and very much on its best behaviour. The till had been covered in brocade to form a lectern, and *thankas* portraying biblical figures hung all around. The worshippers bustled in, gossiping and laughing. I overheard Jogpo, who was in charge of the proceedings, boasting to my father that he had painted all the *thankas* himself. The focal point of the room was a huge painting of Rabbi Chod as Moses, complete with Tibetan-style elongated ears and flowing robes, holding a shepherd's staff in one hand and stone tablets in the other, smiling benignly on a lotus seat. In the background were scenes from his lives, such as the splitting of the Red Sea, the receiving of the Ten Commandments and the opening of his pet shop. In the space above were images of parrots and monkeys.

We took our seats and Jogpo hurried off, smoothing his robes. Gradually, the room filled with Rabbi Chod's followers; Tibetan men of assorted ages and sizes clustered round the benches, preparing for the service by wrapping themselves in ceremonial Jewish shawls and thumbing through their prayer books. There were also a few women and children, grouped together in the corner. Dazel gazed around like a tourist. A few people were confused by his half-Tibetan looks. More and more people came in until the room was packed. Then, at a nod from Rabbi Chod, Jogpo struck up a piping chant which was gradually augmented by voices of varied pitches and levels of musical competence.

The service continued and I amused myself by pushing Plastic Bag around the table. Everybody stood up and chanted (Grandpa Pagpa leaning on his stick); then they sat down again and chanted some more. Then they stood up and bowed to a mahogany cabinet containing the Tibetan Torah; then they sat down again, chanting all the while. Presently there was a period of silent prayer and the congregation rose and stood in quiet contemplation. Some wore expressions of anguish, and rocked to and fro with emotion. Others looked bored and gazed at the ceiling. My father gestured abruptly to me and I put Plastic Bag in my pocket, stood up and pretended to pray. Eventually the chanting ended and everyone sat down again. Rabbi Chod strode to the lectern and took command of the room. It was time for his weekly sermon.

'My beloved and humble congregation,' he began, '*Shabbat shalom*, and indeed, *tashi delek!*' He was answered by a babble of voices. 'I especially welcome Abraham Tulku' – he nodded to my father, who flushed – 'Isaac Tulku, our community oracle' – he waved his arm to indicate Grandpa Pagpa in the corner – 'and Jacob Tulku' – Jogpo smiled benevolently – 'our three reincarnate forefathers. And the rest of you, whom there is not enough time to name individually, welcome. Now, without further ado. This Sabbath is special, as you all know – it is Losar. Happy New Year. *Tashi delek.*' A louder, more frenzied response came this time, and a stray whoop. 'Indeed. Yes, indeed. Top . . . that is . . . Indeed. We are gathered not just to celebrate the Lord's day of rest, but also Losar, the dawning of the year of the Water-Horse.' Another cheer went up, even more raucous than before. 'First,' Chod went on, thumping the till-lectern to restore decorum (there was the ding of a bell under the brocade, and the till opened), 'first, before the main sermon, I shall give a brief exposition of the history of Losar. Silence, please, silence. Silence! Thank you. Now. In ancient times, the blossoming of the peach tree was considered the start of the new year. However, in 1027 the Tibetan calendar was systematised and Losar was reglemented, following the Chinese system of—'

'I'm a Moslemmphthsph,' came a shrill voice. I glanced over and saw Machig stuffing sweets into the piranha-like mouth of her son, while the congregation tutted disapprovingly.

'Indeed! Silence, please. Si—'a huge bang on the lectern, and the sound of a receipt printing'—lence! Now, where was I? Indeed . . . Yes. So. The point I want to make is this. We Tibetan Jews, at a time like Losar, all feel extremely proud of our Tibetan identity. Proud. But. We must, also, never forget our Jewish roots, which stretch back through the mists of history, thousands of years, beyond the boundary of this short life, over many generations, indeed. We were all Jews long before we were Tibetans, I can tell you. We must retain our pride in being Jewish – we must retain our support for the state of Israel – and we must persevere with learning Hebrew, the holy tongue, even though I know that most of you have not made very much progress hitherto, that is, so far. Indeed. For the state of Israel has the best military in the world. We are a strong people, we Israelis, an example for all exiled and oppressed people throughout the world, especially the Tibetans. This is something to be proud of, believe me. We Tibetans must learn to stand up to our oppressors, just like the Israelis have done, and grind our enemies beneath our heel. Indeed. For—' There was another great whoop of approval and the sound of manic laughter.

In the corner, Grandpa Pagpa could not contain his excitement at the rousing rhetoric, and was jumping up and down in his chair, bright red in the face, nodding at top speed, waving his stick in the air and making all manner of noises to display his enthusiasm. He failed, however, to articulate any intelligible words. Jogpo, afraid that the Oracle was going into a trance, scurried over and tried to calm him down.

'Silence, please, congregation. Gentlemen, boys and . . . Silence. Silence! Now. Where was I? Moving on. Next point – tonight, as it is an auspicious occasion, I am going to recognise another reincarnation.' A hush fell upon the assembly. 'I had a dream last night,' Chod continued in resonant tones, 'in which I learnt that the incarnation of Judah, the famous biblical warrior, the Lion of Israel, the son of Jacob, has long been reincarnated in our world.' A hum of excitement rippled through the crowd. 'Thusly, tonight Judah is in this very room. Indeed, he has taken rebirth as a Tibetan. I hereby identify the reincarnation of Judah, Lion of Israel, as none other than' – he swung an arm and pointed – 'the man at that table over there, next to Abraham Tulku and his young son, the half-Tibetan, half-Englishman, yes, the one who answers to the name of . . . Yes! It's you, Dazel! Yes, Venerable Dazel. Get to your feet, my dear sir.'

There was a huge wave of cheers. I was afraid that Grandpa Pagpa was going to have a heart attack, he was getting so worked up. Dazel glanced around in terror as he was hauled to his feet. Instantly, he was draped in a score of *khatags*. His face had flushed a deep mauve, and smoke was spurting uncontrollably from his nose. Everyone wanted to shake him by the hand and wish him *Mazal tov*. He was mobbed, and I had to duck under the table to escape the crush.

After a while the chaos subsided and everyone took their seats once more. Dazel collapsed back into his chair, his eyes rolling and his breath laboured, *khatags* hanging all over his neck and shoulders. Order was restored.

Rabbi Chod resumed his sermon on a lower key. 'In synagogue tomorrow,' he intoned, 'I, my good self, shall read the chapter of the Bible entitled *Teruma*, which deals with the various types of offering and sacrifice that took place within the ancient Holy Temple of Jerusalem – as you shall all hear, no doubt, when you attend the service, tomorrow . . . indeed, on time.' The congregation shifted about uncomfortably. 'In the third verse of the third chapter it says . . .'

With that, he launched into a long and complicated scholarly discourse, and the mood soon became heavy. People leant back in their chairs and picked their teeth. My father pulled his Lax™ Stress Controller out of his pocket and began fiddling with the settings. In the corner, Grandpa Pagpa appeared to have fallen asleep. Even Jogpo was staring listlessly into space. Gradually, Chod's voice became unintelligible and my mind began to implode. I felt as if I was rocking from side to side, and then that I was spinning. My head jerked forwards a couple of times, and I readjusted my angle and propped myself up against the table. Brightly coloured images begin to glide at me out of the gloom, and before I know it I am in hospital. Plastic Bag has been badly burnt. Nobody seems to know which ward he is in, and I am running down thousands of corridors. When I arrive at his bedside it is immensely hot, and I am horrified to see that he is still on fire. Bright orange flames lap round his body. As he turns his face towards me I see, to my horror, that he is melting. Yellow beads of gory molten plastic slide along his brow like sweat. I look into his wide, mournful eyes and cry out; but at that moment he is transformed into Dazel. The flames get hotter and hotter and Dazel disappears in the heat, gasping and shivering. The whole world becomes engulfed in white-hot flames.

There was a great wrenching sensation as I was jerked back into consciousness. I had no opportunity to orient myself while greetings of 'Shabbat shalom!' and 'Tashi delek!' burst from all directions. The Sabbath-Losar service was over. The adults engaged in a long period of post-service socialising, and from time to time grinning heads swooped down and cooed a few words at me. I felt dizzy from the number of times my hair was ruffled. Dazel was the star of the show; everybody wanted to speak to the new incarnation of Judah, and his softly spoken, gentile manner went down extremely well. He looked uncomfortable with his new identity, but seemed to be enjoying the attention none the less. Rabbi Chod had no problem acquiring an audience, and was in his element. Someone brought drinks out, and before long everyone was slightly drunk.

My father, silent as ever, held my hand so tightly that I

wasn't sure who was supposed to be comforting whom. He was relieved when the crowd in the synagogue began to thin. Eventually, the affair was over and we stepped out into the sharp night air.

Chapter Fifteen

'So this old man dies, right, let's call him . . . er . . . Reggie, OK? Ahem! Harrump! And he's lying in state in the under-taker's, dressed in a sombre black suit. So his wife comes to visit him, hack, hack, and she says to the undertaker, she says, look, Mr Undertaker, I bought my Reggie a nice blue pinstripe suit a few months ago, and he only got a chance to wear the damn thing once. And it's such a gorgeous suit. Ahem! Please, I just want to see him in it one last time? So the undertaker says OK, no skin off my nose, so to speak, and she gives him the suit for old Reggie. The next day she comes to see Reggie again, and lo and behold, he's wearing the suit! And he looks lovely. Ahahahahum! But – and this is the thing – when she looks closer, right, she sees that the suit isn't pinstripe. It's a different blue suit. It's different. Hack, hack, hack. So she calls the undertaker, and, ahem, the undertaker says, well, I didn't need to use your suit after all. I had another corpse dressed in another blue suit, and I just swapped the heads over! Ha ha ha ha! Aharahem! Ha ha! Hack, hack, hack.'

Nobody laughed. Dazel hid his face in his hands and there was an awkward silence. We had arrived home from the Pet Shop Synagogue, and were standing respectfully around the table, waiting for Rabbi Chod to open the proceedings. Through the window a string of Tibeto-Hebrew prayer flags could be seen folding and unfolding in the breeze, against the purple backdrop of the night sky; Rabbi Chod had raised them to herald the New Year. My father and Dazel stood side by side, with my mother and myself opposite. Chod was at the head of the table. Solemnly, he lifted the decanter and poured thin grey rice-wine into a cavernous silver goblet.

115

Then he commenced the wine-blessing, which he had adapted from traditional sources. He concluded his chant with a flourish of the goblet and stood for several minutes with his eyes tightly shut and his head inclined upwards.

He opened his eyes and sat down, followed by his guests. Then he took a large gulp of the blessed wine and passed the goblet round the table, wiping his beard with a napkin. As was the custom, everyone took a sip. When it came to Dazel he could contain himself no longer and let out a wrenching hollow cough, thumping the table and apologising with sheepish glances at Rabbi Chod. Eventually he recovered enough to take a sip of wine. Then he passed it on to my father, who received it without acknowledgment, handling the goblet gingerly, like a baby bird. He dipped in his little finger and leant over the table. I felt my mother recoil as his hand came into her personal space. The finger descended and wiped its drop of wine into my mouth. When the rice-wine came to my mother, I dipped my finger in and solemnly fed a drop to Plastic Bag.

Rabbi Chod resumed his prayers, mumbling under his breath and repeatedly raising and lowering his eyebrows. Imitating the adults, I clasped my hands and bowed my head. My mother left the room and presently returned, trembling slightly under the load of a large silver washbowl, a matching jug and a towel. Rabbi Chod glanced up briefly, then continued his prayers while she stood patiently behind him. At length he snapped his prayer book closed, beckoned my mother to the table and allowed her to rinse his fingertips. He dried his hands on the towel and she shuffled over to Dazel, who likewise had his hands washed and dried. My father followed suit; but my mother seemed to forget to give him the towel and continued to me, leaving him to wave his hands awkwardly in the air. My fingers were washed, followed by Plastic Bag's half-cylinders of yellow plastic; then she left the room again, and the sound of water and crockery came from the kitchen.

Without waiting for her to return, Rabbi Chod lifted two

loaves of bread aloft and blessed them in a similar manner to the wine, first engaging in an elaborate chant and then pausing in contemplation. In the background, my mother came back in. Rabbi Chod lowered the bread and tore it apart with his hands, dipping each limb of bread into salt and handing it round. Everyone munched their piece and my mother tore off a morsel for me, which I shared with Plastic Bag. Rabbi Chod sighed and stretched, evidently relieved that the ritualistic part of the meal was done and dusted. Potent alcohol fumes crossed his face as he poured some more rice-wine into his glass and knocked it back. 'Osel, lotus petal, if you'd be so kind?' he said. 'The delicious first course?' My mother obliged. I began to make a protective tepee for Plastic Bag out of a napkin on the corner of the table.

'So, my Venerable Dazel, or should I say, ha ha, Judah Tulku, did you enjoy your first experience of my synagogue?' asked Chod, stretching his hands confidently above his head like a cat. His eyes had a sheen to them, as if they were covered in a layer of oil; the evening's alcohol was taking effect.

'Yes I enjoyed it very much thank you, ahem, very educational.'

'Indeed. If there's anything you do not understand about our customs, our religion or our habits, please do feel free to direct a question, however complex, to my good self. For you are a Jew now, Dazel, a Tibetan Jew. Time to start learning, eh? What do you think of that? Of course there will be a small fee: Jogpo will send you the bill after Sabbath.'

'Well, it's very kind Rabbi Chod, but, I would prefer to remain a gentile. I have a religion of my own, you see, C of E, if only nominally, and . . . I am only half Tibetan, after all . . . hack, hack . . .'

'Oh, I see. You are not in acceptance. My dear Venerable Dazel, of course, of course. Remain a gentile. No pressure. Please yourself, indeed. Suit your good self. No problemo.' He chuckled, and Dazel gave a polite snigger.

'Well, Rabbi, I do have a question, but I think it may be of a somewhat sensitive nature.' As Dazel spoke, small beige clouds left his mouth and thickened the brown haze that was accumulating above his seat.

'Shoot right ahead, my Venerable Dazel. I am a somewhat sensitive Rabbi.'

'Well, OK. How shall I put it? Hack. I was wondering about the Tibetan-Jewish attitude to . . . courtship, between Jews and gentiles.' At this, my father jolted in his chair. His moustache bristled so violently that his whole face vibrated. Dazel shot him a sidelong look.

Having completed the tepee, I tried to break the tension. 'Look, Daddy! Look at Plastic Bag,' I said, affecting my most appealing expression. It made no difference. They were locked in an unspoken, formless clinch.

Rabbi Chod cracked his knuckles in front of him and furrowed his brow, oblivious of the electricity in the atmosphere. My mother came in with a vast tureen of *troma*, the traditional Losar dish that brings good luck. She began to circumambulate the table, spooning it out with a long-handled ladle. Little piles of the tiny bulbous root appeared on each plate. Catching wind of the thunder in the air, she threw me a questioning glance. My father noticed and became even tenser. He stared intently at his glass of water, an unbroken white ring surrounding each of his irises.

'Generally speaking, my Venerable Dazel, marital relations, shall we say, between Jews and gentiles, are one hundred per cent prohibited by Jewish law,' stated Rabbi Chod. My father gave an exasperated splutter, and downed his glass of water. Chod poured himself yet more rice-wine, took a large mouthful of *troma* and continued, chewing. 'You, for example, choosing – against my advice – to remain one hundred per cent gentile, would have zero per cent chance of marital relations with a one hundred per cent Jewess. Is that clear? Likewise, a Jew would have zero chance of marital relations with a gentile girl.' Dazel swallowed uncomfortably and a tiny puff of yellow smoke shot out of each ear. Rabbi

Chod wobbled back in his seat, smacking his alcohol-laced lips lethargically. 'Indeed, my Venerable Dazel, the family of my dear second cousin Menla has endured severe sexual controversies through the generations.'

'Yes indeed, la. How right you are being, Rabbi Chod. *Severe* sexy controversy,' said my father, jutting his jaw.

'Oh? How so?' enquired Dazel, sardonically.

'How so? He is wanting to be knowing how so, la!' blurted my father. Quickly, he poured himself another glass of water and drank the whole thing at once, as if he was quenching a blaze in his belly. This calmed him down. He breathed deeply, closed his eyes and assumed a meditative pose, the steam from the soup spiralling in front of his taut face like an incense offering. He was unsure of what to say, yet determined to say something. Chod slumped drunkenly in his seat, the oily sheen on his eyes so thick that I could barely see his pupils. My mother sat down and started to eat her *troma*, glancing worriedly around. My father produced his Lax™ Stress Controller and placed it on the table, parallel with his cutlery; he adjusted the switches to the Communication setting and resumed his meditative pose. Eventually, words began to leak out of him as if thoughts were slipping out of his head by accident.

'Well, la-la-la. I will now be telling you a story of sexy controversy, Dazel, if you are desirable, la. Sex controversy. Yes. So you are taking it as an example, a warning, la. This story is being about my ancestor . . . What was her name? . . . Pemba, la. She was living at around the beginning of the eleventh century. Her pamily was living in Golog, in eastern Tibet, and were already being as rich as the hills, and very, what you call, very influential, very powerful, la. When she was being a teenager, she was having illegitimate sexy with a local shepherd, an orphan called Ngawang, la. Completely dipprent caste, Dazel, completely dipprent. How shocking, la! Not punny. As was resulting from this appair, Pemba was becoming pregnant, la. Pregnant! The only person she was telling was her older brother. This brother

119

had a very boiling head on his shoulders, and searched out Ngawang, and was killing him in a pit of rage. Killing him, dead as a duck.' He struck the table, softly. 'La-la-la! Dagger through the heart, la. You see, Dazel, what can be happening. Dead as a doo-doo, la.' His moustache shivered as he glared at his adversary, who was breathing two thin jets of smoke nervously through his nostrils. There was a long pause.

'So, my dear second cousin Menla, what happened next? Pray, continue your story!'

'Well, Rabbi, I have now been pinishing making my point, la. No more is necessary, I am peeling.' He glowered again at Dazel, who looked intensely uncomfortable.

'Nonsense, nonsense. Your story's just getting good.' replied Chod drunkenly. 'This tale is fantastic, I have heard it before. The good bit comes later. You know, the bit with the lama. That's the best bit. The best is yet to come. We want to hear it, don't we, Monlam? Don't we, Daz—Judah Tulku? Osel? We could hear it a thousand times, this story. I command you. Go on. On. On. Ha, ha. Do not collect two hundred pounds. Do not. Ha, ha, ha.'

I slid from my seat into the gloom beneath the table. My mother tried to restrain me by clutching at my jumper but I evaded her grasp and squatted against a table leg. Knees and feet were lined up around me, adorned by fingers and napkins. My father's discourse seeped through the table top, just audible above the sartorial rustles and scrapes of shoes.

'Very well, Rabbi, la. OK, la. I will be continuing, la. Although it is against what I am willing, la. All right, so . . . Where was I being? Oh, yes. Pemba was pregnant, but she kept this secret from her parents, not telling, la. And her brother was also saying nothing, la. Instead, she went away from home, to the far-off place called U-Tsang. Then, secretly, Pemba gave birth to a bibby girl. When the, what you call, the bastard child was born, Pemba decided she didn't want the bibby, la. She wanted to get rid of it, but she didn't know how, la-la-la.' The Lax™ Stress Controller seemed to be working, as my father's diction was becoming clearer. He took a mouthful of *troma* and continued. 'One day, she was walking in the village with the child, and she was seeing a big crowd of people. A famous lama called Langri Tangpa was giving a public, what you call, a lecture, la. Pemba ran to the front of the crowd and is pushing the bibby into the lama's lap! "Take your bibby," she is shouting. Then she is running off, quick as a shin, leaving the bibby behind. With the lama! Just like that. La-la-la. Like rabbit.'

'Like that. Whoosh! Like that. Whooomp! Do not pass go,' contributed Rabbi Chod woozily.

As the plot thickened, my father's left knee started to pump up and down. I heard Rabbi Chod grunt under his breath for my mother to clear away the empty plates. There was a soft clink as she put her spoon down in her unfinished *troma*; then her legs slid backwards and began to jerk round the table. I crawled underneath my father's chair and squinted up at him.

'Now,' my father went on, unaware of my mother removing his unfinished plate of *troma*, 'the lama was a, what you call, a celibate monk – not sexy, never – and this scene was causing gossip like nobody's trousers, la. People were thinking he was breaking his vows, la. They were thinking he was having sexy in secret, and he was the real pather. But, to the surprise of his disciples, the lama just nodded, accepted the child, and continued to be teaching as if nothing was happening, wrapping it kindly in his yellow robe, la. Can you believe it, la-la? Everyone began to yabber around, la. The lama took the child home and was caring for it, as if it was his own, for two years. He was getting a very bad reputation, la-la-la.' I peeked out from under the tablecloth and saw Dazel and Rabbi Chod listening intently. Things had calmed down so I climbed back onto my chair and tried to balance Plastic Bag on a fork.

'After porcing the bibby into the care of the lama,' my father went on, 'Pemba was returning to parents' home in Golog, and no one was any the cleverer, la. She tried to be putting it all behind, la. But the problem was, she couldn't be porgetting about her child, la. She was peeling very depressed. Not punny. As time was going by, she was missing her child very much, and deeply regretting giving it away . . . she was starting to be really suffering, la. After two years she had no friends, and was barely leaving her room, la. She was, what you call, a kermit. No, sorry, a hermit, la. Anyway, eventually, she couldn't be standing it one day longer. One night she ran away from home, to find the lama, and reclaim her child, la. It must have been the yabber of community at the time.' Nobody noticed my mother enter the room again, struggling under the weight of a tray of steaming pots – the main course.

'It was taking Pemba several months to be travelling to the lama's house in central Tibet,' my father went on, absorbed in his narrative. 'At long last she arrived and met the lama, and found her child, being happy and healthy, bright as blueberry, la. Like a little apricot. Pemba was so happy. And the lama, smiling, immediately returned the child – just like that, la. So kind. Then, everyone saw he was not the pather, he was just helping. So his reputation was becoming good again, la-la-la.

'Then Pemba became a, what you call, a disciple of the lama. She was practising meditation for a long time, and later she was becoming enlightened in that very lipe, la! And they were all living happily ever after, la-la. Apart from Ngawang, who was dead – killed with a dagger – and reborn as a yak. A yak, Dazel. Mmmm, la. La-la-la.' There was a final string of la-la-la's, and my father's speech tailed off. He had finished. He removed his thumbs from his braces and opened his eyes – to his surprise, his *troma* had been transformed into a plate of chicken and *mo-mo* dumplings. My mother had finished serving the food, and an assortment of savoury smells filled the air. My father looked awkward. 'Sorry, I am being blowing my own gong,' he mumbled.

Dazel sat looking pensive, wisps of yellow smoke leaking gently from his nostrils. After a few minutes, he turned to his food. By this time, the oil was overflowing from Rabbi

Chod's bleary eyes and slipping down his face like tears. His pupils lurked below the surface, flatfish-like. As he dreamily gnawed a chicken leg, an oily trickle dripped from his beard onto his robes.

My father and mother happened to take a mouthful of water simultaneously, and for a moment their eyes locked. Then they both put down their glasses and began to eat. Plastic Bag and I followed suit, relieved that my mother hadn't arranged our chicken in the haunting shape of a smiley face. For many minutes, nothing could be heard but the sound of munching and the scrape of knives and forks.

Presently, everyone had eaten their fill, and in an expression of deep contentment the men reclined their chairs. Rabbi Chod leant back so far that his chair creaked and seemed dangerously close to collapse; Dazel tilted his back just enough to keep his feet on the ground; even my father was sitting slightly further back in his chair than usual. As my mother got up to clear away the crockery, Rabbi Chod took advantage of his new angle to reach hazily for a bottle of chocolate liqueur and some glasses from the cabinet behind him. Belching with effort, he unscrewed the cap and poured out three ample helpings of gungy brown alcohol.

'L'Chaim, to a truly succulent kosher meal, provided by our best friend and companion, the Lord God Himself. Indeed. To God.' he said, articulating his toast with some effort. He dropped his head back and tilted the liqueur down his throat, shaking the glass so that the sticky dregs slid down. My father and Dazel tasted theirs politely, and tried to ignore the enormous burp that Rabbi Chod immediately detonated. In the background, my mother reached for their plates, balancing a stack of crockery precariously in one hand. I noticed both Dazel and my father subtly trying to catch her eye, but her gaze remained downcast.

Dazel tried to gain her attention by proposing a second toast. 'Gentlemen, charge your glasses once again if you'll be so kind. Firstly, let's drink to you, our gracious host and spiritual teacher. Ahem.' Rabbi Chod accepted the compliment with a mini-burp. 'And secondly, let's drink to the beautiful and diligent woman who has been labouring so hard behind the scenes: the lovely Osel.'

My mother smiled sheepishly and reached for his plate. But as she did so he raised his glass and, through a cruel twist of fate, his elbow collided with my mother's arm. The stack of greasy plates slid from her grasp and landed with a crash in her husband's lap. Chaos ensued. Dazel lunged to rescue the plates and knocked over the jug of water, which in turn upended Chod's precious bottle of chocolate liqueur. I snatched Plastic Bag from the brown puddle as it spread swiftly across the tabletop, and looked up to see my father picking his dripping Lax™ Stress Controller from the pool of water. There was a stunned silence. My mother hurriedly picked up the bottle of liqueur, but not before it had begun to ooze onto Rabbi Chod's robes. The Rabbi was speechless, and could only stare at the indignity before him.

'Oh, I'm awfully sorry hack, hack,' coughed Dazel. 'That was entirely my fault, I do apologise. Hack, hack, hack, hack, hack. How careless of me. Aharahem. Not to worry, I'll wash the tablecloth with the nappies when I get home. Hack. Not to worry.' He stretched over to right the empty water jug. My mother reached it before him and stood it on its base.

'I'm sorry, I'm sorry,' she mumbled, gathering up the crockery. Dazel coughed nervously. My father sat still, his wet Lax™ Stress Controller in his trembling hands, while my mother reached round him for the plates. 'Excuse me, Menla,' she said. He moved only the slightest amount while she continued to stretch for the plates in his lap. 'Sorry, Menla,' she said again, but this time he didn't move at all.

'Have you forgotten yourself, Osel?' asked Rabbi Chod. 'On Losar, we are supposed to leave the dirty crockery out all night, as a sign of auspiciousness. Please. What are you doing? Put it all back.'

My mother had been pushed beyond her limit. She flung the crockery back on the table and stood up, tension gathering around her like iron filings to a magnet. A look of unbearable distress distorted her face, which looked as if it was about to split. I felt sick as her contorted expression burnt swiftly through my mind and stamped its impression deep into my unconscious. A stifled scream echoed from her throat. Slowly, she took a plate in both hands, raised it above her head, and brought it down in a great arc on the edge of the table. It divided crisply in two, and a semi-circle of china somersaulted over her shoulder in slow motion and splintered into shards on the mantelpiece.

There was an even more profound silence than before. My mother stood by the table, her head bowed, her shoulders hunched, a half-moon of crockery in her hands. The air was static; no one moved, no one spoke, no one breathed; everyone gaped at her, incredulously. A tiny whine squeezed from her throat.

Rabbi Chod broke the spell. 'Osel!' he exclaimed, in utter disbelief.

The word reanimated my mother. She dropped the broken plate and rushed from the room, clutching her plait to her face. We heard her stumble into the kitchen. The door banged. I began to cry. Rabbi Chod's oily eyes slid from one area of disarray to another. I crept to safety under the table and sat in the shadows with my back against the table-leg, staring at the heavy drops of chocolate liqueur that plopped at intervals from the corner of the tablecloth.

Minutes of silence dragged by and I noted that all three men had their hands protectively cupped over their groins. Still nothing stirred. Then the tension became too much for Dazel and he felt compelled to break the silence, his hands lifting away from between his legs.

'Oh dear. Oh dear. PMT, I expect. I'm sure she'll be right as rain in a day or two. Ahem. Never mind, no harm done, eh? Hack, hack. Thank you for having me, Rabbi Chod, I've had a most wonderful time. I—'

Rabbi Chod glared at him and he fell silent again, his hands returning to his crotch. There was a soft clicking to my left; under the table, my father was setting his Lax™

Stress Controller to Stress Release. Many more minutes passed, and I started to feel like the painted-out figure in an oil painting.

I heard the door open quietly and I peered out from my place of refuge. My mother shuffled slowly into the room, framed by the table-legs and dripping tablecloth, her hair swept back from her blank face and a dustpan and brush in her hands. She crouched behind my father's chair and started sweeping up the shards of china. The jangling as they entered the dustpan was louder than anything I have ever heard. After that she replaced the other dirty plates in their original positions, one by one. Dazel's hands began to rise from between his legs but then hesitated and returned. I heard her put his dirty plate down in front of him again, and then she left the room.

A clattering came from the kitchen, then all went silent again. I felt a slight stinging on the back of my hand, and noticed that it was streaked with blood; a shard of china must have flown at me over the table. There was a soft sound at the door, and I peeked out again. I have never seen a more disturbing sight than my mother padding into the dining room, her face expressionless, her shoulders hunched, straining under the weight of five bowls and a tub of homemade pistachio ice-cream.

Chapter Sixteen

One day my father, who had been getting progressively healthier, took me with him when he went for an appointment with Rabbi Chod at the pet shop. It was summer.

On the way to the pet shop I spotted five police cars. Five! And several motorbikes. My father said that one of them was not a motorbike but a 'scooter'. I practised pronouncing the new word a few times and kept it in my mind for later use.

The past few years had gone by like a dream. 11 September 2001 had come and gone, and the world had changed for the better. I entered a less paranoid, less nightmarish age. Now, in 1999, the world was gearing up for the new millennium. I, of course, remained unexcited. In fact, I was happy to be heading in the opposite direction – I had already seen something of what the twenty-first century would bring, and I was glad to leave it behind.

We arrived at Chod's Animals in good time. It was as cluttered and noisy as ever. Jogpo met us, and told us to wait until Chod was ready. We waited in the aquarium section because I liked the exotic fish. My father showed me a tank where one of the fish had an oversized, puffy forehead. This head was obviously nutritious, because several of the other fish kept taking sudden dives towards it and pecking out little chunks, eating it. He said that Chod was aware that this was happening; apparently he was planning to separate them into different tanks, but he hadn't got round to it yet. Soon, my father said, the fish with the big, tasty head would die. He pointed out that I had left fingerprints on the glass, and let me use the clean part of his handkerchief to wipe them off.

Eventually, Jogpo ushered us into Rabbi Chod's office, lit as ever with butter-lamps and sunlight. Chod showed us the string of plastic Israeli flags that he had just hung across the ceiling, and we were both impressed. He sat down in his leather armchair with a loud squeak; my father lifted me onto one of the green plastic chairs and sat on the other. Then Chod reached down and heaved a large canvas bag onto the desk. Even though it was years since my circumcision, I recognised the bag immediately, and defensively crossed my legs. He opened it and withdrew a bundle wrapped in Tibetan brocade.

'So, my dear second cousin Tashi, you have a problem with your health?' asked Rabbi Chod. I was surprised that he had got the name wrong. My father, however, didn't seem to notice, responding as if he really was called Tashi.

'Health is not being very good, Rabbi Chod, regrettably, not very good, la, patigue, headache, a little nausea, gums stinging . . . not good, la. Something is being wrong, la. I hope nothing serious, but I am peeling worse by the day, la-la-la.'

'Hmmmm,' replied Chod, 'sounds interesting. I will give you a check-up. But first: read this. It is from today's newspaper. Preposterous!' He rummaged in his canvas bag, pulled out a newspaper clipping, and passed it across the table. I craned my neck.

TIBETAN MEDICINE FINALLY HITS THE SHELVES

A Tibetan medication known as Padma 28, which is made from 22 different ingredients, including liquorice, cardamom and sandalwood, finally became available over the counter yesterday. After intensive clinical trials at the Middlesex Hospital, London, the pills have been declared safe and compliant with British Standards. Padma 28 possesses powerful antioxidant and anti-clotting properties, and the trials found it particularly effective in treating peripheral vascular disease, a condition caused by hardening of the arteries in the legs.

Other studies suggest that it might be used in cases of heart disease, and even have implications for hepatitis B and C. The acceptance of Padma 28 is a triumph for the alternative healthcare community, and experts say it may open the floodgates for more alternative medication to be made widely available over the counter and on prescription.

'Preposterous! Off-the-peg medication. Over the counter. Scandalous!' exclaimed Rabbi Chod, pouring himself a mug of tea. 'I am not a cowboy like these people, mark my trousers.' My father put the clipping back on the desk. 'Now, Tashi, to business, without further ado. The traditional, threefold procedure – the examination, the diagnosis, the treatment – I will now do.' He pulled a pair of plastic examination gloves from his bag and rolled them over his hands, snapping them against his wrists. 'First and foremost: the urine.' My father fumbled in his pocket and withdrew a small plastic container filled with a water-like substance. Rabbi Chod accepted it and carefully removed the lid. 'Is this fresh urine? From this morning?'

'Yes, Rabbi, only a few hours old, la.' I could verify that. I had heard my father in the toilet that morning, trying to get a spurt of urine into the tiny container. I was very impressed when he emerged victorious, and he had revelled in my admiration.

'Excellent,' said Rabbi Chod. 'I always think that fresh urine is best. You know, in the old days, in Tibet, the doctor would sometimes have to wait for two weeks while the urine sample was transported by yak. Now, let's see.' He stirred the urine vigorously with a chopstick, held the spinning liquid up to the light and contemplated it, thumbing his beard. 'Hmmmm . . . very clear . . . big bubbles . . .' He sniffed it and made a face. 'Sour smell'. He put it down on the desk, replaced the lid and moved on. 'Tongue? Hmmmm . . . red, rough, and dry. Hmmmmm. Pulse? No, no, left hand first for a man, yes, yes, good. Hmmmm.' He laid his fingers on my father's wrist and applied different kinds of pressure. 'The pulse is like a messenger between the doctor and the patient, Tashi,' he explained. 'Your pulse is telling me everything I need to know.' He closed his eyes. 'Hmmmmm. Just relax. The patient must be as relaxed as possible. Hmmmmm.' He breathed deeply. 'Right hand now? Hmmmmm.' In due course he opened his eyes and my father sat back, rubbing his wrist. Rabbi Chod's face had become very grave.

'My dear second cousin Tashi,' he said, steepling his fingers, 'this is an unusual case, more serious than I thought. I will ask a few questions, if I may. Have you been feeling very nervous lately, Tashi?' My father nodded. 'High blood pressure?' He nodded again. 'Do you often develop a very tight feeling in the chest? Do you have what I like to describe as a broken heart? Do you feel terribly depressed? Is this true of you?' My father nodded emphatically. 'Do you tend to push yourself too hard in everything, Tashi?' More vigorous nods. 'This rigidity causes paranoia, nervous bowels, and a nervous stomach. Right again?' My father nodded so hard I was afraid he might pass out. I patted his hand sympathetically, and he jumped nervously at my touch. 'All as I thought, all as I thought. How sad. Hmmmmm.' He took a sip of tea and wiped his beard contemplatively. 'Tashi, my dear second cousin, I am afraid that things are not looking good at all. I am sorry to say, you are developing a severe *Lung* disorder. *Lung* refers to a special energy, or wind, present in the aura. And your aura, my friend, is particularly dirty. I can see it.' He squinted enigmatically and sighed. 'Your deficient *Lung* means that your immune system is severely damaged. How awful, Tashi, how regrettable.' He sat forward. 'All *Lung* disorders have an underlying psychological cause. The *Lung* patient has what I like to call the "broken heart syndrome". That is, you have too much desire, Tashi, too much longing, too much discontent and restlessness, and your immune system is suffering as a result. You are a victim of your own desire. Indeed, just as you can't defend yourself against your desire, likewise your immune

130

system can't defend itself against infection. This is a serious problem, Tashi. A serious, serious problem.' My father hid his head in shame.

'Now, the treatment,' said Rabbi Chod, perking up. 'The first thing we have to do is to deal with the spirits. You are being haunted by three hundred and sixty female spirits, who are disturbing your aura and giving rise to *Lung* problems. We need to confuse them, to trick them, to bamboozle them, and the best way to do this is to change your name. Therefore, this very day I will give you a new name. This will confuse the spirits like nobody's trousers. If we change your name, they will get lost. How exciting! So I hereby give you a new name: from now on you shall be called . . . hmmmm: "Menla". This name is very auspicious, as it means "healer". From now on, you must tell everyone to use this name, everyone. Indeed, you must go to a solicitor, and change it by deed poll. You must never be called Tashi again. Tashi must vanish from the world, and Menla must live. This is vital, absolutely vital, do you understand me Tash—Menla? Your very life is at stake.'

'Yes, Rabbi, I will do this, depinitely, thank you, la.'

'Second, I will give you some medicine. I will make you some pills, to be taken three times a day with hot water, thirty minutes after food – bearing in mind that lunchtime for us Tibetans means noon, and not later, my dear Tash—Menla. And they must be chewed well. Hmmm . . . I think a mixture of *Aquillaria agollocha*, *Allium sativum*, *Myristica fragrans*, asafoetida, and *Santalum album* should do it.' He pulled out a notebook and jotted this down. 'I'm afraid these pills will be quite expensive, my dear second cousin,' he went on, 'as the ingredients are all imported. This is because the origin of the herbs is vital; only those grown in Tibet possess genuine healing properties. But it is worth the money, to be healthy, do you not agree?' My father nodded reluctantly.

Rabbi Chod rubbed my father's crown and sternum with year-old butter and oily compresses. Also, he massaged the first, fifth and sixth vertebrae of his spine. After this he carried out what he called the 'moxabustion technique', which involved applying heated substances on long wooden handles to various parts of my father's body.

While my father put his shirt back on, wincing from the pain of the moxabustion welts on his skin, Chod gave him the following advice: 'Do not eat what is called "light food". That is: no pork (for us Jews, not a problem), no goat's meat, no milk or yoghurt, no strong tea, no strong coffee' – my father's face fell – 'no soya, no vegetables, no pulses, no skimmed milk. Keep warm and stay in dark places. Your surroundings should be very quiet and peaceful, and there should be beautiful scenery around you.' My father began to shake his head, despairingly. 'Also you should only keep good company, such as lovers and close friends. You should rest a lot, both physically and mentally, without worrying even the slightest bit.' My father rested his head in his hands and moaned. 'And laugh a lot,' Chod continued. 'Laughter is very effective for curing *Lung* disorders. If you are very upset and nervous, laughter will release it. Ha ha! Laugh! Ha ha! Ha ha ha!' As my father raised his head and tried his best to force out a laugh, the whole of the rest of his life flashed through my mind, all the way to his death. His corpse appeared so vividly that I blinked.

At length, my father rose heavily from his chair, thanked Rabbi Chod and started to leave. 'And if this health programme doesn't work, don't worry,' Rabbi Chod called after us. 'I have many other treatments to try. Herbal enemas, for example, which are most helpful for disorders of the lower bowels. Or medicinal powders that are inhaled like snuff. Hnnhhh! Like that. Or the boiling silver poker, or burning cones of paste, or golden needle therapy . . .' We hurried towards the exit, winding our way round cages and tanks, Rabbi Chod's voice fading in the distance. 'Tash—Menla! Menla? Didn't you say that you wanted me to babysit young Monlam this afternoon?'

My father stopped. 'Oh yes, of course, la. Sorry, I was being distracted, la. Mo, please be going and playing with

Rabbi Chod. He is looking after you this afternoon – your mother and I are being very busy today, la-la-la.' Reluctantly, I kissed my father and stomped back towards Rabbi Chod's office.

A couple of hours later, outside a certain small terraced house in Sneath Avenue, Golders Green, Rabbi Chod double-parked, manoeuvring the car violently with his left hand and singing along to Gilbert and Sullivan. The noise of the howling engine, radio and Rabbi was replaced by an almost tangible silence, and the contrast made me feel sick.

'So what do you want for supper, little man? Cereal? Baked beans? *Tsampa*? Hmm, the light is off in the porch. Maybe the bulb has blown. Without further ado!' Rabbi Chod released me from the seatbelt and fumbled his way into the house using an enormous bundle of keys which he had produced from deep within the recesses of his robes. We entered, followed, as ever, by a fat bluebottle.

As soon as we walked through the door, we stopped in shock. An unearthly, indescribable stench filled the house. Simultaneously we clamped our hands to our noses. Rabbi Chod cursed loudly in Tibetan and walked in different directions, trying to ascertain the origin of the revolting odour. The bluebottle buzzed excitedly around, enjoying the intrigue – and relishing the smell.

Chod tried the lights; none of them worked. The electricity had failed. But what had caused the smell? He dashed into the kitchen and, with a splutter of shock and disgust, located the source. I toddled after him. In the kitchen, the stench was unbearable. Gone was the usual aroma of Mr Muscle – instead it smelt as if a horse had died. The padlocked freezer was to blame, as around its base there lay a pool of putrid, brownish water. To get me out of the way, the Rabbi hoisted me into the air and sat me in the sink, with my legs dangling over the edge. Then, throwing caution to the winds, he began splashing about the white hulk, peering behind it and humping it away from the wall. I found it strange that it caused him such distress and abandonment. He began to hunt in his robes, all the time muttering to himself. A bunch of keys gleamed in his hand; he sprang the padlock and flung the freezer open.

An unholy odour instantly belched from its bowels, yet Rabbi Chod was undeterred. Feverishly, he began to rummage through its innards. The shelves had defrosted and were naked, stripped of the blubber-like ice. I craned my neck and glimpsed scores of uniform silver-foil containers with stained cardboard lids, each marked with a three-year-old date and a description of the contents in meticulous blue handwriting: fried fat, *mo-mo*, beef slices. The Rabbi was nearing hysteria. With a high-pitched whine, he tore the cardboard lid from a container of lamb stew, plunged a stubby forefinger into it, and tasted the rank paste. The brief look of hope that flashed across his face was replaced by a troll-like grimace and he violently spluttered brown flecks into his beard. He tore the lids off several other containers and cast them aside in despair. Finally he raised his hands heavenward, dropped the last container of fetid curry into his lap and began to moan, as if to the freezer itself.

'Oh dear God. Oh Ah-ma. Forgive me, Ah-ma. My mother. May the Lord rest your soul. Oh, forgive me, your son, for this . . . this power cut. This calamity.' His wide, high-cheekboned face had become the colour of Cheddar and his hands hung limply from his wrists like burst balloons. He swayed, then plunged his upper body into the freezer, nuzzling into the silver containers and weeping, 'Ah-ma! Ah-ma!'

The bluebottle, obviously worried, flew around his ears, striking up what sounded like a low-pitched Tibetan chant. 'Oh God, what am I going to do?' he burbled into the sauce. 'Ah-ma! All your dear ready-cooked meals are ruined – not even a single frozen *ten-thuk* is left unspoilt. O Lord, hear my prayers. What will become of me – you have taken Ah-ma from me in your infinite wisdom, and I have absolutely no one left to love me . . . Now even the last trace of Ah-ma is gone. The last evidence of her cooking is ruined. Dear Ah-ma! Save me.'

For many minutes the bluebottle continued to float around his head in a state of great trepidation. Then it lost interest and went for the meat. I was uncomfortable in the sink, but didn't dare to climb out. I pulled my T-shirt over my nose and mouth and stayed silent. Chod's sobbing slowly subsided and he lay in the puddle, lonely and exhausted, his head resting in the freezer. The stench was almost unbearable. After a while, he turned and gazed at the photo of the amber-eyed woman on the wall, draped in a *khatag*. This he stared at for a long time.

After a while, he dragged himself out of the meat and stumbled upstairs, mopping his beard on his robes. I climbed out of the sink and went into the sitting-room. The sound of a shower came from the first floor. When he reappeared he had recovered his dignified air, and was sporting a clean set of emerald green robes. He lifted me onto his shoulders and strode towards the door. 'Let's get out of here, young Mo,' he guffled. 'Let's go for a drive. I can deal with this mess later. I'll take you to a restaurant for supper. Solly's? Marcus's? Not Kosher Fried Chicken – I've been banned from there.'

He reached the front door and paused, turned to the urinal and hitched up his robes. Then he emptied his bladder indulgently. I clung on to his hair for dear life, foreseeing a decidedly unpleasant situation in the offing. But I had nothing to fear. He gave a final shake, left the house (I ducked as we passed through the door), and strapped me into the front seat of his car. Then he revved the engine until the street was submerged in a foul grey cloud, and we sped off down the road.

Chapter Seventeen

'Uma' means 'middle way', but, as I discovered at her funeral, the name by no means described its bearer. A world in which she actually represented the middle way would be in a sorry state indeed. Of course, I arrived at the funeral from the other direction; I didn't know her. That, I assumed, was to come. During the service I tried to piece her character together from what people said about her. Although the mourners spoke of her kindly I felt sure that the photograph of her face, with its solid amber eyes, clenching jaw and jutting chin, must have represented her more accurately. Even so, her funeral was well attended; people had loved her for her pragmatism, and were infused with a die-hard loyalty.

But now she was dead. The grief was tangible. Tribute speech followed tribute speech. The sudden demise of such an indomitable character had been a shock to all concerned – apart from myself, of course. Nevertheless, I tried to look suitably morose. Her son was particularly affected; he was an only child and had relied on her strongly since his father had died at the hands of the Chinese. So when Uma unexpectedly died, it sent Rabbi Chod into a state of devastation.

Only I knew how Chod would react to his mother's death. I knew that the first thing he would do would be to install a urinal by the front door, marking his territory; then, in a gesture of reverence, he would pledge to leave her frozen meals and bedroom untouched. Then, slowly but surely, he would come to terms with his loss. He would realise that his mother was no longer affected by his gestures of either respect or defiance. He would begin to see that her life was a closed story, viewable in retrospect; his grief would be driven underground. He would clean her room out after all, and the urinal would become less a statement of rebellion than a personal eccentricity. Her frozen meals, however, would remain sacrosanct; he would always claim that he intended to dispose of them, but would never seem to find the time. And only I knew that one day, when she had been dead for two years, her frozen meals would be mistakenly defrosted and would rot, bringing Rabbi Chod's grief flooding back. I knew all this – but no one would have listened to me.

When I arrived home from school on the afternoon of the funeral, my mother flung the door wide almost before I had rung the bell. She worried about me even though there were no roads to cross on the way home from school, and usually loitered around the front door for twenty minutes in anxious anticipation of my arrival. She was wearing pure white clothes which filled the hallway with a radiant glow. I had never seen her wearing plain white before, and at first it confused me. Unlike most exiled Tibetan twentysome-things she had a fondness for traditional clothes, but she usually wore a haphazard combination of colours and mat-erials. As the door opened, the scent of Samsara wafted down from her armpits. She had a sharp-edged, post-shower look, and her cheeks were redder than usual. I was surprised to notice that the silky shoulder of her blouse had a small rip in it and was about to point this out when something in her expression stopped me. She gestured for me to follow her into the house and called up the stairs to my father.

'Tashi? Mo is home from school.' There was no answer. My satchel skidded along the hall to nestle beneath the over-loaded hat-stand; then she led me upstairs, the red coral and turquoise ornaments in her plait bouncing at the level of my eyes.

I was slightly unwell, which I was used to by now. A recur-ring headache had developed, and I was often tired. I had my suspicions about the cause of this discomfort, but tried to ignore it. I had managed to live a relatively normal life until now, given the circumstances, and hoped to continue.

My backwards life was leading towards better times; I refused to let my health deteriorate and spoil it.

My mother opened the door of my parents' bedroom through the force of her glow alone and my father came into view, also in pure white, the mid-afternoon light settling in the creases of his clothes like fireflies. It was even more disconcerting to see him in plain white. He didn't have my mother's attachment to Tibetan clothes and thought Western suits and shirts gave him a sharper, more fashionable image. He was looking in the mirror and combing his hair, which was thick and healthy. His moustache was growing thinner as the hair on his head got thicker – it was as if the different parts of his head had an arrangement worked out. He turned to the side and smoothed his shirt over his flat stomach; then he spoke to me, ignoring my mother.

'Monlam, my son, I am hoping that school was being as good as the day is long, la? Your white clothes are on your bed. Please be putting them on, la.' The whiteness of his clothes made his skin appear swarthier, and as he turned around I noticed that he, too, had a rip in the shoulder of his shirt.

Two hours later, everyone was wearing white and I was glad my father had made me do the same. Branches grasped at the sky above us like the roots of an upside-down forest, and our whiteness blurred into the watery air. I had never experienced an occasion like this before. The service was offici-ated by Jogpo, whose chanting was continually snatched by the late autumn wind that was blowing from all directions at once. He looked unusually solid, as if he was growing in the ground by the gaping hole. Rabbi Chod stood beside him, his white robes fluttering, his eyes fixed on the brassy leaves dancing in small vortexes above the oblong chasm. I noticed that even the bluebottle – or a distant ancestor – had been moved to attend and was squatting solemnly on Rabbi Chod's shoulder. Grandpa Pagpa, who had an especially soft spot for the deceased (and, some said, romantic inclinations), stood sadly beside Jogpo, without the aid of a stick. From time to time the leaves vanished into the earth, and I felt we were being sucked in after them. But the leaves had nothing to lose, that was the difference.

Once Jogpo had concluded his prayers, Chod stepped forward to speak. It was the first time I had ever known him to make a speech without relishing it. In his shaking fingers he held a tea-stained piece of A4 paper that had been folded and re-folded many times. The white-clad congregation clustered closer to the brim of the grave like a bleached iris contracting, straining to hear his hoarse voice as his words tumbled into the wind and fell into the hole. He had written a poem. I overheard my mother say later that he had been up all night composing it. I cannot recall its words; all I can remember is that it was written in strict rhyme, and sounded like the kind of thing you would find inside a greetings card. But the uncharacteristic dullness of his voice and the red blotches round his eyes infused the poem with the gravity that it otherwise lacked. Here and there, handkerchiefs flurried round eyes and noses. Grandpa Pagpa hid his face in his jacket.

I couldn't connect Rabbi Chod's sentimental valedictory verse to Uma's actual demise, for I had overheard my parents mention that she had died on the toilet; she had squeezed her consciousness out by mistake while the shit remained inside her body. She had sat there motionless for several hours before her son discovered her, going stiff with rigor mortis, a clump of rose-scented toilet paper still in her hand. This image didn't sit with the fervent words that tumbled on the air: 'queen of hearts', 'God's angel', 'there for me through the rain and the pain'. The post mortem had been unsatisfactory, establishing the cause of death as 'accidental'. To me, the accident was no more than the accident of existence, which comes with the unpleasant precondition of mortality. Nevertheless, from that time on I was especially careful when excreting.

Rabbi Chod concluded his poem, folded it and weighed

it between his fingers. Then he said a few words, freestyle. He spoke about how his mother, being the reincarnation of the Holy Mother Miriam, embodied the virtue of kindness better than anyone he knew. He gave the example of how she always prepared lamb stew and *ten-thuk* and froze it 'for days in which the rain falls'. He mentioned that her 'passing on' had been peaceful and, so far as he could tell, she hadn't been in any pain. As he stood over the hole, each gust of wind eroded his energy. His face had a grey, drawn look. His robes hung loosely around his midriff, shimmering in the late afternoon light. There was a communal concern that he would never recover. I knew that he would regain his exuberance in time, and said something to that effect. But nobody listened to me.

As the funeral went on the people got sadder, and the sadder they got the more ironic it seemed. They were treating death as if it were an anomaly, like a natural disaster that had managed to bamboozle them by a terrible fluke. However, I knew, in a way that no one else could, that these people were all being slowly reeled in. I had no memory more vivid than those of my parent's deaths. Uma's death was a shock to people who thought they were safe within an enclave of the living into which death occasionally infiltrated, like a fox into a chicken coop. Yet the reality was quite different; their everyday life took place in the palm of death's hand, and the fingers were gradually closing.

Rabbi Chod released the dog-eared square of paper into the air. It zigzagged on the wind and disappeared into the chasm. Then he dropped the first hunk of mud into the gloom. For a moment it inexplicably gleamed turquoise, then it was gone. It struck the lid of the coffin with a loud, resonant bang, making everyone jump. Slowly, the congregation filed past, dropping earth and tributes into the grave. I hung back behind my mother and when our turn came around I caught a glimpse of the crumpled poem lying on the black shiny coffin, surrounded by a corona of mud and leaves. I held my mother's skirt and turned my face away from the clutching hole.

We got a taxi home in silence. My parents had a brief conversation about death, then cut it short for my sake: my father said he wondered when he would die, and what it would be like to be dead, and my mother said she was never going to die, and that when we got home she would make me some hot milk. A sharp ache was dancing in my veins and I drifted into oblivion, the streetlights streaking into my dreams.

'Are you really never going to die?' I asked my mother that night, before bed.

'No,' she replied, 'not someone young and healthy like me. I'm going to live to a ripe old age, and sit around all day playing cards and wearing outrageous clothes. I will wear purple. And eat lots of sweets with my false teeth. I'm sure that by the time I'm an old woman Tibet will be free and we will be back in our homeland. You mark my words, little Mo. When I die, I will be buried in Tibetan soil. Maybe I will even have a sky-burial, you never know. This is my dream.' She kissed me on the top of the head, turned out the light and closed the door behind her, softly.

The next day was the day before. When I opened my eyes to the light and remembered where I was, I felt relieved that Uma's funeral was over and done with, having not yet occurred. I went down to breakfast to find the solitary figure of my father sitting at the kitchen table, contemplating his mug of coffee in front of him.

The familiarity of the breakfast routine was comforting, and I was especially pleased to find a yellow plastic space creature nestling in my Frosties. The Creature and Plastic Bag became instant friends, and I discovered a way of making them ride on each other's backs. My father suggested that, instead of going to school, I accompany him to the café to help with the morning rush. His eyes were lonely and desperate. I agreed; anything was better than school. Before we left the house he typed a note and left it on the table for my mother, who was still asleep. It read:

141

'G●●●d_m●rn*IngHp●e_y●u_slept_wellk.
_ I _ p r O ● m i s ” e
again,_I_n&ever_di*d_sexy_wit%h_
an●t%her!!1!._NO^_TRU&E!!
Justa_rum●ur!!!DONT^LISTENING!!_
N O T % T R U E ! ! 1 _ P l e a s s e
beli&eve_me._(Osell,_d●n@T_f●rjgtet_
u m a s _ f u n e r a l k
t●m●rr●we,_rabi_chO()D_saywe_need_
w h i t e _ & C L ●^ t h e s . _ ! ! _ I
INN●c&ENT!Seee_y●u_t)ONig%htL●vetashii'

As we left the house he closed the door firmly, trying to shut something ugly away.

I searched the bright pavement unsuccessfully for conkers while my father gazed in the shop windows. He was especially interested in the Lax™ Stress Controller in the window of Argos. The sweeping wind invigorated me, but it kept catching my scarf and flinging it wide. My father avoided this predicament by tucking the ends of his scarf into his braces. I felt superior when I noticed an ungainly gaggle of children in school uniform on the other side of the road, and let go of my father's hand. We walked side by side. The sun glinted off the paving stones. My father pulled his trousers up every few steps while I kept an eye out for conkers and double-winged sycamore seeds.

When we arrived, I was surprised to see a large spiral of dogshit in a pool of light outside the front door. My father accepted this with equanimity, stepping over it as we entered the café. He raised the blinds and turned on the lights; I went into the kitchen for the WD40. While I was lubricating the cash drawer he modified his daily routine to accommodate the large turd, drenching it in torrents of Dettol while angry flies spiralled away. My father, who had failed to appreciate the danger it presented, came back in and gave the counter a final wipe.

I was never paid when I worked in the café, and I never

expected to be. I enjoyed serving the customers their coffee and watching them drink in their individual ways. I wound the white apron straps three times around my waist as usual, and began to take bets with myself on who the first customers would be. I decided it would be Grandpa Pagpa, reincarnation of Holy Isaac, and his friend Ishmael, who came to play chess in Hush Hush three times a week. The chess was, of course, secondary; the main aim was to give Grandpa Pagpa a feeling of being connected to his son in between his occasional visits to our house. An image of them came into my mind: Grandpa Pagpa with his leathery skin and the huge mahogany chessboard under his arm, and spindly Ishmael towering over him, clutching the small ivory box of chess pieces and peering at the world through glasses which shrank his eyes to the size of lentils. They both wore large woolly hats when they played chess, Ishmael's pulled down over his forehead and Grandpa Pagpa's perched on his crown; at moments of particular excitement they hunched so closely over the chessboard that their hats rubbed against each other. By the end of the day they would fall asleep in this position, their heads propped up against each other and a shimmering thread of drool slipping from the lip of each man.

But I was wrong. The first customer of the day was Madeline. It was strange for her to arrive this early; she didn't usually appear until the afternoon. She always looked tired but today she looked exhausted, her face blotched orange and her mascara creating an impasto around her eyes. The paleness of her face and the darkness of her eyes gave her the appearance of a depressed panda, and her thin lips made a bright red slash across her face. She tottered in on her pink stilettos, wearing a scarlet top and black PVC miniskirt – a sort of tragic Petrushka doll. Even though she looked a few years younger than she had done on the front of her funeral programme, she was one of those people who the more you look at them, the worse they seem to look: before my very eyes she became thinner, pastier and older, and her hair more straw-like and brittle.

My father's head snapped up, the cloth falling noiselessly from his hands onto the carpet. I picked it up. Madeline made her painstaking way through the café and mounted the platform at the back. She lowered her frame onto a stool by the pool table and slumped into a smooth, worn patch on the wall. As was her habit, she rested the fingertips of her right hand on the edge of the table, let her left arm hang limply and rested her head to one side. During the course of the day she would alternate the hand that touched the pool table, and the side to which her head was inclined. Nothing else would change until she left at the end of the day. I turned and saw that my father had already disappeared through the curtain. Presently he emerged, gingerly holding an ancient coffee cup covered in clumps of dust and grime, full of ancient coffee that had gone solid. He ascended the three shallow stairs and placed it beside her fingertips. There was a flicker of recognition in her face. The cup looked at home, the grey hue of the dust matching that of the table. I saw Madeline's eyes spring up to meet my father's; then he turned, came back to the counter and slipped through the curtain again.

The silence continued. Madeline was one of those people who can sit utterly still for incredibly long periods, and I respected her for it. She became part of the furniture wherever she went, taking the world in through glazed pupils which were incapable of passing judgement on anything. I forgot she was there and reached into my pocket to retrieve Plastic Bag.

The door opened again. I could tell from the sound that this wasn't a regular customer, as it was pushed open all the way, allowing the maximum amount of traffic noise into the café, and no care was taken to deaden the noise of the hinge. Immediately the atmosphere changed; whereas Madeline had entered like an air current, without a sound or a gesture, the air became agitated when this character entered. In fact, I think the air had become agitated even before the door opened. A rhinoceros man with a heavily tattooed face came striding towards me, his gait stiffened by leather trousers. The sight of him gave me a profound sensation of déjà vu. I clutched Plastic Bag, afraid of what the man might do. My father had not yet emerged from the kitchen. Rhinoceros Man reached the counter and angled his blue mirror shades towards me so that an upside-down image of myself slid into view. The tattoos on his face seemed to ripple; then he pointed a thick finger at the faded photograph of the coffee, bared his teeth and slunk off to sit by the window. I marked his order down in the notebook and was about to go into the kitchen to pass it on when my father emerged through the curtain. Madeline's coffee was steaming in his hands, and he had a white tea towel over his forearm.

Madeline was never charged for her coffee. She and my father had built up an inextricable bond that could never have been verbalised. Every day she came into the café and sat in the same place, a sentinel over the decrepit pool table, gazing into the middle distance; every day my father obliged her by feeding her incessant cups of coffee. Every day she stayed behind after closing while my father wiped the surfaces and put the chairs on the tables; every day he completed his chores by taking the ancient, dusty coffee cup back into the kitchen, and she left the café. This was their routine, the silent dance that they rehearsed day after day, in perfect unspoken harmony.

I handed over Rhinoceros Man's order and my father glanced at him suspiciously. The Hush Hush clientele were an eccentric bunch, but this man was not a Hush Hush type of eccentric. I could almost feel my father willing him to make a noise so that he could be ejected. But so far he had sat in perfect silence. My father disappeared into the kitchen to prepare the coffee.

I was about to bring Plastic Bag into the open air when I noticed a nasty odour contaminating the dusky aroma of coffee. I looked over at Rhinoceros Man and saw, to my horror, a thin brown trail looping from the doorway to the counter and over to his seat. I put my fingers in my mouth

145

to stifle a giggle as my father walked noiselessly past me, holding Rhinoceros Man's coffee. He was concentrating so hard on the coffee that he didn't notice the brown trail until he trod in it. He stopped still in the middle of the café like the Tin Man on the yellow brick road and his head darted confusedly around. It took him a minute or two to make the connection between the odour, the brown trail, the dogshit and Rhinoceros Man; then, his face turning a slow red, he returned to the counter, placed the full cup carefully on its surface and reached for his Polaroid.

When the ensuing flurry of activity had died down, I was on my hands and knees beside my father, scrubbing the carpet, flecks of beige froth flicking unpleasantly into the air. I may have imagined it, but I think admiration had seeped into Madeline's blank features as she watched my father courageously tackling the tattooed villain and pinning his picture on one of the noticeboards behind the counter. My father's outrage at the state of his carpet had empowered him. As he scrubbed, his face assumed the boiling lobster colour for the second time that day.

The hours wore on and gradually the damp trail on the carpet disappeared. My father drew a large circle round the shit with red chalk. The shit itself now had a large cliff in its centre and a caked flat section stamped into it where Rhinoceros Man's boot of ill fortune had fallen. Nobody else stepped in it that day. Business was quiet; for hours no customers came in until Grandpa Pagpa and Ishmael arrived for their after-lunch game of chess. My father allowed me to serve their coffee, but I doubt they recognised the difference between us anyway. For what felt like hours I leant on the counter, fascinated by their game. It was like a somnambulant tai-chi session, yet fiercely competitive. They used no clock. Although they were fundamentally different in appearance, they were united by a common grimace of determination and concentration which spread seamlessly across their faces. Ishmael's glasses kept slipping down his nose, and Grandpa Pagpa rubbed his dry lips repeatedly with a stumpy forefinger. After several false starts, one of them would make a move. They slid their pieces aggressively across the board, inevitably knocking over other pieces. The process of retrieving them from the carpet severely hampered the flow of the game. They had never managed to arrive at a conclusion; in fact, I doubt they even knew what a checkmate was. Neither of them would ever back down. It was this inability to finish anything that perpetuated the cycle of their daily games.

Slowly the sun went down and the whiteness of the café turned lemon. Then the edges of all the objects glowed pink and we were reliant upon electric lighting alone. Night and yesterday were approaching; today was on the cusp of evaporating into the past-future. Once the sun had set and dawn had broken, I would never be able to refer to it again, since it wouldn't yet have happened for anyone else. This wasn't so bad; apart from the incident with the dogshit it had been a thoroughly uneventful day, one worth forgetting. At least, that's what I told myself. But even though nothing much had happened, I hadn't played with Plastic Bag. In fact, I hadn't done anything at all. It was easy to remain motionless for hours on end in the soporific atmosphere of Hush Hush, letting time swallow itself. The dying moments of the day felt static; the café seemed to exist in a single moment lifted out of the continuum of time that was flitting by the windows. My father started to put the plastic chairs on the tables and he nudged Grandpa Pagpa and Ishmael awake. They were so used to sleeping in the café that they awoke without a sound, glancing around and massaging their loosely fleshed faces. Ishmael gave his milk-bottle glasses a swift wipe on his woolly hat while Grandpa Pagpa had a thorough scratch of his head; then they both collected their respective chess game components and disappeared into the night.

I sprayed the windows and wiped them with a J-cloth while my father swept the carpet (hoovering was never allowed); the fumes from the acidic cleaning fluid irritated my lungs

147

and I wheezed slightly. On the edge of my field of vision I noticed my father stepping onto the platform at the back of the café and sweeping round the blotched legs of the inscrutable Madeline, who was on her fourth cycle of head and arm alternations. He paid particular attention to the area around her stilettos, and then he stopped sweeping and leant on the broom, gazing into her face. A ripple of recognition flitted across her brow and her eyes stuttered up to meet his. For several long seconds they peered at each other, as if for the first time. Then my father resumed his sweeping and the dead sheen returned to Madeline's pupils. Something about their interaction made me feel deeply nauseous. The subtle look of admiration I had noticed on Madeline's face earlier was eroding her introverted detachedness. I closed my eyes and continued to wipe the windows.

A fine rain began to spray on the outside of the glass as I sprayed on the inside. Car headlights dragged bright smudges along the road. I finished cleaning and my father beckoned for me to follow him into the kitchen. Behind the sliding door, he spoke to me in hushed tones, perching on the corner of the battered red table, the pipes stretching out behind him on the wall. There was something in his face that I had never seen before – a mixture of anxiety and suppressed excitement.

'Mo, my son, I am thinking it will be being best if you are making your own way home tonight, la-la-la,' he said.

'Why? Are you not coming back?'

'I am, I am, of course I am, but I have some paperwork to be sorting out here first, la. Not punny, you know? No relaxation for the crooked, la,' he replied. I was reluctant to cross the roads by myself, especially at night. But I agreed. A childish effort to expand the limitations of my freedom, I suppose. And I was tired. My blood had become a thick, dark paste. I wanted to get home. I was looking forward to seeing my mother. I was even looking forward to sleep, though I knew it would inevitably catalyse the reversal. I had become resigned to the loss of the day; by now I was used to the evaporation that followed in my wake. My father handed me a stumpy blue umbrella and without a word I followed him through the sliding door and white curtain. He tried to give me a reassuring smile. I stepped out into the darkness and glanced over my shoulder to see him walking towards the pool table, beckoning to the motionless figure in the scarlet top, stilettos and rubber skirt.

I hunched under the shelter of the umbrella and made my way along the deserted street. I felt protected in my little slot of dry air but also anxious at being alone in the darkness. My headache was deepening and I was sick with tiredness but I had a feeling of animal alertness in the hostile city. My intestines felt as if they were slowly coming alive. The image of my father and Madeline locked in unspoken empathy kept drifting into my mind. I was getting short of breath, and when I came to the corner of my road something made me stop. A string of terrible memories crept into my mind and united. My mother's death, and her diary entries. Grandpa Pagpa crashing on his typewriter, accusing my mother while my father collapsed. Madeline, thin, fatigued, in stilettos and a rubber skirt – and her funeral programme. My father, lonely, with a *Lung* disorder, filled with desire. Dazel making advances to my mother, and my mother rejecting him. The rumours about my father. My headache, gripping me in its talons, and the fatigue. It all made horrible sense. At that very moment, the disease was poised to attack our lives.

I dropped the umbrella into a hedge, turned on my heel and hurried back along the road to the café. The rain slapped against my legs and the orange mist from the streetlights clung to my body like poison gas. Eventually, the light of Hush Hush came into view and I skidded through the shit and flung myself against the door. It was locked. I stumbled down the side of the building and squeezed through a gap in the railings. Falling against the wall, I peered through the kitchen window, cupping my hands round my eyes to protect them from the rain.

The scene within curved round my mind like a wrap-around cinema screen. Madeline was sitting on the red wooden table, her thin legs dangling, her skirt rucked up round her waist, her shaggy head resting on her shoulder. Her gluey lips parted and her eyelids fluttered. Her top had been pulled across her body in the frenzy of the previous moments, and one of her breasts was flopping out. My father was clamped between her legs, his pasty, shivering buttocks reflecting a sickening glare into my eyes. His face was nestling in her neck. My blood seemed to be scabbing in my veins and the rain pierced my skin like a thousand syringes. Helplessly, I watched as the disease that I had inherited seeped into my father's body. I could have made a difference, but I was too late. I had arrived too late. I had missed the chance to rid our lives of the disease. In the kitchen of Hush Hush – at that one tiny moment – our fates had been sealed.

Chapter Eighteen

When my parents got married, according to the Tibetan tradition, they were young. Even though they were already living together, they wanted to legitimise their relationship. They both seemed mature for their age; partly through death (my mother was an orphan and my father's mother, of course, had died in childbirth), and partly because they were adults, making a commitment, getting married. I myself was struggling with puberty and adolescence; my first patches of pubic hair caused me immense embarrassment.

The wedding took place on a snowy Tuesday, and I had been given the day off school. It was 1994; Nelson Mandela had been released some years before, and the first multiracial elections had been held in South Africa. My mother had been particularly moved by the images of unity broadcast on the television – the black and white hands clasped aloft, the smiling faces, the rainbow flags. She said she liked the idea of Truth and Reconciliation. Then she began to talk about her hero, Gandhi, and said non-violence was the only way to peace. My father wasn't so sure. He said we Tibetans had to be strong, like the Israelis. Only then could we really deal with the Chinese. Nothing would be achieved without bloodshed – Rabbi Chod said so. Truth and Reconciliation? Non-violence? Pah. We need to stand firm and treat the Chinese like dogs, just like the Israelis should treat the Palestinians. Only then will there be real peace. Peace can come only with victory, and victory can come only through war. My mother said he sounded like Grandpa Pagpa. My father didn't reply. Together, we watched Mandela's speech on the television, surrounded by ambiguity, the light flickering against our faces.

The community of Chod's followers, while smaller than it would later become, had a kernel of dedicated members and felt strong and unified. At that time everyone was immersed in their routine. Everyone was trying to forget something. We were deep in the freezing heart of winter, and my body felt filled with snow.

The wedding gathering took place in the Pet Shop Synagogue, which was cold but had been decorated gaily. Jogpo had painted several *thanka*s for the occasion, and they hung in prominent places around the room. One depicted my mother and father standing under a *chupa*, a Jewish wedding canopy, holding hands, while Rabbi Chod and other Holy Forefathers gazed benignly down from their lotus seats in the sky. A second featured a wrathful image of Yahweh in vivid primary colours, with bared fangs and bulging eyes. White *khatag*s, offered by members of the community, hung from every available protrusion. My parents had been receiving gifts all day, and these were piled in the corner of the room to form a mound of toasters, cutlery sets and packages.

The synagogue was about half full of Rabbi Chod's disciples. They stamped the snow off their shoes and blew into their hands as they entered. Some of them were resplendent in traditional Tibetan attire, all reds, greens and golds, while others wore Western suits and dresses. As a wedding tradition invented by Rabbi Chod, the men wore sky-blue skullcaps and the women had turquoise ornaments sparkling in their hair. Chod had clamped my skullcap to my head with a hairclip which pulled my fringe, and my oversized navy suit and pinching shoes were cripplingly uncomfortable.

The service began beneath the *chupa*, which was covered in *khatag*s and heavy folds of multicoloured silk with bright tassels and fringes. Under this stood the shining figure of Rabbi Chod, enrobed in his best satin cloak and wearing a ceremonial hat, which was brought out only on exceptionally auspicious occasions. Jogpo hovered around the outside of the *chupa*, looking busy and alert. His mousy hair gleamed golden in the butter-lamp light. My parents stood on either side of Rabbi Chod, pale and dizzy; as is the Jewish custom, they had been fasting in honour of the great day. Their necks were draped in scores of *khatags*, and from time to time well-wishers would scurry forward from the crowd to add yet another. My father was wearing a pristine white suit which gleamed with occasion, complemented by a pale yellow tie which looked as if it had been stripped off the top of a Battenberg cake. His blue skullcap was immense and radiated round his head like a patch of sky. My mother was in traditional Tibetan costume, her customary plait nowhere to be seen. Instead her hair was drawn up into two great wobbling wings, wound strand by strand with white hyacinths (orange blossom was out of season) and studded with large chunks of turquoise. She kept catching eyes with me and smiling reassuringly through her make-up. Beside her, in a cloud of smoke that was thinner and less intrusive than usual, was Dazel, the best man. My father had given him the role to force him to witness his own defeat, and was eyeing the smoker smugly. Jogpo whispered in Dazel's ear and he apologetically went to stand beside my father, mumbling something about how Chod's religion was far too complicated.

Rabbi Chod was chanting prayers with special gusto, drowning the tweets and grunts coming from the next room, where the animals had been stored. Every time he took another breath, his lungs were so inflated that his elbows rose in the air and shoved against my parents beside him. They looked increasingly nervous. Now my father was trying to give me reassuring glances, too. My mother circumambulated my father seven times, according to Jewish custom; Dazel reluctantly handed my father the ring; my father slid it onto my mother's finger; my parents' hands were bound together with red string; Jogpo gave a great blast on his conch shell; my father stepped on a glass to commemorate the destruction of the ancient Jewish temple; someone jokingly remarked that it was the last time he would ever put his foot down; and the service was concluded to cries of '*Mazal tov*' and '*Bâgma dâng mâgba nyila* ('To the bride and groom').' Somebody struck up a tune on a cheap keyboard. People started dancing and I lost sight of my parents as I got jostled into the centre of a frantic, spinning circle of men and boys.

The small community of disciples relished the opportunity to lose themselves in the celebration, and danced for at least an hour. Eventually, people spilt out into the snow-speckled air and I was bundled into a car which formed part of a procession down Golders Green Road. I didn't recognise anyone around me. After a short drive, the car stopped and I was bustled into a large hall with 'Tree of Life Banqueting Suite' inscribed above the door in Hebrew. I overheard someone remark that Rabbi Chod had pulled off a miracle in managing to hire it, as the mainstream Jewish community generally would have nothing to do with Chod or his followers.

I was sat in front of a set of plastic cutlery on a trestle table. Somehow, the man with the keyboard had got there before us and was playing an oompah tune while the guests filed in to sit behind white paper tablecloths. Rabbi Chod lowered his bulk into the chair next to mine, throwing an offhand '*Mazal tov*' in my direction and ruffling my hair violently. A strong smell of detergent and rabbit shit accompanied him. When everyone was seated, there was a great cheer as my parents entered the room. My father's tie was askew and my mother's great hair-wings had developed a fine corona of hairs that had come loose. They looked nervy and overwhelmed as they took their seats at the high table, with Dazel and Jogpo on one side, Rabbi Chod and myself on the other, and Uma and Grandpa Pagpa, who were deep in conversation, near at hand.

The microphone squealed with feedback, then fizzed and echoed with reverb. 'Rabbis, family, ladies and gentlemen, *bâgma dâng mâgba nyila*,' declared Chod. The salute was echoed by the audience as the Rabbi lifted his goblet to the ceiling. 'We are gathered here today, as you full well know, to celebrate the joyful marriage of our dear friends, my second cousin Tashi and his new bride, Osel.' More cries of felicitation. 'The Holy Lord, blessed be His Holy Name, gave us a holy commandment to enjoy ourselves on such holy days. We must not renounce worldly pleasure, as do the Buddhists, but instead we must enjoy it, in the name of the one true Lord. Indeed, Buddhist monks do not even officiate at weddings. Not so my good self. Not at all. That is, we must enjoy wine, women and song. Or at least wine and song. It is up to Tashi to enjoy the woman, is it not, my dear friend? Girl just wanna have fun?' There was a great wave of uproarious laughter and everyone started talking at once. My father studied the ceiling and Dazel flushed. 'I think we can say that Tashi is indeed lucky to have put in his net such a fine figure of a woman to be his lifelong love, I am sure you all agree. A fine figure,' continued Chod, receiving another burst of laughter and cheers. My mother hid her face in her hands. 'Good luck to them, I say. *Mazal tov!*' bellowed Chod, and the crowd, once again, responded in kind. 'Now, without further ado, before commencing this wonderful wedding banquet, I would like to call on a man, the best man, indeed, the very best of all men, that is, the gentile Dazel, to say a few humble words.'

Dazel had been sitting at the table, agitatedly breaking the prongs off his plastic fork. I had been impressed at his self-control. Nevertheless, the extent of his attachment to my mother was evident from the way he always stood as close to her as possible. Whenever she moved away from him, flames flashed in his pupils. When Rabbi Chod beckoned him to the microphone, Dazel's face went startlingly pale and he dropped his stump of a fork back on the table. Tilting his chair, he signalled frantically to the Rabbi by waving a napkin in the air. Rabbi Chod leant over and his voice echoed faintly over the loudspeakers. 'What? Dazel, you . . . But I was assured that . . . Indeed! Really? Well, all right, then, may the Lord protect you.' Rabbi Chod drew himself up and addressed the audience again. 'Ladies and gentlemen, I am afraid that the best of all men has sadly forgotten to prepare a speech. Forgotten. These things happen within the life. So without further ado: on with the meal.' There was a short, awkward silence and Dazel's face turned all colours at once; then the keyboard struck up another oompah and everyone's attention shifted to the procession of Eastern European waitresses bringing in steaming pots of soup.

Rabbi Chod knocked back a drink – where had he got it from? – and prepared to receive his food. I glanced at Dazel, who smiled weakly back. My parents shot reassuring smiles at anyone who happened to catch their eye. Everyone ate, everyone drank, everyone danced. My parents never lost their edginess. Dazel's depression deepened and he stopped following my mother around. Rabbi Chod taught everyone a new dance. I felt sick. The celebrations went on deep into the night.

Chapter Nineteen

When I awoke the next morning, it was very cold. My parents were excitedly preparing for the big day. My mother flung open the curtains onto the dazzling urban snowscape, and said the snow reminded her of Tibet. My father said that snow is more beautiful than cherry blossom, but still less beautiful than her. They kissed. I tried to prevent the image of his bare buttocks gulping in the disease from breaking into my mind, and did my best to share their enthusiasm. For months I had been plagued by that image, eaten up by regret, sleeping fitfully, plagued by nightmares. For once in my life redemption had been within reach, but I'd missed it. If only I had run faster, or realised sooner what was happening, I could have thrown myself between Madeline and my father, I could have stopped them. But I hadn't. I'd failed.

When it was time for breakfast I left my room and heard my parents having sex. I plugged my ears with scraps of newspaper, went downstairs and ate my toast alone, gazing out of the condensation-dappled window at the snow. Later my parents went into the sitting room and hunched over the seating plan, discussing who should be next to whom. Glaring winter light struck them through the window, highlighting the shrine behind them with its picture of Rabbi Chod and its fresh offerings of alcohol and curd. I said goodbye and left the house to go to school.

My feet left luminous impressions in the soft white pavement and my breath became visible in the air. I remember thinking that, although snow seems pure, in fact it has been created by water soiled by centuries, even millennia, of digestion and excretion. Snow is a whore masquerading as

157

a virgin. The street was muffled, lucid and silent, like an extension of my father's café. It was bright and effervescent, as if I was walking in the sky. What would it have been like if I'd never been born? What was it like before birth? I couldn't remember. I imagined my existence before this life – a state of blissful light, bright and untainted, without form, without conception, without time, without any of these contaminations, these bases of suffering. At intervals the snowy world blurred into my imagination, and the state of peaceful expansiveness in my mind enhanced the glow of the street. Soon I was lost in a never-ending ocean of light. I could no longer tell what was mind and what was not. The sound of my feet in the snow and the regular jolting in my legs made the luminosity seem even bigger. I don't know how much time passed.

I turned a corner and the traffic noise increased. A barely visible trail of smoke hung above my head, and its impurity made the glowing vastness seep away from the street. I realised that I was running late. I speeded up, my satchel thudding against the stiff material of my new school blazer. The increase in speed made my tie flap out and bounce around in front of me. I had not yet discovered how to make it hang in a respectable manner; either it reached only halfway down my chest like a sort of mangled cravat, or it poked out the bottom of my blazer and dangled between my legs. My mother had offered to sew it together at an optimum length and thread it on a piece of elastic, but it wasn't worth the risk with the older boys. That morning I had spent almost an hour standing on the frayed patch of carpet in front of the mirror, tying and retying my tie. It had proven impossible to get any compromise between the two extremes, and in the end I had gone for the longer option. Also, I had unpicked the manufacturer's label so that I was in no danger of being 'de-tagged' by the fifth-formers.

The trail of smoke above the cold, creamy pavement thickened as I followed it. Eventually it became a hazy pillar of cloud, shimmering in the morning glare. In its centre was the indistinct figure of Dazel, sidling distractedly along the street. His neck had disappeared in a thick blue roll of scarf and he was sporting a Sherlock Holmes deerstalker. In one blue hand he clutched a white plastic bag. It had become stretched and transparent and I could see its contents: a pint of milk, a carton of apple juice and a loaf of bread, surrounded by about twenty packets of rolling tobacco. His other hand continuously deposited lugs of smoke into his mouth from a shrivelled, hand-rolled cigarette. He was going the same way as me but I didn't feel like talking. I reduced my speed so that I wouldn't have to pass him, calculating minutes in my head.

Gradually I became aware of something in Dazel's gait that I had never seen before. He usually walked with a chain of measured steps, as if he was wearing invisible shackles. Now, however, instead of plotting a straight course along the pavement he was veering from side to side. Several times I was afraid he would topple into the road. On occasion, the hand holding the cigarette ran itself across the dome of his deerstalker, releasing another thick cloud of dust-like smoke into the air. He seemed oblivious of everything around him. I ventured closer, ducking round the thickest areas of smoke. Even so, my lungs began to grate and I pulled my scarf over my nose. My breath grew yellow in the air.

We passed Hush Hush, and I peered in. The windows had triangles of snow in the corners, as if they had been sprayed for Christmas. Three thick icicles hung from the doorframe, and the sign was faded with frost. Someone had built a snowman outside, complete with a carrot positioned between its legs. Inside, the only customer was Madeline, slumped against the back wall by the old pool table as usual. I saw the gangly, youthful frame of my father bending over her, tightening his braces and setting a grimy coffee cup on the table. The window ran out and the image was gone; we continued our journey, two figures in a cloud in the whiteness.

Dazel began to speak to the air in high-pitched, agitated tones. I could make out only snatches of his monologue, but what I heard worried me. Cautiously I tried to walk closer to him, tucking my tie into my blazer. The snow deadened my footsteps and he didn't hear my approach. Initially his discourse seemed to be on a loop, repeating the name 'Osel' amid scores of curses. Then he began to bark oaths into his scarf. He swore that she'd re*gret* it. He promised that if she went *through* with getting *wed*, he'd never see her again. Then he went on a rambling muse, muttering that she'd come to him in the end, her *knees raw* from *crawl*ing. Finally he began repeating over and over that he'd be united with her in the *end*, if not *here*, then in *heav*en, if not in *heav*en, then in *hell*. I felt sick to my stomach and we walked on.

We crossed the road. Dazel didn't look up once, but by a stroke of luck he coincided with a gap in the traffic. Exhaust fumes mingled with his smoky aura and then we were on the pavement again. As we walked, passers-by began to emerge out of the foggy whiteness and dissolve again behind us. I gazed straight into the hollow, distracted eyes of the hordes as they rushed towards and past me, in desperate search of the X that marks the spot, in search of vanishing, somewhere in the distance. I was the only one who wasn't blinded by the glitter-dust falling like snow all around.

Once again I was brought back to physicality by thick smoke, but this time from a different source; a plume of blackness was billowing into the sky in the distance, made ominous by Dazel's incessant rambling about hell. Soon we came to the source. A building site lay next to the road, surrounded by a high fence. A section of the fence was missing, and a large bonfire was visible through the gap. Compelled by the fire, Dazel stopped, and I came to a halt behind him. Orange and red sheets were gobbling the snow from the air. Dazel stood for a long time, his head cocked, mesmerised by the flames. His voice had dropped to a mutter, and was largely unintelligible. The only words I could make out were 'heaven' and 'hell'.

When he removed his deerstalker and pressed his chin into his scarf, I realised that something was seriously wrong.

His complexion had become an odd pale blue and his breath sounded like a blunt saw, both inhaling and exhaling the same grief while the cause remained immovable. Flames flickered in his eyes as if they were covered in a layer of mirror glass. They were surrounded by scarlet blotches, the like of which I had only ever seen on Rabbi Chod when he was in mourning. Passers-by flitted like ghosts through his field of vision, and part of my mind became aware of an unidentified clicking approaching from behind.

I am not sure if the events that followed actually took place in slow motion or have merely been stored that way in my head. Maybe they were slowed down every time I recalled another detail. Either way, the entire memory is speckled with infinite flecks of falling snow. Dazel unwinds his scarf and throws it into the fire, where it vanishes in the flames. Then he sweeps his arms above his head and declares something that sounds like he wants to meet my mother in hell's bed and breakfast. I see my own arms, speckled with snow, floating towards him as if on an air current, reaching towards his coat, my tie leaping out again from my blazer. But I grasp empty space as he throws himself towards the pillar of fire, his face glowing orange in the heat, his eyes closed.

At this point I clearly remember concluding that he was doomed, and being amazed that I had been able to form a coherent thought in such a tiny splinter of a second. Then I remember being amazed that I had time to be amazed at being able to form a thought in such a tiny splinter of a second. Also, I needed the toilet. As I was in the process of contemplating this, Dazel was gliding towards the bonfire, snow swirling around him on the disturbed air. Meanwhile, the strange clicking was getting louder and louder, invading more and more of my mind. Suddenly a bicycle shot into view. It collided full-on with Dazel's midriff, tangling him up and propelling him clumsily away from the heat. Two things spurted out; a loud squawk of distress from the rider of the bike, and a collection of books and cosmetics from

161

the bag in the handlebar basket. I felt like a spectator as the tangle of limbs and metal came towards me in dreamy slow motion; I experienced nothing but numb surprise as the world suddenly spun and chunks of ice and frozen snow sprayed into the air.

There was a brief period of stillness. We lay in disarray on the pavement while the back wheel of the bike rotated with a sullen clicking. The fire thrashed noisily on. Damp began to seep through the parts of my blazer and trousers that were buried in the snow, and my lungs began to crackle and whistle as smoke slid into them. Anonymous Londoners continued to ghost past; nobody stopped. Eventually, as one body, the mass of limbs and metal began to untangle itself. Several minutes later it separated into three individuals and a bike. Three clouds of breath gently rose into the air. No one was seriously hurt. Dazel had a thread of blood on his hand and I had a swelling on my left cheek, but the cyclist emerged unharmed. Our attention simultaneously turned to sartorial matters; Dazel put his deerstalker back on and brushed down his coat while I straightened my creased tie and dealt with my errant shirt flaps, which had spread themselves ignominiously over my thighs. As I was buttoning my blazer, I looked up at the third figure. A diminutive girl in her early twenties with a heart-shaped face and industrious-looking hands, she seemed unaware of the vital role she had played in saving Dazel from the fires of hell. For a moment I started to thank her in Tibetan; then I realised that she was one of those Westerners whose features have merely combined in an Asian-looking way by some odd coincidence. She gathered her belongings into her corduroy bag and dragged her bicycle upright, obviously shaken. It seemed undamaged; it must have been cushioned by the snow. As she rode away, however, it displayed a worrying wobble and produced a grinding squeak, which gradually faded until she was out of earshot.

Dazel and I were left alone again, bound together by a clutching brown vapour in the whiteness. He was scuffing his feet guiltily in the snow and I noticed that the glassy shield over his eyes had dissolved.

'I say, it's young Mo,' he began. Expression was returning to his face – it was as if he had purged something. 'What a to-do, what a to-do. Ahem! Hack, hack. What a business. Tomorrow never comes, what? Oh dear oh dear oh me. Vixen weather. Hack. You're on your way to school, are you?'

'Yes. Are you . . . ?'

'I'm fine, fine, just fine, thank you very much. Thank you very much indeed. Aharahem! Oh dear oh dear oh me, hack, hack, hack. Well, oh, goodness, is that the time? Lovely to see you, and give my love to . . . er . . . Must be off. Tomorrow . . . Hell, vixen weather. Ahem! Yes, yes, don't worry. Got to be off.' He hurried away into the brightness, turned a corner and was gone.

I blinked and looked around, stunned by the speed and slowness at which everything had taken place. Had it really happened? A large brown puddle caught my eye and I saw that in his embarrassment Dazel had forgotten his bag of groceries; it lay crumpled against the fence, leaking apple juice. I salvaged its remains and walked in the direction that Dazel had gone, glad to leave the fire behind. I felt too unsettled to go to school on time; the drama of the last few minutes had pushed the threat of Mr Barratt's wrath to the back of my mind.

Although Dazel had disappeared, his trail of smoke was still visible, stretching off down the road. As I followed it, I checked my body again to see if adrenalin had masked an injury. Surprisingly, there was no pain anywhere. The luminosity in my mind had been banished by the image of Dazel falling in slow motion towards the flames, which was replaying from all angles in my head. I became completely immersed in the recent past. The words 'Osel' and 'go through with it' and 'hell' hummed around me, dragging comet-like trails after them.

The yellowish smoke trail thickened as I went on. It curled round several corners and into a side street, the signpost of which was obscured by a deep white pad. Eventually the smoke settled at the door of a small, squat, 1950s building which looked like a block of concrete with windows punched in. Dazel's nappy van was parked outside, rounded by the snow. A legend had appeared on the bonnet; it read, 'The end of collection is dispersion.' I wondered if the words had been inscribed by someone or if they had appeared naturally, as the snow fell.

The ground-floor flat made a chilling scene. The inside of the icy windows was covered in a jumble of hand-written signs. They were scrawled in an assortment of pens, in different-sized lettering, on scraps of paper and torn-off pieces of cardboard; it was as if Dazel's mind had sprayed in a haphazard collage across his house. Between the signs, like mortar round bricks, were layers and layers of blankets, secured with foot-long strips of grey carpet tape – I assumed for insulation purposes. The centrepiece of the collage was a square flap of cardboard surrounded by streaks of grey tape. On it was inscribed a statement in thick black marker: 'This flat is full of torture for me.' Below was a newspaper clipping containing a survey of battles in the Second World War. Surrounding this sign were smaller ones, like side plates round a dish. One, on a piece of lined A4, read, 'I am only a nappy launderer, not rich, I am poor, I live with my father, a disabled war veteran trying to live on meals on wheels three times a week and four days live on odds and ends and he is very cold and cannot last much longer.' Another, on what looked like the inside of a cereal packet, said, 'Tourists from Australia, New Zealand, the USA, Canada, all welcome to see wartime art book to commemorate the battle of El Alamein 23 October 1942. Please ring this telephone number 081 203 9764 for time to view. Maybe time for chat with battle veteran. Admission free. Dazel and Stan, flat 25.' Next to it was another, more violently written: 'Please help 8th Army war veteran to get some food. Flat 25,' and another, 'I would not vote for any of them Lab-Tory-Lib, they are all past their sell-by date, new parties are what is needed

164

now.' And on the very edge, penned in strict red felt-tip, was 'Old war veteran would like anybody to call on him just for a chat. Thank you. Flat 25, Stan.' But worst of all were the postcards crammed on the side of the window nearest the path, which caught my eye as I approached the door. They were covered with slogans in anxious blue Biro: 'N for O now and for ever,' 'I love you, I need O,' 'Don't take her away from me, please,' 'matches made in heaven are the first to burn,' 'we will be together, if not this world, then heaven, if not heaven, then hell.' I began to feel sick. Dropping the mangled bag of groceries on the path, I backed away from the door and hurried off into the muffling snow. For the first time in weeks I fumbled Plastic Bag out of my pocket and held him tightly to my chest.

When I arrived at school, I was over an hour late. Registration had been and gone. I stood alone in the foyer, dwarfed by the high ceiling and vast, gleaming floor, and pulled my crumpled timetable from my bag. The crackle of paper felt like a giveaway in the subdued mid-lesson atmosphere. I saw the first lesson on Monday morning, and my stomach turned. Chemistry with Mr Barratt. Why did it have to be that, of all things? I crept up the stairs, shivering slightly from the snow, clutching Plastic Bag to my heart as I went. Passing classroom after classroom I heard the echo of facts being declared, answers being demanded and chalk scratching on boards. The wet patches on my sleeve and trouser leg clung to my skin, and the ceiling seemed to be slowly rising higher and higher. At the end of a long shiny-floored corridor was the lab. It had a blue door with a square window in it. There was a large crack in the glass from when Mr Barratt had slammed it after forcibly ejecting a fourth-former who, legend had it, had been scratching a penis on the desk with a compass. I steeled myself and tapped on the door.

Mr Barratt rotated his wrist and the tongs turned. The eyes of the class were on me. Nothing could be heard but the hiss and flicker of the Bunsen burner. Inside, my stomach was folding in on itself. My face felt numb and expressionless. I fixed my eyes on the teacher's shiny patent shoes with their evil, pointed tips. I was glad I had spat on my lace-ups before entering the lab, as dull toecaps always made him furious.

Again, the tongs turned. A thick, syrupy drop of molten yellow plastic thudded onto the safety-mat beneath the Bunsen burner. Plastic Bag's round black eyes had become streaks on either side of his glowing head and his mouth had stretched into a gaping smudge. The corners of my mouth felt as if they were being pulled down by tiny chains as one of Plastic Bag's crescent hands dropped from its cracked socket and bounced onto the table. The tongs turned once more, and his head fell away from his body, hanging like a boiling globule of phlegm above the flames. Another turn and his head came to rest on his back, which blackened and writhed in the heat. The other hand extended from its arm on a long melting thread and disappeared into the heart of the flames. Plastic Bag was unrecognisable. The blue of his body mingled with his legs and head to form a single purple lump. Finally, Mr Barratt turned off the Bunsen burner and dropped the bubbling remains on the table.

Throughout the rest of the lesson I couldn't take my eyes off the small plastic mass as it smouldered and cooled. It was molten sadness. After a while, Mr Barratt swept it onto the floor and kicked it into the corner of the room with his sinister pointed shoes. I waited for the bell to ring, and as we filed out I secretly retrieved the mangled corpse, covered in tufts of hair and dust. I slipped it ruefully into my pocket and followed the line of uniformed figures down the stairs, my anonymous textbook clasped to my face to mask my swelling eyeballs. My vision was becoming watery and blurred.

I never liked sports at school. My left foot always poked out sideways when I tried to run, and I was informed that my arms flapped like a girl's. Also, physical exertion tired me

166

out, and trying to keep my eyes focused on small moving objects gave me a headache. When we were supposed to be playing football I used to dig for worms in the corner of the pitch, and during cricket matches I sat in the shade by the boundary and pondered things. That Monday afternoon it was running. The snow had begun to thaw and the morning's immaculate white carpet had become icy piles of slush. I set off behind everyone else, shuffling reluctantly along beneath the white dome of the sky. When the last runner was out of sight I walked back, retrieved my bag from where I'd hidden it under a bush and headed for home, wondering what would happen if one were to hold Mr Barratt in a huge throbbing flame.

Several hours later, warmed by home and supper, I was standing once again outside in the cold, between my mother and a large green recycling bin. My father had, in his youthful wisdom, reminded me that Plastic Bag was no more than a piece of plastic – just like an actual plastic bag – and not a real human being. My mother didn't seem to understand the depth of my loss, either; after offering what sympathy she could, she took me to the recycling bin. Against my instincts, I agreed to go. I did not want to be a child any more.

The night had arrived in wintry earliness, creating a murky, inhospitable afternoon. I stood peering up at the hulking bin, my tie fluttering in the breeze, cupping Plastic Bag's charred remains in my hands. I was surprised at how heavy he was in this state. I fixed my eyes on the exact circle of the porthole. When I contemplated dropping him into the hole, his body got heavier and heavier. The wind danced cruelly around my face as I tried to force myself to set Plastic Bag on his last flight to his doom. But my arm was paralysed, I couldn't galvanise it into action. Slowly, my fingers became numb with cold.

A white cloud floated over my shoulder as my mother spoke into my ear. Her voice sounded flat and impatient. I closed my eyes and opened my fingers; without a word she plucked Plastic Bag from my palm and dropped him into the porthole. I didn't hear him hit the bottom. I imagined him suspended for ever in space. Plastic Bag had given his life for Dazel, I thought. He was a martyr. My mother turned away and led me down the pencil-drawn street. I felt naked and alone as we walked briskly home.

Chapter Twenty

Soon winter slipped into autumn. Then autumn was surprised by summer, and summer faded into spring. Then it was winter again, and autumn, and when a few cycles had passed my father and I were the same age. It was bound to happen sooner or later. We were in our mid-teens. My mother, of course, was younger.

It was morning. I was sitting at the kitchen table alone, watching how it glowed in the autumn sun. The walls were plastered with pictures of Tibetan and Chinese pop stars, as well as pages of poetry which my mother had ripped out of books. Beside the typewriter was the novelty radio in the shape of an elephant, and an entire cupboard was dedicated to baked beans and rice.

My parents were still in bed. The previous night they had gone to a midnight screening of *The Silence of the Lambs*, which had just been released (billed as the 'Big Film of 1991'); they had managed to sneak into the cinema even though they were underage. The state of the sitting room was going from bad to worse. Not only were the walls covered in dog-eared pin-ups, but my parents weren't getting any tidier as they got younger. Coke bottles, crisp packets and the odd beer can littered the corners of the room; only the centre of the carpet was clean, as they were in the habit of kicking the rubbish to the edges.

Breakfast time yet again. As usual, dawn had broken on the day before, and I could do nothing about it. There was a riddle at the centre of my life, and that made me lonely, but no more so than anyone else. How did they see the world? How did they see me? I had no way of telling. I had begun to realise that, deep down, everyone has to accept that some things are just unexplainable, and there's nothing you can do but live with them. Like everyone else, I could control my direction in life no more than I could control my gradually deteriorating health. From my point of view, however, it seemed as if my parents were getting steadily healthier. Especially my father, who now had a rowing machine in his room. I tried not to think about the irony of his physical fitness – I tried to ignore the fact that he was the instigator of my disease. Breakfast. The glowing table. A couple of bits of toast and half a bowl of cereal.

After breakfast I left the house. As I closed the door I heard my father's alarm clock ringing and his voice saying, 'Hello? Hello?' – as usual, he had mistaken the alarm clock for the telephone and tried to answer it. I thought about calling goodbye up the stairs, but didn't feel like speaking to either of them. Especially my father. I didn't even feel like seeing him, most days. Instead, I typed a short note on the typewriter and slipped it under their door.

The oily October leaves sprang at me as I walked in the direction of the local plate factory, where I worked. I worked mornings, as my energy levels were too low to do any more. I didn't make much money, but it was enough to pay my way. The factory was filled with the tinnitus of machinery, and its artificial lighting turned your flesh orange. All the workers had their hair and feet in sanitised plastic bags. I arrived, clocked in, put my plastic bags on and went out onto the factory floor. I worked in the quality-control department; my official title was 'Junior Product Monitor', known amongst the staff as the 'Second Spotter'. I was situated at the end of the assembly line and my job was to spot and remove damaged plates, or 'peanuts' as they were known, as they slid by on the conveyor belt. The 'First Spotter', or 'Senior Product Monitor', a bespectacled German with a stoop and an asymmetrical face, did exactly the same job about three metres in front. Being the first line of attack, he was the one to filter out most of the peanuts. This meant that I did virtually nothing apart from enter a trance as a result of the constant, regular flow of plates, hour after hour after hour. I retrieved one or two peanuts a day, that constituted the highlight of my working hours.

It was a Friday. There was no doubt in my mind; for everyone else in the factory, Fridays were deceptive, cheating, snake-like days, because they heralded the promise of the weekend. They hyped it up like a PR team, making it seem that everything would be OK in the end. 'Don't worry, soon it will be the weekend, the marvellous, fantastic weekend', they say, 'coming soon to a cinema near you, the two-day bonanza of relaxation and fun, the answer to all your prayers. You see, we ourselves, the Fridays, the final boring days of another boring week, are not the monsters we seem, the taskmasters, the torturers. We are the salvation of the bored. Sure we're pretty vile, but in reality we are your friends, because once we've passed, the pressure will be lifted all at once. The weekend, the joyful weekend, the blissful weekend, will be here. It will soothe your aching brain with the universal balm of long afternoons, late lie-ins, walks in the park and the Sunday papers.' But what Friday fails to mention is that by Sunday night you'll be sitting on the sofa in the dark, wishing it all would end. For me, however, this was not the case. For me, Friday promised nothing but more days of numbness and suffering. I was not taken in.

I returned home at lunchtime, feeling a twinge of sympathy for the German, who would go back to work in the afternoon and then be subjected to the weekend. The kitchen table was still glowing like a pool of electricity, but this time plates of food protruded from the glare. My father was at work, but my mother welcomed me with a high-pitched salute as she flitted round the table, her plait wagging behind her; it was tied with a glittering pink ribbon. She was working to the rhythm of Leslie Cheung's new album, *Dreaming*, which was blaring from the elephant-radio. I recognised it instantly; I had become familiar with popular music through my parents. I wondered why she had gone to so much effort, as my father always stayed at Hush Hush for lunch. The room was unusually cold; I bunched my shoulders against the chill, and saw that the windows were open wide. I was about to push them closed when I noticed an extra plate on the table. The penny dropped. Dazel was coming for lunch. I hadn't seen him for a while. I left the windows open.

My mother and Dazel were in the habit of having 'poetry lunches' together from time to time. As they ate they would treat each other's verse like cigarettes; lighting it, sucking it, taking it in deep, blowing it out. They were careful to keep these liaisons secret from my father, and whenever Dazel came to visit he always left a couple of hours before my father got home, to give my mother time to air the house and get rid of any evidence.

I tightened my collar against the autumn chill. As my mother was putting the finishing touches to the table, a shimmering cloud of smoke announced Dazel's arrival. My mother turned the music off. He came into the kitchen and sat opposite me. The pillar of smoke immediately streaked off to his right, dragged out of the open window. I squinted slightly, blurring the figure of Dazel and watching the cloud of smoke form a huge grey banana as it curved on the draft. Dazel seemed somewhat agitated, and was finding it difficult to catch his breath after the walk. His eyes flicked anxiously around the room as my mother heaped steaming, glutinous piles of *dofu dang tsay*, *phing sha* and *mo-mo ngopa* on his plate. Fat, savoury smells appetised the air. As my mother had become more youthful she had become a less conscientious cook; much of the food was revived leftovers of previous meals. Each dish was passed to me after Dazel had taken a spoonful, and my mother poured him a large glass of beer. Then we began to eat, while Dazel gathered his energy and revealed the cause of his distress.

'They found out about it, chums, and they've been going mental with me all morning,' he said, lifting an overloaded fork to his mouth.

'Oh, Dazel, fuck! You're joking!' My mother sat back in

her chair with a girlish giggle, clamping her hands over her mouth.

'I wish I was, Osel. Last night I got out of the shower and walked smack bang wallop into my dad as he was coming up the stairs.' He glanced at me, noticing the blank expression on my face. 'Osel, didn't you tell Mo about it?'

'Of course not. I thought it was, like a secret?' Both of them turned to me, fixing me with four gleaming eyes. I gave a slight shrug.

'Well, I don't suppose it matters now,' grunted Dazel. 'The cat's out of the bag in any case.' He stood up from the table and began to untuck his shirt. 'Prepare yourself, Mo.' He pulled his shirt up over his head. A burst of smoke emerged and cleared, revealing a pasty slab of chest. In the very centre, level with the nipples, was a sore patch of red skin, and in the centre of that was a fresh cluster of scabs. Underneath the scabs I could just make out an image; a Benson and Hedges packet, tattooed in black lines about four inches high. Dazel picked off a few more scabs to give me a better look. From what I could tell, the artwork was good; the lid of the box was flicked insouciantly back, the cigarettes inside protruding in the classic ʌ formation. I gasped and shook my head in disbelief. As Dazel released his shirt, something on his inner arm caught my eye. It may have been my imagination, but I could have sworn that I glimpsed several deep scratches crisscrossing his skin; and I could have sworn that they spelt O-S-E-L. He sat down and continued to eat. 'It hurt like the fires of hell but it's not so bad now,' he said. 'I reckon Dad will ground me for ages. But it was really inspiring. Look.' He pulled some wrinkled papers from his back pocket and laid them on the table beside my mother. They had been scribbled over with verse. I realised why I hadn't seen him for a while. He was indeed going to be grounded.

We finished the meal in silence while my mother perused Dazel's poetry, her fork gliding pensively to and from her mouth. The glow on the table had begun to dim as the world tilted. I tipped a couple of paracetamols into my hand, and for an instant two chivalric heroes flashed before my eyes, straightening their cartoon helmets and combing their plumes. I swallowed them, and the knights charged despairingly into my bloodstream.

Generally, I regarded my mother's poetry with amusement. Sometimes I found it entertaining to sit in on her meetings with Dazel, observing their emotive declamations from my vantage point on the sofa. But that afternoon I was keen to get away from the table as soon as possible and shut myself in the quietness of my room. I wanted to be alone. I had developed a taste for sitting; often I would begin to read a magazine, or tidy my room, only to be distracted by the action of sitting itself. I suppose it was the result of the hours I spent in Hush Hush as a small child. Nowadays I sat motionless on my bed for long periods, my back against the fading wallpaper and my legs stretched towards the door. In some strange way, it made me feel in control.

'Mo, you'll like this one.' My escape was foiled before I'd even made a move. 'Can I read it to him, Dazel? It's called "Decay". Ready?' I nodded resignedly, and she cleared her throat and began.

'The trees bloom
Then boom
They're gone. Decay
Decays us all.
My lungs are hurting,
My pain is growing,
The unspoken desire
Remains unspeakable.'

She giggled and glanced at Dazel, who looked slightly embarrassed. His face took on a deeper shade of blue and he began to make excuses for what he called his 'lack of a muse'. I nodded, went over to the typewriter, typed, 'very good, see you later, got to go', pushed the paper across

174

the table and made my way upstairs. The door of my parents' room was ajar, and as I passed I glimpsed several porn magazines spread on their bed. That kind of thing always made me feel uncomfortable. Especially as I was medically prohibited from any form of sexual activity. When I closed the door of my room behind me, the relief hit me like a feather pillow. I drew the curtains. Nausea was setting in.

At times like these, it became clear to me that the fabric of the world was only an extension of my mind. Buffeted by the queasiness, crushing headaches and dizziness, my experiences were not contained within my body and mind alone. All the objects around me became injected with the substance in my blood, and were transformed by my ravaged mind. There's no doubt about it, mind and matter are the same. How could they ever be separate? Everything was in flux, in motion; my world alternated between incredible buoyancy and unbearable weightiness. Things would float in and out of each other and then, without warning, force themselves determinedly into the ground. My bed became a desert, an ocean, a peanut field, the back of an alligator; everything was sickeningly mobile and everything was part of my mind.

A couple of hours later I felt slightly better, and decided to get out of the house for a change of scene. I had been sitting on my bed, feet towards the door, for longer than usual, and my legs were stiff. When I went downstairs Dazel had gone; my mother was spraying suffocating air freshener into every cranny in the house, and had opened all the windows to clear away every trace of his visit. A cold draught whipped around my ears. I walked out of the house without saying goodbye, and as I went down the path I glanced back at the sitting-room windows. They were blurred with condensation and a pithy message had become manifest on the centre window, surrounded by a zigzag: 'The end of rising is falling.' I was becoming convinced that these slogans appeared at random, quirks of the atmospheric conditions. I set off aimlessly down the road.

175

For some reason, I was drawn towards Hush Hush. I didn't intend to go there but my feet were compelled. For a moment I thought that my future was indeed mapped out for me in my parents' past, determined by their experience. I shook myself out of the thought and entered the silence of the café.

It was late in the day, and the only customers left were Grandpa Pagpa and Ishmael. They were sitting in their usual places, sound asleep with their heads propped up against each other. Another unfinished chess game lay between them. Apart from that the place was empty. I was surprised not to see Madeline anywhere. I was used to seeing her sitting at the disused pool table, guarding the strange, stagnant cup of coffee. Neither was there any dust on the pool table. The balls, which had never been moved during my lifetime, were in different positions; they, too, were free of dust and grime, splashing the table with their gaudy reds and yellows. There was even a turquoise cuboid of chalk on the side.

My father looked glad to see me. His thinning moustache could no longer bristle with delight, but he made the pleased expression that would cause it to bristle in later life. It irritated me. All that was left of the glory of his upper lip was a dark smudge, as if he'd wiped his face on the handrail of an Underground escalator. My own moustache was coming along nicely, a stripe of curious, wispy hairs that was clearly noticeable when you got close up. I didn't want it to become the same as his, and fully intended to shave it when it became more developed. However, my resemblance to my father was grimly unavoidable; his moustache would get thinner and thinner over the next few months and soon would disappear altogether, so whether I decided to shave mine or keep it, either way I would be echoing him. He beckoned me in and I went all the way to the back of the café and mounted the platform next to the pool table. He turned back to whatever he was doing behind the counter. I sat.

Soon the interior of the café began to blush, and outside the world took on the dreamy feel of dusk. There was still an hour or two left until closing time. My father finished what he was doing and stood motionless at the counter, staring into space. Two figures laden with luggage emerged from the swirl of colours outside. The first was Madeline, and the second a lean, androgynous-looking man in denim. They approached the counter to order their coffee, and I could tell from the suspicion with which my father scrutinised her that he had never met her before. Fascinated, I sat in the shadows, unnoticed, and watched.

My father took their order and pushed his way through the white curtain to prepare the coffee. His gait was nimble. The continuum of his life had unfolded clearly; over the years his limbs had become energised, and smooth, and untwisted.

The bedraggled pair scanned the café, looking for a place to put their bags. The man headed for the pool table, urging Madeline to follow him with a toss of his hair. They mounted the platform and dropped the bags noisily in the corner, causing Grandpa Pagpa to let out a sleepy moan. Half of me expected my father to expel these two from the café, as they were evidently unaware of the fact that silence was required. On the other hand, I knew that Madeline, at least, would become a regular. Neither of them noticed me sitting in the corner in the shadows. Denim Man had a pair of train tickets in his long fingers. He put them on the side of the pool table and clattered the multicoloured balls into the triangle. He was reaching for a cue when Madeline went over to him and put her arms round his waist. They stood in silent embrace, pink in the late-afternoon sun. Then Madeline whispered in his ear; the words were clearly audible in the stillness of the café.

'You're my rock, babe, I'm so excited. I'm not going to kill myself. We're getting out!'

Presently Denim Man unclasped Madeline's coiling arms and plucked a cue from the wall, weighing it in his hands. Finding the balance to his satisfaction, he twisted a greasy lock behind each ear and placed the white ball carefully in the D. Stooping, he attached his frame to the table and spidered his fingers. The cue slotted perfectly into the cavernous dip between his knuckles. He began to slide it rapidly back and forth like a piston. Meanwhile, Madeline plucked a second cue from the wall and leant on it, watching him admiringly. He continued to aim. I faded into the wall.

What happened next can only be described in great detail. I have thought about it so many times that it is even more vivid in my memory than it was when it occurred. Before Denim Man struck the ball, my father reappeared from the kitchen, balancing two steaming cups of coffee on a huge tray. He came over to the platform and climbed the stairs. Denim Man saw my father approaching. He stopped aiming and stood up, receiving his coffee with a twist of a lank forelock. Then my father walked round the table towards Madeline, and from my vantage point in the corner of the room I could just see Denim Man take a sip of his coffee, scowl and place it on the side of the pool table – in the very spot, in fact, where the stagnant cup would be placed every day from then on. Denim Man smacked his lips and my father reached over to hand Madeline her coffee.

It was at that precise moment that it happened. A sharp noise stung through the air, so loud that I jolted upright. It was a spoken word, and sounded like 'Woja'. Madeline and my father both spun round to face the Denim Man, who was staring down the café towards the window, his mouth agape, twists of hair obscuring his eyes. His hands were clasped in a knot and stuck out directly in front of him. All three of us turned our heads, following his line of vision to the window, but nothing unusual could be seen. Grandpa Pagpa and Ishmael were still fast asleep, the street was still running along the window from right to left, the slanting light was still pinkish and clear. Simultaneously, we wheeled our baffled heads back towards Denim Man. He was gone. I got to my feet, and Madeline let out a high-pitched gasp. Where he had been standing was nothing but empty space. The cue was leaning against the wall, the coffee was on the side of the pool table, the steam curling lazily into space; but Denim

Man had vanished. Disappeared. Madeline reached weakly into the air and my father, in a rather ridiculous way, had a quick glance under the pool table. But the man had gone. There was no way he could have made it out of the shop in those few seconds without us seeing him. But he was nowhere to be found. And I, with the benefit of hindsight, knew that he would never be seen again.

Over the years, I have tried to analyse, and re-analyse, that single word. Woja. What did it mean? Was it a slurred form of 'What do you'? Or a Rastafarian 'O, jah'? Or was it really an 'Oh dear'? It was hard to tell, not having any familiarity with his accent or way of speaking. Also, I gave a lot of thought to the tone of his voice in that single word. Afraid? Determined? Shocked? Exasperated? Loving? I tried to think back, to re-create the exact sound of the word and to hear it again in my mind, fresh, as if for the first time. But it always changed in my memory. That sound was the only piece of evidence left, the only clue, but it was reinvented whenever I recalled it. It existed only in memory, a ghostly trace of a decayed emotion. And how was I to interpret his hands held out in front of him, his fingers twisted together in a never-ending knot? Madeline must have scrutinised her memory far more intensely than I did mine. She had more at stake. The ambiguity of that moment was unbearable; the floating fragment of time was impossible to pin down. For a while I came to the conclusion that the exclamation had been fearful, and that the hands were held out in defence; then I changed my mind and thought that it had a ring of deep determination, or even surprised innocence, and that the hands were extended in a welcoming salute. In the end I had to concede that I'd never know. Nobody would discover what happened in those few bizarre seconds, and there was no way anybody could; some things just happen, they are unexplainable, they are riddles. I don't know if my father came to the same conclusion. But I knew for certain that Madeline would never accept it. She couldn't. I had witnessed the birth of Madeline's tortured future.

She slumped into a chair by the pool table – the scene of so many listless hours over the years – while my father conducted an absurd search of the café, peering under the tables and behind the counter. From time to time he glanced at me for help, but I didn't have the heart. I knew it was useless. I accepted it. Defeated by the mystery, my father returned to the security of his familiar spot behind the counter and resumed staring into space.

Madeline sat motionless by the coffee cup. The steam had subsided, and a wrinkled skin was beginning to creep across its surface. The way she was sitting was eerily recognisable, but there was something in her posture I had never noticed before. A deep tension swelled beneath the skin and flesh. Gradually I formed words around what I saw in her. She was waiting. Waiting hopefully.

Madeline sat as the sky darkened, alternating the arm that made contact with the pool table. My father went about his usual procedure of waking Grandpa Pagpa and Ishmael and lifting the chairs onto the tables. He had wiped the surfaces long ago. I sat in the deepening shadows, trying to blot out the constant prickling sensation on my skin. When all the chairs were up and the 'Closed' sign had been turned to the world, my father stood gazing inscrutably at Madeline. She hadn't moved, and I could see dust settling on the pool table and coffee cup like snow. My father disappeared through the curtain, and reappeared with two hot cups of coffee. He mounted the platform, put one of them in front of Madeline and sat opposite her, staring into her eyes. I saw her pupils bulge, then focus. I had been forgotten. He sipped his coffee and for an instant his face was engulfed by a cloud of steam. By way of response, Madeline reached out a spindly arm and drew her coffee cup to her. She sipped. The steam brushed her cheeks, gently. They replaced their cups on the table and sat motionless once again, waiting together in silent empathy.

I knew that Madeline's forlorn hope would touch my father deeply. He would accept her into the system of his coffee world without hesitation, wrapping her in his routines like a comfort blanket. They waited together deep into the night, and she wasn't charged for her coffee; the system itself was enough, and they experienced it together. Together they experienced the initial sting on the tongue, the tartness on the throat, the sharp twinge of the stomach. Together they experienced the gradual heady flow of caffeine, the shakiness and the nausea; and together they came down into the murky depths of a low. Yes, the coffee system acted infallibly, as it had for decades; it was reliable, it could bring people together. The dregs in the bottom of their cups congealed in mysterious constellations and the rings round the rims became stains. They sat deep into the night until the effect of the caffeine had completely dissolved; the high passed into the low and the low had passed into normality. Starlight soothed the café. After a long while, Madeline raised her awkward body from the chair, heaved her luggage onto her shoulders and disappeared into the night, leaving my father alone. Some time later he rose, piled the empty cups onto a tray and took them into the kitchen. Then he returned and delicately raised Denim Man's abandoned coffee cup from its place on the table. It had adhered slightly and there was a quiet click as he pulled it away. He carried it gingerly down the three shallow stairs and into the kitchen. I emerged from the shadows and left the café secretly, glad to be shocked by the cold and obscured by the darkness. The moon was orange, and unusually low. I headed for home.

Chapter Twenty-one

Eventually, there came a point when I was older than both my parents; our ages had overlapped. I was seventeen, and not getting any younger. My father was heading for his early teens. I wanted my independence. My parents' incessant juvenile chatter and petty arguments were getting me down, and the way they assumed that they knew better than me was infuriating. My father couldn't understand why I never wanted to row on his machine, and my mother had stuck so many pin-ups on the walls that there was no point in having wallpaper any more. They were developing a disregard for Tibetan tradition – the shrines around the house had not been cleaned, and the offerings had not been refreshed, for weeks – and the amount of junk food they consumed rose almost daily. What's more, my health wasn't getting any better, and the more I mulled over the cause of my illness, the more my parents became walking reminders of my doom. It was getting difficult to bear. I decided my parents could look after themselves.

I left home while the sun was setting on another Friday. I had been sitting on my bed all afternoon, watching as the shadows crept across my body and gradually filled the room, hating the scents of normality that passed on the air. I heard my father arrive home from work, heaved myself from the bed and went downstairs. My mother was sitting in front of the TV, vacantly. My father sat down next to her and they kissed; then he grabbed the remote control and changed channels. My mother protested and they had a scuffle, laughing and shouting, until the remote control burst out of their hands like a bar of soap and hit me on the chest. They tumbled off the sofa and dived at it, almost knocking me over in the process. My mother grabbed it and dashed out of the room, plait flying, followed by my father, red in the face and laughing hysterically. I started to watch TV, then changed my mind and went into the kitchen, then changed my mind again and went back upstairs. Shouts and thumps came from below, followed by loud music; 'You Have Placed a Chill in My Heart', the Eurythmics' latest single. They had been playing the same record over and over again, incessantly, for weeks. Suddenly the realisation hit me. I was no longer part of their lives.

I sat on the bed again, leaving the door open. The entire *Savage* album played from beginning to end, and then it was replaced by the clatter of plates and the odd snatch of speech. I assumed they were having supper – pizza and Coke yet again, no doubt; they always had pizza and Coke. I mustered the energy to push the door closed and lay down on the bed.

The image of my adult father having sex with Madeline came into my mind again, yet instead of making me feel regretful it made me angry. These days, I no longer took the blame. I realised that the notion that I could have made a difference to our fate was ridiculous. I took heed of my twisting sinews and throbbing pulse, and understood that I could not shoulder the responsibility. I had no control over my fate; there was no way I could have prevented the disease from being transmitted, because I was experiencing its effects every day. My symptoms were testimony to the fact that the transmission was set in stone and could not be avoided. I had experienced my parents' future, so it could not be changed; likewise their past was sealing mine. Our futures were locked, sealed, irrevocable.

Someone was to blame, though, for the disease. My father. And, indirectly, my mother. I somehow felt she was involved. Their relationship was to blame, that was the true source of the suffering. Grandpa Pagpa was to blame, too – he contributed to the defunct relationship – and so was Rabbi Chod, and everyone. They all created this together. The whole lot of them were tainted.

Resolutely, I got to my feet and packed everything I needed into three plastic bags; underwear and T-shirts in one, trousers and pyjamas in another, and personal effects in the third. These consisted of my toothbrush and toothpaste, soap, shaving kit and pills. I put on my jumper and coat, and slid a chewed Biro into my pocket. Before going downstairs, I deliberated for many minutes over how to carry three bags and remain balanced. I even considered stuffing a fourth bag with newspaper, to even things out. But in the end I decided that I would put two bags in my right hand, since it was the stronger of the two, and carry the other in my left. This worked all right once I got used to it. I had a couple of trial runs up and down my room. When I felt sufficiently confident, I made my way downstairs.

My parents were sitting on the sofa in the sitting room. They were watching TV and clutching at pizza with their teeth. The room was littered with discarded packaging. My father had changed into a Tottenham Hotspur T-shirt. My mother stole a chip from his plate, and they had another minor scuffle. A huge tub of what looked like strawberry swirl ice-cream partially obscured them from view. I cleared my throat and they peered round the tub, noticing my bags and coat. There was an uncomfortable pause. I could tell from the wide-eyed expressions on their wrinkle-free faces that they understood this was serious. Mind you, their surprise could have been because of my startling appearance. For one thing, I was carrying three plastic bags, when I never usually carried anything. Generally speaking, I felt weighed down enough as it was. Also, that afternoon I had re-styled my facial hair, and this made me look quite different.

Red was creeping into the sky when I left the house, and red was beginning to flood my head as well. The sky was slowly starting to resemble my parents' ice-cream, and crept into me as I walked. I had heard people identify the sensation of redness with anger, but that wouldn't be wholly accurate; I wasn't just angry. I was experiencing a great redness, together with a powerful clenching in my chest. I picked my way over my father's bike, which was lying sloppily across the path, and headed down the street. I had no particular plans, but I knew I wasn't going to return. My parents could look after themselves, they had the resources, and they certainly didn't need their son hanging around and spoiling the atmosphere at home. It would be better this way. I would seek out privacy and independence. I turned onto Finchley Road and withdrew some money from a cash machine. It was pleasing to feel the small bundle nestling in my left inside pocket, as it went some way towards balancing the weight of the extra plastic bag in my right hand.

My upper lip was still stinging, fresh from the shave. My skin was sensitive and unused to the harshness of the razor. Actually, to be more specific, only the left side of my upper lip was stinging; I had only shaved half of my moustache, and half of my beard. The opposite halves. For a couple of months I had been growing whiskers all over my face. I had even managed to grow a few real bristles on my upper lip and around my ears, which is unusual for a Tibetan. I suppose I got my hairiness from my father. When I had returned home from work at lunchtime, I went straight into my room with my razor, shaving cream and a basin of hot water. I held up the blade to the window and for a moment it was lost against the steely grey of the November sky. Then it flicked back into view and I scraped a line of smooth, speckled skin from the white cake on my lip. I paid great attention to getting the cut-off line below my nose absolutely straight. Then I shaved off the right side of my beard, leaving another crisp line down the centre of my chin. The next half-hour was spent with plastic gloves, silver foil and bottles of dye; finally I stood back and admired the contrast between the vulnerable skin and the haggard, shaggy whiskers – dyed the colour of wine.

This style was by no means perfect, but it was the best I could come up with. I had no other choice. To allow my moustache to grow would be to set myself in my father's future footsteps; to shave it off completely would invoke his present childish self. I wanted neither. I didn't want his face infiltrating mine. It was bad enough that I was being consumed by sickness, his sickness, Madeline's sickness. I didn't want his face to be transmitted as well. Granted, by worrying about facial hair in the first place I was still trying to assert my independence on my father's terms, I was playing his game. But there could never be a complete escape from his influence, there was no outside. And short of decapitating myself or having a sex change, I couldn't come up with a better solution.

I ignored the sting as I ambled aimlessly through increasing layers of red cloud, along roads and round corners. The cityscape was all angles and surfaces, in burning hues of cherry and scarlet. Dark silhouettes of passers-by jostled me, their extremities splashed with light. Something was compelling me onwards. Looking back, I suppose it was merely the force of my destiny, which was pinned down by other people's pasts. All I could do was follow. At times I was possessed by the rhythm of my feet and the faint crackle of the plastic bags. I don't know how long it lasted.

I found myself in a train station. I was tired and dazed from the walk, and I sat on a bench in front of a dazzling information board. Destinations were flicking in great yellow waves across its surface, and I began to feel queasy. But the effort of focusing on words and numbers cut through the vermillion haze. Gradually I became aware of the dimensions of the place, the fluorescent lighting, the crowds. Many troubled figures were flitting to and fro, and announcements klaxoned on tangents through space. As my head began to clear, the information board was obscured by a group of people standing in front of me. Their backs were turned and became a wall of coats, apart from a single figure, a small child, framed by legs and scarves. Her head was cocked in suspicion and three pensive fingers drooped from her mouth. One of her feet was corkscrewing into the ground. I stood up and she spun on her heel. A train ticket was in her hand. She came to a standstill and held it up above her head.

Without fully realising what I was doing, I plucked it from her fingers and perused its details. Platform six. I couldn't see the destination. It seemed appropriate to accept the gift. I nodded my thanks and shuffled off in the direction of a huge metal archway with 'TRAINS' inscribed on it in three-foot letters. The girl ran headlong into the coat of an adult and was whisked bodily into the air.

I mounted into the train and sat on a seat which felt like a huge yellow toothbrush. I had no idea where I was going. As the train drew out of the station, condensation appeared on the window and I was surprised to see words slowly forming in the mist on the glass. Maybe someone had written a message on it previously and the fog was collecting around the imprint. Or perhaps the message was appearing for the first time. Gradually, the words became clear: 'The end of meeting is parting'. Scarlet eyelids closed on me like a blind and the matronly rocking of the train sent me slowly to sleep.

I dreamt no dreams. Pure oblivion dragged me down, engulfed me, then slowly raised me back to the surface again, towards the waking world. I was greeted by an intercom announcement I couldn't make out. There was a jolt, a hiss and a lot of banging. Figures writhed past my seat. I found myself out on the platform: I had left the train. I checked my belongings. All three plastic bags had disembarked with me, but I had left my coat (with Biro) on the train. I caught a glimpse of it lying limp and forlorn on the seat as the carriage moved away.

The people on the platform showed great collective purpose. They were in a huge pack, all striding at high speed in the same direction as the train. I was slightly giddy from the recent sleep, or awakening, and was sandwiched on the edge of the platform between the blur of the train and the blur of the crowd, my feet akimbo on the yellow safety line. For a moment I felt perfectly still in the midst of the frantic rushing on both sides. Then motion returned, and I began to walk in the opposite direction. At first it was difficult; I felt as if I was swimming against the tide, being dragged backwards by the will of the masses. The train disappeared behind me, a sudden expanse of black air appearing in its place. I pushed my way into the crowd and through some barriers. Then I stepped out onto another grimy pavement.

By that time, the city had turned into a maze of purple, stained in the shadows with threatening black. The relief at being away from my parents was tempered by a profound uncertainty. My legs had begun to shake uncontrollably, so instead of continuing my journey I sat on a bench. My plastic bags flopped beside me. Time passed and I wrapped my arms round myself for warmth. At one point, a bearded face peered at me from the shadows. The eyes were filled with concern and, although I couldn't fully understand what was being said, I realised that the man was offering help. I shook my head repeatedly. Eventually he gave a defeated shrug, adjusted his yarmulke and disappeared back into the murky gloom. I sat.

I realised that I had been sitting on the bench far too long. The slats were hurting my legs. The bench obviously wasn't built for lengthy periods of sitting. That frustrated me, and the red cloud began to make a return. Why didn't they build benches that allowed the sitter to determine the length of the sit? Why should the environment dictate what you do? I shifted my pose, uncomfortably. Still, I thought, every chair becomes uncomfortable in the end. In which case, freedom is a mirage.

A second figure emerged from the swirl of the street. A pale smudge became a shock of peroxide hair, and a turquoise blur turned into a short leather skirt. She set her hips at a jaunty angle and said, 'Hey man, you lonely?' She was affecting an American accent.

'No,' I said.

'Well, fine, I'll just go take an overdose,' she replied, and was starting to walk away when she paused and turned back. 'Hang on . . . What . . .' she came closer, her American accent vanishing. 'Monlam! Mo! Is that you? God, you look terrible. What on earth are you doing?'

'I real,' I replied, my rubbery tongue faltering before I could add 'ly don't know.'

As the bearded man had done, she bent and gazed at my face. I was finding it increasingly difficult to perceive external things; it was difficult to focus, difficult to feel and difficult to discriminate sounds. I think she sat next to me. Gradually, the dizziness passed and eventually I understood what she was saying.

'Are you all right? Why won't you answer? Are you sick? God, somebody give me some Prozac. What are you doing out here, away from home? It's no good round here, you know. This is enough to make me want to throw myself into Clapton Common pond.'

There was genuine distress in her words. I recognised her. Younger-looking, perhaps, more beautiful, less fragile, but certainly the same person. The same red gash for a mouth, the listless eyes, the sallow cheeks. Madeline. It was definitely her. My future was unfolding into her past. The familiar face jolted me from my stupor and I sat up straight.

'Madeline,' I said.

She furrowed her brow. 'What's up, then, Mo? Are you OK? You look really spaced out. God, this is depressing. I'm going to have a nervous breakdown in a minute. Do you want me to take you home?'

'Home?'

'Yeah, to Turk's.'

I gave this some thought. 'Don't know.'

'Do you want me to leave you here, then?'

'No.'

'So?'

'I . . .' I lost track of my thoughts. She helped me to my feet and I followed her, my plastic bags skipping in my hands as I walked.

I found the solidity of the paving slabs somehow grounding. Madeline made no attempt to engage me in conversation. It was strange seeing her out of the context of the Hush Hush café. She looked different, less vulnerable. A fine rain began to fall. My hair clung to my head. After a while we turned left between two monstrous hedges, and a turreted Victorian building emerged from the shadows. It was made of carrot-orange brick and was surrounded by a high wall, topped with broken glass. The doors were toothed with bolts, and the windows were covered with turquoise paint so that no one could see in or out. We sheltered from the rain under the porch while Madeline fumbled for her keys and struggled with the stout front door. A vicious-looking Alsatian guard dog was chained to the wall. It nuzzled up to me in a familiar way, and tried to lick my hand. Madeline petted it, calling it 'Savio'. I held my bags to my chest.

The door swung open. We walked along a narrow hallway and came to another locked door. It had a keypad. Madeline typed in a code – 1568 – and it clicked open. Then we stepped into a dingy room with high ceilings, which Madeline briefly introduced as the 'Great Hall'.

An odd smell of roses and sweat seeped from the carpet. Battered sofas and coffee tables were everywhere. The slightest movement was mocked by scores of mirrors lining the walls. I watched as thousands of Madelines shut the doors quietly behind them, then took me by the hands and led me towards the corners of the rooms. An anticipatory stillness hung around the place. She poked her arm into a shadow and there was a burst of cold air. Then she threw me a glance and disappeared. Presently, the shadow was pierced by a light, revealing a spiral staircase. I followed her up the steps, which began to twist up a turret. The crackle of my plastic bags was deafening.

By that time my mind had become sufficiently lucid for me to wonder where I was. I tried to recall any landmarks I had seen on the way. It was difficult. I recalled Madeline mentioning Clapton Common, and guessed that I was some-where in Hackney. I wondered what kind of house I was in. To that, I had no answer. I continued to climb up the turret.

The stairs ran out and we stepped into a dark space. Madeline pulled a cord. There was a click. A bathroom fuzzily materialised. The light came from a single scarlet darkroom bulb dangling from the centre of the ceiling. The floor was

190

covered in tiles, and the ceiling was covered in mirrors. I glanced up to see myself glancing down, and glanced down to see myself glancing up. The wall facing me, being the turret wall, was curved, and had a thin rectangular window in its centre that archers could shoot from, painted over with turquoise like all the others. On my right was the only decoration in the room; a glass frame, displaying a gargantuan Red Admiral butterfly. Below it stood a Victorian bathtub, mounted on four brass feet. Somebody had obviously been using it as a bed, because it was filled with blankets and a pillow. It gave me an eerie sensation of déjà vu. On my left there was a sink and an old-fashioned toilet, with a tank connected by a pipe, and a rusty chain. Everything was given a reddish hue by the scarlet light-bulb. The air was unbearably hot and stuffy.

'Unpack those stupid plastic bags, Mo, and settle down,' said Madeline. 'What are you playing at? Fuck. Don't worry about Mama. I'm sure she didn't mean what she said yesterday. She was just in a rage. Depressing. Makes me want to flush my head down the toilet. Just carry on paying the rent as usual, and before long things will die down.' I nodded, wondering who Mama was. 'Good,' she said. 'Sort yourself out and get an early night. I'll try and speak to Mama for you. But Mo,' she wagged her finger in the air, 'if you're going to run away in the middle of the night, just say so. Tell me now. I can take it. I don't care if you abandon me. That would be bloody brilliant, that would. Abandon me. Leave me to rot here at Madame Turquoise's. Typical of my life. Depressing.'

I walked over to the sink and put my bags in it, peering around in the airless gloom. Given my sporadic diarrhoea, it would be good to have a room with a toilet. I turned round and tried to smile.

'Good,' she said. 'I'll see you tomorrow. Depressing.' She vanished downstairs.

I needed some air. I went over to the window, opened it and looked out. The cold breeze stung my face. Millions of tiny raindrops cascaded below me. From the top of the turret,

I could see for miles. A long crocodile of insect-like figures moved along the road, in and out of the streetlights. In the foreground a solitary figure in white and green scurried along, arms raised as protection from the rain. I looked again and the figure had vanished. I crossed the room, sat in the bath and gathered the blankets round me. All at once, I felt completely at home.

At that point I must have fallen asleep, because the next thing I knew, I was waking up. It was pitch black outside the window and although I had no watch I guessed it must be about ten thirty or eleven at night. My body-clock was usually accurate. It was the one part of my body that worked properly. It was ironic that the only fully functioning part should be the one that measures the horrors of decay. I shook my head from side to side until I was fully conscious. I needed to eat something. The normality of that thought comforted me. I pulled myself out of the bath, left the room and made my way down the spiral staircase.

The Great Hall was very different from when I had seen it an hour or two earlier. Far from being deserted, the room was full of men and women. Jarring voices and the clink of glasses filled the air, riding on the beat of Duran Duran's Top Ten single, 'I Don't Want Your Love'. My parents played that song all the time. The smell of alcohol and smoke mingled with the aroma of roses and sweat. The women were in a great variety of poses, all wearing bright, glittery turquoise. They were nervous and agitated. Bare flesh gleamed. Their lips and eyes were painted blue. They swayed forwards and backwards, at times drinking, at times dancing, at times laying their hands on the men. The men were generally slouching, and scratching, distracted, and desperate. They wore a great variety of colours, and gulped aggressively at their drinks. Sometimes they grabbed hold of the women. From time to time, a turquoise woman and a man would get up and go through the double doors at the back of the Great Hall together. I noticed one man leading two girls away, his chest jutting out like a robin's. He was dressed in white and green, and laughing loudly. I couldn't see Madeline anywhere. A thin, steely figure was reclining in a shadowy corner, surveying the proceedings from a throne-like armchair. An orange glow flitted around her face as she sucked on a cigarette. Every now and then Savio's barks would announce a stranger, and the steely figure would get up and interrogate them before they were admitted. Everything was multiplied thousands of times in the mirrors. Nobody noticed me. I sidled round the edge of the room and escaped through the front door and into the street.

I walked towards the main road. The rain had stopped, and the streets were covered in an oily skin. At a late-night chip shop, I purchased a cod and chips, and stowed it in my pocket. Then I headed back. After about five minutes I became aware of footsteps behind me, just audible over the distant hiss of the traffic. They were uncomfortably close. I glanced over my shoulder – and recognised him instantly. It was a strange coincidence. It had been strange enough bumping into Madeline earlier. But in my experience coincidences tended to cluster together. We caught eyes, and I felt obliged to speak.

'Hello, Dazel,' I said.

His eyes widened. 'Mo! Hello, chum. What on earth brings you here?'

As I shook his hand, I was surprised that his smoky cloud was nowhere to be seen. For the first time, he was sharp around the edges. He was younger, and healthier, and wore a jacket with big, fashionable shoulder-pads. He looked almost normal, but rather weak; he reminded me of Samson after his head had been shaved by Delilah. I realised that Dazel's smoke had given him, if not strength, at least protection. He fell into step beside me and as we began to talk I felt that something else was different. It took me a while to put my finger on what it was, but then it came to me. There was a kind of frustrated energy in his eyes. Previously his emotions had always been hidden beneath a veneer. Now he seemed wilder, less restricted.

'What are you doing here, Dazel, so late at night?'

'I . . . Well, I'm visiting friends, you know. What about you?'

'I just moved into the area. I've got a turret room in a house down there. I think it's called Madame Turquoise's.'

Dazel looked flustered and coughed into his sleeve. The cough was so mild that I almost laughed out loud with agony, knowing what it would later become. He pulled out a golden box of Bensons and clumsily opened the lid, his fingers inexpert. 'Want one?'

'Are you sure you want to smoke, Dazel?'

'Oh, Christ, not you as well. Do you want one or not?' A strange look came into his face that I can only describe as being a mixture of rebelliousness and sexual frustration. And self-hatred. That look touched me deeply. It was like looking into a mirror. I saw my hand rise in front of me and pluck a cigarette from the box.

'How long have you been smoking?' I asked.

'Oh . . . months,' he replied, rummaging in his pockets for a light. I put the cigarette gingerly between my lips. The texture of the filter felt strange in my mouth, like a shard of broken bone. He raised his hands and an amber flame flashed, igniting our cigarettes and our eyes.

Then the moment was over; our Bensons smouldered quietly. Smoke rose in sinister shapes above us. I tried a drag. Unsure of what to do, I held the smoke in my mouth and then released it with a soft flap of the cheeks. The taste of nicotine was unpleasant, yet there was something pleasant in that fact. I felt like a trainee dragon. Dazel threw me a sidelong glance then, without warning, stopped still, poised on the pavement. For an instant I wondered if he was about to perform a gymnastic routine. I turned and watched. He inhaled with a violent suck, then, his upper body inflated so much that his arms were raised from his sides at an angle, tilted his head back and expelled a chain of smoke rings into the air. After they had dispersed, he stood perfectly still for several seconds. Then he lowered his chin and continued to walk, a triumphant wiggle in his neck, as if being applauded. I followed him, a strange feeling in my stomach; I wanted to laugh and scream at once.

'Like that?' Dazel asked.

'Yes,' I lied.

'That your first ever ciggy?'

'No,' I lied again.

'I'm on ten a day, me. I've been like that for months. More if something pisses me off. And tonight I'm pissed off.' He took another drag. He had begun to affect a slight cockney twang.

'Why are you pissed off?' I asked. My own cigarette burnt away in my fingers.

'Nothing. Doesn't matter. Ask no questions . . .' He looked at me sidelong again, and his eyes looked even more lascivious, and rebellious, and self-loathing. A cloud was beginning to accumulate round his head, making it look bigger than it was.

'Mo, I'll show you something. Tonight I'm really pissed off, right, so I'm going to smoke in a really cool way. A way that really hurts.'

'Dazel, you don't have to,' I said, knowing full well that he did.

'Mo, Mo, Mo. I have to show you what real life is about.'

'What are you going to do?'

'I'm going to breathe smoke out my ears. My ears, Mo. That's what I do when I'm really pissed off.'

For all his determination, I could not imagine this to be biologically possible. 'Have you tried it before?' I asked. The expression of supreme confidence on Dazel's face slipped for a moment. 'Course I have,' he grunted.

He stopped in the middle of the pavement again. I leant against the wall to watch. Madame Turquoise's was only five minutes away. I could have walked on, and spared Dazel the embarrassment. But my feet were rooted to the spot, my tongue paralysed. Anyway, I was powerless, I couldn't change anything. All futures were fixed.

Dazel bunched up his courage and took an immense drag on his Benson. His cheeks bulged. Then, with as much force as he could muster, he closed his lips tight and constricted his whole body, as if trying to expel a watermelon from his rectum. His face went puce with effort. As the pressure built up, his eyes bulged and the veins swelled on his forehead. Several seconds passed, and a strange croaking came from his throat. I found it impossible to move. Then, all at once, a gush of smoke exploded violently from his mouth and he collapsed in a heap on the pavement.

'Christ, that was good!' He croaked. His face was pale and a thin trickle of blood came from his nose. 'Did you see it? Did you see the smoke coming out my ears?'

I thought about it. I wasn't sure. 'Yes,' I said, 'very good.'

As I walked away, a sound of violent retching came from behind; Dazel was throwing up in great grey plumes on the pavement. I dropped my cigarette, turned a corner and hurried back to Madame Turquoise's.

Savio was friendly, but I remained on my guard. The front door was unlocked, and I remembered the code for the inner door. I sneaked in. The Great Hall was busier and rowdier than before. Duran Duran was still playing. There was a bar that I hadn't noticed before, all chrome and pictures of American cars, with electric guitars on the wall. The bartender looked familiar with his denim jacket and lank, greasy hair. He noticed me and raised a finger. I nodded in reply. As I sidled round the edge of the room towards the turret, a drunken man blew smoke in my face, laughing like a demon. I ignored it and found my way up to my room. I was tremendously tired, and my lungs grated with smoke. But I was hungry. I sat on the toilet seat, unwrapped the cod and chips and ate half of it. I felt sick, and closed my eyes. I had been thrust blindly into my future, and I had no idea what was going to unfold.

PART II

Chapter Twenty-two

A single speck of light tumbles from the sun and streaks down to earth. It breaches the atmosphere and makes its way down through the clouds, past an international flight, past a flock of bedraggled gulls, down until it slips through the city air, and in through a window, and, magnified by the glass, bounces off the smooth pate of Grandpa Pagpa and illuminates the trepidated faces of the congregation facing him.

The room is filled with fragrant clouds of blue smoke. The crowd is standing back, apprehensive, as one body, pressing towards the edges of the Pet Shop Synagogue, away from the centre of the room, where Grandpa Pagpa is sitting in a trance. Even Rabbi Chod and Jogpo are subdued. Behind Pagpa, cast in his long shadow, is the mahogany cabinet containing the Tibetan Torah scrolls, surrounded by vibrantly painted *thanka*s. The room is dim, and shifts quietly in the light of the butter-lamps. Incense billows from every corner. Pagpa seems larger than life.

Grandpa Pagpa has his eyes tightly shut and is rocking to and fro, moaning softly. He is dressed in traditional finery, wearing several layers of multicoloured Tibetan brocade, complete with fringes, tassels and pointed shoes, giving his body a layered, patchwork effect. In the centre of his chest there is a domed mirror, in which can be seen a kaleidoscope of butter-lamps and onlookers' faces, a ghost world. Suddenly, Grandpa Pagpa raises himself; his eyes snap open and he stiffens. A cloud of incense smoke billows in front of his face and he smiles, vacantly, a smile I haven't seen before. He raises his hand; the sleeve flaps. This is the signal. Chod, Jogpo and two other men scuttle timidly to the shrine and heave a huge metal hat onto their shoulders, grunting under the weight. Chod gives instructions through gestures alone. They carry it over to Grandpa Pagpa and lower it carefully onto his head, strapping it tightly under his chin. They pull so hard on the straps that Pagpa's jaw is clamped shut and his face begins to crumple; the hat wobbles slightly. At a signal from Chod, they let go. This is the test. If the spirit is not in him, his neck will snap.

I am sitting on a windowsill beside my father, surveying the proceedings from a vantage point. This is where we always sit for Grandpa Pagpa's invocations. Brocade drapes hang either side of us, and we are partially masked from view by the rising incense smoke. We are raised above a sea of about fifty heads, all bowed nervously in the direction of the Oracle. Grandpa Pagpa's eyes roll in their sockets and he sways uncertainly on his seat.

All at once, there is a huge commotion as, without warning, Pagpa gets violently to his feet, his eyes flashing, the immense hat shaking but secured. Then he begins to dance. Loud whoops echo round the synagogue as Pagpa works himself up into a frenzy, thrashing his limbs and whirling round the room, onlookers scattering as he approaches them. Someone tries to move a table out the way, but too late; Pagpa dives into it and it overturns with a splintering crash. People begin to cry. Pagpa takes a few steps backwards and charges in the opposite direction, knocking a couple of people over, arms flailing. His whoops are becoming screams, and his face is bright red.

Pagpa prances round the shrine, letting out a gurgling shriek. He catches hold of somebody and shakes them violently, before letting them fall to the ground. Then he sits heavily back on his chair, gurgling and spitting, moaning, stamping and gnashing his teeth.

'Line up in front of the Oracle, quickly now, quickly,' announces Jogpo, his voice wavering, glancing apprehensively at Grandpa Pagpa, whose eyes are glaring from side to side. Drool covers his chin. Tentatively, a small cluster of people gather in front of him. Some are weeping, some are hiding their faces, some are staring around, shakily. No one wants to be first and they jostle one another. At length a teenage boy steps forward, a sick expression on his face. Pagpa fixes his eyes on him, screeches, and lunges, gripping his head between his hands. He plunges his face into the boy's neck, pulls it back and spits a gob of black liquid onto the ground. The boy sags in his hands, then straightens. Pagpa stalks back to his chair, roaring, and the boy staggers off. His illness has been purged.

Next a woman meekly approaches, two plaits stretching down her back. She holds a small pile of handwritten papers, and begins handing them one by one to Pagpa, who screams, grabs them out of her hand, and eats them. Eventually he shrieks and waves one piece of paper aloft; then he hands it back to her. She flinches, but takes it, reads it, smiles nervously, and melts back into the crowd. Her question is answered.

Rabbi Chod pushes his way over to the windowsill and helps my father and me down. My heart begins to pound. We join the people waiting for Grandpa Pagpa's attention.

Soon it is my father's turn. He approaches. Pagpa flicks his head up, bellows, and slaps him a resounding blow on the face. 'A blessing, a blessing,' murmur the crowd, as my father walks dazedly back to the windowsill.

At last, there is no one left but me. I pluck up my courage and step towards the Oracle, my legs weak and my blood pumping in my ears. I am aware of tears on my cheeks. Pagpa glares at me intently with fiery eyes, and beckons me closer. Reluctantly I comply until I am within range. An electric energy surrounds him. Without warning he grabs my head in his hands and pulls my face towards him, gazing at me intently. I try to shut my eyes but cannot. His grip is monstrous. My mind begins to spin. He releases me, grabs a *khatag* and wraps it tightly round my neck. I can barely breathe, and begin to croak. It is painful, and there is a commotion in the crowd. Just before I lose consciousness, Pagpa releases his grip on the scarf and throws his head back, laughing manically. I collapse onto the floor, pulling the *khatag* away from my neck.

'Beware, beware, beware!' he says in a high-pitched wail. 'Beware the circle of sky-blood! Beware the circle of sky-blood! You must beware! You must beware! Or you will die!' I scramble away and he gets to his feet, yelling and screaming horribly. His face gets redder and redder, and vivid veins appear in his eyes. He clutches his throat and spins once, twice, on his heels. Then he leaps high into the air and falls heavily to his knees. By this time he is gurgling and spitting, and looks as if he is going to explode. His tongue is hanging out, covered in flecks of blood. He gives one final, terrible shriek and keels over backwards, his metal hat hitting the floor with a sickening *thunk*! All at once, the crowd move away from him and Rabbi Chod, Jogpo and their two assistants rush over, trying to cut him loose from the heavy hat. The trance has ended. Pagpa is unconscious. The hat is rolled off and his limp body is carried into Chod's office and laid on the floor, his head supported by cushions. He is tiny now, and the extravagant outfit looks ridiculous. They gently remove his ceremonial clothes. An hour later he will be back to normal, his usual silent self, the most unlikely of oracles, and will be unable to recall even the slightest detail of the event. It will be as if nothing has happened.

The memory of Grandpa Pagpa's invocation was so vivid that I was beginning to see the *thanka*s appearing on the shadowy walls of the bathroom. The event had been reproduced exactly in my mind, realistic down to the smallest detail. It was as if it had actually taken place a second time. Gradually the ghostly *thanka*s faded, to be replaced by the smooth, blank walls of the bathroom. Dawn was breaking, casting streaks of light across the ceiling. I turned over in the bath and tried to get back to sleep.

Quite certainly. Nescafé. Definitely. I was a coffee-shop owner's son, I could recognise the smell anywhere. I hated Nescafé. With a massive effort I wrenched my eyes open and turned my aching head to the side. I had slept fitfully. I was swathed in blankets, in the bath. Morning light was humming in through the open window. Gradually, the details of my life returned, accompanied by footsteps increasing in volume. Madeline appeared in a skimpy turquoise outfit, stained all over with unsavoury colours. I tried to sit up. She was carrying two cups of coffee. She perched on the edge of the bathtub and handed one to me.

'You still sleeping, Mo? In the land of Nod? Aren't you going to work today?'

'I . . . Yes, I suppose I am. What time is it?'

'Seven thirty. In the morning, by the way.'

I shook my head woozily and tried to collect my thoughts. 'What are you doing in my room?' I asked.

'Just bringing you a coffee, what's up with that? Don't be so unfriendly. Mo, you look like shit. You look depressed. Are you depressed? Believe me, if you are, you're not the only one. Fuck!'

I took a sip of the coffee. It was so weak that I could barely taste it, but the heat began to wake me up. 'Thanks for the coffee, Madeline.'

'God, *Madeline* he calls me! You haven't called me that for years. What happened to old *Mad*? Don't get all formal on me, Mo, I know you can get all formal sometimes and it makes me want to puke.'

'Sorry. OK, then. Mad. Listen, thanks for bringing me here last night.' I realised, too late, that 'last night' would have been wiped from her memory, lost in the eternal tomorrow.

'Bringing you where? What . . . ?'

'Sorry Madel—er, Mad. Yes, Mad. Sorry. I think I'm still half in a dream. I haven't woken up properly yet.'

'Yeah, whatever.' She eyed me suspiciously and sipped her coffee. The sight of her holding a coffee cup to her mouth brought hundreds of memories into my mind at once, so many that I couldn't identify them. The absurd American accent kept fading out of her voice, only to return when she became defensive. 'Look, Mo, you've been behaving real strange recently. But I'm too exhausted to deal with it now. So give it a rest, yah?' She sipped her coffee again. The image of her and my father locked in embrace flickered into my mind, then dissolved. 'I haven't slept a wink all night, and I'm not in the mood,' she went on. 'Barry didn't even call, either. I almost had a nervous breakdown, I thought something had happened to him. Fuck. Turns out he was working late on his secret project, and couldn't get to the phone. Apparently.' She got up and closed the window, cutting out the sounds of the street. 'You'd better hurry up if you're going to get to work. Beth was right about you, you're naturally lazy.'

'Beth?'

'Hello? Mo? Anybody there?' she tapped her forehead, her nails leaving moist imprints on the skin. 'Are you sure you're not getting depressed? Suicidal? Eh? Like Beth? Fucking! Beth – remember? God, this is obscene. You're going downhill. Get it together, Mo. I'm too exhausted for all this. I've haven't slept a wink all night – for a change. Four turds last night, *four*! Fuck! And when I managed to get to bed, I couldn't sleep because of the noise next door. They were at it all night, the whole damn room was shaking. Weird noises, too. Jesus H. That woman's into all sorts of weird shit. The turds love it, though, believe me, fuck. I couldn't even bang on the wall – not allowed. You have to suffer in silence, you know? It's depressing. Depressing. That's the word. It's a really depressing life. I might as well just slit my wrists. Fuck!' She took another clumsy sip of coffee. 'Shit, I spilt it on your bed. Sorry. I'll go downstairs and put my head in the oven, shall I?' She didn't move. There was a pause. 'I hope that last turd isn't going to complain to Mama about me. I wouldn't . . . He wanted me to do some weird shit, you know? Should have sent him next door. Fucking. I hope he doesn't complain. Mama would go mental. It makes you want to batter yourself to death. Or stick your head in a mincer. All hell would break loose.' We gulped simultaneously. Every mouthful seemed to bring me more down to earth.

'Mama sounds like a bit of a tyrant,' I said.

'No shit. And since when have you called her Mama? You sound like one of us girls.'

'What am I supposed to call her, then?'

'Oh, come on, Mo, you've been here long enough. Get it together. Call her the same as you always do, as all the turds do. You're being really weird lately. What's up with you? You've been really distant. Just don't go and kill yourself, OK?' I nodded. 'Seriously. You've got loads to live for. You're lucky. Mama likes you. Fuck! And if Mama likes you, God likes you. You're, like, her favourite, I reckon, even though she can't work you out.'

'I'm sure she doesn't like me that much.'

'Oh, don't talk about it. I don't want to think about it, it makes me want to choke in my own vomit.' She put her mug down on the floor, shifted closer and looked at me intently. I held my coffee defensively to my chest. It felt sore with heat. 'Mo, I'm going to tell you a secret. Don't tell anyone else, OK?' I nodded. 'I'm getting out of here. Soon. I'm going to escape – with Barry. He's my rock. As soon as he gets the cash together. He's got plans, Barry has. He's not just a barman. He's working on a secret project.' She leant conspiratorially forward. 'You want to know what his secret project is? I'll tell you, only you mustn't tell a soul, or I'll top myself, I swear. He's' – she leant even closer – 'setting up a business. He's just launched it. He gave me a snap to prove it. Have a look . . . Here.' She fumbled in her bosom, pulled out a crumpled photo and handed it to me. In the centre was a large vending machine. On the front was the slogan 'Bazza's Disposable Underwear. All Sizes and Styles. Quick, Slick, and Does the Trick. Only £2.' Standing in the foreground, proudly holding a pair of semi-transparent Y-fronts to the sky, was the androgynous Denim Man. Instantly, another piece of Madeline's puzzle clicked into place. A nauseous feeling welled in my gut. I returned the photo and looked away. 'Of course,' continued Madeline, replacing it in her bra, 'as you know, Barry is a rock but he's not perfect. He can be weird sometimes. That's the depressing thing. But at least we're getting out of this place.' I drained my coffee. She took the empty mugs and got up. 'Look, Mo, go to work. Don't just sit around. I'm going to bed. I'm exhausted, I didn't sleep a wink last night. *Four* turds, I tell you. I'll see you later, if I don't croak in my sleep.' She left the room and tottered down the stairs. I breathed a sigh of relief.

I got out of the bath. My room looked very different by day. Without the light on there were no red shadows. The daylight made everything seem more real, more organic. I became aware of the sounds of the building; the groaning pipes syncopating with banging doors and voices. Everything sounded as if it was at once mocking and being mocked, and everything sounded like one body.

The plate factory seemed far away. I had no idea how to get there. I left the house and found a tube station. You can always get to your destination on the tube, even if you have no idea where you are. You just have to follow the lines, join up the dots. By the time I got to the plate factory and punched in, I was only ten minutes late. I squeaked out onto the factory floor with my bagged-up feet and hair. An image of my parents came into my mind – I cut it off. I took up my position at the end of the conveyor belt and nodded cordially to the First Spotter. He winked a greeting – a bizarre sight on such an asymmetrical face – and turned back to the procession of plates. I wondered how many peanuts would come my way that morning. As was my habit, I set myself an incentive, Tibetan-style. If I spotted fewer than three peanuts, that would be inauspicious and I would die young and impoverished. Four or more would be auspicious: a long and prosperous life would be in store. I adopted my familiar plate-spotting pose. The working day began.

I had only a few fragments of information about my new

life, but evidently, so far as everyone else was concerned, I'd been there a while. So I had no choice but to reconstruct the situation from the shreds of evidence I had picked up. As the plates trundled somnambulantly by, I examined the clues. Madeline, or rather Mad, had been behaving as if we were good friends, so a relationship must have developed. Or be about to develop. Was that a good thing? Before I knew it, my mind had begun to wander. A snatch of conversation came into my head that I had overheard in Madame Turquoise's; two drunken men, referring to everything as 'shit'. Good shit, bad shit, all that shit, so-and-so and shit, and so on and so on. It struck me that everything can be seen in terms of shit. Life is a continuous process of substitution of old shit for new shit, pretending that the new shit isn't really as shit as the old shit. But even new shit is still shit. There's no point in getting excited about it. A peanut trundled past, and I bagged it. A good sign – only two more to go. It was tiresome thinking in this way, trying to focus, trying to piece the clues together. But I suppose it was no more confusing than usual, in the last analysis. No one knows what's coming for them. If truth be told, they're always just reading the clues. I tried – in vain – to collect my thoughts.

I continued my scattered musing all morning, and as a result I must have missed quite a few peanuts. By the end of my shift, there were only two in the bag, damning me to an inauspicious pauper's death. Rabbi Chod would have advised me to make an offering to the spirits, to avert the bad luck. I unbagged my hair and feet, punched out, left the factory and headed to Madame Turquoise's – headed home.

It took me just over an hour to get there. Auspiciously enough, I didn't get lost. When I arrived, Savio was slobbering and affable. I patted his matted head, gingerly. Then I released all the locks and stepped inside.

Even though it was early afternoon, the house had a thick, heavy atmosphere. The working night was yet to begin. So far as I could tell, everyone was asleep. The place was deserted. The sunlight took on an aquatic hue as it filtered through the turquoise paint on the windows. I was alone – the only one reflected in the mirrors. There were thousands of me. But I was not alone; as I crossed the room towards the turret door, I heard a chink of a glass and turned round. A scrawny female figure unfolded from the shadows in a corner, blowing smoke into the air. She was almost obscured by a coffee table laden with great shimmering piles of money. Then the gloom withdrew to reveal a shrivelled lady in a black sequinned dress, which hung uneasily on her bony frame. She was wearing jewellery like armour, and had heavy make-up on. Her lips were painted dark blue. A gin and tonic glowed potently in her hand.

'Mo,' she began, 'I was hoping you would come.' Tension underlay her friendliness. Her voice sounded taut, as if un-accustomed to speaking affectionately. 'I want to speak to you. I want to . . . ask you something.' She tipped her head backwards and drained her glass, then banged it down sternly on the table. She seemed nervous. Adjusting her glimmering tiara, she squeezed her lips into a tight indigo smile. 'Mo, Mo, Mo. I'm in charge, but . . . Have you ever . . . Do you feel . . . Are you lonely, Mo?' Her lined face crumpled as the blue smile grew. At the edges, her lips were quivering. She looked rather drunk.

'I'm not sure what you mean, Mama,' I replied, cautiously.

She broke into a dry laugh. 'Mama! He calls me Mama!' She coughed, and rubbed the back of her neck uneasily. 'I like it, I like it.'

'What should I call you, then?'

'Yeah, Mo, whatever. Want a drink?'

'No, I'm . . . I'm fine, thanks.' My voice sounded flat and ingenuous.

'Mo, I want to talk. My husband died fifteen years ago, you know?' she said, supporting herself on the table. 'Since then, I've been . . . alone. Alone. I've been working too hard, maybe.'

'Well, I—'

'Everyone sees me as an iron lady, everyone's scared. No

one understands me. I can never open up. But you . . .' Tears sprang into her eyes.

'Er . . . I . . .'

'I can't be alone any more, Mo. I don't want to die alone. I can't take it any more. I need a man in my life. I am . . . dead.' She stopped, swayed on her feet, and rubbed her eyes. 'My husband was killed with a knife. It was stuck into him, six times, like that. But I wish it had been me. There is no one on the face of the earth who cares for me any more. I'd have preferred the knife. I wish I was dead. I am dead.'

'I think you've had too much to drink,' I said. I felt uneasy. I couldn't bear the sight of this hollow-eyed reflection of myself. I felt I should stay with her and comfort her, but I was overcome by the desire to get away. She'll be all right, I told myself. She just needs to sober up. I made my excuses and hurried towards my turret, leaving her standing in the Great Hall alone.

Once in my room I spent half an hour on the toilet as my excrement streaked into the bowl like toxic waste. For a while, I listened to the muttering of the house. I swallowed two paracetamols, sipping from a couple of bottles of Yakult I had bought on the way. The Yakult turned my stomach again and I staggered over to the bath and lay down, gasping. Everything began to spin.

There was a turquoise square of light on the wall opposite the window. I watched it peel itself from the wallpaper and drift over the bath. It expanded until it was about five foot long, and developed a bulge at one end. Limbs separated and details appeared. I found myself looking at a luminous figure with large emerald eyes and a prominent, downturned mouth. Its fingers and toes took the form of long fringes, floating gently on the air currents. I gazed up at it for a while, and it gazed down at me. Its eyes were full of curiosity and sadness. Then it faded back into the square patch of light on the wall. Little by little, it disappeared.

The afternoon stretched before me. I wasn't sure how to fill it. After I'd lain in the bath for a while, the dizziness subsided and I felt capable of getting up. I was curious about the house; all I had seen of it was my turret room and the cavernous hall downstairs. Tentatively, I made my way downstairs and was relieved to find Mama, or whatever she was called, nowhere present. I crossed the room and pushed the double doors through which I had seen many men and women pass. They scraped open to reveal a dingy flight of stairs. I crept up the stairs and entered a maze of corridors flanked by rows of doors. On each door was a showbiz-style name-star. I could just make out the names in the gloom: 'Santa Maria', 'Sexy Suzie', 'Big Fun Sally', 'Busty Bridget'. I made my way up another flight of stairs and entered an identical beehive of corridors. They were all poorly lit, and as I approached the heart of the building a faint smell of vomit developed and increased. 'Striptease Sandy', 'D-D Debbie', 'Erotic Emily', 'Lapdance Linda'. The faint sound of snoring could be heard from many of the rooms, making it feel like late at night, even though it was early afternoon. Occasionally, I found myself illuminated by beams of turquoise light streaking across the corridor from the painted-over windows. I passed an open door with a sign saying 'Common Room', and looked in. Three or four moribund figures sat listlessly in the corners, smoking and eating sandwiches. One was painting her toenails. They didn't look up and I walked on.

Eventually I passed what I took to be Madeline's room; it bore the name 'Mad-for-it Mad'. I peered through the keyhole but couldn't see anything. Her neighbour was 'S&M Seraph'. No wonder Mad-for-it Mad was kept awake at night, with S&M Seraph for a neighbour.

The next door was ajar. This surprised me, as all the other doors were shut tight, apart from the Common Room's. The name on this door was long: 'Bouncing Beth The Psychic Witch Bitch'. Beth . . . I peered gingerly in. It was dark inside and it took my eyes a while to adjust. The room materialised. Something was uncannily familiar about it. Curiosity overcame me and I slipped in.

It was like entering an Egyptian pyramid. There was dust everywhere and it was cluttered almost beyond belief. Great grubby sheets of multicoloured Indian materials, covered in embroidery and exotic designs, were draped over every surface and wound round every object. Everywhere were incense holders, as well as candles, crystal balls, skulls, statues of Hindu gods and goddesses; the whole thing was like a New Age Oxfam. A stuffed alligator presided over the grimy bed. I glanced around, trying to pinpoint what it was that felt so familiar. Suddenly, amid the thick, stagnant air I smelt something fresh. Perfume. I followed it across the room. It led to a vase of fresh flowers. They were on a table, along with multicoloured candles and handwritten notes. In the centre of the table was a photograph of a deep-eyed, red-haired girl, staring at the camera as if about to speak. Something was written in the dust on the picture frame; I peered at it, trying to make it out. It read, 'The end of birth is death.' I wiped it clean. A dim glow appeared in the space above me and I looked up. The turquoise figure was hovering sadly in the air again. It gazed at me silently with tragic emerald eyes, its fringed fingers and toes waving gently to and fro. I heard the door open and footsteps entered the room. Instantly, the turquoise figure vanished. I stood up.

Madeline emerged from the darkness. 'I thought I heard someone in here. Mo? Is that you?'

'Yes. I was just, er . . . well, you know.'

'Yeah, Mo, I know. Believe me, I know. I come here a lot. It's depressing. I miss her, too. Even now.' She came over and sat on the floor in front of the picture. She seemed to expect me to sit beside her. I lowered myself to the dirty carpet. 'I miss her so much, you know?' she went on. 'These days I'm a right insomniac, I can never sleep, because all the time I'm thinking about her. Fuck. Why did she have to do it, Mo, why? She was so sweet, she never harmed anyone but herself. You must miss her, too.'

'Well . . . not . . .' I paused, and thought better of it. 'Yes, of course I do,' I said.

'It's good to hear you say that,' she replied. 'You're always so cold about these things. It almost gives me an epileptic fit, you're so cold. Are you ready to talk about it now? You've been bottling it up for so long, it's depressing.'

I didn't know what to say. 'Well . . .'

'Come on, it'll be good for you to get it off your chest. I've spoken to you enough about her, haven't I? I've confided in you? Come on. It'll help. What's your favourite memory of her?'

'Well, I . . . I couldn't rightly say. What about you?'

'Me? Turning it round, Mo, as usual? Ha ha. Oh, all right, if it'll make you feel better. I think my best memory of Beth is' – she rolled her eyes – 'the time when she refused to fuck that weird religious turd. Do you remember? She said he had bad karma. Bad karma! It was so funny, you know, it was just so Beth. Mama almost hit the roof. But Beth wouldn't do it. She just refused, point blank. The funniest part, though, was that the turd was actually a bit of a dish. Relatively speaking, of course. But for some reason Beth reckoned his karma was worse than the old bald turds she used to fuck!' She giggled weakly. 'So, come on, then, I've told you my best memory. What's yours?'

'OK, let me see. Beth. Right. Well, I suppose I just . . . treasure my memory of Beth in general. Herself. Her personality.'

'What do you mean?'

'You know . . . how she . . . how she was,' I said, lamely. I was fighting a losing battle.

'Go on,' she prompted.

'Look, Mad, I'm sorry but I can't do this right now. It's just too . . . difficult for me.' I put on a bit of an American accent to try and evoke some sympathy from her. She rubbed her face in her hands. I got up and walked towards the door.

'That's OK,' she called after me. 'Some other time, yah?' The back of the door was covered in tribute messages to Beth, scrawled in all sorts of colours and styles. I pushed it open and headed off down the corridor. As I walked away, I heard Madeline muttering to herself.

It took me a while to find my way back through the maze of corridors. At long last, I pushed my way through the double doors and entered the Great Hall. I froze. Mama was standing by the stairs to my turret, cradling another glass of alcohol. It was impossible not to be seen, especially as I was multiplied infinite times in the mirrors. She saw me and broke into a wide, anxious smile.

'Mo! You've come back! Can we talk?' Her voice was desperate.

'Thanks, Mama, but I've . . . got things to do.' I slipped past her and climbed the turret stairs.

She came after me. 'Why have you started calling me Mama? Call me the Turk, as usual, like all the other men, OK?' she said. 'Do you know what it is to be lonely? It's like acid inside, eating me away. It's killing me, Mo. I'm dying. I'm in need . . . I'm empty inside. I'm tired. I need someone to save me.'

We reached the top of the stairs. I stood in the doorway, unsure of what to do. She looked at me with moist, sad eyes. There was a moment of silence.

'I think . . . I think I might be in love with you, Mo,' she whispered.

'Turk,' I said, 'I'm not sure if . . .'

She put up her hand and stroked my face gently. Her bracelets jangled. Although she was unattracive, lust stirred deep inside me, and I almost moved towards her. But I couldn't. I was imprisoned within a bell jar, torn in half, repelled and attracted at once. I wanted to grab her and caress her frail body, but that very thought was filled with pain. I loved her and hated her; in the same moment I felt compassion and fear, resentment and lust. I longed for intimacy, and knew I could never have it.

'I'm sorry,' I said, my throat dry. 'You make me . . . but I can't. I can't do this.'

The Turk pulled her hand away and clutched her fists to

her chest. 'What?' she said, her voice rising, 'Do I disgust you? Am I just an old hag to you? Is that it?'

'No, it's not that.'

'What is it, then?'

'You make me . . . I'm sick.'

'I make you sick? What? Well, sorry to be so foul!' She turned to walk down the stairs, then paused and turned. Without warning, she slapped me a stinging blow across the face. I recoiled in shock, throwing my hands up for protection, and one of my fingers caught in her bracelets. For a moment, our limbs tangled. Then she lost her footing and tumbled backwards, thudding painfully down the stairs until she came to rest on the landing. I rushed down to her. Her head was bleeding, and she was in shock. I bent over her, but she pushed me firmly away.

'Get the fuck out of my house,' she said in a low, threatening voice. 'If I see you again, I'll have you killed.' She got shakily to her feet and descended the spiral staircase, crying. I didn't follow her.

Silence returned. I sat on the landing in the shadows for a long while, not knowing what to do, adrenalin pumping. I wished that the turquoise figure would appear again – there was something comforting about its presence. But it was nowhere to be seen. I had to leave the house as soon as I could. But where could I go? I got up and went into my room. My reflection appeared in the mirror and I cursed my illness. I would have done it, I told myself, if I wasn't sick. I would have gone through with it. I blinked, but my eyes stared unblinkingly back at me. I turned away from the mirror and got back into the bath. Tomorrow, I thought, it would all be OK. Today would fade into the future as soon as the sun came up. The Turk, as she was apparently called, would be back on good terms with me again. There was no need to leave – I was safe. When time reverses, the danger will pass. I just had to wait for the dawn. I lay back and breathed easily again, a lonely Tibetan cold in a bath.

214

Chapter Twenty-three

I settled into the Turk's, and tried to establish some form of life for myself. As the months passed, my work routine became stable and I found ways to take the loneliness out of the empty hours. My favourite places were museums, where I wandered for hours on end, enjoying the sensation of voyeurism and anonymity. At home I read every book I could find about Tibet. While my days were filled with an incessant flow of plates on the conveyor belt, my evenings were spent turning over page after page of dramatic mountain photos, and studying information about youth hostels and monasteries. I cut out the most evocative pages and kept them in a large envelope by the bath. When I felt homesick I allowed myself to look through them, and I usually felt better after that. I bought all my books at charity shops; the faded covers and finger-softened edges made me feel connected to the previous readers, as if our emotions were shared.

On the whole, I kept myself to myself. My only friends were Savio the dog and Madeline, who was on startlingly good terms with me. She would barge into my room as if it were her own, and want to chat for hours on end. Initially I found it invasive. After all, I didn't know her all that well; she had known me for longer than I had known her. From her point of view I was a good friend, but from my point of view she was a stranger. But I got used to it. My life became simple and predictable, and although this was tedious it made me feel grounded. I allowed myself to be dictated by routine, and the pain began to fade.

One April evening, in the '80s, when I had been at the Turk's for many months, long enough to feel like the last

Tibetan on earth, I came home one afternoon to find Madeline waiting for me at the bottom of the stairs to my turret, leaning against the wall, drinking a cup of something. I nodded to her.

'I've been waiting for you, Mo. Where've you been? Want a cuppa?'

'What, tea? No thanks, Mad, I can't stand English tea. Too watery. Too dry.'

'What do you mean, watery and dry? You're mental, Mo. How can something be watery and dry at the same time? Water's wet, isn't it?'

'Well, wine can be dry, can't it? Dry wine?'

'So what's wrong with wine, then? I actually happen to like wine, if you don't mind.'

'Mad, there's nothing wrong with wine, it's just that you can have dry wine, you know? Like tea.'

'So tea's no good either, then? You're a really depressing person, Mo. I'll just go and hang myself.'

'No, nothing's wrong with either of them, I just don't—'

'All right, all right, let's drop it, OK?'

I made my way up to my room, and Madeline followed. I would have preferred some privacy, but she gave me no choice.

'Mo,' she said as I was taking off my coat, 'I've had enough of being a performing monkey. I want to be free.' She sat on the edge of the sink. Her skirt was short, and her knickers, like a flag, were exposed. She began to swing her legs.

'I've got escape plans, you know,' she went on, 'and an accomplice. But I can't tell you about it. I promised. It's a secret.'

'OK,' I replied.

'Well, I might tell you – if you really want to know.'

'No, thanks, Mad. You keep it to yourself.'

There was a silence and she drank some more tea. I was getting hungry.

'Do you think there's any such thing as freedom?' she asked suddenly.

'What do you mean?'

'Freedom. Do you think it's possible? I mean you're free when you're born, right? But when I look around, everyone's in chains. Especially me. It's fucking depressing, and I want to die. Or at least I want to be free.' She laughed nervously.

I found her irritating. 'Mad, we're not born free. We're born in chains. We pop out the womb, and our sentence begins,' I replied. I didn't feel like talking.

'But freedom is possible, right?'

'No, Mad. It isn't.'

There was another, longer pause, and she looked at me searchingly, lost for words. 'But I'm going to be free,' she said at last.

'No you're not. You're not going to be free. No one ever can be free. The Tibetans aren't free. Look at the state I'm in. I haven't spoken my own language for months, not since I moved here, in fact. I'm not even free to like English tea – I only like Tibetan tea, which in case you don't know is thick and salty and fills you up for hours. If you tried it, you wouldn't like it – you're English, you're not free to like Tibetan tea. Even if you escaped from here, you still wouldn't be free. Believe me. Life's controlling you. And one day it'll kill you.' She looked at me blankly for a few moments, her mug dangling from her fingers. 'And when you die, you won't be free, either,' I heard myself say. 'All death will bring you is a new prison. So I don't know where you got the idea of freedom from, but it's nothing but a stupid fantasy. Freedom is impossible even to imagine. I know this, Mad, believe me.'

Her lip trembling, she got down from the sink and left the room without a word. I picked up a book and tried to read the tension away.

The next day, I felt guilty about what I had said, but there was nothing I could do about it; for Madeline it hadn't happened yet. I decided to make myself some Tibetan tea, as a treat, as a comfort. I bought the ingredients at Waitrose: Lapsang Souchong, butter, salt, and so on. I saved money because the butter, being almost out of date, had been reduced in price. I borrowed a small kettle from Madeline and set to work. I mixed and folded all the ingredients in a large copper pot, using a huge salad fork, trying to remember how my mother did it. The mixing was strenuous on my shoulder muscles but I managed, taking frequent breaks. Eventually, through a process of trial and error, a familiar smell began to fill the bathroom. When everything was ready, I poured myself a mug of the precious liquid and took a sip. Surprisingly enough, the taste was almost exactly right. I sat on the tiles and drank, luxuriously, facing the toilet. The toilet was no longer a toilet; I had made it into a shrine. The taste of the tea and the presence of the toilet-shrine were comforting.

The shrine looked quite authentic, given the circumstances. Not having the right materials, I had improvised. First I had covered it with a cloth I found in a skip, then I had arranged a few small statues I found in a charity shop. It didn't matter who the statues were of, so long as they created the right kind of feeling. I had a metal image of the Hindu god Ganesh, a ceramic figurine of the Virgin Mary, and, between these two, a small wooden duck. I didn't have an image of Rabbi Chod to put on the shrine, but in a way I was glad of that. I used eggcups to hold the offerings of water and yoghurt, and the finished effect was striking – almost as good as a real shrine, if I didn't scrutinise it too closely. I sipped my tea, savouring its taste.

I am in my den behind the sofa, crouching down, secretly. Today I am the famous Tibetan warrior-king Songtsen Gampo. I have a cardboard sword. I have one of my father's belts slung across me. My socks are pulled up to my knees, and my trousers are tucked in. I have one of my mother's scarves tied round my waist. I have a shield made out of a cardboard box. All I need is a helmet. Songtsen Gampo always has a tall helmet of solid gold, decorated with precious stones. I need to get one from somewhere, then my powers will be complete. I sneak out of my den and go in search of a helmet, my sword drawn to defend myself against wild rhinos. Stealthily, I enter the kitchen. My parents are sitting at the table. My father is drinking coffee and pawing through the local paper. My mother is absently munching toast and combing her hair. No threat there. But no helmet, either. Sword at the ready, I slip under the shadowy table and enter the forest, weaving my way between the ancient oaks that grow there, careful not to touch the magic golden leaves that can paralyse you for life. There are thousands of butter-flies everywhere I look, like a carpet. I take care not to disturb them. I make it through the forest unscathed and sneak out from under the table, sword first. My parents do not notice me. I remain on guard. My father sneezes and I jump back into the forest; when all is quiet, I slip across the kitchen, trying not to let my feet squeak on the lino. I creep down a couple of concrete steps and into the toilet.

I survey the area. On the ground is my plastic potty, golden and encrusted with precious stones. It has a small horn which sticks up between your legs when you sit down. This, I say to myself, is a perfect helmet. I will put it upside down on my head, and the horn will protect my nose, like a real warrior. I look around. All clear. I lay my sword on the radi-ator. It slips down the back. I retrieve it and balance it against the wall. Then I take the potty in my hands, turn it so that the horn section is at the front, lift it up and place it on my head.

It is an unpleasant shock. Instantly, I am drenched in urine. I begin to howl, loudly. I am so shocked that I can't move, I am paralysed, frozen to the spot. I am soaked and stinking. I need my parents to rescue me, to comfort me, to protect me. They burst into the toilet and I raise my arms to receive their sympathy.

But they laugh. They laugh so hard that they have to support themselves on the doorframe. My father's moustache vibrates, he jumps up and down like a piston, and my mother clutches her stomach and swings her plait from side to side. I wail even louder. I have been betrayed. I totter towards them for reassurance. They will not even allow me to touch them. I remove my helmet, go upstairs to the bathroom, get undressed and have a bath, all by myself. It takes me a long time to do this because I am not used to having to do it on my own. In the end I manage it and I am washed clean. When I get out of the bath, my mother wraps me up in a huge yellow towel and carries me into my room. Then she puts me into my pyjamas and gives me a big hug. But now I want her to go away. The damage has been done. I stay in my room, by myself, for a long time.

I finished the tea, having drunk a little too much, and went to bed. It was cold. I had been away from my parents so long that I wasn't even sure if they still existed. I felt mildly nauseous, and hoped the butter wasn't off. I tried to read, but couldn't. Little by little, my consciousness dissolved.

Suddenly, I found myself standing up, engulfed in a tangible blackness. Pure darkness was all around me, above me, below me, within me. I had no idea where I was, or how I'd got there. I held my hand in front of my face and could discern not the slightest movement. I began to doubt that I even had a hand. I felt my eyes to make sure they were open. They were. I thought I had gone blind. Then I thought I'd died. The eternal blackness – how naïve! The darkness was solid, opaque, oppressive. The moan filling my brain dropped out of my mouth, a strangled squawk, onto the floor.

A chink of light appeared, a tiny slit, which slowly widened into a dazzling rectangle of luminosity. A figure appeared in the light and called me by my name. Then it called me again and approached me. I braced myself for a journey across the Styx, into whatever lay beyond. The next life. Then the figure raised her left hand and a flame appeared, illuminating the hallway. Madeline stood in front of me, surprise on her wan face, a cigarette lighter in her hand. Dim rows of doors appeared in the flickering light.

I had been granted a new lease of life. I had been reborn, or born again, but only into the life I'd died from. I felt like a new person. The fact that I had sleepwalked didn't occur to me till later. As the details of my life came back to me, I noticed how awful Madeline looked. I could see that even in this light.

'Mo, Mo, Mo, where have you been?' she whispered, walking slowly towards me. She buried her head on my shoulder and began to sob wordlessly, holding the trembling flame above us.

'Don't cry, Mad,' I said, still disoriented. 'It can't be that bad.'

'Beth's dead, Mo, in case you didn't know,' she retorted. 'I'm not sure how much worse it could get.' She resumed her sobbing, harder this time, and I wished I could have thought of something to say. Eventually her tears subsided and she asked me to sleep with her for comfort. The ethereal turquoise figure appeared behind her, wrapping fringe-fingers round her waist in sympathy. She couldn't feel it. I said she could sleep on the floor of my room if she liked. She turned abruptly and disappeared down the hall. Darkness enfolded me once more and I picked my way back to my turret.

The turquoise being had begun to hover above my head much of the time, and I had become quite used to it. Its presence was comforting; it provided the kind of silent companionship that I had not experienced since the demise of Plastic Bag. I began to refer to it as 'Yakult', which I had been drinking when it first appeared. I had begun to see other things, too; dull lights around people's heads, figures crouching behind their backs, dark patches lurking in corners. These seemed to supplement life, like discovering a secret species among one's own. Every night, when I went to bed, Yakult watched me from above until I melted into oblivion.

When I awoke at dawn, Yakult was gone. Only a few flecks of light remained in the air. I remembered instantly that it was the day before – the day on which Beth was going to die. I went to work as usual, and spotted a resounding six

221

peanuts. Afterwards, I went to the British Museum to visit my favourite exhibit, a brass statue of the ferocious Buddhist deity Mahakala. It was on a low shelf and I had to squat to get a good view. It didn't matter how often I looked at that statue, it always had the same effect: as soon as I saw it I was surrounded by a heavy, thick energy, protective yet frightening, like hot snow. The statue had billowing, flaming hair, terrifying spherical eyes and a fanged snarl. It was grossly overweight and was caught frozen in a violent dance, clawing the air and screaming. It made me feel at once scared, secure and Tibetan; it made me feel at home. It gave me hope.

I bought a tuna sandwich and a couple of bottles of Yakult and walked around Bloomsbury, browsing through second-hand bookshops. The end of the winter had arrived, and I was sad to see the back of spring. The blossoms had been sinking back into the trees daily, and now the branches were almost bare. I didn't want to go back to the Turk's and confront the aftermath of Beth's death. Tomorrow it would be over, anyway.

I bought a book called *Tibetan Signs and Symbols*, a dog-eared copy with an ugly red cover and a coffee stain along the spine. I had it already, but this was an earlier edition. I wanted to find somewhere to sit and read, but nowhere seemed right. For a long time I was mesmerised by the beat of my footfalls. The world rolled up like a ball of plasticine.

It was rush hour. The roads gradually became busier and busier, and the traffic slowed to a crawl. Before I knew it I was walking faster than the cars, and then the traffic came to a complete standstill. The air was dense with petrol fumes. Horns bayed like hounds. I passed row after gleaming row of cars, all inert and buzzing with frustration. Drivers sat corpse-like in their seats. Everyone looked troubled. The pavements became fuller; the pedestrians multiplied, as if by magic. Soon I couldn't walk any further because of the hordes. The road was gridlocked and everywhere there were crowds, coughing on exhaust and glaring impatiently.

I clambered onto a bin, supported myself on a lamp-post

and peered over the heads of the people in front. A line of plastic police-tape blocked off the road, and policemen stood like ravens, holding back the crowd. The streets beyond were empty. Everyone was staring at a particular concrete building. The building was deserted apart from three figures on the roof. In the centre stood a girl, her head haloed by a fluttering cloud of reddish hair. I could just make out that she had clambered over the railings and was leaning precariously forward. Behind, at a cautious distance, were two figures on the other side of the railings. They were bent slightly towards her, as if trying to smell her fear. I wondered what they could be saying. So far as I could tell, the girl was oblivious of them, gently rocking back and forth.

The crowd's mood was volatile. Car horns wailed, and people muttered and shouted at each other.

'Bloody selfish cow,' snarled a man, clutching a newspaper to his chest with the headline 'TRAGEDY IN CHERNOBYL'. 'Holding everyone up like this.'

'Too right,' said someone else. 'We've all got homes to go to, you know. Things to do. Bitch.' More and more voices joined the clamour. The man with the newspaper threw his head back and yelled at the lonely figure on the bridge, punching his fist in the air.

'Just bloody well do it! Get it over with! We've all got homes to get to! It's been a long day! You selfish fucking cow!' he screamed. His wet ears trembled with rage. Car horns blared like a church organ. Other voices joined in, sending a volley of shouts up to the bridge. 'Do it! Do it! Get on with it! Get it over with! Jump!'

The girl raised her head, scanning the crowd. For a moment, the chanting was subdued. Then she rocked forwards and let go of the railings. The two figures behind clutched vainly at the air. She entered space, revolving gently and waving her arms. The people in front obscured my vision – I didn't see her hit the ground. A weak cheer arose from a few of the harder onlookers, and the man with the newspaper laughed nervously. Then all was silent. Somebody began to cry. We waited for a long time. An ambulance came into view, picking its way painstakingly along the pavement. The ravens raised the tape to let it through. After a while it re-emerged. Then the barriers were lifted and with a huge cheer of relief the commuters were allowed to continue their journey.

I found a pub in Victoria and sat in a fuggy corner, trying to absorb myself into my book with the aid of a pint of bitter. But I couldn't focus. I felt as if I had been in league with the commuters. The fact that Beth would be alive the following day gave me some comfort, but I couldn't help imagining the scenes of mourning that would take place that evening. I drained my glass, and began to feel giddy. The pub was unbearably stuffy. I left, and walked in the general direction of home. The sky was darkening, and home was a long way off. At some point, I would need to catch a bus or a tube. Smoke and fumes clung to my clothes, reminding me of Dazel. I looked around for a park or open space to get away from the oppressive swell of the traffic. I passed the ostentatiously lit Marble Arch, surrounded by a corona of McDonald's and newsagents and homeless people with plastic bags and bottles of cider. I realised I had left my book at the pub. I couldn't be bothered to walk all the way back. I decided to cut across Hyde Park, and climbed over the railings into Speakers' Corner.

It was deserted. The rain bounced off the concrete like salt, and the grass beyond was barely visible in the growing darkness. A few placards had been left propped against trees and railings, and there was even an abandoned soapbox. I stopped and gazed at it, wondering why it had been left behind. Maybe the speaker had been hauled away and crucified on the London Eye, forever rotating, mouth lolling with each oscillation. But the London Eye hadn't been built yet, and wouldn't be built for many years. Nevertheless, it would have been wiser not to have spoken in the first place.

I wasn't the sort of person to get up and tell the world what I thought of it; I wasn't even sure what I thought. But if I did, and if there was a crowd here, and if they asked me to get onto a soapbox and tell the world what I thought of it, I'd talk about how skeletons are walking all the roads of London, sitting on all the sofas, in all the rooms of the world. I would tell them how the flesh is dug up and peeled back on the bones, and the corpse is set off once more to fumble around until, one day, it is gone. Moments fade even before they have occurred, they disappear dream-like into the eternal yesterday, the eternal tomorrow. I would tell them that everything is nothing, everything is empty. I looked down and saw that I was standing on the soapbox, my hands gesticulating in the stinging air. My voice was hoarse. I had been ranting. The concrete was no longer deserted: an old woman with prominent bones was standing in front of me, cocking her head to listen, her Scottish terrier licking its balls. No, she was adjusting her hearing-aid and gazing, half-blind, into space. She didn't know I was there. I was about to go on when I looked down again and saw my feet on the concrete. I hadn't moved; my hands were by my sides; there was no sound in my throat, my voice was not hoarse; there was no old woman, no Scottish terrier licking its balls. I was gazing at the soapbox. It had begun to drizzle; the rain was bouncing off the concrete like salt, and the grass beyond was invisible in the darkness. I wasn't the sort of person to get up and tell the world what I thought of it; I wasn't even sure what I thought. But if I did, and if there was a crowd here, and if they asked me to get onto a soapbox and tell the world what I thought of it, I'd say nothing. I'd never mix my own projections into the pot. If I had my way, I'd never leave my room, I'd never be lured into pretending that meaning exists, because every extra word adds to the confusion, and fate is deadly and inexorable. I stopped my thoughts, blinked and looked again. The soapbox had disappeared. The rain got heavier. My hair became a second skin and water blurred my eyes. I walked through the railings and into the park, to get escape the sound of bones grinding.

I walked across the wet grass, my feet sinking into it.

Skeletons were multiplying all around me. I stopped and took some paracetamol, swallowing the pills without water. Then I carried on. The skeletons faded and I rejoined the collective insanity. I crossed the park and stepped once again onto the street. I felt it was late. I brushed past pleading hands at the tube entrance, joined the dots and sat, jolting in a carriage. I think it was the last tube of the night.

Eventually I was on the street again. The rain had stopped and I was in familiar territory. My body was heavy as I walked the last few streets to the Turk's, hoping to slip in unnoticed. I passed the jagged wall and the building came into view. All the windows were dark. It was strangely silent. Unusually, Savio growled at me. I entered nervously. The Great Hall was dark and deserted. It was a relief that there were no mourners to deal with. I felt my way round the edge of the room, making for my turret. The air was thick with spent emotion, and I could see bright flecks of anguish still spiralling about the ceiling.

I climbed the stairs, took my sodden clothes off and cocooned myself in blankets. I was wet and shivering. I wanted to read, but my mind was too scattered and exhausted. The toilet-shrine was just visible, silhouetted in the darkness. Work tomorrow morning was not a pleasant prospect. But I was looking forward to meeting Beth. I lay down. As the world began to spin, Yakult appeared in a turquoise glow above the bath, obviously distressed. The long fringe-fingers flailed agitatedly from side to side, and the large emerald eyes darted about the room. I had never seen Yakult so anxious before. The turquoise figure glided around the room, settling nowhere, peering around as if lost and frightened. Then it disappeared. I fell asleep. My mind continued to wander restlessly, as my body had done, through the night.

Chapter Twenty-four

I am at my parents' funeral. It is in the sitting room of their house in West Hampstead, but out of the bay windows I can see a snowy mountain range. This does not strike me as odd. They are going to be buried in the front garden; two dark graves gape under the pine tree. There are lots of relatives and friends there whom I don't recognise. Rabbi Chod is officiating, reading something in a foreign language from his battered prayer book. But my parents are still alive, standing in the corner of the room, the guests of honour, dressed in traditional white shrouds. Their faces are freshly washed and their hair is brushed, all ready for death. It is their big day. They stand there peacefully. They accept the fact that their time has come. At a certain point in the service, everyone strikes up a chant and my parents walk quietly out into the garden with two men dressed in white. Some people start to cry. The men stretch a blanket out beside one of the graves. The mountains tower over them. I try to scream but my throat is locked, frozen solid. My mother is first. She lies down on the blanket. The men pick it up by the corners and lower her into the grave.

Only twelve hours after Beth's reanimation, a bedraggled-looking woman came into my room unannounced. It was a Saturday, about eight in the morning. Birds were singing outside. I awoke, my heart pounding, and sat up in the bath, trying to shake the fog out of my head. For a moment, my dream remained vivid; I could still see my mother disappearing into the ground, transposed over the bathroom wall. Then it began to fade. I rubbed my aching face and leant against the wall. The bedraggled woman crossed the small room in a disconcertingly familiar manner and sat on the edge of the bath, in the very spot where Madeline usually sat. I looked up at her. It was Beth.

In the photos, she had looked spirited and vibrant, but now she looked a different person – exhausted and anxious. But it was undoubtedly Beth. Folds of her heavy velvet skirt fell into the bath. Her fingers fiddled incessantly. Yet even this husk of a person was beautiful, the turquoise light from the window highlighting her hair. As soon as she opened her mouth, I was in love. Whatever that means.

'Sun shines yellow today,' she began. Her voice had a northern tinge. She had a habit of lowering her head and widening her eyes as she spoke, like Princess Diana; but the pain in her eyes tempered the seductive effect. Twisting round, she dragged a matted carpet-bag into view. She plunged her arm into it and dropped a heavy object onto the blankets.

'Look, Mo. Pick it up . . . and gaze.' I shook the last of the mist out of my head, reached down and retrieved a small crystal ball, covered in smudges and fingerprints. 'What do you see, Mo? The same as me? Tell me.' Her emerald eyes were restless and had an ingenuous clarity. They reminded me of something I couldn't quite bring to mind. I sat up and held the ball to the light. The window contracted and spun. 'See, Mo? See? That figure . . . it's you.'

'What?'

'It's you, in the ball. Can't you see?' She plucked the orb from my hand, polished it vigorously on her skirt, as if that would help, and returned it to me.

I gazed hard. Still nothing. 'It's just glass,' I said. 'I can't see a thing.'

'Uh-huh,' she replied sceptically, lowering her head. She took back the ball and dropped it into her bag. Then she leant forwards with a conspiratorial whisper. 'I know about you, Mo,' she said. 'I know how you're living.' Her intensity was startling.

'What do you mean?' I asked. 'Are you talking about the crystal ball?'

'How did you know that?' she demanded.

'What?'

'Oh, don't play innocent with me,' she muttered through desiccated lips. 'I'll put that in my psychic journal.' She got up and walked over to the window, collecting her thoughts, her fingers twisting like worms. Then she returned to the bath and sat down again. 'Mo, I know about you. You're not ordinary, are you?' Her mood had darkened. 'I haven't slept for three days, and not because of the work, either. I've had no turds recently, but I don't care. I've had a revelation, I know the truth. The truth about everything – the whole world, the universe, the galaxy, the lot.'

I cleared my throat, not knowing what to make of it.

'What's my name?' she asked suddenly.

'Beth, isn't it?' I replied, caught off guard.

'Yes, yes, but my last name?'

I gave it some thought. 'Sorry, I couldn't tell you.'

'But I told you yesterday,' she said, new energy coming into her face. 'Surely you can't have forgotten.'

My heartbeat began to speed. 'Well, I . . . Yes, I suppose I have. My memory isn't—'

'What day was it yesterday?'

'Friday.' She wouldn't catch me out that easily. I had been following the week backwards all my life.

'And what did we do yesterday?'

'Why the twenty questions?'

'Answer me.' I didn't reply. I was pinned down by her relentless stare and I didn't know what to say. Suddenly she sprang to her feet and carried out a bizarre series of hops on the tiles, her fingers wiggling in the air. 'I knew it, Mo, I knew it! The crystal ball was right, my experiment worked. You don't remember yesterday at all, do you? You don't remember hanging out in Mad's room.'

'Oh yes, Mad's room,' I said lamely.

'What music was it, then? Whitney? Prince? Starship?'

I couldn't answer. She knelt by the bath and took my hand in both of hers. 'Yesterday,' she said in a hoarse whisper, 'hasn't happened for you yet, has it? It hasn't arrived. Your yesterday is my *tomorrow*. That's right, isn't it?' I was too stunned to speak. She pulled away and sat in front of the toilet-shrine on the far side of the room, swaying back and forth with her head in her hands.

I reached into her bag and looked into the crystal ball again. Still nothing. I put it back.

She started talking as if she had a tiny version of herself in her lap. 'What does this mean, Beth, what does this mean?' she asked. 'Beth, you've got to . . . Beth, what does this *mean*?' There was a pause and more rocking, then she began speaking in a broken whisper. 'What's the point, Beth, what the fuck's the point? I can never be in . . . and they can never be in . . . Everyone's trapped. Fucking shitting fuck! I can't . . . no one can . . . just . . . in my own head.'

I climbed out of the bath, my heart pounding, crossed the room and gripped her wrists with shaking hands. 'So you know . . . you know about me!' I said.

She wasn't listening. Her eyes were staring wildly. 'Mo, tell me everything you know about my future,' she hissed. 'What's going to happen to me? I have to know.'

'Promise you'll spend all day with me, Beth,' I replied. 'You're the only one who knows. Tomorrow it will be too late.' For the first time in my life, my isolation was thawing.

'Mo, my future . . . What's going to happen to me? Tell me,' she begged, baring her teeth. 'I can't take it another moment more. I can't live in uncertainty, Mo, I'm too weak. If this had happened a few years ago, I'd never have started with all this crap – I'd have known the fucking results. And I wouldn't be in this shit hole now – I'd still be on the rails. I can't take a chance with my life any more, I can't face it, I'm too weak. What's going to *happen*? Tell me what you know, Mo, you *have* to!'

I let go of her hands and turned away, pressing my forehead against the bathroom tiles. The ceramic was cool and silent. I could feel her waiting for my response, watching me like a vulture. The minutes passed, and I was paralysed. How could I tell her that in twelve hours she would be lying dead on the road? And in twelve and a half hours the grim cargo of an ambulance? I couldn't tell her that, I couldn't do it. I couldn't tell her she wasn't going to see another dawn. For all I knew, the information might cause her suicide, and I wasn't going to have that guilt on my shoulders. What's more, her future had already happened, I had seen it. Surely her suicide would be impossible to avert? But on the other hand . . . Maybe there was a chance.

'Beth . . .'

'Yes?'

'I'll tell you what I know.' She seized me with her eyes. 'I don't know very much,' I went on. 'All I know is, you'll be OK. You won't be here for ever. You'll . . . All your dreams will come true.' Instantly, I realised I'd blown it.

'You're *lying!*' she spat, grabbing me by the arms and pulling me viciously towards her. *'Tell me.* Don't give me any fucking shit now, Mo. Tell me what you know. I know when you're lying, I'm fucking psychic, you know. Fucking tell me. Fucking *tell.*' I closed my eyes and tried to blank my mind. There was a pause. Her fingers dug sharply into my skin. Then she pushed me violently back against the wall and shuffled into the corner of the room, staring dazedly into space.

'I'm sorry, Beth,' I whispered. 'You've made a mistake. It's not true. I can't help you. I'm sorry.'

We remained like that for a long time, saying nothing. Then she walked wearily over to the door. Her eyes shone a beautiful turquoise in the light.

'I'm going,' she said. She turned and left the room, almost floating on the air currents. I could almost see her fringe-fingers. I realised that I already knew her very well.

For the next hour or so, I sat motionless in the bath. I told myself that whatever happened, however cold, hot or uncomfortable I got, I'd not move, even slightly, for a whole hour. I resisted the urge to browse through my Tibet books. As the minutes passed, my knees began to ache and my back developed searing pains below the shoulder blades. But I didn't move. I tried to stop all mental activity. I would not allow myself to be affected by my thoughts. I permitted not a single thought to arise; no good, no bad, no comfortable, no uncomfortable, no images, no memories. No conception. I tried to smother everything. If everything was neutral, nothing could cause me pain. There was nothing else I could do.

I let my consciousness seep back, and got out of the bath. I could barely move because of the numbness in my legs. I rested against the sink until my strength returned and the ache subsided. I took some paracetamol, and gallant knights flashed before my eyes. Then I went downstairs to the Great Hall.

It was deserted, as was usual at midday. The place hadn't been cleaned since the night before; everywhere were empty glasses and full ashtrays. Skeletal fingers of wax protruded from the bottom of the candleholders. Everything was stained, and the mirrors made it all worse. I sat on one of the sofas in the corner. It stank of stale cigarette smoke mingled with roses and sweat.

I was hungry. I had lost a lot of weight, and my clothes hung off me like bin bags. Sometimes I didn't recognise my gaunt face when I glimpsed it in shop windows. It was rare for me to feel hungry nowadays and I took advantage of it. There was a half-eaten sandwich and a plate of cold chips on the coffee table next to the sofa. I took a bite of the sandwich. I wasn't sure what was in it – I couldn't identify the taste – but it was edible. I tried a few chips, scraping off the congealed streaks of ketchup with a knife. Then I returned to the sandwich. Soon I was thirsty. The first glass I tried had a cigarette butt floating in it. The second smelt too foul to consider. I stopped eating. Within a few minutes, I felt nauseous. It was always a gamble whether or not I'd be able to keep my food down. I shut my eyes and tried to clear my mind. The feeling passed.

After a while, the double doors at the other end of the

hall swung open and Madeline came in, wrapped in an assortment of towels. Beads of water slid over her skin and her oversized pink turban wobbled precariously as she walked. She didn't notice me.

'Hello, Mad,' I said.

She started. 'Oh my God, Mo, you almost gave me a fucking heart attack. What are you doing down here?'

'Nothing. Just saw Beth.'

'Yeah, she's looking a bit depressed. But don't worry, she'll get over it. Seems like everyone's depressed round here anyway.' She sat beside me, produced a cigarette from somewhere and lit up. Instantly I felt queasy, and images of Dazel lying in a grey pool of puke swam before me. I hadn't seen Madeline smoke before.

'I'm about to give these things up, they're killing me,' she said. 'Although I'll probably kill myself before they get a chance.' She gave a dry chuckle and turned towards me, spurting a jet of smoke out of the corner of her mouth. 'I'm waiting for Barry, he's coming in a few minutes. When he arrives, tell him to go straight to my room, OK?'

'OK. How's he doing?' I asked.

'Me and Barry . . . Well, I guess it's going pretty well. It's weird at the moment. I don't know whether to laugh or take some Prozac. He says he's going to take me away from here, as soon as he gets his business up and running. He says we can escape to America and start a new life together. He's my knight in shining armour. He's starting a . . . Sorry, I can't tell you about it. It's a secret. OK, I'll tell you if you really want me to. You've twisted my arm . . .'

'Thanks, Mad, you don't need to tell me. It's quite OK. Really.'

'Oh. OK, then. Anyway, on one hand that's cool, you know. I mean, I would give both my kidneys – and probably my spleen – to be out of this fucking pit. But on the other hand, Barry's got a hell of a temper. I've known that ever since the beginning. And he's obsessive, too. You weren't around when me and Barry first got together, were you?' I shrugged again.

'In the beginning, he sent me these wonderful love letters every morning. He said it broke up his day. Made it less dark. But then he sent me more and more, and soon it got beyond a joke. Fuck! I mean it was all very nice, but after a while he was letting me know about his every move. He must have spent a fortune on stamps and envelopes. It got to the stage where I got hundreds in the post, twice a day. He sent me these weird fucking letters saying, "Breathing in" and "Breathing out". He got violent, too, and did strange things. He used to hide in skips and shoot policemen with home-made potato bazookas, things like that. Anyway, when I asked him to cool it, he lost his mind. He went mental and took it out on me. I was in agony for weeks. It made me want to gas myself. Fucking A. But I got through it in the end.' She drew heavily on her cigarette, fingering an invisible bruise on her face. 'So I don't know whether to trust him or not, you know? And to make matters worse, he says that I'm *his* girl now, and only his. He wants me to commit to him, and say no to all the other turds. How am I supposed to make a fucking living? He can't support me – his business isn't up and running yet. But I want to get out of here, Mo. Really. I do. So I'm holding out for him. Holding out for a hero, you know?' I nodded, knowing that this was the beginning of the end for her. 'Anyway,' she said, standing up, 'I'd better go and dry my hair. Tell Barry to come straight up, yah?' The American accent had come back into her voice. As she walked away, I overheard her mumbling something about dropping the hairdryer in the bath.

All went quiet and I finished the rest of the sandwich and half the chips. I began to feel nauseous again, so I sat back and waited for the food to settle, without making any sudden movements. I was furiously thirsty. My mother drank lots of water when she was ill. I remembered it clearly.

Barry sidled in through the front door like a smell. He stopped in front of the sofa and wrapped a greasy lock of hair behind each ear. 'Mo.'

'Yes,' I replied.

'How's it going. Can I sit down.' He had an odd way of making questions sound like demands; his sentences always finished on a downward lilt, and always sounded very definite. He pulled at his denim knees and collapsed into the sofa. 'Mad told me to ask you to go to her room,' I said.

'Yeah, OK. I'm just going to chill for a bit first.' Spreading his hands across his denim thighs, he tried to catch his breath after the exertion of the walk. His hair swung loosely in front of his face and he pursed his lips with effort. 'Cor, I'm not fit and no mistake. Can I smoke.' I shrugged. He pulled a leather tobacco pouch and some rolling papers from his pocket. 'Want one.' I declined. He stretched a hairy clump of tobacco along the fold of a rolling paper and began to manoeuvre it into a cylinder with a skilful rubbing of his fingers. He smelt strongly of cheap aftershave. His shirt was unbuttoned almost to the navel, exposing a pale-blue chest crisscrossed with cobwebby black hairs and adorned with a large gold medallion. He slid the rolled cigarette between his lips, pulled his hair behind his ears again and fumbled in his pocket for a lighter. His jeans were so tight that he had to tilt his whole body backwards to allow access. He produced a rusty Zippo, clunked it open and lit the cigarette. As he did so he gave me an odd, sidelong look. His pupils were very large, like black holes. He sat back in the cushions, took a drag on his cigarette and spoke, his words riding on puffs of smoke.

'So Mo. What do you think I should do, then. I'm in a bit of a fix, if you know what I mean,' he said, with a man-to-man air.

'What's up?' I asked.

'Look, don't tell Mad about this, OK. It's between you and me, yeah. But I've got to decide what to do about my wives. Should I leave them. I want to take Mad away from this cesspit but I don't know how my wives'll take it.'

'Do you love your wife?' I asked, wondering about his plural usage.

'Of course I do. They're my wives. But I'm also really into

235

Mad. She's a sexy bitch, don't you reckon?' I made no reply. He cracked his knuckles anxiously. His hands were too big for his wrists and grease was visible on his forehead. 'The thing is, Mo, I want them all. I want Mad and my wives at the same time. But I don't want any of them fucking anyone else. I want them all to myself. You're a bloke, you understand that, don't you. You don't want other blokes fucking your birds.' I didn't know what to say. He continued without looking at me, his eyes fixed on the floor. 'You see, Mo, I'm an open-minded kind of bloke. Completely open minded. I want them all. I have no discrimination, me. I'm not a racist. Blacks, whites, Jews, Muslims' – he pronounced it 'Mozlems' – 'it's all the same to me. Men, women, boys, girls, what the hell's the difference. Gays, lesbians . . .' Even his breath smelt of aftershave. 'When you get down to it,' he said, 'everyone's the same, no matter what sex or race, or whatever. Everyone wants to fuck, or get fucked. That's the way it is. Who cares where your hole is, you still want someone to stick something up it. And I just want to be that person. I want to be the person sticking it up. To me, no one's better than anyone else. Equal rights, that's what I say. Equal rights. Women's lib. Gay pride.' He finished his cigarette and dropped it with a sizzle into a pint glass. 'So that's the long and short of it. For me, Mad and my wives are equal. I want them all. I'm not a racist, me, I'm not a fucking racist. So what do you think I should do?'

Before I could answer, the double doors opened and Madeline appeared, carrying half a bottle of vodka.

'Barry!' she exclaimed. 'Why didn't you come straight through? I've been waiting for ages. Fuck. Makes me want to eat my head.'

'Oh, for fuck's sake. I'm coming, you bitch,' he said, hauling himself out of the sofa to greet her. She wound his hair round his ears and they embraced briefly, then settled down on a sofa on the other side of the hall, taking occasional swigs of vodka. My throat was burning with thirst. I hunted around among the glasses on the coffee table and found an almost full glass of tomato juice. I drank it all. It had a kick. I sat back into the dirty sofa, and gradually became drowsy.

When I awoke it was evening and the Turk was lighting candles around the Great Hall. It took her about half an hour to get them all going, and the hall slowly filled with bronze shadows. A succession of girls emerged from the double doors, all in skimpy turquoise uniforms, ready for work. Their shadows danced on the ceiling. Music filled the room: it was Bonnie Tyler's 'Holding Out for a Hero'. I knew that one. Barry came in and started work behind the bar. When the men arrived the girls went to meet them, giving them drinks and flirtatious glances, all under the watchful eyes of the Turk. She sat imperiously in the corner of the room, sipping a gin and tonic, from time to time getting up to interrogate a newcomer. The air filled with smoke and noise, and soon the party was in full swing. I sat. Nobody noticed me.

After a while Beth appeared in the crowd, dangling a glass of wine from her fingertips. She was wearing turquoise hot pants, and her hair was fluffed up above a turquoise headband, the same shade as her eye shadow. We caught eyes and she hesitated, a strand of hair stroking her face; then she came and sat next to me. For a few minutes we sat in silence, surrounded by the noise and the chaos. She was beautiful, even with sunken eyes and cheeks. Her lips shone in the candlelight. She broke the silence, speaking as if to herself.

'Look, Mo, I'm sorry about before. I think I lost it a bit. I think I'm going a bit mental.'

'Never mind, it's OK,' I said. 'Don't worry.' There was a pause.

'It's weird, you know,' she said, lowering her head. 'I always thought you were so open-minded, such a good listener. But the truth is, whenever I speak to you about the past you haven't a clue what I'm talking about, have you? It's got nothing to do with being non-judgemental. You can't judge because you don't know. Or so it seems to me.'

'You're making a mistake, Yakult,' I said.

237

'What did you call me?'

'Never mind. Sorry. Anyway . . . Beth, you've made a mistake. I don't know what you mean with all this backwards stuff. I just get forgetful, that's all.'

She looked uncomfortable. 'Mo, stop lying. This backwards stuff is enough of a headfuck as it is, and I can't take it right now. I'm too weak. OK?'

'What do you mean, weak? Look, my situation is just like everyone else's, really, it's not that different. But I have to deal with it alone. That makes it worse.'

'Believe me, Mo, everyone has to deal with their shit alone, not just you. Everyone lives and dies alone.' She closed her eyes and raised her face to the ceiling. 'Your backwards thing proves it.'

I thought for a while. There was no point in pretending any more. 'Beth . . . can I ask . . . How long have you known me? What will I . . . What have I . . .' She opened her eyes and gave me such a fearsome look that the words froze in my throat. 'Mo, enough. Stop it, OK? I can't take it. It fucks with my head.' Our eyes locked for a few seconds. Then she gulped her wine and turned away. I sat back, tired all of a sudden. My whole body was covered in pins and needles.

We sat in silence for a few minutes until a flash of green and white by the front door caught my eye. I was shocked to see Rabbi Chod swaggering in like a cowboy. I began to panic. My old life was intruding on my new one. My hiding place had been discovered. But I couldn't run – it was too late for that. He went over to a sofa opposite us, and was startled when he saw me. A few girls trailed after him. He waved them away with his drink. His eyes flicked over me and I cringed – then they moved to Beth and lingered on her as she sipped her wine. He was drunk and distracted, and hadn't recognised me. After a while he smoothed his eyebrows, took a gulp from his glass, got to his feet and came over to Beth.

'My dear girl. Good evening to you.' She glanced up at

him and looked away. He squeezed himself onto the sofa and I was rammed up uncomfortably against the arm. I strained to eavesdrop on their conversation. 'My dear beautiful thing, what is your name?' he asked. Beth didn't reply. 'Name your price for the night, just name it and I will pay. I . . . You are beautiful. Let me take you away from this.'

'Sorry, mate, I'm waiting for someone,' she said, abruptly. I felt a wave of relief. But Rabbi Chod wasn't satisfied. 'But!' he replied. 'You are the one I choose. I choose you. I want you. I need you. Surely you cannot refuse me?'

Beth looked him full in the face. 'Look, mate, I'm not up for it. You've got bad karma. I'm psychic, see? Now get going. Try someone else. Just fuck off, yeah?' She pushed him, hard, and turned away, and he dropped his drink on the carpet. Inwardly I smiled. He stood up, gasping as if he'd been given a parking ticket.

All the girls in the immediate vicinity stopped what they were doing and stared. Uncharacteristically, Chod was speechless. The noise died down; even the music stopped. Out of the corner of my eye, I saw the Turk slowly unfold her limbs and come towards us, her dress shimmering like a layer of scales. Everyone seemed to grow tense. Somebody coughed nervously.

'Sir, is there a problem?' asked the Turk, curtly.

'No, indeed, not at all. Nothing at all, no, no, no indeed. No,' Chod replied. She scrutinised the two of them. Rabbi Chod folded his hands uneasily across his chest. Beth put her nails in her mouth.

'Did you want this girl, sir?'

'Well, that is . . . er . . . indeed, we were just talking, that is, after a fashion . . .'

She bent and snarled at her under her breath, 'Beth, you bitch. You give this man a full service, get me? Full service. Half price.'

'Look, Mama,' pleaded Beth softly, 'I'm not feeling great at the moment. This man has bad karma. I can't do it. Please don't make me.'

239

'What are you playing at?' muttered the Turk. 'You want to lose your fucking job?'

Beth was about to reply when Chod butted in. He appeared to have gathered his wits about him, and drew himself up. 'Actually, I've changed my mind, as, I would remind you, is the client's prerogative. Let her be. She is very nice, but I have seen someone nicer. How about . . . you? Your good self? Us two, tonight? How much for the night?' He glanced at Beth who was gnawing her fingers apprehensively.

The Turk stared at him for a full ten seconds. She was poised between being offended and being flattered, and didn't know how to react. All eyes were upon her. Cigarette smoke wound round itself in the space between them. Then, all at once, she regained her authority. She glared around and clapped her hands.

'Mad-for-it Mad! S&M Seraph! Here, now!' she commanded. Madeline gave Barry a nervous look and went demurely over to the Turk. Barry's face tensed, but he stayed where he was. Madeline was joined by a large, pouting black girl with a startling white afro and scarlet lips. I wondered if she and Madeline shared a lipstick.

'These are my two best girls,' said the Turk. 'They'll definitely show you a good time. I am not a working girl. I don't do that stuff any more . . . for personal reasons. But tonight I'll give you two for the price of one. What do you say?'

'Two for the price of one?'

'Yes.'

'At once?'

'Mmmm-hmmm.'

Rabbi Chod looked as if he would instinctively refuse, but stopped himself. He ran his eyes slowly up and down Madeline and S&M Seraph. Madeline stood impassively, her arms at her sides, as if she could physically feel his gaze. S&M Seraph, however, pouted and winked at him. He winked back, and the matter was decided.

'OK, OK. I accept,' said Rabbi Chod, glancing sheepishly

at Beth. Simultaneously, Beth breathed a sigh of relief and Barry clutched his head in distress.

S&M Seraph took Mad and Chod roughly by the hand and led them briskly towards the double doors. The crowd parted to let them through. Madeline caught eyes with Barry as they went by. Then the three of them disappeared through the doors, into the darkness. I prayed that this was Chod's first visit, and I would never see him again.

Gradually the party atmosphere returned. Barry downed his drink and left immediately. The Turk waited until the moment had passed, then turned her wrath on Beth.

'What are you doing!? What are you fucking *doing*? You're fucking crazy!' she hissed. Beth rose and hurried away, pushing through the crowd. The Turk swept back to her chair. I got uncomfortably to my feet and went up to my room.

On the edge of the bath, I sat rubbing my eyes. Boisterous voices floated up from downstairs. Soon I would lie down and go to sleep. I could see a splattering of stars through the open window, an unusual sight in London. The limp red light-bulb spread a pinkish wash over everything. I looked up at my face in the mirrors on the ceiling. For a moment I saw it impartially, then my gaze was invaded by self. I was surprised at the darkness of the smudges round my eyes and the prominence of my cheekbones. Was that a lesion on my cheek? I felt it with my fingertips. No, just a patch of sore skin. I retrieved some paracetamol from under the bath and swallowed a couple. Images of the day began to crowd my mind. I tried not to think about what Rabbi Chod was up to with Madeline and S&M Seraph. Would he be in danger of catching the disease from Madeline? She might not have contracted it herself, yet. In any event, I knew Rabbi Chod had many healthy years ahead of him. And, considering his obsession with hygiene, I was sure he would be scrupulous with contraception. But what of the Turk refusing him? I remembered when she had tried to seduce me. She must have felt tragically humiliated. Part of me wished I had gone

241

ahead with it. I was tired, but my mind was too active to sleep. I decided to read *The Eyewitness Guide to Tibet*, hoping that the dense prose would help me drift off. I picked up the book, cracked the spine and began to read, waiting for sleep to descend.

Chapter Twenty-five

As the years passed in a blur of monotony, my relationship with Beth and Mad improved. They got to know me less, which made me feel less crowded. And I got to know them more, which made me feel closer to them. I learnt to overcome my hesitancy and began to enjoy their company. I finally felt I had found some friends. For a long while we all got on very well, and the homesickness-envelope by the bath was left happily untouched.

It was a mild Sunday afternoon in January and the New Year was approaching. I was in Beth's room with her and Madeline, the three of us sitting together on the floor. Madeline had been antagonistic recently, but I didn't take much notice, because she was prone to mood swings anyway. Today, however, she seemed in a good mood. All around us was Beth's bohemian detritus: crystal balls, incense holders, stuffed animals, swathes of coloured cloth. It was late afternoon, and the girls were going to start work in a few hours. The air was stuffy. We were sharing a bottle of whisky which burnt our throats as we talked.

'Well, I think it's all just a lot of bollocks, Beth, mate,' said Madeline, blowing smoke through her nose.

'That's exactly what I mean,' said Beth, 'that's a typical Cancerian response.'

'OK, then, try it on Mo. Then we'll see.'

'Fine,' said Beth, rising to the challenge. 'Mo, what's your favourite colour?'

'Grey.'

'*Grey?*' guffawed Madeline, rubbing her eyes.

'Yeah, grey. So what?' I muttered, taking a hot sip of whisky.

'OK, then,' said Beth, 'grey. If you say so. It's quite possible, Mad, why not? OK, what's your favourite food?'

'Er, beans,' I said, picking the first thing that came to mind. Madeline giggled behind her hand and took a long drag on her cigarette.

'Favourite number?' asked Beth, undeterred, lowering her head.

'Zero.'

'Zero? You fucking freak, Mo. Makes me want to jump off a bridge. Fuck.'

'Shut it, Mad. Hmmm . . . let me work this one out.'

'Face it, Beth, it's a load of rubbish,' said Madeline, pouring herself another drink.

Beth was lost in thought. Then she clicked her fingers and rested her hand on my knee. 'You, Mo, are . . . a Pisces. Right?'

'I don't know.'

'What do you mean, you don't know?'

'I have no idea. I don't know.'

'You don't know your own fucking star sign?'

'Afraid not.'

'Oh, oh, that reminds me of this joke,' interrupted Madeline, swirling her drink in the glass. 'This bit of string goes into this fucking bar, right, and the bartender says, sorry man, I don't serve bits of string in here. So the bit of string ties himself into a knot and ruffles his hair, and tries to get served again. So the bartender says, aren't you the same bit of string I spoke to a moment ago? And the bit of string says, no, I'm a frayed knot. A frayed knot. Ha ha ha ha!'

'Yeah, Mad, very funny,' I said, as she laughed uncontrollably.

Beth started rolling a joint in sensitive, expert fingers. 'Anyway, Mo, how come you don't know your star sign?' she said, her eyes not moving from the rolling paper.

'I just don't.'

'OK, then, we'll work it out for you. When were you born?' She slipped the joint between her lips and squinted at me.

I looked at the ceiling. 'Don't know.'

'What? You must know! How can you not know your own birthday?'

'It's a long time ago. I've forgotten it. I've wiped it out of my mind. I can't remember.'

'Mo, you fucking freak. Makes me want to . . . Fuck.'

'Well, we'll have to make you a new birthday, then,' said Beth. 'How about today?'

'Thanks, Beth, but no. I'm fine without.'

'Mo, you're one year old today. Congratulations. Happy birthday to you, happy birthday to you—'

'Look, Beth—'

'Come on,' said Madeline, 'let's get out of here. Let's go and have a smoke on the steps outside.'

'Mad, it's too cold,' Beth objected.

'Rubbish,' retorted Madeline, 'come on. We're going to be inside all night, we might as well catch the last bit of sun. Jesus.' She led the way downstairs and we huddled outside in the crisp winter air, passing the joint round. Savio had been on bad terms with me recently. When he saw me, he snarled and his fur stood on end. Madeline calmed him down, softly telling him that he was jealous, and that he'd get used to me in the end. She told me it sometimes took him years and years to feel comfortable with someone.

When the joint was finished, I sat against the side of the porch. Sun pooled around us. The shadows were dark and vivid, and the light was very bright. The traffic noise was dull and constant. My head began to ache. Beth said she would heal it with a crystal, and pulled one out of her bag. The sun glinted off its angled surfaces.

Madeline sat cross-legged on the ground in front of us, leaning back on one arm, a cigarette between her fingers, drinking a can of Coke. 'Beth, man, give it a break. That fucking crystal stuff does my head in. Fuck. It's clearly not going to work.'

'Shut up, I'm doing Mo a favour here. Don't be such a peasant. Mo, where does it hurt?'

'It's only a headache, Beth, no big thing,' I replied.

'Which part of the head?' I gestured to the back of my cranium, just above the neck. That was the source of the pain. Beth cupped her right hand gently over my forehead and pressed the cool crystal against the back of my neck, rotating it carefully.

Madeline groaned and sucked hard on her cigarette. 'I don't believe in all this voodoo mojo shit, Beth. Why doesn't he just take a paracetamol, like every other normal person?'

'Paracetamol's bad for you, Mad,' said Beth. 'You're just a heathen peasant and you know it.'

'Smoke another joint, that'll do the trick.'

'OK, thanks Doctor Mad, we'll bear that in mind. Now shut up – I'll scramble his brain if you're not careful. I need to concentrate or he'll end up retarded. Shut up. It's not funny. Don't make me laugh.'

I was dizzy, but Beth's hand felt good on my forehead.

'I'm feeling a bit weird, Beth,' I said.

'You are weird,' retorted Madeline, dropping her cigarette butt into the Coke can.

'Don't worry about that, Mo,' says Beth, 'don't worry, weird is normal, weird is good. It means the headache's leaving.'

Suddenly there was a loud spluttering and Mad sprang to her feet, dancing as if the ground were on fire and clutching her hands to her throat.

'Mad, are you OK? What's wrong?' asked Beth. 'Are you taking the piss? Shall I call an ambulance?' We hurried over.

She was retching and gagging. 'Fuck me. Fuck me. Fuckadoodledoo,' she croaked, spitting hard on the ground. 'I just took a mouthful of that Coke! That fucking Coke!'

'What's wrong with it?'

'It's not the Coke, it's the cigarette. I put my fag out in the Coke, then I forgot, and I fucking drank it. Mouthful of fag. Fuck. Fuck me!'

Beth began to laugh. It was infectious. The sight of Madeline in her tiny skirt, doing a ridiculous, contorted dance, spitting and coughing, made even the slightest thing hilarious. My stomach began to ache with laughter. After that, my headache disappeared.

That evening I was reading in my room when I heard footsteps on the spiral staircase. I peered into the unlit gloom and Madeline emerged from the shadows, wearing skimpy work clothes and carrying a glass of wine. She brushed woozily past me and leant against the sink. Her glass, brimming with gold, turned crimson when she set it on the red tiles. She peered at me over a raised shoulder. Her eyes were kaleidoscoping, as they often did; I wondered if it had been dope, a pill, or something heavier.

'Thought I'd come clean,' she said in a low voice. 'I've got to come clean. I can't take this any longer. Fuck. I have to tell the truth, I can't bottle it up or I'll drown myself. Fucking fuck. Mo, I've been noticing your . . . your signals over the past few days. You *like* me, right?' Before I could muster a reply, she leant closer. 'And I like you, too,' she whispered. 'You're really . . . sexy.' She got up like an inflating balloon, raised her left hand and, without warning, pulled up her top. White breasts flopped limply out, the veined flesh instantly becoming goose-pimpled in the draught from the window. Tilting her head enticingly, she took my hand and squashed it onto the bare skin.

That was the first time I had ever felt a female breast. I was surprised at the coolness and softness of the flesh, the way it yielded so readily to the touch. Also, its physicality surprised me; until now the only breasts I had encountered were imaginary. Madeline threaded her arm round the back of my head and pulled my face towards hers, my hand still clutching the flap of flesh. For an instant I was captured by my own desire. Months of longing for Beth, for Mad, for anyone, for fulfilment, had come to fruition. Adrenalin shot through me. Our lips glued. I was trembling. We parted and gazed at each other. But as our eyes met, I was repelled. She wasn't Mad any longer; she was Mad-for-it Mad. Like a spirit, her working persona had possessed her. The jaded eyes reminded me of my own; a screen had gone up, there was no empathy. I left her grasp and took a step back – absurdly enough, wiping my hand on my jumper. She giggled and followed me, and I retreated. She stopped for a moment, not comprehending; then she leant against the sink again, suddenly vulnerable.

I could feel my blood heavy in my veins, my infected blood. I wanted to explain, or apologise, but no words would come. My blood was becoming denser and denser, buzzing with contamination. I was fighting to contain the flood of my desire. Mad had her hands over her face. I watched myself as I walked across the room towards her, my loins thumping, and touched her bare shoulders. She hesitated, then lowered her hands. I saw myself stroke her cheek, then lift her face awkwardly to mine. I tried to stop but I was bewitched. My mind became numb, I couldn't think any more. My whole body was trembling. Mad's hands slipped across my thighs and unbuttoned my trousers. 'Small, but perfectly formed,' she whispered, and giggled. As soon as her fingers touched me, wave after wave of tense, stinging bliss shot through my body and I felt myself gulp wet stickiness into her palm. She laughed, slipped off her top and pressed it between my legs. Then she dropped it onto the floor, took me by both hands and led me towards the bath.

I shouldn't be doing this. I watched myself despairingly as I tore Mad's clothes off and we locked in a furious, tangled embrace. I shouldn't. Our tongues wound again and again, like snakes, and she raked her fingernails bitterly across my back. Shouldn't. I could not stop. All I could do was hope the disease wouldn't be transmitted this time. After all, there was no blood present, or not that I knew of. I'm sure it will be OK. Yes, it will be OK. She gripped me between her legs and I slid into her, racked with relief. For a couple of minutes we rocked together, flesh and skin thumping. Our hearts pumped in deadly unison. I mustn't go through with this. I must stop this now, before it's too late. We swayed franti-cally, and Madeline began to pant. I heard myself groan and the stinging bliss began to rise again. I'll pull out before it's too late. I'll pull out. I didn't pull out. It was too late. Every muscle in our bodies tensed simultaneously as the bliss speared us like a single fish. My body convulsed into her. Then it was over and we lay twisted together, gasping in the bath. Our blood had mixed. The loop of fate was complete.

The mist passed. Madeline's body felt clammy and disgusting in my hands. I had done what I had never wanted to do. I had completed the circle. She lay there without speaking, quieter than I had ever known her, smelling of sex. I couldn't find anything to say.

Round my head a ring of skeletons begin to dance, skeletons with human faces, holding hands. One by one, they come into view. First are my mother and father, looking blankly ahead while their bony bodies skip and jig. Next in the circle is Madeline – and then me. My skeletal frame dances more manically than the others; my right hand clasps Madeline's bony fingers, and my left hand grips my mother's. I got the disease from my mother, who got it from my father, who got it from Madeline – who got it from me. I complete the ring. I have given it its power.

Suddenly I bolted from the bath, my face wet with tears. 'Mad, this never happened. It never happened,' I sobbed.

Madeline sat up in shock. 'What? Mo, what's the big—'

'Don't fucking answer me. Just get out. Get out! Never mention this ever again, to anyone. You hear me, Mad? Not to anyone. This didn't happen. This never happened. This isn't true.' A fist punched up inside me and I threw up, violently, in the sink. Thick liquid netted the enamel. When I turned back, Madeline was gone.

That incident was the closest I had ever got to love. In the bizarre few days that followed, I saw Madeline interpreting my bumbling embarrassment as evidence of infatuation. I could feel her planning to seduce me. But before long it wore off and things returned to normal – for the moment.

Chapter Twenty-six

As the years went by, I began to lose my friends. I had left my family behind years ago, and every relationship was fated to follow suit. At first the change was barely noticeable; a few less familiar words, less openness in conversation, more suspicion and distance. But over the months I was faced with the painful truth that my friendship with Mad and Beth was disintegrating day by day, and there was nothing I could do about it. They were starting to forget me. Even though we had been such good friends, the longer I knew them, the shorter they knew me. My closest friends were turning into ghosts before my eyes. When I popped into their rooms for a chat, they began giving me strange looks. Eventually they asked me to knock before I came in. However friendly I tried to be, the following day all my efforts would be erased. Madeline's phoney American accent appeared again, the final barrier. I saw less of them, and found myself with a great deal of time on my hands. The empty hours were difficult to fill. I began to look at the pages in the envelope again. They became my companions. I pored over them for longer and longer every night.

I wondered what my parents were like now that so much time had passed. I fantasised about meeting them again. My resentment took second place behind my loneliness. One weekend, unable to bear it any longer, I took the bus to West Hampstead. I had no intention of making contact with my family. I just wanted to catch a glimpse of them. One glimpse, that would be enough.

I recognised my surroundings. Memories linked with objects. I got off the bus. Instantly, a crowd of images sprang at me. The feeling of being in a familiar area after such a long time opened the sluice gate, and old memories came flooding back. My mother arranging my food in the shape of a smiley face. My father pretending to eat Plastic Bag, and then hoisting me into the air. Grandpa Pagpa bashing his typewriter.

I am on the metal bridge that leads to the Heath, the one that echoes like a spring when you stamp on it. I am holding my parents' hands, my father on my left, my mother on my right. We are walking, two of my steps to every one of theirs. It is spring, and the birdsong forms a sphere around us. The sunshine feels like feathers. From time to time I stop in my tracks, and they carry on walking; then they swing me, in a great swoop, up into the air, and I see the sky beneath my feet. I come down again, slapping my feet hard on the bridge, making a loud, cheeky sound that startles the birds overhead.

Yes, I remember now. I play on the helter-skelter. At first I am afraid; my father lifts me halfway up and runs alongside as I slide down, and my mother catches me. Then I get my confidence and my father helps me climb the ladder all the way up to the top. He persuades me that I will be all right, and I can see my mother waiting to catch me at the bottom. I steel myself and take the plunge, sliding down, winding round and round, my breath catching in my throat, until I shoot off the end and my mother is there to make sure I don't hurt myself. My parents cheer, and they celebrate my first slide down the helter-skelter by doing a little shoulder-to-shoulder Tibetan dance round the roundabout. I do a somer-sault on the tarmac. It is the sort of tarmac that is soft, in case you fall on it. By the end of the afternoon, I am able to climb up all by myself, and slide down with no problem at all. From the top of the helter-skelter I see my parents sitting on a bench, chatting, and I call for them to watch me. I slide down as fast as I can, showing off, and when I land on the ground I stumble and graze my knee. They rush over, and my mother holds me in her arms while my father picks out the grit and bandages my knee with a handkerchief. When I have recovered, I have a go on the swings.

I turned a corner, and the roads opened towards the Hush Hush café. No doubt my father would be there. My gut twisted. I didn't want to speak to him. I stopped and wondered what I should do. How old would my parents be now? Would they be children? Toddlers? Babies? I had lost track of time. I decided not to go and speak to him. He might expect me to move back in, and there was no way I was going to do that. And why should I? I was ill because of him. Anyway, he might become dependent, and that would make things worse. The best thing would be for him to learn to be independent, to manage on his own. It was only sensible. I should leave him and my mother to get on with their lives, that would be practical. I shouldn't rock the boat. I had to be responsible about this. And anyway, my appalling predicament was their fault. Grandpa Pagpa was probably still there to look after them. Probably.

I walked along the pavement towards the familiar white façade, crossed the road, went into Regent's Park Café and sat by the window. From there I had a clear view of my father's café. It looked exactly the same as when I had last seen it. There was nobody behind the counter. An unpleasant cocktail of emotions shook violently into my mind. I didn't want to speak to my father. I considered paying him a visit.

A waitress sauntered over and raised an eyebrow. She had a badge on her chest that said, 'Hello, my name is Pandora. Can I help you?'

'Vixen weather, bean,' she said, 'but it might be just an April shower.' It had begun to drizzle outside. I nodded. 'What you so interested in that place for? Hush Hush?' she asked. Her words were garbled, as if she was speaking several sentences behind herself. I didn't reply. 'Hang on,' she said. 'Don't I know you from somewhere? You look really familiar.'

'I don't think so,' I replied. I'd never seen her before. But that didn't mean she hadn't seen me. She hummed through her teeth, corrugated her forehead and tried to place me. I turned away and she let it go. 'Whatever. They're awful over there in Hush Hush, bean,' she jabbered on. 'They kick you out for the slightest thing. They kicked me out ages ago, for no reason at all. I did nothing. Bastards. You'll be glad you came to this café. Here at Regent's we're more laid back. We've got our heads screwed on.' There was a pause. 'I'm not really a waitress, you know. I'm a pert.' I wasn't in the mood to talk. I glanced around and saw that I was the only customer in the place. I'd better get rid of her while I could.

'Black coffee, Pandora,' I said, without looking up.

'Look, you may be in love with me but you don't have to be so . . . terse,' she retorted. I pretended not to hear her. In the reflection in the window, I saw her make a bulgy-eyed face and walk away. Still nobody appeared in the window of Hush Hush. I waited, wishing my father would come over to the counter so that I could see him. To check from afar that he was OK.

There he was. For an instant, I didn't recognise him. He was far shorter than the last time I had seen him. He couldn't have been much older than a toddler. His skin was smooth and unblemished and his features had been strangely foreshortened into those of a child. He went behind the counter and stood on an upturned milk-crate to reach the surface. His elbows stuck out awkwardly at his sides as he tried to rest his forearms nonchalantly on the counter. A customer came over and made a gesture. He scribbled on a notepad in his familiar way, nodded and hopped down from the milk-crate. Then he disappeared through the white curtain.

It was strange to see his mannerisms in the body of a child. The pecking of the head, the upright walk, the disapproving glower; all were there, though he was using a different-sized set of limbs to express them. Should I go and see him? I was in two minds. My thoughts began to race. On the one hand I wanted to run over and have a dramatic reconciliation. But that was the stuff of fantasy. I wasn't sure I wanted a reconciliation, anyway. My father could never be completely innocent in my eyes. But he could never be conclusively guilty, either – he was controlled by fate like everyone else. And his affair was years and years away, in the distant future. Could

I blame him for his future in the present? And wasn't I equally to blame? My thoughts wound round me, getting tighter and tighter.

The waitress appeared and slid my coffee unceremoniously across the table. I accepted it without making eye contact and she walked away, muttering under her breath. She turned the radio on, offensively loudly. I ignored it.

I had to go into Hush Hush. For all I knew, my father wouldn't recognise me. If that was the case, it would mean he'd never met me before, and that would be the beginning–end of our relationship; if I was not in his past, he would not be in my future, for his past and my future were the same. Then I would have no choice but to forget about my parents altogether. Simply walking into Hush Hush would give me the answer. I had to do it. If he recognised me, we would have a relationship in my future. If he didn't, I would never see him again. Either way, fate would prevail – whatever was mapped out for me in his past was inevitable. But I had to know.

I had an idea. I would go halfway; I would phone the café. If my father recognised my voice, we would meet again in my future. If he didn't, I could seal our relationship and push it to the back of my mind.

It took me several attempts to persuade Pandora to come over to my table again, and when she arrived it was with a lackadaisical flick of the lip.

'Sorry . . . Do you have the phone number of Hush Hush?' I asked, raising my voice above the music.

'Hush Hush? What for?'

'I want to call them.'

'I'm composing a perm, you know,' she said. 'I'm busy. I'm not a servant.' I turned away. She shrugged, loped off and scrawled a phone number on a napkin in Biro. I paid and left the café. As I closed the door, she turned the music right down. I stepped out into the street, hunching my shoulders against the drizzle, and took up my surveillance post in a phone box across the street from Hush Hush. I cupped my hands against the glass and squinted at the café. My father was nowhere to be seen. I had to wait. To preserve the silence in Hush Hush, the telephone didn't have an audible ring. Instead, a small green light had been installed below the counter and flashed whenever someone phoned. This meant that my father would have to be behind the counter when I made my call. If he noticed the flash – which he rarely did, even as an adult – and if he could be bothered to answer the call – which he rarely could – he would need to go into the kitchen, where the phone was. I waited, gazing out of the smudged window. The drizzle settled on the glass of the phone box like a spray of cleaning fluid. The waitress was watching me listlessly out of the window of Regent's. I ignored her.

A woman in a suit, huddled against the rain, ducked into Hush Hush and approached the counter, collapsing her umbrella. A man approached to take her order; at first, merely through the force of expectation, I thought it was my father. But it was not. It was a man with a gleaming pate and a pecking manner. Grandpa Pagpa. It was the first time I had seen him doing something useful in the café. Needless to say, he looked younger than before. I gazed incredulously at his nimble movements. The order was taken and both figures disappeared from view. For a long while, nothing happened.

I needed the toilet. Not too badly, but enough to increase my impatience. The drizzle made it worse. I even began to consider forgetting the phone idea and walking into Hush Hush, to end the agonising wait. With some irony, I noticed how difficult it is to be still when you're waiting for something, when satisfaction is deferred. I tried to imagine I was at home in my bath, in my blankets, not waiting for anything, reading an absorbing book. This settled my mind a little.

My wait ended. The miniature figure of my father toddled over to the counter and started fiddling in the drawers underneath. It was now or never. My heart pumping in my ears, I dialled the number. I saw his head give a jolt of recognition as the green light flashed. Then he went back to rummaging in the drawer. The line went dead. I dialled again. The green light sparkled. My father gave a small, irritated shrug, closed the drawer and disappeared through the white curtain.

A quiet voice answered the phone, in a high octave. It was my father – his voice had un-broken.

'Hello?' he asked. 'Is anybody being there, la? Anybody being there?'

'H . . .' I cleared my throat. 'Hello.'

'Yes, Hush Hush café, can I be helping you, la?' I couldn't reply. I wished I had rehearsed some opening lines. 'Who is this, la?' my father asked.

'Hi . . . this is . . . er . . .'

'Mo? Is that you, la? Mo? Hello?'

That was it. He knew me. Our relationship wasn't over. Conflicting emotions flooded my mind.

'Hi, it's me. How . . . how are you?'

'OK, OK, very well, very well. Where are you calling prom, la la la?'

'Work,' I lied.

He sounded happy to hear from me. 'When are you coming home, Mo? Hello? Hello?'

I knew he wouldn't see me for many years. I hung up.

The waitress wasn't looking at me any more. I pressed my forehead against the glass and gazed at the Hush Hush café, my breath misting all around my face. My father re-emerged and continued rummaging beneath the counter. The sprightly Grandpa Pagpa came over and joined him. Suddenly, their heads snapped up, identical expressions of shock on their faces. I watched as they hurried over to the woman in the suit and ejected her from the café, my father frantically snapping her with his oversized Polaroid, Grandpa Pagpa frogmarching her out by the arm. She must have made a noise, probably by rustling the newspaper she was clutching to her breast. The scene had a kind of comedy to it, like a silent film or a mime. I left the phone box and walked towards the bus stop, the rain beginning to annoy me.

The vision of my childish father stuck in my mind. He looked as assiduous and industrious as he had when he was an adult, but all his actions seemed a struggle. The milk-crate, the tiptoes, the awkward elbows; he was clearly finding it difficult to manage. A far-off voice told me I should be there, helping him. I tried to block it out. Grandpa Pagpa might be making things easier for him. But I knew he was probably being more of a hindrance. Should I be responsible for my father, in the way he had been responsible for me when I was a child? And what of my mother? How was she coping with the descent into youth? With a start, I realised that I didn't know if they were still living in the same house. I had no idea about their lives at all. And yet my father had recognised my voice on the telephone – we had unfinished business. I was certainly destined to see him again. I found myself wishing I were part of his life. I had missed so much of it. So many wasted years. I reached the bus stop and waited. The rain thickened.

My mother sits down on my bed, tossing her plait over her shoulder. 'Would you like me to tell you a bedtime story, Monlam, sweetie?' I nod. 'OK. This is a story that my mother used to tell me. And it used to be your father's favourite story, too, when he was a boy. It is about a very famous Buddhist lama called Ponlop Rinpoche.' She settles herself on the bed and strokes my hair as she speaks. 'Once upon a time, Ponlop Rinpoche was going to give a series of teachings in Lhasa, around the time of the Saga Dawa festival. His teachings attracted large crowds, and people would travel from miles around just to catch a glimpse of his holy face.

'One particular woman, by the name of Lhamo, was travelling all the way from eastern Tibet to hear his teachings. She was a poor peasant woman, and had four children with her. She couldn't afford very much food, so many days she went hungry so that her children could eat.' Her voice is soothing and resonant, and makes me feel warm.

'On the road, she met a monk who was also on his way to Ponlop Rinpoche's teachings. Since they were heading for the same place, they decided to travel together. The children instantly liked the monk, and he helped Lhamo to look after them. It was a great relief for her to have somebody else to share her burden. The monk helped her to carry the bags and buy the food, and the journey became a lot easier.

'When they got to the outskirts of Lhasa, the monk said he had to leave her to join the other monks from his monastery for the duration of the teachings. He promised to travel back with her afterwards, and they arranged a place to meet.

'That evening, Lhamo and her children attended the first of Ponlop Rinpoche's teachings – and she was amazed to see the very monk who had helped her all the way from eastern Tibet climb onto the throne and begin to teach. She had been assisted all the way by none other than Ponlop Rinpoche himself. She was very surprised, and very happy.'

My mother bunches her shoulders in excitement and smiles broadly in the half-light. I want to ask her if Ponlop Rinpoche travelled with Lhamo all the way back to eastern Tibet again, but I am drowsy and starting to nod off. She kisses me softly on the top of the head, turns out the light and leaves the room, closing the door gently behind her. With a warm feeling in my heart, I fall asleep.

The bus arrived and I boarded. As I sat resting my wet head uncomfortably against the cool, vibrating glass, my mind swimming with images of my father, dusk beginning to fall outside, adverts and people jolting past, the engine loud in my ears, I came naturally to a decision. I decided to leave the Turk's. I decided to go back to my parents.

This decision, which I had been fighting for so long, now came to me surprisingly easily. There was nothing to keep me at the Turk's now that Madeline and Beth – and even Savio – had become strangers. For the first time in a long while, I felt comfortable in myself. I understood that my father was nothing more than a link in the circular chain of suffering. No longer was there anything to resent; the blame for the disease fell equally on all those involved, including myself. The responsibility was shared. Ultimately, nothing but mortality was to blame. For years I had been too afraid to allow myself to forgive my father; but once I allowed forgiveness to emerge, it was sad but profoundly peaceful. We were all puppets controlled by unseen forces; the forces of desire, of anxiety, of fate, of mortality. These things were the real masters of our lives – we were all victims. Even my father.

A couple of hours later, outside the Turk's, Savio barked at me more viciously than he had ever done before. Flecks of foam flew into the air from his teeth. Hurriedly, I felt in my pocket for the key but it was nowhere to be found. I assumed that I had left it in my room that morning. I swung the heavy brass knocker and thudded on the door. There was no answer for a long time. At last it creaked open to reveal a thin, deathly white face with hair scraped back and a single blue lip.

'Yes?' I recognised the honeyed gravel voice. It was a disfigured-looking Turk, in the midst of her beauty routine. 'Who are you?' she demanded.

'It's me, Mo. You know – Mo,' I said, confused.

'Ah yes, Morris. You're renting the room, yes? Very good. Come in.' I followed her into the Great Hall, wondering what was going on. She leant on a sofa and spoke as if she didn't have much time. 'I am Madame Turquoise. Girls call me Mama. Clients call me the Turk. I call clients turds. You, Morris, I won't call you a turd. I'll call you Mo. Maybe you'll become a turd later, but to start with, I'll call you Mo. Get me?' I looked into her eyes; her gaze was cold. She was looking at me like a stranger.

All at once, my throat went dry. 'Pleased to meet you, Madame,' I croaked.

The gleaming blue lip rippled in response. 'Your room – there,' she said, gesturing towards the turret with a powder puff. A white cloud flew from it and was absorbed into her face. 'I want to use it for the girls, but it's not big enough for work. But it's perfect for you. You go up, make yourself comfortable. I am the boss, I am busy. I am the landlady. I'll come up later, I'll speak to you properly later, OK?' With that, she strutted off through the double doors.

Deep in my mind, a leviathan awoke. My mind was fuzzy and I was tired, but my decision to leave the Turk's flooded me with adrenalin. I went up to my room, leant against the sink and looked up at my face looking down from the mirrored ceiling. I looked different – my eyes were brighter. Suddenly, I feel drowsy. My mind begins to wonder. I start to think I can fly. I can do it in dreams, so why not while awake? I get up from the sink and balance on one leg. All I have to do is slowly lift that foot off the floor, and that will be it, I will be hovering. All I have to do is lift the foot. But I can't do it, however hard I try. It is as if my foot is glued to the floor. I give up.

Footsteps came up the stairs, getting louder and louder. A cloud of perfume burst into the room, stinging my eyes. Then the Turk appeared, striding purposefully across the tiles. Behind her was Madeline, balancing three cups of coffee in her hands. Her face was bruised. The Turk planted her feet in the centre of the room and looked me up and down. Madeline distributed the coffee, leant on the basin next to me and blew the steam away from her mug. I took a sip. Nescafé. The Turk waited until she had our full attention, filled her lungs, and began to speak. I felt ridiculous.

'Mo, you've decided to move in. Is that right?'

'Well . . .'

'Rent's three hundred a month. Is that OK?'

'Yes.' In the background, Madeline looked surprised at the figure. I was leaving, I didn't care. There was nothing I could do about the years of overpriced rent I had already paid her.

'You'll need to pay on the first day of every month. No delay. Cash. That clear?'

'Yes.'

'It's cheap, very cheap. You're lucky, you've got an en-suite bathroom and everything. Very cheap. Very good deal.' It seemed pointless to mention that the en-suite bathroom lacked an en-suite bedroom. I was leaving for ever, anyway. 'Good,' said the Turk, relieved at my lack of resistance. Smugly, she gestured to Madeline. 'This girl is one of mine. She'll show you round. I am a busy woman. The boss. I don't have time for you, Mo.' She bustled out of the room and down the stairs. There was a pause as the air settled.

'Hi,' said Madeline in a standoffish, fake-American voice. 'Can I call you Mo, too?'

'Yes, of course,' I replied, uneasily.

'Nice to meet you. I'm Madeline. You can call me Mad. Mama's always like that. I hope it's not too depressing for you. Fuck me. I see you've unpacked your stuff already . . .' She glanced around the room. I looked for a glimmer of recognition in her eyes, something that would suggest our relationship hadn't completely vanished. But there was none. She didn't know me in the slightest. I was lost in her future. She set her hips at a jaunty angle and petulantly rolled her eyes. 'Look, Mr Mo, don't look at me like that. I'm a person, too, you know. Fuck. Mama told me to show you round, so I'd better do it. This is supposed to be my day off, you know, it's depressing. Not a minute to myself. Fucking H. But there you are. Come on, I'll show you downstairs.'

'Madeline, you don't have to show me around,' I said, calling her Madeline for the first time in years.

'Look, Mr Mo, let's not make this more painful than it already is. Call me Mad. Come on. Let's go.'

My mouth moved but no words came. I followed her down the stairs and into the Great Hall. It was cavernous and empty.

'OK, this is called the Great Hall,' she began, in Americanised tour-guide tones. 'Business hours are from nine in the evening until nine the following morning. There's a party here every night. We're quite busy at the moment, it's depressing. You can join us whenever you like, but you've got to pay for any services we provide. No freebies.'

Beth came through the double doors, sucking a smoking stump and carrying a pair of mini-bongos. 'Beth, put that away. You'll give us a bad impression.' I wasn't sure if Madeline was referring to the joint or the drums. Either way Beth took no notice. She approached us surrounded by a herbal aroma, glancing at me without recognition or acknowledgement.

'Who's the turd?' she demanded, her voice slurring.

'This ain't no turd,' replied Madeline. The American accent was beginning to fray my nerves. 'This is our new lodger. He's moving into the top of the turret.'

There was a pause while Beth absorbed the information. 'What, the loo?'

'Yeah. Don't ask me.' Once again, Madeline made the introductions. 'Mr Mo, Bouncing Beth The Psychic Witch Bitch. Bouncing Beth The Psychic Witch Bitch, Mr Mo. The bouncing bit is ironic by the way.'

We shook hands, briefly. Beth's eyes were opaque and guarded. For a moment, I felt panicked. I wanted to force her to remember her future, to be my friend again. But that was impossible. I remained silent.

'Call me Beth,' said Beth.

'Through those double doors on the far side,' Madeline went on, anxious to get the tour over with, 'are the girls' rooms. Beth and I live on the third floor. During working hours, there are always people going in and out. We sleep during the day, mostly.' I looked at Beth, who didn't react. 'And one last thing,' she added, pulling herself together and gesturing to the Turk's seat, 'don't sit in that chair. Ever. OK?'

I nodded and her duty was done. Without a word, the two girls began to walk away. 'I'm fucking depressed, Beth,' I heard Madeline say, her normal accent returning. 'Barry's been acting really fucking weird. Look at my face, for fuck's sake. It's mashed. Can I have a drag?' The double doors banged and they disappeared, leaving me alone in the Great Hall.

Thousands of images of myself flashed mockingly in mirrors all around. I decided to spend one last night at Turk's,

262

in the bath. One final sleep. Then, in the morning, first thing, I would leave for ever and go to my parents' house. I went upstairs to my room and began to pack. Ruthlessly, I disposed of anything that wasn't absolutely necessary, and managed to fit all my worldly possessions into a single plastic bag. I decided to leave all my Tibet books behind, and only take with me the treasured homesickness envelope. The task complete, I turned off the light and got into the bath, clutching my envelope to my stomach.

My sleep was deep and dreamless. The following morning, I awoke with the dawn. The face in the mirrors on the ceiling looked awful. The skin had a yellowish pallor and the cheek-bones were prominent. Mornings were always the worst. My head was pulsing. I got up and sat aching on the toilet for twenty minutes, as had become my habit. Then I folded the blankets neatly and laid them over the taps. I took a deep breath and, holding my plastic bag at shoulder height to prevent it rustling, crept down the turret stairs, across the Great Hall and out of the front door. As I closed it quietly behind me I could feel all my reflections being reabsorbed into my body, never to appear again. My heart was fluttering like a bird. Luckily, Savio was asleep and I didn't wake him up. I made my way through the golden morning light, along Seven Sisters Road, towards the tube station. Not many people were around. I passed a mangy dog with a split tail, lying beside a man unconscious in a suit. My head was throbbing.

When I arrived at the station, I had a feeling of profound foreboding. I bought a ticket and entered the catacombs. The ominous feeling grew, knotting my stomach. There were few people about. I stepped onto the escalator, leaning heavily on the handrail. As I descended into the earth, the appre-hension turned to terror. The deeper I went, the more frantic I became. I couldn't bear being under the ground; the earth was sucking me in, tomb-like, eating me. Soon there would be no escape. I turned and bolted back up the escalator, the descending wave of stairs pushing against my steps. It took a great deal of effort to reach the top. I rushed onto the open pavement and collapsed on a bench, my lungs ballooning desperately. A passer-by stopped and peered at me, his eyes filled with concern. He asked through his beard if I was OK. I nodded and he walked on. I sat. I needed to stay in the open air.

After several minutes, I felt better. My descent into the abyss had been postponed. It would be a long walk to West Hampstead. I set off through the dappled morning light.

It was late afternoon by the time I arrived at my parents' house. Everything looked the same, only much, much bigger. I felt dwarfed. I hadn't seen my parents for years, and had no idea what they would be like. But I was returning home. Would it be everything I wanted it to be? Would it really be home? Or would it have changed? Had I been away too long? Three times I approached, only to lose my nerve and run off down the street. Eventually I managed it. I put my trembling hand on the gate and eased it open. It didn't squeak, and opened without a sound. The lights were on and I could hear faint sounds of activity within. The walk up the path took an age, and several times I almost turned back. The noise of my feet on the paving slabs thumped in my ears, and a thousand memories poured in from every angle. It was all too much; I spun on my heel and bolted down the path, but managed to stop when I reached the gate. I leant against the wall. My eyes were stinging with sweat. I passed my desiccated tongue around my mouth and forced myself to return to the front door. Then I raised my hand to the doorbell.

I couldn't bring myself to push the button. Through the frosted glass I could see figures moving about in the kitchen, and I could hear laughter and the sound of pots and pans. My finger remained poised above the doorbell. I was beginning to feel queasy. I sprinted back down the path, through the gate, down the road, and was violently sick in a neighbour's dustbin.

I sat on the kerb, wiped the flecks from my mouth and

264

regained my composure. I felt better, and my head began to clear. I went down the road to a corner shop, bought a can of Coke and drank it slowly. This settled my nerves. Then, with measured paces, I blocked everything out, strode down the road, through the gate, along the path, and pressed the doorbell, hard.

Then I ran off again.

After that I walked round the block thirty-three times, each time turning up my collar and peering out of the corner of my eyes when I passed my parents' house. My heart got into a rhythm, beating faster every time I passed their gate, and slowing down as I left it behind. In this way, some hours passed. I told myself I would try one last time, then I would give up. Night was approaching, and shadows were beginning to cluster in corners. I hid behind a tree outside my parents' house. The curtains had been drawn. Soon it would be bedtime. It was now or never. I focused on the square of yellow light in the centre of the front door, trying to infuse it with all sorts of inviting qualities. My mind rebelled, throwing up thousands of negative memories instead. But I knew this was my last chance. It was all or nothing.

My blood pounding in my ears, I walked unsteadily up the path and stepped onto the porch. So far, so good. Just ring the bell. Just ring the damn bell, damn it. I raised my hand and held it, trembling, above the button. My arm felt heavy and light at once. A moth appeared, tumbling about my face and batting against the window. The doorbell seemed to get further and further away. I swallowed, dryly. Something moved within the house.

A shadow appeared in the window, the door swung open and I turned to run away. But it was too late.

'Mo? Is that you?'

Like a guilty schoolboy I looked back over my shoulder. In the doorway, silhouetted against the rectangle of yellow light, was a man propping himself against the doorframe, a fork poking out of his mouth. I squinted into the light. I didn't recognise him, but he obviously recognised me.

'My dear Mo!' he said. 'Where on earth have you been? We had to start our meal without you – that is, we were all, in fact, without exception, hungry enough to eat a mouse! We were worried about your good self. Please, do come in, without further ado.' He beckoned me in and I followed him into the hall. His robes were nowhere to be seen; instead he was wearing fashionable bellbottoms and a long-collared shirt, and his hair was unusually straggly. Nevertheless, as the light fell on Chod's distinctive cheekbones and upright posture, I easily recognised him.

He ushered me emphatically inside. The smell! I hadn't smelt it in years, it was the smell of my childhood. Everything seemed bigger. It was like walking into a memory. I caught a glimpse of my mother's familiar red velour armchair through the sitting-room doorway, picked out by the light from the hall. I followed Chod into the crowded kitchen. It was warm and muggy, the air heavy with the smell of home cooking. The heat clung to me like a sock. I felt profoundly nervous, not knowing what to expect. The anxiety made me giddy. Many people were sitting round the table, and debris from a meal littered the tablecloth. I was bustled to a chair and made to sit down.

'Ah, Mo, you're arriving back, la!' came my father's shrill voice. He stood up on his chair and waved a podgy hand.

The matronly woman sitting beside him gave him a disapproving look. 'Sit down, Tashi,' she drawled, 'that's no way to behave at the table. There's a good boy, no?'

My father obeyed, taking his seat once more and lifting his glass with both hands to drink. It was cumbersome, and liquid coated his chin. He put it down, gasping with effort. I took a deep breath and tried to identify the people around me. I felt as if I had just walked into an old family photo. The matronly woman had amber eyes and a jutting chin. I unfocused my eyes and imagined a few more pounds round her face; then I recognised her as Uma, Chod's mother. At right angles to her was Grandpa Pagpa, silent and furtive as ever but with a full head of hair. His bristling moustache was longer than before and fashionable, stretching all the way down to his chin. He was nursing a thin glass of lemon tea. Opposite Uma and my father sat Chod, looking around with an air of seriousness which evoked his future self. Then there was me. That was all. Not so many people after all.

'You're late, Mo, where have you been?' called Uma. 'Don't worry, there's lots of food left. I'll make you up a plate, no?' She went over to the stove and began to spoon out steaming piles of *phing-sha*, *sham-day* and *chi-may mo-mo*. The thick smell of hot Tibetan food moistened my tongue, and I felt sick with nerves and hunger. I sat back, knocking a spoon to the floor.

Chod pressed a glass of *châng* into my hand. '*Châng toong-na go-na, ma-toong-na nying-na*,' he muttered, patting me on the back. I searched for the translation: 'If you drink *châng*, you'll get headaches, if not, you'll get heartache.' I took a gulp, the alcohol heating my throat like a butter-lamp. Uma lowered a weighty plate in front of me. The steam cleared and I dug in, heartily. For a few minutes, nobody spoke.

I tried to take stock of the situation. Their reaction had been casual when I walked in; they were expecting me. I drank some more *châng* and it spoke to me: so far as these people were concerned, it whispered, I hadn't left. For them, that would happen tomorrow. I breathed a sigh of relief and put another heavy spoonful in my mouth. At least I wouldn't have to deal with their interrogations or accusations; I would be able to slide easily and comfortably back into family life. I took another gulp of *châng*, and it confided in me again. 'Tonight is a special night,' it murmured.

I carried on eating. Something troubled me, something I couldn't put my finger on. Something about my mother.

'Hey, Mo,' Uma said from across the table, 'I bet you're glad I cooked the meal this week, no? Makes your life easier, no? It must be hard for you, cooking the food, week after week. No?'

I smiled and took another mouthful of *châng*. No inspiration came from it, this time. Maybe I had overworked the magic.

'Will you be telling me a story after we are eating supper, Mo?' piped my father. Before I had time to respond, a harsh clacking came from the other side of the table; Grandpa Pagpa was banging on the typewriter. He tore off the page and slid it across the table to me. It said, 'n● st●ry all●ud he must g● strait t● sleep its late ●k d● n●t undermyne me again alrite m●'

I glanced apprehensively at Grandpa Pagpa, who typed again: 'n● Leg● eether'.

He glowered at me and returned to his lemon tea. Chod put down his glass of *châng* and stood up with an air of ceremony. His belly was as flat as a board. He couldn't be more than twenty-five, I thought. He tapped his glass with a spoon. 'Ladies and gentlemen, may I humbly request the pleasure of your attention for a few humble minutes?' The room was hushed. 'I have to inform you of some extremely important news.'

There was more typing from Grandpa Pagpa, and he passed a note to Rabbi Chod. I caught a glimpse of it over his shoulder. 'grate ch●d ive been wayting f●r this m●ment g●●d luck g●●d luck my b●i I am with y●u all the wai'

Rabbi Chod smiled appreciatively. 'Thank you, holy Oracle, for your most sincere and generous support,' he said. 'Indeed! For this is a most significant hour; and support for my cause is imperative.' He glanced around the room, and took a sip of *châng*. 'Thank you all for supporting me this evening. I shall not forget your loyalty. In a few minutes, I am expecting Jogpo to arrive, accompanied by a select group of eminent Tibetans; then the formal proceedings will begin. But before they get here I would like to disclose to you good people, my mother and cousins, my family, my blood, the . . . the news. The important news.' He coughed, nervously. All eyes were upon him. 'I would like to announce that I, Chod, a humble Tibetan from Golders Green, have had a divine revelation. A vision.' There was a gasp. Everybody sat up in their seats. Uma put her hands over her mouth. Chod continued. 'Three nights ago, while asleep in my very own humble bed in Sneath Avenue, Golders Green, the Jewish God came to me in a dream. Yes, the Jewish God! And He gave me a prophecy – no more, no less! And He spoke to me, saying, "Rabbi Chod," – yes indeed, He referred to me by the title, "Rabbi". "Arise, Rabbi Chod," He said, "for you are indeed the saviour of my people. Rabbi Chod, you are . . . none other than . . . the Messiah, *the reincarnation of Moses.*"'

'Poses?' asked Uma. 'Who is this Poses?'

'Not Poses, Mother, *Moses* – Leader of the Israelites.' replied Rabbi Chod.

'The who?'

'The Israelites. The Jews. I, my good self, am Leader of the Jews. Moses.'

Uma smiled broadly, as if she had known all along. Grandpa Pagpa was nodding enthusiastically.

'Indeed!' Rabbi Chod continued. 'The Lord spoke to me and revealed to me my true identity – and also the identity of various other members of our community. We, my dear friends, are, each of us, reincarnate Jews. We are the Lost Tribe of Israel. In my dream, the Lord showed me, in symbolic form, the identity of our former incarnations. You, Pagpa, appeared to me lying on a stone altar – indeed, you are none other than our Holy Father Isaac. Little Tashi appeared to me in a tent with four doors, bandaged about the loins – he is our Holy Father Abraham. Jogpo, who has not yet arrived, appeared drinking lentil soup – he is our Holy Father Jacob. And you, Mother, appeared sitting by a well – you are our Holy Mother Miriam.'

My father had slipped under the table. I peered down and saw him sitting beside my chair, surrounded by a forest of legs. He had acquired a banana and was fruitlessly trying to peel it, frustration on his plump face.

'Tonight,' came Rabbi Chod's voice from above, 'once Jogpo and the eminent Tibetans have arrived, Pagpa, being the community oracle, will perform a special invocation and divination, to ascertain whether or not my vision was authentic. Thus we shall know the truth, once and for all.' Grandpa Pagpa nodded even faster. He was going red in the face.

I peeled the banana and my father gobbled it up, then grabbed my hand and quietly led me out of the kitchen. Rabbi Chod's oratory, Grandpa Pagpa's typing and Uma's expressions of enthusiasm faded as we went upstairs. I sat on my father's child-sized bed. He tried to get onto it, and I lifted him up. The double bed that I was familiar with was nowhere to be seen. We played with his Lego; I helped him build a house for his Lego spaceman. Later the doorbell rang; Jogpo and the eminent Tibetans had arrived. Later still, the sounds of Pagpa's invocation floated up the stairs – shrieks, bellows and crashes. My father was scared. I tried to reassure him by telling him a story, the story of Ponlop Rinpoche, as I remembered it, which my mother had told me many years before.

The hubbub died down. My father yawned and lay down in the moonlight. He had enjoyed the story; he had clapped his hands with delight when he found out that the humble monk was, in reality, the great Ponlop Rinpoche. But it had made him sleepy. I said goodnight and tucked him in. I sat on the corner of the bed and his breathing became deep and regular. I could tell he felt safe, and this gave me a sensation of peace. I sat watching him until he fell asleep.

There was another commotion, outside in the garden. My father was snoring, and didn't stir. I went to the window and parted the curtains. A colourful crowd of Tibetans was spilling out of the house, and the grass and flowerbeds were getting trampled. Grandpa Pagpa, having finished his invocation, had collapsed at the end of the garden; a group of men were trying to remove his heavy metal hat. All along the road lights flicked on and neighbours' heads appeared in windows.

At length Grandpa Pagpa's hat rolled away and he was propped up against a tree, sipping water. Rabbi Chod became the centre of attention; he was treated like a celebrity. He jumped onto an upturned flowerpot and raised his hands; there was a cheer, then the crowd fell quiet, listening closely. Neighbours were massing at their fences.

'My dear congregants,' he began, 'the Oracle has spoken. Tonight has been a great night – an extraordinary night, a monumental night – of global significance. A landmark, no less, in the history of the world. A landmark.' Another great cheer went up. I suspected that Chod had been drinking all evening. 'Over the following weeks and months, I would encourage you all to bring your friends and colleagues – Tibetans only, of course – to my good self, in order that I may divine whether or not they are a Jewish *tulku*. In this way, our community will definitely flourish.

'We, the newly formed Tibetan Jewish community, have a testing time ahead. We must, each one of us, learn Hebrew, and become familiar with the Jewish faith, as interpreted by my good self. We must find a synagogue, and hold weekly meetings. We must appoint officials. And carry out circumcisions. And so on and so forth. But. But. That is. But. We can take great comfort from the fact that we are now part of the Jewish people – a strong people, a mighty people. We are no longer weak, helpless Tibetan refugees, abused and shitted on by the bastard Chinese, we are a strong and brave people. We are a proud Jewish race. I feel certain that all Jews will welcome us with open arms. We shall unite. The future is bright. The Lord is smiling upon us tonight. The Messianic Age has dawned.' There was a final burst of applause and Rabbi Chod got down off the flowerpot into the arms of the excited crowd. They all poured back into the house and the merriment continued downstairs.

Eventually the last guests left and the house became quiet. Some time later I heard Grandpa Pagpa go into his room and shut the door. All was still. It was late. I went to my old room, unpacked my things and took some paracetamol. I took my precious pictures from the homesickness envelope and stuck them up on the walls with Blu-Tack. Instantly, they

271

looked as if they belonged. I crumpled the envelope and threw it away. The bed-springs creaked with a familiar melody as I lay down. It felt strange not to be encased, snail-like, by a smooth shell. The room was very warm. As my mind drifted towards sleep, my body felt light and buoyant, as if freed from a heavy load. My father was getting younger, and needed help; now I was there to give it to him. I was at home with my family once more. But something, at the back of my mind, was bothering me. Something about my mother. I fell asleep.

Chapter Twenty-seven

Morning light made my eyelids go orange and I was forced awake. For a full five minutes, I couldn't remember where I was. My stomach felt as if it was filled with bleach and my tongue was covered in a thick white film. A skeleton hung in the air above me, its discoloured bones fanning out across the ceiling. It evaporated, piece by piece. Then the details of my life came back. I was in my parents' house, in my old bed. I hadn't woken up in a bed for years. I swung my legs over the side, a movement I had forgotten during my time at Turk's, and opened the curtains. Strangely enough, it was light outside – for the first time in a long while, I had slept through the dawn. I didn't know what time it was, as the sun wasn't visible from my window. I pulled my trousers on and left the room.

I made my way along the landing, leaning on the banister. My father came out of his room with a dummy in his mouth, his face creased from sleep. We went downstairs and found Grandpa Pagpa sitting at the kitchen table, fully dressed, munching a bowl of wet rice-porridge. In the light of day, the kitchen looked in even better condition; the signs of dilapidation that I remembered from years ago were nowhere to be seen. The stains on the wall had vanished, the worn-out patches in the lino had healed; the fraying on the chairs had woven back into place and the wallpaper had peeled itself up again and smoothed itself out. As I sat at the table and lifted my father onto his chair, I tried to adjust my memories to fit in with the present. Grandpa Pagpa saw me, gave a disapproving scowl, loaded a piece of A4 and began to type in an irritated fashion. The phone rang, and he interrupted his typing to go into the hall to answer it. I glanced at what he'd written so far. It read, 'whats r●ng with y●u m●, I had t●● get mai ●wn brekfast, y●u re getting up s● lait y●ure getting laz'

I looked in the cupboards. Everything was in its familiar place. I began to prepare breakfast. No sound came from the hall; Grandpa Pagpa was, as usual, receiving the call silently. The speaker must have known him, because when he refused to respond, they merely imparted their message to the silence. After several minutes he hung up and returned to his place at the table. I asked him if the phone call had been anything important. Impatiently, he typed his reply, unrolled it from the machine and handed it to me.

'nufing t● d●● with y●u but anywai, it was just uma calling t● let me kn●w that sherab and drime up in manchester have just had a baby girl this m●rnin'

I felt afraid. My blood seemed to thicken, clogging my veins. 'A baby girl? What have they called her? What's her name?' I asked, dreading the response.

Grandpa Pagpa rolled his eyes in exasperation and went to put the kettle on, ignoring me. But I persisted, and eventually he returned to the table and grudgingly typed a single word. I leant over the typewriter and read: 'Osel'. My intestines jerked. Suddenly, powerfully, I needed the toilet. I stumbled into the bathroom, and left it only when my entire system had been squeezed to the point of collapse.

I finished my breakfast in a daze. My father had finished his and was playing behind the sofa in the sitting room. Grandpa Pagpa sat watching me as I ate. Then he typed me another note: 'Are we g●ing t● the café t●day, if s● wen'

'I suppose so, Pagpa, why not?' I replied. 'What day is it?'
'Friday d●nty●● n●'
'OK, then . . . What time do we open up?'
'd●n't play silly buggerz its nine asy●● n●'
'All right, we'll leave soon, I suppose.' I washed the dishes and helped my father dress. Then all three of us left the house.

It was the kind of February morning that felt like May, apart from the few leaves that creaked underfoot from time to time. The sun glinted off the paving stones. I had lost weight through illness; I had to pull my trousers up every few steps, while my father kept an eye out for conkers and double-winged sycamore seeds.

Grandpa Pagpa and my father walked a couple of paces behind me. I kept slowing down so that they could catch up, but they slowed down in turn and gazed at me blankly. I had difficulty remembering the way, and made a couple of false turns. Grandpa Pagpa and my father simply followed me. At one point, just to see what would happen, I made an about-turn and walked a few feet in the opposite direction. Without a word, they followed. Then I spun on my heel, enacting a little pirouette, to see if they would do the same. They stared at me, nonplussed. I sighed. I felt like a mother duck. We continued our journey.

We arrived at the familiar white door. We all stood there for a while, on the pavement. The other two were looking at me, and I was unsure of what to do. There were ten minutes until it was time to open up. I looked at Grandpa Pagpa. He looked back at me.

'Er, keys?' I asked. He looked at me in disbelief. 'Do you have the keys, Pagpa?' I repeated. He shook his head, and pointed at my pockets. I checked. They were empty. I pulled them out in little white tufts. Pagpa rolled his eyes. 'Are the keys at home, do you think?' I asked. A shrug. 'Would they be at home, somewhere? In the key drawer or somewhere?' Another shrug. I gave an exasperated sigh. 'OK then, Pagpa, you wait here with Tashi while I go home and get the keys. OK?' Again, a shrug.

I glanced at my father. He was peering into the darkened café, making fingerprints on the glass. Pagpa pulled him roughly away from the window and gestured for him to sit on the step. He looked chastened, but didn't cry. I set off once again for home.

Once there, I realised that I couldn't let myself in without the keys. The sun was bright in my eyes, and a formation of birds animated the sky. I checked underneath the big stone by the front door, and to my surprise found the spare key, first time. I entered the house and opened the key drawer. There were hundreds of unmarked keys in there. I tipped them all into a plastic bag and made my way back to the café.

When I arrived, there were a few silent customers waiting outside on the pavement, looking soberly at their watches. Grandpa Pagpa was standing, arms folded, looking up at the sky. My father was still sitting on the step, looking miserable. When he saw me approaching he got to his feet, but Grandpa Pagpa pushed him roughly back down. I reached the door. My father clung to my leg. I tried the keys, one by one. Pagpa remained in his place on the pavement. The minutes slipped by. I could feel a silent wall of impatience building up behind me as more and more customers joined the noiseless crowd. Perspiration stippled my forehead. At last, the door swung open and we all entered.

I searched for the switch, and the lights came on. Then I lifted the blinds. The chairs were all legs-up on the tables, like dead insects. I took them down, one by one. Everyone stood and watched me, silently. I carried on. Sweat dampened my middle back. A few more customers came in and joined the spectators. I motioned for Grandpa Pagpa to help me, and he did so. After that, a few of the customers began to take the chairs down, too. When everyone was seated I began to take orders, encouraging my father and Grandpa Pagpa to do the same.

Little by little, the systems came back to me. I was surprised how quickly I remembered how to run the café. I could recall where everything was, how to work the coffee machine, and the procedure for ejecting customers.

My father did his best to help me, wiping tables and serving coffee. But he found it difficult. His age was against him. He couldn't reach the tables very well, and his physical co-ordination had deteriorated to the extent that he dropped several cups on the carpet. When the customers settled down and the café became less busy, I told him to play with his Lego in the corner, quietly. His pride was hurt but he obeyed.

The morning passed in a haze. The breakfast rush came and went, and the café was deserted. Brash sunlight beamed through the window. My father continued to play with his Lego, and Grandpa Pagpa paced the room restlessly, waiting for Ishmael to arrive.

A customer came in – it was the waitress from Regent's Park Café over the road. It took me a while to remember her name. Pandora. She strolled to the counter and glanced at the menu, with its single option of black coffee. Then she looked up and asked me in a low whisper if we did cappuccino. I felt my face draw into a frown of disapproval. It was my father's frown. I looked at him. He had finished playing Lego and was at the other end of the café, standing on tiptoe to wipe one of the tables. He almost knocked a bowl of sugar cubes onto the floor. I looked back. Pandora whispered the question again. I swept my hand towards the sign that demanded silence and pecked my head vigorously. Bewildered, she walked away and took a seat by the window. I went through the curtain to prepare her coffee.

As the coffee brewed, its heady aroma filled the room. I could feel it seeping into my clothes, my hair, my skin, making me one of its own; my father's spirits were giving me strength. The thought was strangely empowering. I poured out two cups of dark liquid and took a gulp of one. It burnt my tongue and coated my throat in a rich, heavy film; then, as the caffeine entered my bloodstream, my heart beat with more power than usual. Coffee is so reliable, I thought. It always has the same old taste, the same physiological effect. A source of order in this chaotic world. It made me feel in control. I understood my father. I took my paracetamol out of my pocket and washed it down with coffee. Then I took both cups into the café.

Ishmael had arrived. He was sitting head to head with Grandpa Pagpa, the chessboard between them. I gave Pandora her coffee and took the other mug over to my father, who was sitting under the counter. I knelt beside him on the floor and offered him a sip. He took one, then wrinkled his nose and stuck out his tongue in repulsion. I could understand his distaste; he was a child, and the coffee was bitter. But that was the joy of it. I persuaded him to drink. He managed about half the mug. Kids, I thought. No appreciation for what's really important in life. In the end he finished the coffee, and to encourage him I did a little dance of approval.

In the afternoon, I began to panic. As I went back and forth through the white curtain, taking orders and serving coffee, my mind felt locked inside itself. I had forgotten that my mother was several years younger than my father. Today she had been born, and when the next dawn broke she would disappear from my world altogether.

I decided to rush to Manchester to see her one last time. I phoned British Rail, to check the times of the trains. A recorded voice informed me that there had been an incident on the line. All services to Manchester had been suspended. A coach would never have got me there in time.

I made myself another cup of coffee. For a second time, my mother was lost. She had slipped out of existence while I had my back turned, and there was nothing I could do to bring her back. And no one else knew. As far as they were concerned, she had her whole life ahead of her. Tomorrow, she would vanish from their lives.

Now the café was quiet; there were no customers apart from Ishmael, who was still playing chess with Grandpa Pagpa in the corner. My father was at the window, looking through the glass at the pedestrians as they hurried past. I went up onto the raised platform at the back of the room and sat in one of the chairs. I closed my eyes and tried to loosen the connection between my mind and my body. Slowly I let my mind waft into the air. An image of a hospital mat- erialised and I floated to one of the windows on the fourth floor. Reaching the pane, I peered in. Everything was very

278

clear. In the bed, propped up with pillows, was a woman cradling her new baby. Her hair drooped in two black plaits across the bedspread. A man was kneeling beside her, playing lovingly with the child's fingers. They looked blissfully happy. I became intensely jealous. I shot back into my body and sat up straight. Nothing had changed. My father was still gazing out of the window, and Pagpa and Ishmael hadn't moved. All was still. I got to my feet and took up my position behind the counter.

The atmosphere in the café became lethargic. Everyone seemed to fall asleep at once. Grandpa Pagpa and Ishmael were resting head to head, breathing deeply; my father had curled up under the counter. Ishmael woke up and, without even a nod of acknowledgement, exited the café, leaving Grandpa Pagpa asleep, sprawled across the table.

I was losing everyone around me. My father was certainly on his way out; he had only a few years to go. Then it would just be Grandpa Pagpa and myself left. Memories of Madeline and Beth spun before my eyes, mingling with those of my mother.

The sun was going down, and the café was blushing. I decided to call the Turk's. Deep down I knew no one would recognise me, but I had to try. I needed to hear a familiar voice. The late-afternoon sunlight gave a vivid, defined edge to all objects. Leaving the café in slumber, I stole through the curtain and sat on the un-battered lipstick-red table in the kitchen. I took the phone in my hands again and dialled the number of the Turk's. It rung for a long time, and my despondency grew. Just when I was about to give up, a voice answered.

'Hello? Hello?' I recognised the voice straight away. It was a stroke of luck to have got straight through to Mad. Her voice was fast, as if she were chewing her words. She was on speed; I had seen her like this many times.

'Hello . . . Do you . . .' I began, hesitantly. As usual, I wished I'd prepared some opening lines. 'It's Monlam here,' I said, finally.

'OK . . . What . . . ? Who . . . ?' came the puzzled reply. 'I was just ringing to speak to you.'

'What, about the room?' she asked, her voice racing. 'You saw the ad, then, in the paper? Well, you're the only one who has rung up so far. Morris, was it? Bathrooms aren't particularly popular rooms to rent, you know. I wouldn't like it myself, it'd make me suicidal. But if you want, I'll arrange for Mama – she's the landlady – Madame Turquoise – the Turk – Mama – to see you the day after tomorrow. Six thirty. How does that sound? Good? What do you think?'

'Mad, I—'

'Great. I'll write you in the diary. I'll do it now. You know our address, yah?' The line went dead. The dialling tone howled in amusement.

My mind felt frantic, as if I was experiencing the effects of Mad's speed. I had just made an arrangement in my past. I sat on the table for a long time before going back into the café.

Chapter Twenty-eight

Mornings followed mornings like a backwards reel of film and I traced my life through the world's yesterdays. As I got used to my new lifestyle, time blurred into itself. My world was made up of two places – home and the café – and two people – my father and Grandpa Pagpa. I settled easily into a routine, and the routine stopped me thinking. Each night I crumpled into bed, sick and exhausted.

I checked the temperature of the milk with my elbow, and poured it into the bottle. My head felt as if it was in a vice. I took the bottle through the white curtain. Grandpa Pagpa and Ishmael were playing chess, as usual. I went behind the counter. In an open drawer, beside the cash drawer, my father was lying, wrapped in a blanket. He was awake, but silent. He was good at being silent. He was a very quiet baby. I slipped the teat into his mouth and he began to suck greedily.

I laid my head on the counter, still holding the bottle, and allowed my mind to drop to unconsciousness. Immediately, skeletons appear, crawling out of the air and multiplying all around me. I woke up. There was a customer waiting at the counter. I put the bottle on the counter, took the order and went back through the white curtain to prepare the coffee.

I had never felt as ill as this. Every day, it was getting worse. I was desperate. I had a constant ache in my head and my stomach; I barely ate, and was prone to dizzy spells. A perpetual cold dogged me, and I had developed the habit of going everywhere with a roll of Andrex under my arm. My gums bled. Everything about my body was wrong, every-thing was malfunctioning.

As I was placing the cup below the coffee nozzle, I caught sight of my reflection in the side of the coffee machine.

Usually, I tried not to look in mirrors. So when I saw my face, I was shocked. My skin had a beige pallor, and was speckled here and there with unsightly lesions. Calluses had appeared round my nostrils. My eyes were sunken and grey.

I awoke on the floor, the cup lying broken next to me, a black pool of coffee creeping towards my face, my head hurting from the fall. I pulled myself to my feet, and almost fainted again. But it passed. I swept up the shards of china and threw them away, and then mopped up the coffee. As I was brewing another cup, I decided to go to hospital. I had never been to the doctor in my life, but something had to be done – fast.

I closed the café at lunchtime, walked an irascible Grandpa Pagpa home and set off for the hospital. I took my father with me because I didn't want to leave him with Grandpa Pagpa, who was going from bad to worse. These days, whenever he saw my father he gave him a vicious glare and bared his teeth like an animal; his son, who came into the world just as his wife left it, whose birth had killed his beloved. He had become unnaturally moody, and sat up all night typing abuse on his typewriter. By breakfast time, A4 sheets of obscenities were littered all around the house, and I would find him slumped over his typewriter at the kitchen table, snoring. Once, when I went to wake my father up at dawn, I found that several pages had been slipped under his bedroom door in the night. The first page was covered in the words, 'my wife c●m bak c●m bak c●m bak c●m bak c●m bak c●m bak c●m bak c●m bak c●m bak c●m bak c●m bak c●m bak.'

Then, right at the very end, it said, 'why did y●● g● and leave me with tashi, y●u dyed s● hee c●uld liv, ha● cud itbe it wurthit ?@'

I threw it away. The paper felt slimy with grief.

The walk to the hospital took longer than I had expected, as a result of having to rest many times along the way. But eventually the great concrete building loomed into view. Ambulances were going in and out, beetle-like, and there were people in hospital gowns outside the entrance, smoking. This is where everything happens, I thought: people being born, and later dying, being cared for by people whose suffering was yet to begin.

It was busy. Taxis swarmed round the entrance. I got into one of the lifts. The smell of disinfectant was strong. The lift rose with a jolt and my father, who had fallen into a doze, whimpered with surprise. A nurse smiled at us. One of her teeth was missing.

The lift stopped at the seventh floor and I got out, clutching my father to my chest. He was fast asleep. Hospital noises laid siege to my ears. I walked along a short stretch of gluey lino and went through to Reception, where I registered. After a period of gazing at the hospital-issue coffee machine, the loudspeakers called me to Dr Thromby's room. My father was still asleep.

Dr Thromby was a compact man with tiny hands and red cheeks. His defining feature was a pile of tightly curled chestnut hair which grew dramatically to the right as a result of a severe side-parting. He lifted his spectacles as I arrived, and peered at me under the frames.

'Aha . . . Monlam? Please come in and take a seat.' His voice was strangled and academic. I followed his instructions. I felt slightly faint, and my head was pounding. I sat down and blew my nose. 'Do you have a surname, Monlam?'

'I've forgotten it.' And I had.

'Aha, you've forgotten it?'

'Yes.'

'Well, then.' He asked me questions about my health for a few minutes while I sat quietly with my father in my arms, replying as best I could. I could see Dr Thromby's thoughts rising in a haze in the space above him. Images appeared; flappy-mouthed diseases and gleaming knights, together with vague scenes of how he imagined my future to be. His thoughts were remarkably vivid.

I described my headaches (aha), nausea (aha), bleeding gums (aha) and all the rest. As I went on, his ahas stopped and his face grew increasingly grave. I raised my chin to show him my lesions and pointed out the colour of my skin. His face became stony. He walked over to my chair and took my blood pressure. He arranged for a nurse to pull some blood from my arm. He examined my skin, my muscles and my tongue. He did some more tests. He asked me lots of questions about my eating and sleeping habits. All the while, his jaw became more and more set and he kept glancing at the sleeping baby in my arms.

As the minutes pass, tiny skeletons appear in the corner of my vision. They approach the warty viruses and the knights, bowing low and offering their hands. One by one, they pair off and strike up elegant ballroom dances to secret, silent rhythms. They spiral round and round Dr Thromby's knotted hair in a whirl of bones, warts and armour.

He sat delicately back and slid his glasses onto his forehead. As I focused on his face, the images above his head became invisible.

'Aha, Monlam,' he said uncomfortably, 'I have to say . . . to be honest . . . things aren't looking . . . how shall we say? . . . you are a very sick man.' My father awoke in my arms with a small gurgle, making Dr Thromby particularly uneasy. 'Is that your child?' he asked. I didn't reply. He leant closer. 'Monlam, can I make a suggestion? I think it would be a good idea if . . . if you got someone to help you look after your child . . . for the future.'

For the future? My heart jolted. What did he mean?

'What do you mean?' What did he mean? I stood up with a start, and my father began to cry. Dr Thromby didn't answer. What did he mean? I got up and backed towards the door. Dr Thromby's mouth was gaping like a fish's; his lips were working but I couldn't hear any words. I hurried from the room and took the lift back to the ground floor, my heart thudding in my mouth.

All the way through the corridors, my father cried. In my haste, I had left the roll of Andrex in Dr Thromby's room. Liquid began to run across my upper lip. I stepped into the street, ignoring the spectre-like figures around the hospital entrance. I tried to absorb myself into the street. Crowds milled about me, and my father's wails throbbed incessantly in my ears.

I walked for twenty minutes. Then I became crushingly tired. An Underground sign conjured itself up in front of me, hanging like an emblem in the murky sky. Below it was a set of stairs, stretching grimly into the ground. For some reason, the sight no longer filled me with dread. I felt a strange desire to be submerged in the earth. The depth appealed to me. For the first time in months I left the safety of the pavement, crept down the stairs and picked my way through the hellish network of tunnels and bridges. Curved adverts jostled for my attention as my father's shrieks resounded off the walls. Posters peeled and strained against their glue as if about to leap off the walls to smother me. The air was thick and hot in my mouth. A dirty odour of transience clung to everything. A rat ran across my path. Nothing seemed right, everything was uncomfortable. Everything felt as if it was swarming with spiders, all objects had a shifting skin. I looked closely at my hands, and saw that they were covered with millions of tiny skeletons, locked in an ungainly dance. The world was teeming with them. Dazed, I stopped walking. The world spun in all directions, lights streaking like a web around my mind.

I think that was when I collapsed.

Chapter Twenty-nine

Much time passed before I came to. I awoke in hospital, in the middle of the air. From the sign on the wall beside me I realised that I was in Intensive Care. Below me was a bed with a transparent plastic tent over it, surrounded by medical gadgets. I managed to sink downwards until I could peer into the plastic bubble. I was in the bed. There were tubes coming out of my nose and machines monitoring my every movement. Or, rather, the machines were monitoring my breathing and the ebb of my blood, for there were no other movements. There was a continual bleep, and a loud sucking sound accompanied my breathing. My hair had been scraped back. I was in a regulation hospital smock, and my wrist was tagged. I looked much thinner than I remembered. Unnaturally thin. I wondered how long I had been there. My face appeared strangely asymmetrical. I was almost unrecognisable. My skin had a consumptive sheen and my eyes seemed glued shut, as if they had never opened. I looked profoundly peaceful. But I didn't feel it.

A hospital orderly came in, wheeling a huge plastic sack mounted on a trolley. She was wearing rubber gloves and had a plastic bag over her hair. Her face was obscured by a green mask. For a moment I doubted that she was human. She dropped the sack and let her mask fall round her neck. Her skin looked rubbery and artificial. She fumbled in her pocket, brought out a small object and touched it to her breasts, forehead and belly. Then she placed it on the small table beside my bed. It was a tiny picture of the Madonna. I glanced at myself. Needless to say, there was no reaction. The orderly went over to the window and pushed it open; she leant out and lit a cigarette, blowing the smoke downwind so that only a few wisps fluttered into the room. Nevertheless, my body began to cough, and something bleeped faster. But I didn't feel a thing. I was a spectator. The orderly finished her cigarette, closed the window and picked up her rubbish sack. She crossed herself again, put the Madonna back in her pocket, and left the room.

She wheeled her trolley into the corridor and I floated after her. The hospital was busy; everything was almost blue with whiteness. We turned a corner and entered an adjoining ward. It was full of elderly people, their worlds shrunken around their beds. Their eyes had a certain hollow indignity to them, and their hair was ruffled. The orderly placed her Madonna on the windowsill and started emptying the bins. The aged patients watched her as if seeing into their own pasts. Colours blended into each other and nurses flitted to and fro. Curtains were drawn round beds and there was the occasional shout or jerk. The orderly emptied the last few bins into her sack. Life is a bin, I thought, and this hospital is the sack. She completed her work, picked up her Madonna and moved on.

I slipped down a couple of flights of stairs and ended up in the hospital café. Patients were sipping from paper cups, looking as if they had never worn anything but pyjamas. The food was laid out precisely on surgical steel trays. One man was hobbling around the sandwich section, wheeling a stand with a bag and a drip. Whenever he lowered his arm, a thin thread of blood crept into the bag. Dr Thromby was sitting in the corner, looking at his reflection in a window and puffing up his hair. He smoothed the wrinkles round his eyes, his brow creasing as they reappeared. He began to apply lip-balm.

More corridors. More people. I couldn't believe how many people there were. I never saw the same person twice. More stairs. Another ward, this time full of rows of small, egg-like incubators. The walls were painted with pictures of clowns and balloons. Flowers were positioned like talismans. Two nurses at the far end were fiddling with a capsule. As I approached, I overheard a snatch of their conversation.

'Poor little bugger,' said one.

'Yes, poor thing. Oh, it's sad, to be born without a mum. And as for the father, he hasn't said a word since he got the news,' replied the other. They finished their work and walked off, their voices fading.

I glided down to the incubator and peered in. A maroon baby lay there unmoving, tubes coming from its nose and hands. I looked at the wristband. 'Tenzin Tashi, born 04:37pm, 26 March 1975, parents Tenzin Pagpa, Tenzin Pagmo.' My father. I looked more closely and could just recognise his features. My mind filled with spirals, shot upwards through three floors and darkened into unconsciousness again.

When I next awoke, I was in a waiting room. I felt as if I had been unconscious for only a couple of minutes, though I had no way of telling. A few drunken men were sleeping in the far corner. Large, bright windows looked out into the London blackness. I looked below me and saw a crumpled figure slumped against a soft drinks machine. The machine was buzzing loudly, but the man seemed oblivious. I slid down in front of him. It was Grandpa Pagpa, gazing listlessly into space. His fingers were pulling absently at the handles of a large holdall at his feet, which gaped open like a mouth. A selection of women's essentials was revealed – nightdresses, Tibetan ribbons, a pair of flip-flops, some pastries wrapped in a vest. Alongside these were several sets of baby clothes, brand new, still in their packets. Grandpa Pagpa didn't move, apart from his fingers. I had never seen him with such a stunned, faraway look on his face. Beneath his eyes were deep purple indentations that spread over to his temples like bruises, and the whites of his eyes were full of red webbing. He didn't seem to notice when a nurse approached. She cleared her throat to catch his attention.

'Sir? Your wife . . . The doctor said you'd like to view your wife before you go home tonight?'

Grandpa Pagpa's eyes closed and he nodded as if his head

was too heavy to hold up. He got up and followed her slowly out of the waiting room.

I went after them into a lift. As the steel box slipped downwards, Grandpa Pagpa stood in heavy silence, making the nurse pick at her hair uncomfortably. There was a lurch, and the doors slid open. They were met by a doctor, and the nurse instantly vanished. The doctor shook Grandpa Pagpa sympathetically by the hand and led him slowly into a cold, brightly lit chamber full of surfaces. In the centre was a steel bed covered in a white sheet that rose in peaks over the cadaver. The doctor pulled the sheet back. Grandpa Pagpa stood motionless. I drifted over the bed. I could see the similarity between this woman – my grandmother – and my father. She had the same colouring, the same industrious-looking face and assiduous hands. Her hair lay coiled in a fat plait beside her head. There was something uncomfortably fascinating about that plait. Grandpa Pagpa was expressionless, silent. For the first time, I understood him. I could see his whole life at once, and I felt a profound acceptance. Almost a forgiveness, if there had been anything to forgive. A whole life of causes and effects mingled in that single moment. The doctor pulled the sheet up over the body and led Grandpa Pagpa slowly from the room.

Suddenly I felt a deep desire to get back to my body, post haste. I needed to get back to it. At first I couldn't find my way and I felt increasingly panicked. Eventually, however, I arrived above the intensive-care tent. My body hadn't moved; it was lying there as peaceful as a pebble, sucking in breath with a regular rushing sound. But the beeping was faster than before. There was a powerful disturbance in the air all around me, accompanied by a feeling of fading. I was pushed downwards and lowered towards my body; all vision stopped as I clicked together.

I am lying sleepily in my mother's lap, her hair gently brushing my face. We are sitting in the red velour armchair by the big bay window in the sitting room, and snow is falling outside, patting the windows softly. But inside, we are warm.

My mother is singing to me in a low, rich voice, a traditional Tibetan folksong, rocking me gently in her arms. The melody wraps round me like warm cotton.

'Over the highest mountain
The moon rises, pure as a conch shell
It is not the moon
It is the face of my Guru
Of my Guru Tsongkhapa.

'In the highest valley, in the sun,
Corn and water laugh
This is not a worldly valley
It is the valley of Amitabha Buddha
It is the valley of the Blessed One

'On the hills around the valley
Lamas are discussing the holy Dharma
It is not they who are talking
It is my Guru who is talking
It is the pure voice of Guru Tsongkhapa.'

My mother kisses my forehead softly. Then I am in a valley, in an ocean of crisp, clear air, vast mountains stretching protectively above me. Tiny blue flowers are scattered on either side, nodding and bowing in the wind. In the sky above me appears the statue from the British Museum, the ferocious bronze Mahakala; it has grown to an incredible size, and fills the sky with flames.

The fading continued. Sensations appeared where they had never existed before, and disappeared from life-long limbs. I was fading upwards, and the whole world was fading with me. Everything began to go numb. Desert mirages appeared all through my mind, followed by wisps of smoke, billions of sparks and candle flames. I was absorbed into everything that appeared. All went white. The whiteness was stained with an infinite blood red, stretching out and around to the ends of space; then there was a profound blackness, and I swooned.

The swoon parted to reveal a vast, clear light, like the dawn. All was still. In the immense spaciousness, my whole life entered my mind. Moments piled upon billions of moments, chronologically. That's what's important at times like these, when your life flashes before you. Chronology. Let's begin at the . . . Now I've seen it all, in order, as it happened. It's about to disappear.

My life is beginning to fade. I remember . . . what? What was I remembering? It's gone. What was the point? Nothing exists now, apart from the present. Was there ever anything else? Suddenly there is motion; I am moving fast, in all directions. Where am I going? When am I?

Acknowledgements

Thanks to:
Isobel Sallon, Camilla Hornby, Hugh Andrew, Helen Simpson, Neville Moir, Alison Rae, Alexander McCall Smith, Louis de Bernières, Beryl Bainbridge, Maggie Gee, James Buchan, Patrick Neate, Pascal Khoo Thwe, Siân Gibson, Jan Rutherford, David Del Monte, Richard Gollner, James Daunt, Tina Gadoin, Catherine Shoard, Natasha Fairweather, Maggie Phillips, Lucinda Aris, Patrick French, Jane Khin Zaw, Danny Angel, Phil Oltermann, Sara Ribeiro, Ben Seifert, Kilian Weinberger, Andrew Staffell, Boris Saunders, Savio Noronha, Shailee Jain, Burt Baskerville, Stuart McVinney, Sam Bain, Lydia Rainford, Mei Ling Choo, Judith Simons, Toby Wallis, Binyomin, Chana, Abe, Miriam, Michael Sallon, Diana Sallon, Tony Simons and Ruth Simons.

In memoriam Giles Gordon